FACE OF OUR FATHER

Face Of Our Father

G. Egore Pitir

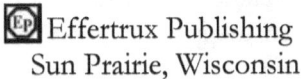 Effertrux Publishing
Sun Prairie, Wisconsin

Effertrux Publishing
P.O. Box 694
Sun Prairie, Wi 53590-9998
www.Effertrux.com

Library of Congress Control Number: 2014948319

ISBN: 978-1-940251-12-7

Cover design by Cid Fretag

Cover image montaged using licensed photographs:
© Estate of Stephen Laurence Strathdee | iStockphoto.com
© Robert_harrison | iStockphoto.com
© Steven Love | Dreamstime.com
© Robyn Mackenzie | Dreamstime.com
© Stockmateapp | Dreamstime.com

To my reader

For I am merely the storyteller

I did not write this tale

You did

ACKNOWLEDGMENTS

My wife. What am I to say? How can I explain? She reads the very worst. Finds the gentlest way to explain that a scene just doesn't work. She can never really enjoy the story the way a reader can. She always understands why I'm not really there, even when I'm sitting right next to her. And yet sometimes when she reads, she cries. And I instantly know that this particular passage never has to change. Know that I will never let it change. Because, she cried.

My writing coach. What she initially saw, why she later endured, what she sees now, I do not know. Yet, when this struggling writer looks at his own words and wonders who could ever enjoy them, whenever he thinks to quit, he is encouraged by the fact that she still sees something. And when someone believes in you, well, it's magic, isn't it?

My betas. Many a beta reader endured the most tortured versions of this novel, smiled bravely through the pain, and encouraged me onward. In no particular order, they are: Brian, Christine, Mike, Suzy, Kathy, Daila, Matt, Schlossman, Sue, Jacob, Roger, Terri.

My super beta, Patricia. I've lost count of how many times this gracious woman sallied forth to take on one more read. A special friend, indeed.

My fellow novelists, Rich and Michael. We exchanged novels, hacked and whacked, and spurred each other forward. I am the first of us to publish. If I have a writer's fantasy, it's to achieve sufficient notoriety, that by lending my endorsement to their amazing novels I would cause readers to take note, and to read.

My WBTL classmates. From characters, plot and theme, to page, paragraph, sentence, and word, the following students of the storyteller's art continually challenged this struggling writer to work harder, reach deeper, to find, and hopefully please, the reader. The generosity of these folk is my constant reminder to give my all: Sylvia, Kathleen, John S., Peetie, Jan, Bobbi, Emily, John W., Kim, Robert, Walter, Linda, Anne, Erin, Matt, Patricia, Richard.

My proof editors, Terry and Bob. Any mistake that slipped past was due to the overwhelming abundance of errors that these two had to sift through.

My copy editor, Marisa. What a mighty task this miraculous woman performed. I doubt that any writer has ever had a more talented, invested, dedicated angel protecting his words.

My cover artist, Cid. Talented, imaginative, and patient. Everything I needed in an artist.

My publisher, Diana. A superb novelist. A creative businesswoman. Without her hard work, you would not be reading this.

All credit to those above for any successes in this novel, all failures wholly and solely this author's.

For those readers interested in following the tale you've written toward its conclusion, please note that I've included an excerpt from the sequel at the end of this novel.

PROLOGUE

Two things always drove Zuehb Azwad to search the dead. Hope and hate.

Today, mostly hope, a dogged faith that hidden amidst the unearthed bodies lay some means to a better end. But as Zuehb rode his camel out of camp, his brothers' jeers brought forth a bit of the hate. Still, only a little. The sands had raged all night, the type of storm that reshaped the land, uncovering the old battlegrounds and restoring in Zuehb great hope.

He made a rapid clicking sound with his tongue, then whipped the camel's flank, spurring the lazy animal toward the ancient battlefield ahead. The old storytellers recounted how the Roman Emperor Augustus had once ordered ten thousand conquering legionaries into the heart of the Nabataea. But wherever the Romans marched, the Bedouin clans vanished, leaving behind only poisoned wells. Six months of searing sun and flesh-rending sandstorms drove the Romans steadily mad. Somewhere between Medina and Mecca, the united clans struck. Like dust devils the Bedouins whirled, withering the Roman flanks until the vaunted legions broke. Weeks later, a few hundred legionaries were allowed to stumble back to their emperor with tales of endless sand and dry death. The Romans, like the Greeks before them, never tested the desert sands again.

Zuehb's father loved that tale. A good reason to hate it.

Cursing aloud, Zuehb released his camel's reins and pinched its right ear, yanking until the stubborn creature angled across the scorched dunes toward the lone metallic glint amidst a field of sun-bleached bones.

The tale was a lie, Zuehb knew. Poisoned wells, searing sun, sandstorms, all believable. Bedouins defeating thousands of Roman legionnaires? Laughable. Not so much the destruction of Roman legions. But uniting the clans? Just another storyteller's lie. Yet one part of the old tale had fired young Zuehb's imagination. The raging sand. He'd seen a storm bury a caravan in minutes. Why not Roman legions? Roman treasure? This kept Zuehb searching.

Most often, he found only a bit of rusted sword or broken shield, but once, while still a young boy, he discovered a jingling leather pouch.

Little Zuehb decided that the pouch, embossed with a great eagle, was the perfect place to keep safe his collection of colorful rocks. But long years beneath the arid sands had drawn every bit of moisture from the old leather, leaving it shrunken and stiff. And its mouth, shriveled tight about hardened twine, defied his every attempt to open.

Bringing the pouch to his father's tent, he pleaded for help. One shake sent his father's eyes wide and his knife screeching from its sheath to slash at the old leather.

Crying out, Zuehb lunged for the pouch and met the back of his father's hand instead, knocking him to the ground. Spilling to the floor next to Zuehb came coins, gold, silver and copper, and something more, crystal rocks, green, red and bright blue. They sparkled more colorfully than any Zuehb had collected, and he managed to clutch a handful before his father's foot stomped across his wrist, grinding against his bones until he released the gems. At his father's command, Zuehb's two older brothers tossed him from the tent, the empty pouch landing in his lap.

From that moment, his father's status steadily rose until he became head of their clan. And on that day, his father had three rings fashioned from the Roman gold. Two bore their family's symbol of crossed spears above a five pointed star. These he gave to each of his first-sons. Upon the third ring, mounted above the spearheads, lay a bright red gem. This he kept for himself.

At the time, little Zuehb understood none of the implications. He only knew that his father had ruined his leather pouch. Later, he learned of first-wives and first-sons, and that whether his father took three or four or ten more wives, all of them were mere second-wives, and that he was fated forever—a second-son. And Zuehb also learned of the shackles placed on one's life by the simple misfortune of dropping from some second-wife's womb.

What difference, first womb or second? Was not the measure of a man his deeds? Zuehb pulled hard on the camel's reins, halting the lumbering animal. For perhaps the thousandth time in his adult life, he examined his wrists and felt about his neck. Invisible chains, yes…yet stronger than any ever wrought in a forge master's hearth. "Koosh!" he yelled into the camel's ear, ordering the stupid creature to lie down.

Slipping from the camel's back, Zuehb knelt beside the glint—the point of a blade. Digging through the sand, a mere hand's length down, he found the hilt. Below the shiny tip, the remainder of the knife was tarnished near black, the edge dull yet smooth, with not a single pit marring the metal. He hurriedly fumbled through his pockets, located and drew out a sharpening stone. A single stroke did for the edge what last night's raging sand had done for the tip, leaving it shining bright as the sun. Zuehb sucked in a quick breath of air, then hid the silvery blade beneath his robes as he searched the ridgeline for his father's thieving eyes.

No one. Of course not. They'd left Zuehb behind, descended the other side of the ridge to the caravan road below. Zuehb's fate mattered little to his father, and not at all to his father's first-sons. No reprieve for second-sons.

Twenty years trying had proven it so. Who had figured out the scale master's cheat in Mecca? Zuehb. Who had spotted the shipwrecked trading ship south of Aqaba? Zuehb. Whose secret route across that very ridgeline saved them a day's travel on every trip between Medina and Mecca? Zuehb's. But always the praise and favors fell on the first-sons. Though he bore the name Azwad, they all saw Zuehb as a fool.

Only last month, at the height of the festival of Al Qaum, his father had called him such to his face. After gaining private audience with the Prophet Mohammed, Zuehb brought to his father good tidings—all followers were now permitted to attack and plunder the caravans from Mecca. His father declared the Prophet a frenzied zealot whom Mecca would eventually crush, and that he, as leader of their free clan, needed no man's permission to carry out raids. At great length, Zuehb calmly argued the merits of associating their clan with the Prophet, both the numerous political advantages, and the oasis of protection that the Prophet's many followers afforded against retaliation. His father responded, "Only two types of men knowingly mount a rabid camel, the demented or the foolish. You do not appear to have lost your wits, Zuehb." Despite the intervening weeks, the memory of the first-sons' raucous laughter still burned Zuehb hotter than the sun.

Ignoring the searing sands, Zuehb dug long and deep, first uncovering the skeleton of a horse, then below that, the bones of a hand surrounding a lump of silver sculpted like an eagle. The rider's death grip upon his saddle horn, Zuehb surmised. A single jerk freed silver horn from rotting saddle. Another hour produced the dead man's armor and weapons, all corroded beyond value.

With his treasures tucked beneath his robes, Zuehb crossed over the ridgeline and began the treacherous descent. Two hours and dozens of switchbacks later, he caught sight of carnage below. "Koosh, koosh, koosh," he whispered. Sliding from the camel's back, Zuehb crept forward until he obtained a clear view of the entire valley and surrounding hillsides.

Silent. Mostly still. The battle done, the only signs of life were the few surviving camels nuzzling at the twisted bodies littering the sand. Then came a sniffling sob. Zuehb crawled closer. Beyond the farthest camel, he made out his father, tears wetting his cheeks, sitting against a boulder and cradling his oldest first-son's head in his lap. For the first time, Zuehb saw his father as old and weak.

Telling himself that the marauders might return at any moment, Zuehb retreated to his camel and searched the hillsides for spying eyes while listening to the old man's sobs.

At sunset, he brought out his sharpening stone and silver knife. With each of Zuehb's strokes along the edge, his father called out, "Who's there?" Zuehb did not answer. Instead he listened for footsteps, and studied the horizon for the glow of torches. As the night wore on, his father stopped asking. Sunrise brought circling vultures. The hovering scavengers would soon bring others, mounted and armed. Zuehb could delay no longer.

Tying a cloth over his nose and mouth to ward off the growing stench, he grabbed his spear and crisscrossed the battlefield until he found the youngest first-son. After hacking off his brother's ring finger, he hurried to his father's side. The oldest first-son lay lifeless, skull open, flies feeding at the brains. Zuehb hacked off another ring finger, sneering, "I'll remember your laughter well, my brothers."

His father stirred from unconsciousness. "Zuehb? Is that you?"

Zuehb dribbled water across his father's cracked lips and washed the caked blood from his forehead and eyes. The circling shadows now seemed everywhere. Looking up, he guessed the vultures numbered some thirty or forty, probably more, a dark column visible for many leagues. And in the distance, above the farthest hill along the caravan road, a cloud of dust rose. Camels, moving fast.

He estimated barely time enough to finish the deed and retreat to the switchback trail above to determine whether the camels bore friend or foe. Either way, his choice remained the same. Act now, or accept his shackles forever.

Leaving his father gulping from the water bladder, Zuehb pulled his oldest brother's sword from the chest of the nearest marauder, then jammed his spear in its place. After prying loose the spear-crested rings, he dropped both of his brothers' fingers atop the marauder's chest.

His father gasped. "You'd rob your own brothers…with your father as witness?"

"Yes, father, but I'm no fool." Backhanding his father across the face, he stomped down on the old man's ring hand. "To sever my chains, I'll need your ring too."

CHAPTER ONE

When Stuart Pierce was a boy he prayed for two things: First that God would love him; second that he would be a good guy, a hero. This was a particularly unfortunate combination for which to pray.

"That's it." Stu nodded one firm nod, his nod of respect. "Don't quit until you're dead."

Despite dragging a bloody, mangled hind leg, the rabbit scurried past the front of Stu's car and across the driveway, disappearing into Angie's rosebushes. Stu stepped out, closed his car door, and glanced up at the vulture circling overhead. "So that's why. Well, he ain't carrion yet, pal." Reaching through the window, he grabbed his snack from the console, took a bite of the apple and rolled it into the bushes.

Stu checked his watch. Plenty of time to pluck one of Angie's caramel wrappers from her wastebasket, fashion his good luck charm, and swing by the airline's pilot lounge to grab his flying gear before heading up to Boston.

Opening their front door, Stu yelled, "Angie, it's me, forgot my wings." She didn't answer. Down the hall, he tapped on their library door and paused before turning the knob. "Angie?" The room was empty. "Angie!" he yelled louder. No response. Must be out back.

As he approached her wastebasket, he stopped and stared at the surface of Angie's desk, his teeth starting their habitual grind. Not ten minutes earlier, when he left home for the airport, her desktop was clear. Now this thick file, three empty caramel wrappers, and the burqa. The morning barely begun and Angie was already gnawing sugar and begging answers from a scrap of black cloth. More and more she shut him out. And the proof was likely inside that file.

Stu shook his head, thinking that he had a thousand good

1

reasons to open the file. For months, every time he returned from a flight, his welcome home was delayed by a series of clicks, shuffles and clunks—Angie minimizing websites, stuffing computer printouts into folders and slamming file drawers shut. Seconds later, only a few caramel wrappers remained. Desk sanitized, she embraced him, her lips pressing too hard, lingering too long, then burrowing her face against his chest. All of it, just too much. At meals, her jaw often paused, food half chewed. His "Penny for your thoughts?" always answered with an unconvincing "Oh, nothing." And Angie's signature knitting of brows had become almost perpetual. His soothing thumb across her forehead earning him a thankful sigh, but a shrug always dismissed any mention of his concern. And the quiet. Everything was too quiet between them. Alone, each reason was insufficient, but lumped together, they argued loudly for opening the file.

Yes, he had a thousand reasons to open it and only one to walk away—an honorable man doesn't spy on his wife. An honorable man is honest and direct. He could thank his mother for that burden. Ingrained in him since he first contemplated stealing a cookie, the tenets of his personal honor often left him feeling like an aging stallion hauling a load of uncompromising rules around society's increasingly pragmatic track. Yet, with one exception, his code had served him well. Angie was that exception. She named him "the uncompromised." His silent rejoinder—"with everyone but you."

Of course, Angie meant "uncompromised" to convey the biggest of compliments. He'd married a born idealist. From grade school hemlines to co-ed dorms to the Russian invasion of Afghanistan, small to great, any cause was cause enough to fall upon her sword. She died many deaths between the Iowa Basics and the LSAT. But in law school, she was forced to stomach compromise, her advising professor giving her cherished ideals little respect, saying, "Perfection is God's work," and "One person's God is another's devil."

Stu snorted. Perhaps idealism was, in fact, Angie's devil. How does one rid a person of her devil? Did he really want to?

Stu bent low, his forehead almost touching the desk, wondering what name his idealistic wife would assign him if he was caught investigating the contents of her file. Surely, not complimentary.

The file was thick. An inch and a half, he judged. Looked old too. The original manila color had decayed to uneven shades of yellow dinge, its edges soft and frayed. He sniffed. Even smelled stale. A tattered and curled tab hid the label. Sliding a finger underneath, he pressed it flat. Perhaps a lowercase "c" and "o"…or maybe eight and zero…then one or two more scribbles long since faded away. Recycled from some old case, he supposed.

Releasing the tab, Stu gave it a sharp flick. Early retirement bliss? Load of crap. Angie had simply traded a horror-a-day prosecutor's job for a nightmare cause. He'd pictured a life…no, damn it…she'd painted him a picture of her life as a hobby-lawyer. A little pro bono work—a child custody case or two, maybe advocating for those she called "the voiceless women of the world."

Angie had made her retirement pursuits sound pleasant enough. Problem was, most of her "voiceless women" wore some type of veil. And defending those women made Angie some very serious enemies, a death threat soon arriving and ringing the opening bell on the second biggest fight of their twenty-five year marriage.

But that was all ancient history. So why did it pop into his head now? Seemed silly. Yet he had a nagging feeling in his gut, prodding him to not dismiss that event so quickly.

Stu let his mind run. As he recalled, that argument degraded into a regular knockdown, drag-out brawl. Mostly his fault. He threw the first sarcastic punch. "Funny, I don't remember asking our financial advisor about the impact of death threats on your early retirement plans."

"A card wishing me well in my next career isn't a death threat, Stu."

"An unsigned card. Who sent it? And what about the package I received? How do you explain away an anonymous gift of white cotton sheets?"

"Who's the former prosecutor? I know what a death threat looks—"

"Card and sheets were both postmarked from The Realm. The card read 'next life,' not 'next career.' And simple white cloth is how they shroud their dead."

"I've been threatened before."

"Look around, Angie. This isn't the ivory government tower. You're no longer the 'Queen of Prosecutions' commanding a cohort of loyal knights. No detectives following up on threats. No police cruiser at the curb all night. We're alone here. And my next trip is the day after tomorrow. What about when I'm gone?"

"Then you're gone, Stu. The threat's half a world away and I can—"

"The threat is an airplane ride away. I've shared meals with the sort of men that send this type of message. They brag of 'honor killings.' You're naïve if you think they wouldn't—"

"And you're letting the past cloud your judgment. Sharing a kabob of goat meat at The Realm's airshow twenty years ago hardly makes you an authority on Islamic culture. If you're correct, then this threat confirms I'm doing some good. I'm not running away because my husband thinks—"

"Now who's letting their personal history affect them? Is this 'hobby-lawyering' about doing good or making up for the big one that got away?"

And that ended any scrap of civility. Her "goat meat" jab might have landed a little below the belt, but his "big one" was a true sucker punch—no prosecutor liked reminders of the monster that went free. Nothing intelligible followed.

The next day they negotiated a Cold War style truce. When the Carter-like peace treaty was reached, what had been their library became her fortress. He agreed to leave the lawyering to her and she vowed to share any real threats with him. But that trusted her definition of real. He wasn't three steps out of her sanctuary before a wrenching twist had grabbed his gut, leaving him wondering if this was how opposing attorneys felt shortly after agreeing to one of Angie's truces.

And there it was, the prodding nag fully developed—that same wrenching twist, grabbing his gut again. Their truce was bullshit. What he needed was a renegotiation, an agreement more along the lines of a Reaganesque "trust but verify."

But to revisit the terms of their truce, he needed more than just a feeling in his gut. No, with Angie his arguments required physical evidence, the type beyond words. The sort he might find just beneath that faded manila flap.

Reaching for the file, Stu flinched as the rabbit limped out from below the bay window, hobbled across the driveway and disappeared into the hedge on the other side. Damn. Spooked by a wounded rabbit? Sure didn't bode well for the remainder of his day. Up in

Boston, he had a full schedule awaiting him. Hand-to-hand combat training followed by a simulator evaluation.

If he got spooked in the simulator, he'd fail. And the evaluator would confiscate his badge and weapon. He'd have to count on others to defend his airliner. Bottom line—failure in the simulator meant shirking his duty. Stu nodded his respect toward the hedge. It took a near-dead bunny to remind him where the day's priorities lay. Today, he'd focus on the evaluation. Tomorrow—Angie and the bullshit truce.

Snatching up a caramel wrapper, he slammed it down onto the file and began rubbing out the wrinkles. A lucky wrapper is what he'd driven back home for, and the only liberty an honorable man could take.

He'd be out the front door in less than a minute. Lots of experience. For more than twenty years he'd shaped the waxy papers, first flattening and smoothing, then twisting the center tight, finishing by folding and refolding each half fanlike to form his lucky angel wings.

But minutes later he was still flattening and smoothing. And half a minute after that he was still asking himself why, when the grandfather clock chimed seven times, providing the answer.

Angie routinely snacked on one or two caramels between lunch and dinner and nibbled a few more late at night. She gobbled handfuls when preparing a closing argument, and consumed entire bags along with a bottle of "Old Grandpa" the few times she'd lost a case. But just like her bourbon, she never indulged in caramels before noon.

Stu's mind argued in circles until he finally accepted that the only honorable option meant finding Angie and demanding to see what had gotten her so riled within ten minutes of his leaving the house. But challenging her right now? Minutes before he left for the airport—not knowing what lay inside the file—without a clear battle plan? Likely result—days of useless bloodletting—most of it his. Nope. Time to beat a hasty retreat, before he did something foolish.

Stu yanked the flattened wrapper and the front of the file came along for the ride. In the split second it took to slam the file closed, his mind registered a woman's photo—her head nestled in ripples of windblown salt, face painted a puffy patchwork of purple splotches and red streaks, a halo of dark gems gleaming around her shimmering

5

black hair.

Slamming the file shut protected his honor but did little to guard his thoughts, his mind holding fast to the woman's image and casting it down upon the desk as clearly as if he'd pulled the photo out and laid it atop the file. Windblown salt? No. He'd seen this type of photo before. The ripples were sections of bunched up cloth, remnants of the woman's white veil torn away, shredded in the sand. The purple splotches—bruising from direct impacts, and the red—cuts from glancing strikes. The halo—her executioners' stones, some the size of a large man's fist, others small and jagged. All of it neatly arranged and carefully photographed to convey a specific message.

He shut his eyes tight and willed his imagination to turn off. But in the darkness of his mind the woman's black hair became auburn, the face, Angie's. And the photo came to life—Angie tucking chin onto chest, raising her hands against the torrent of hurtled stones. For every blow she deflected from her face, another slammed her breast, dug into her stomach and bit into her thigh. She sunk to her knees, arms flailing. Twenty, thirty, forty impacts, and her arms lifted no more. An earsplitting crack shot through the air as a small stone, no bigger than his thumb, impacted directly between her eyebrows. Her head reeled backward, exposing her neck. The next stone, flat and sharp, spinning like a saw blade, cut into her throat, snapping her head forward. Eyes wide, mouth drooping open, Angie crumpled to the sand and lay quiet, the rocks still caroming from her skull, while he just stood there…watching.

Unclenching his eyes, he found the woman watching him. The file was open, his offending right hand resting alongside the photo. Fragments of stone protruded from her skin just below the hairline, adorning her with a cruel, prickly crown. A single tiny shard, poking outward from her lifeless pupil, prevented her left eye from closing. She winked up at him like they shared some final secret.

As if locked in one of his too-frequent nightmares, he watched his hand move unbidden, pointlessly pushing at the rocks, smoothing her veil and brushing at the tangles in her hair. Fingers scraping at the tiny shard, he tried to coax her eyelid shut. His thumb gently rubbed at the purple swell between her eyebrows as if this woman were Angie and he could smooth all of her troubles away.

Stu clenched both hands into fists, and pounded them down along either side of the photo. This isn't Angie, he scolded himself.

This is a photograph. Angie is safe.

At the top of the photo he noticed a scrawl, scored in the sand. Part of a letter—looked like a "P." And next to it, a bit of another. Hard to tell which. Vertical ticks and horizontal slashes continued across the sand just above the woman's veil.

Stu checked the wastebasket. Right on top. Nearly half an inch of sliced away photo. Fishing the fragment from the basket, he aligned it carefully across the top.

Written in the sand, "PIERCE OF DEATH?" Next to it, a gritty smiley face.

Clutching the edge of Angie's desk, Stu steadied himself as his heart began hammering out an old familiar rhythm.

CHAPTER TWO

During the last moments preceding each college football kickoff, and as he bowed to his opponent at the start of every karate match, Stu's heart had always hammered out the same strong cadence. In his ears, he felt the pounding heartbeats—six beats growing louder and then six softer, over and over, until the crash of the first tackle, or the impact of that first blow.

While leading the initial wave of aircraft over Baghdad, the cadence had pounded so powerfully that the radio calls became unintelligible, his heart not calming until he launched his first missile. Right now, the rhythmic crescendos cycling through his skull grew so loud that he clamped his hands to the edge of the desk and squeezed, waiting for the hammering to subside.

But it just went on and on, up and down, pounding. He had no one to crash his helmet against, no opponent to snap kick, no aircraft to shoot down.

Bolting from the study, he turned left away from the wide-open front door and headed for Angie. The pounding quieted. At the end of the hall, Stu heard running water, darted into the bedroom, cornered around the bedpost, and twisted the bathroom doorknob. Locked.

Locked? Angie never locked the bathroom door. Hell, out here in the hill country, he could barely get her to lock any door. Stu raised a fist, but the file, caramels, burqa, death threat, and locked bathroom door kept him from knocking. There was too much he didn't understand. And what exactly would he say? He could hear her answers already. "The caramels—a moment of weakness. And the burqa—my new client is Islamic. The photo—a threat to my client.

8

PIERCE OF DEATH—Come on, Stu, pierce means pierce, as in piercing stones, not Angela Pierce." Every answer reasonable...but for knitted brows...half-chewed mouthfuls...and the quiet. And she'd never believe he opened the file accidentally. He wasn't prepared for that battle. A fight sure to rival the top two on their all-time list. The water turned off.

Stu stepped backward and sat on their bed, his mind picturing every motion of Angie's post-shower ritual, listening for any deviations from normal. The sliding shower door—always opening just a few inches. The towel bar squeaking as she pulled her towel into the mist. The door sliding closed. First, her face, gently dabbing the droplets, then her neck and shoulders and breasts. Always too rough on her breasts. A turn to the side, and the towel slipped down each thigh and shin, but never an instep. Another slide of the door to grab her robe. First her left shoulder, then right. The belt, cinched rather than a loop and pull. And with a full bow tied taut, Angie's dripping feet stepped through. The door slid closed.

Every sound normal, but still, the locked door. Nothing added up. He needed a plan. Most battles were won long before the first bullet left the barrel. He needed time.

At the sound of the hair dryer, Stu retreated toward the front door, but stopped at the study's threshold, drawn by the face inside the file. The oaken floorboards creaked beneath his feet as he shifted his weight from left leg to right and back. From this distance the file appeared to hold at least fifty more sheets. Of what? Emails, legal documents—photos? Perhaps the sort of proof she couldn't explain away.

The floor gave up one last groan as he reentered Angie's sanctuary. What did it matter now? One photo or a dozen? She'd never believe he hadn't rifled the entire thing. Well short of her desk, Stu loosened his tie. Twice he stepped toward the file, then back. If he didn't examine the remaining contents, then everything he'd seen could be written off as mere happenstance. His honor still intact.

Stu searched the carpet at his feet, located and retrieved the flattened wrapper from beneath Angie's desk. After smearing off the remaining caramel residue, he twisted the center tight and sat to complete the folding. Finished, he examined the photo one last time.

The woman seemed so young, her neck slender and flawless. What crime does a child commit? Stu's elbow nudged the photo. The mere inch it slid confirmed the presence of many more photos beneath. Stu muttered a violent "no" and closed the file. The wrapper was why he'd returned. And so far, he'd pushed no further than chance afforded.

Closing his eyes, he recalled the study as it appeared when he first entered, and then set out to duplicate that image.

File folder? He pushed it dead center on her desktop.

Burqa? He lifted the headdress from the corner of the desk and paused, staring at the black cape, his fingers probing the dark cloth. A big mistake, Stu reflected. Real big.

When he first saw Angie struggling to understand the mindset of the women she defended, the solution seemed obvious to him. She needed a simulator.

As an airline captain, simulators had allowed him to safely test all manner of aviation theory in order to perfect his flying. If Angie wanted to "get into their heads," as she put it, she needed a headdress. So, on a layover in Detroit, he rented a car and drove out to the suburb of Hamtramck. Found an Islamic clothing shop. Inside he discovered hijab, chador, niqab, veils and grilles, and much more. In the end, he decided that the burqa, with its full face-covering grille, provided the most challenging simulation.

Made the strangest birthday gift ever. Angie, at first skeptical, eventually grew to love the damn contraption. Draping the silky cloth over the back of the beechwood client's chair, she sat for hours, legs woven in a pretzel, more patient than a Tibetan monk, staring across her desk, literally asking the burqa questions aloud, searching for answers.

Holding the burqa at arm's length, Stu wondered if Angie had ever just looked at this thing. Instead of posing endless complicated questions, had she ever asked herself the simplest? What did she see?

Stu searched the cloth for his own answers. He mostly saw a great blackness. Darker than charcoal or tar. So dark it seemed to define itself by the absence of all light. Within its folds his hands lost their fingers, became hacked-off stubs entangled in a shifting darkness. Stu pulled one hand free. Four fingers and a thumb. He frowned. What did he expect?

After reviewing his mental image of Angie's undisturbed desk, Stu carefully placed the burqa just above the file, stretching the cape up and to the right.

Last item. The caramel wrappers. Crap. There'd been three, not two. Stu opened the right-hand drawer, took a mental snapshot and pulled out the caramel bag. Only one remained. He studied the sharp folds of his lucky wings. Impossible to remove those creases.

Peeling free her last caramel, he plopped it on his tongue, and set the wrapper on the top right corner of the file. Returning the empty bag exactly as he'd found it, he noticed a small screwdriver at the bottom of the drawer. Not his. Doing her own mechanical work now? The woman was damn determined to exclude him from her fortress. Stu chomped down on the caramel. Sweet and salt. Just like Angie.

Back on the creaking floorboards, he surveyed the study. With the exception of the caramel sticking to his teeth, everything was as if he'd never crossed the threshold.

Stu quietly closed their front door, slipped behind the wheel, and slid the lucky wings into his pants pocket, only to find another wrapper. Like he'd hit a mnemonic rewind button, his mind flashed back to this morning's goodbye kiss, then backed a few frames farther.

Yes…he'd fished an old wrapper from the garbage and crafted a near perfect set of paper wings. Holding them up, he joked with Angie that he should pull the golden metal pair from his shirt and replace them with this fine set. Her response—a faint, faraway smile. He'd shrugged, kissed her forehead and headed for the car. Not five steps away she asked him for a kiss. Chuckling, he scooped her up, but her return kiss seemed distant as her smile. More salt than sweet.

And somewhere between that salty kiss and five miles down the highway, he'd forgotten the lucky paper wings in his pocket. Forgot and returned home. Pressed the sticky side of the wrapper to the top of the file, flattened and flattened, then yanked. Saw the lifeless child wink up at him. An accident?

He didn't believe that bullshit any more than Angie would. Yet, he was glad. Trust but verify. Well, he'd verified she couldn't be trusted. How was that photo not a real threat? And if he hadn't invaded her study, how would he have ever known? Now he could demand to see the rest of that file. Shove the proof in her face. Help her see that she was in over her head.

And his personal code? Intact. He could only damage his honor with a conscious act. He'd premeditated nothing. No dishonor here.

None.

Stu compared the old wings with the new. The newest one looked all wrong, unlucky. He stuffed the old pair back in his pocket and threw the latest onto the floor mat. As he eased the old Mercedes past the bay window, a shadow shot up the length of the hood, straight at him. Startled, he spun the steering wheel left, brushing up against Angie's rosebushes with a crunch.

Shaking his head at his jumpiness, he spun the wheel back right, and pulled away. A second crunch sent his foot to the brake. He threw open the door.

Behind the rear tire the rabbit quivered, eyes blinking, hips and hind legs mashed. Stu knelt down in the rocks, brushed the pebbles and dust from its fur, and watched until the blinks stopped.

The words "I'm sorry" almost left Stu's lips, but he was immediately struck with their insulting inadequacy. Instead, he nodded his head in respect. "Now, you can quit," Stu whispered, thumbing the rabbit's eyes closed.

In the branches above, he heard a scrabbling of claws. Stu snatched up a stone, sighted and fired. As soon as the rock left his hand, the young woman's bruised and lacerated face flickered before him, her open eye asking Stu, "Why?" After all, the vulture was just a vulture. Did what vultures did. They didn't kill. They simply waited to clean up the mess.

The stone impacted hard, the vulture hissing and flying off.

"Starve, you flying rat." Stu picked up the rabbit, placed it inside the trunk and started down their long gravel drive. The rearview mirror showed a closed front door, the study's bay window empty. All calm. The only disturbing reflection—his eyes.

Swatting the mirror askew, Stu turned onto the highway and stomped the accelerator, swerving until the tires caught hold. His jaw ground as he reviewed his carefully constructed self-justification. He'd begun with a secure foundation—Angie couldn't be trusted. Then fabricated four thick walls—she'd hidden a real threat— invading her study was the only way to know—now he could confront her—for her own good. And then cleverly roofed his self-told lies—declared his honor still intact. Built a nice little house for his bullshit.

More like a liar's hospice. The place where trust goes to die.

CHAPTER THREE

Stu shuffled backward, blocking the training instructor's blows, never leaving too much of his one hundred ninety pounds weighted to either foot. His fifty-year-old reflexes were not as quick as his young opponent's, but thirty-five years practicing the martial arts brought something faster—patience.

The more he retreated the quicker came his opponent's fists and feet. Well-timed sidesteps avoided the kicks. Swirling forearms deflected the punches. And the more casually he diverted the blows the more forceful they became. Stu ducked and parried, moving steadily backward. Watching. Waiting.

Soon each strike came accompanied with an audible grunt. The instructor's neck bulged, veins popping outward under the strain of delivering such powerful blows.

Stu smiled at him.

The kicks turned vicious. Always the kicks. Punish the timid defender with the nastiest weapon. One raked across Stu's hip, leaving a searing burn along his skin. Another kick, and then another. A flurry. The instructor's kicks coming so fast and hard they seemed more like a set of bamboo whipping canes than human legs.

But only leverage delivered kicks that strong. Leverage gained by too much forward lean, too much weight on a single leg.

Stu suddenly reversed direction. Darting inside a whipping leg, he tapped the back of the instructor's weighted knee, throwing him off balance, drawing him closer, and then drove the heel of his hand deep into the man's solar plexus.

A rush of air gushed from the instructor's throat as he tumbled backward to the mat, gasping for breath from lungs that no longer cooperated.

Reaching down, Stu grabbed the man's belt and pulled upward, lifting his hips slightly from the floor, alleviating the pressure on his spasming stomach muscles. He loosened the chinstrap of the instructor's headgear and pulled the plastic guard from his fish-out-of-water, gulping-for-air mouth. These small kindnesses were all that he could provide until the nerves that controlled the man's midsection recovered, allowing him to breathe again.

Stu looked around the room. Everyone else still fought. Charging back and forth across the mats, each pair of combatants switching from offense to defense and back, a fury of blows delivered and received, all of them hurrying to finish their opponents. Stu shook his head side to side. Patience was faster.

"Knock it off," boomed a voice from the corner of the room—Mash, the lead hand-to-hand combat instructor, issuing the training manual's sacrosanct command for all attacks to immediately cease.

Most blows froze mid-strike. But arcing leg whips, with far too much momentum to freeze, snapped heel against hamstring, swinging harmlessly past their targets, yet spinning the attacker like an ice skater finishing a twirl. One lost his balance, stumbling to the mat and bringing a few laughs.

The loud whack across Stu's hand told him that the instructor had regained control of his lungs. He released the man's belt.

"I said knock it off." Mash stalked over, looked down and pointed the young instructor toward the door. "Everyone, take five."

"My fault," Stu offered. The last thing he needed was a break, his heart already starting to ramp up. Throughout the entire drive to the airport, the flight to Boston, and the cab ride to the training facility, every moment since he opened that file, his heart had never completely ceased its mad cycle.

Even as he'd warmed up, the slow pace of his push-ups reflected the low background pounding. Six beats up—he extended his arms. Six beats down—he lowered his chest to the floor. The hammering continuing until he blocked the instructor's first punch.

Stu tried again. "Agent Mash, really, I was holding onto his—"

"He didn't knock it off." Mash growled and then pursued the young instructor out into the hallway.

But he's just a kid, Stu wanted to say. He'll learn. Go easy on him. Young people make mistakes.

As Mash slammed the door shut, Stu's mind flew open, the woman's battered face immediately filling the void, sending his heart hammering higher. Hours had passed since he'd studied her photo. The details should fade. Shouldn't they?

Instead the details grew ever more vivid, the stark contrast between her beauty and her suffering dominating Stu's thoughts, becoming his meditation.

If he covered her face, all appeared serene. Soft rippling sand. Sheer white veil. Wavy black hair, thick and shimmering in the sunlight. A silky, flawless neck.

Then uncover her face and see the pain. The winking eye, held open by a sliver of stone. Alongside her broken nose, a contusion, purple and puffy, swollen like a boil about to burst. An open gash lacing one cheek from temple to chin.

And if he closed his eyes, he could count the stony fragments of her prickly crown. Did they really number thirteen? What could someone so young have done to deserve this? How old could she be? Fourteen, maybe fifteen. Sixteen at most. What crime does a child commit? Six up. Six down. The pounding.

Mash returned. The young instructor didn't.

Stu's next opponent seemed tired, worn. A former field agent, Stu guessed. Mash introduced him simply as "Ice." That couldn't be good. The man looked bored. As if he'd seen so much covert action that anything short of dying didn't interest him.

Mash took up a position directly behind Stu. "Fight's on," he commanded.

Ice just stood there. Didn't even raise his arms. That was bad.

Stu lashed out, testing. He delivered three quick combinations, nine total blows.

Ice swatted all of them aside, like so many flies. He still looked bored.

Stu toyed with the idea of unleashing his best assault. Dispatch the man quickly. Show the hovering Mash that his personally selecting Stu's next opponent made little difference.

But what if Ice tossed aside his best attack? What then? No. Patience is faster, he reminded himself, and switched styles, planting both feet, waving the man forward, grinning.

Ice's eyebrows rose. A slight smirk pursed his lips. He came, dancing lightly on the balls of his feet, feinting, weaving, delivering one controlled blow after another, never striking too hard, yet punishing Stu's forearms. Ice switched to Stu's legs, targeting thighs and calves, every impact sapping a little more strength. He stepped back and examined Stu's defense like a wood carver considering his next chisel placement. High and low, Ice chipped away until a fist penetrated, flying past Stu's late block and crashing into his headgear at the temple. Stu slung a counter, but Ice was gone.

Stu rolled and spun, came up with forearms raised, weight spread evenly across both legs, expecting a follow-up attack. Nothing. At the far edge of the mat, Ice waited. Over his shoulder, Mash looked on, his face seemingly saying that Stu could practice another thirty-five years and still get his ass kicked. Mash was probably correct. Stu nodded Ice his respect.

Ice smiled.

Mash winked.

And Stu launched. No control. No balance. No patience. He flew forward.

Ice's smile and Mash's wink together triggered a flash of revelation. The fragment in the girl's eye was no chance bit of flying stone. Some bastard had carefully chosen that sliver, maybe even took the time to shape it from a larger rock, then lifted her dead eyelid and jammed it through her cornea. It wasn't enough just to execute her. No. The bastard had to dominate her. Defile her. Use her to send a threat that promised Angie no mercy. This child did nothing to deserve this. How could she? What crime does a child commit? She was no more than a prop to them. A mannequin. Disposable.

His fists a blur, his legs whipping, Stu's body strained to satisfy the needs of a single emotion—rage. His punches met blocks, his leg whips missed. The counter attack was brutal, an elbow catching him square in his left bicep, his arm going numb. But the girl's battered face commanded him, driving him forward, demanding an answer. What crime does a child commit? Stu pushed through the elbow's crushing impact, his knee smashing into Ice's thigh, buckling him over.

"Knock it off," Mash ordered.

Ice didn't, swinging another left hook at Stu's temple.

"Knock it off," Mash repeated.

Stu ducked below the arcing fist, rolled and slammed a forearm

16

into Ice's hamstring. "What crime?" he grunted, hammering a fistful of knuckles into Ice's Achilles tendon, collapsing him to the ground. "What crime?"

Somewhere, far off at the outmost edge of Stu's awareness, a gravelly voice bellowed, "Knock it off!"

CHAPTER FOUR

One steaming hot shower, two tubes of analgesic, four painkillers, and a long lunch did little to reduce the throbbing in Stu's left shoulder. But the ache was worth it, his pulse now running slow and steady. Much rather suffer the aching throbs than the mad pounding.

Strapped to the captain's seat of the flight simulator, Stu waited impatiently for *something* to go wrong. As an FFDO, a federal flight deck officer, his job was to protect the flight controls at any cost: his life, other lives, all lives on board. But as he waited, the real enemy worked tirelessly against him—boredom.

His first flight instructor preached that flying airplanes for a living meant hours and hours of abject boredom interspersed with moments of sheer terror. The simple act of paying attention, staying focused on the *here-and-now*, was the professional pilot's biggest test.

The simulator magnified that challenge. Nothing in this *here-and-now* was true. Everything, a manufactured reality. The throttles were hooked to a computer, and that same computer controlled the engine gauges, which fed information back into the computer, which produced the airspeed readouts that told the pilot he was going too fast, or too slow, and so the pilot moved the throttles, which fed information back into the computer, which....

It all seemed real enough. As did the men acting as terrorists. Well-rehearsed men performing the scripted scenarios of government-paid playwrights. Confidence-building terrorist plays based on ancient history. Plays crediting the enemy with no intelligence and no imagination. Worst of all—no patience. Every script a slightly different version of the same self-conceived story, hero pilot defeats crazed terrorists. Pilot after pilot, day after day,

18

starred in these feel-good plays, everyone from playwright to terrorist-actor to computer technician deceived by simulator after simulator of simulated success.

The truth? Intelligent, imaginative men watched and waited. Patient men who defined their lives, their sons' lives, and all the sons of sons for lifetimes uncountable, by a single word—jihad—the struggle. Design one hundred scenarios, one thousand. No matter. These men had an entire lifetime to adlib one line, effect one plot twist, and the curtains came rushing down, the critics booing as the airplane crashed…into the towers…onto the banks of the Potomac…onto the amber waves of grain.

If a simulator crashed, nobody jumped from the top of the World Trade Center, or burned to death at the Pentagon, or plowed their graves into the Pennsylvania farmlands. Sure, men lost jobs, but no one died. And no matter how real the cockpit throttles, or how Oscar-worthy the performances of the terrorist-actors, some part of one's mind never let go of that fact. One's mind wandered.

But Stu knew all the tricks to remain *here-and-now*. After leveling at cruise altitude, he checked the list of diversion airports, picked the safest two based on terrain and weather. Close places to land in case *something* went wrong. In the simulator, *something* always went wrong.

Next he scanned the engine instruments looking for a fuel flow too high, an oil pressure too low, or any of the dozens of other abnormalities indicating impending *somethings*. Between scans he scrutinized the cockpit door. In every scenario, the playwrights consistently followed the same plotline. The *something* that went wrong always started at that door.

Yet why? How about an empty airplane? Middle of the night. Patient men waiting for the ground crew's shift change. Sneaking aboard and starting the engines. Airborne in minutes. Crashing into the White House minutes later. Or the patient flight attendant, learning all the proper codes and procedures, already standing inside the cockpit, stabbing and stabbing for jihad. How does one stem the spurts from a severed carotid? That's the script Stu would write. That and many more just like it.

But that scenario doesn't make any sense, the playwrights would argue. Who would fly the airplane? Who would stop the passengers from retaliating? Sensible questions. But they were yesterday's questions.

And yesterday, Stu would've rebutted their sensible questions with sensible questions of his own. Why can't a flight attendant learn to fly? If one flight attendant can fight for jihad, why not two or three? Why not the entire flight attendant crew? Stu's script made plenty of sense if one flight attendant flew while the others sliced up the passengers. But that was yesterday.

Yesterday, he married Angie. Yesterday, they raised Maggie and Andrew. Yesterday, everything made sense. As of zero seven hundred today, nothing did.

Today, he'd rebut all of their sensible questions with just one. What crime does a child commit?

Stu stared at the blackness beyond the simulator's cockpit window. Placing a hand on the cool, flat glass, he covered up the haunting face floating there, leaving only hair and sand and veil—a simulated serenity. Dropping his hand, he uncovered the brutal truth and asked himself again, what crime does a child commit? Like a nagging song lyric, he couldn't get the question out of his head. He'd pondered many questions since this morning. Vital questions. Why did Angie insist on hiding threats? Who threatened her? How could he find them? How to stop them? All questions he must answer. So why did the only question he didn't have to answer, a question that had no answer, keep demanding an answer, right now?

A thump at the door snapped him back to the *here-and-now*. Mumbling a "damn it," he twisted halfway around in the captain's seat. With head hawked over right shoulder, Stu peered through the cave-like darkness toward the cockpit door, listening. Only the usual sounds met his ears, a constant low roar of rushing air and a mind-numbing electronic hum. No more thumps.

As Stu stared, the handle seemed to rotate, the cockpit door to bulge inward. Mind games. He leaned out, hanging from his harness, arm stretching, fingers grazing the cold, gray metal, confirming his suspicion. The door didn't bulge. The handle hadn't turned. But the mind games grew worse, the young woman's face appearing at his fingertips, winking. A face that with every passing meditation looked more and more...like Angie's.

Stu's fingers fell away from the door. He knew why the face wouldn't go away, and why the question wouldn't go away. He'd seen hundreds of photos depicting the same sort of ritualized brutality. Many, much worse. But none directly threatened Angie. Now, the face was Angie's. Now, the face mattered.

Stu turned his back on the winking eye and turned up the lights. Too much light in a cockpit destroyed night vision. Filled the windows with reflections of dials and gauges and switches. Made it hard to see outside. He turned them up brighter still. Seeing outside? Precisely what he didn't want.

He needed to focus on *here-and-now*. At any moment *something* would happen and the scripted scenario would play out. A terrorist pretending to be a flight attendant. A real flight attendant entering the cockpit without proper warning. Perhaps a Federal Air Marshal pounding on the cockpit door, or a hijacker disguised as one. Every year, new scenarios. Yet always the same question for the hero pilot. Shoot, or don't shoot? Dead terrorist—good job. Dead Federal Air Marshal—probably a long debrief culminating with dismissal from the FFDO program.

And occupying the copilot's seat for Stu's evaluation, the unluckiest of draws—Agent Strickland, the program's director. Rumors were the old patriarch took a bullet during the Bay of Pigs fiasco, pioneered the Navy Seal program, and worked the CIA's Middle East desk for over three decades. Called out of retirement after 9/11 to start the Federal Flight Deck Officer program, he'd set a standard for FFDOs that some joked rivaled the FBI. Advice was—don't believe Strickland's grandfatherly smile. Make a mistake and those pearly teeth tore off large chunks like a great white shark.

Right now Strickland did nothing. He sat. And looked. At Stu, at the door, the window, the floor, and back to Stu, circling. Impossible to tell what the man was thinking. No emotion on his face. Everything about him said…absolutely nothing.

Stu's left hand located the lucky angel wings in his pants pocket and gave them a pat, then wrestled with his harness—first snugging it tight, changing his mind and loosening, finally releasing it to the floor. His right hand adjusted the pistol at his hip and reached up among a forest of knobs to select the autopilot speed control. One click clockwise increased the Mach reading from point seven-eight to point seven-nine. Alongside his right thigh the throttles ghosted backward in response. Not what he thought he'd asked for.

As he looked up to confirm the Mach setting, an odd sparkle of light bounced from the glass and drew him toward his reflection in the cockpit window. Good. Something *here-and-now* to keep him *here-*

21

and-now. Stu glanced at the door. All quiet.

He faced the window and searched for the source of the light. A kaleidoscope of bright colors showered from the instrument panel, coloring his chest. Shifting and leaning, he generated repeated flashes of the golden sparkle, zeroing in.

By sitting perfectly still, balanced in his chair, Stu coaxed the odd trick of light to remain long enough to study the strange phenomenon. Even moving his right hand back six inches to the holster, it scampered away. But if he sat straight of spine, centered, facing himself unflinching, the sparkle glowed steadily. Its source, the wings above his heart, the wreath that surrounded the star mounted there. The captain's wreath burned brilliant, a tiny halo around his star.

Stu frowned. He was a most unlikely candidate for a halo. And where did one's star head after betraying a wife's trust? Doubtful the direction was a good one. He shouldn't have opened that file. Never seen the girl's face. But he did. Can't change that. Could tell Angie. He should tell her. Such a tiny halo. Maybe he could earn it.

Transfixed on the mirrored image, trying to freeze everything except his arm below the elbow, Stu's hand abandoned the small comfort of the paper wings in his pocket and reached up toward the light. A loud crack sounded from the cockpit door. He rose and spun. Three men rushed him. Too late to draw and fire, his hands gripped the backs of the cockpit seats as he delivered a powerful snap kick into the first assailant's sternum, propelling him against the two trailing behind. All three fell backward onto the galley floor. Stuart stepped from the cockpit, drew his weapon and fired. One shot, point blank, to each of their chests as they sprawled helpless. Rotating back through, a second red explosion appeared on each of them. Two more pulls left him with an empty chamber and the dead sound of metallic clicks as he continued firing into the last body, wanting just one more live round to finish his painting.

Laughter erupted behind him. "Whoa there, Tex. Nice shoot'n." Agent Strickland pointed at Stu's still-pulling index finger. "But you're out of ammo. Stop yanking that trigger."

Stuart forced a smile at the white-haired patriarch.

Agent Strickland smiled back and offered a helping hand to the tangle of men struggling to rise from the slippery red paint. "And just look it here at my fearsome terrorists, all three painted up nice and pretty."

"Gramps, you can just kiss my...." The man's reply was cut short by his slip back onto the floor.

"Now, now boys, no need for profanity. No self-respecting Islamofascist would cuss. He might cut off your head and piss down your neck, but he'd never speak like that, now would he?" Gramps asked with a laugh.

Agent Strickland was called "Gramps" by everyone who worked at the training center. By all accounts, an appropriate nickname. Gramps was top-down loyal and defended his men against all outsiders.

Stu reminded himself that he didn't work at the training center. And whether he got Gramps or Strickland for his debrief depended on his performance. Pilots who screwed up got the sharp-toothed Agent Strickland behind the debriefing room door.

Gramps patted Stu on the back, smiled and reached down to aid the recipient of the snap kick. "Captain Pierce, let's help these three gentlemen up. Mind the paint though." Strickland's smile looked a little stiff as his eyes slipped from Stu over to the cockpit door and then down at Stu's pistol.

Stu shoved the empty RAP4 back into his holster. The cockpit door was wide open behind him. He stood in the center of the galley, more than two full steps away. No arguing with facts. He could only hope the results outweighed his mistake.

Stu bent down, offering the last terrorist-actor his hand, and got it smacked away. As the man lurched to his feet, a single drop of red dribbled from his chest protector toward Stuart's white shirt, falling onto his wings. Rubbing only spread it deeper into the crevices of his tiny laurel wreath.

"Captain Pierce?"

Stu rubbed harder, but the golden light was gone.

"Captain Pierce?" Gramps, phone in hand, examined him. "Maintenance wants to know if you got anything for them?"

"Maintenance?"

"Yeah, you know, that flying stuff you do."

Stuart's right hand slipped from his wings, found his tie and straightened it. "Why, have they had complaints?"

"Nope, just checking. An inspection's coming up."

"No, nothing." Stu shook his head. "Well, possibly. Have them check the interface. I thought I saw the throttles move backward when I asked for more speed."

Gramps spoke into the phone, then turned to him laughing. "Maintenance says you pilots are always looking for speed. He says you need a little patience, a bit of faith."

"Yeah, yeah, a funny guy. Just tell him to check it out and get back to me."

The laughing Gramps morphed seamlessly into a shark-smiling Strickland who covered the phone's receiver with his hand. "Captain, why don't we take a good, long break?" His gaze circled from Stu to his wristwatch and back to Stu. "Half hour or so. Grab yourself a cup of coffee and collect your thoughts. Meet me in debrief. There's a few things we need to cover." Strickland returned the phone to his jaw. "Maintenance, you still on? Captain Pierce was wondering if you guys wouldn't mind taking a good look at the throttle interface anyway, and get back to us. He'd sure appreciate it."

Heading for the break room, Stu reviewed his simulator session, searching for the errors. All his previous evaluations had concluded with "Nice work. See you in debrief. Five minutes." But this time, he'd gotten "a good, long break" and "a few things we need to cover." Same as ever before, he'd successfully accomplished the basic duty of an FFDO—no one had reached the flight controls. But he'd discharged his weapon outside the cockpit. A clear violation of federal law. Stu pushed open the door, turned the corner and stared. Not at a coffee machine, but a wall of urinals. Behind him, a whoosh of air signaled the door opening again.

"They're 'frinking' urinals, 'Ironman.' Used for unloading the byproducts of copious quantities of beer or coffee, evening and morning respectively, but sometimes I get confused by drinking 'til dawn." As he so often did, Carl laughed at his own wit.

An honest smile formed on Stu's lips. Felt good. He let it grow into a chuckle. "'Frinking?' I see you've found yet another pronunciation for your favorite word."

"Just keeps on giving, Ironman. Most versatile word in the English language. Frinking. It rhymes with drinking. Pure poetry." Carl laughed again, walked past, unzipped and bellied up. "Hey, speaking of drinking, did you ever get Buzz that case of beer?"

Stu's chuckle faded. "No...I...forgot what he drinks. Need to call the control tower over at Reagan National and ask someone."

"What? You kidding me? You've known the guy forever. Drinks that dark crap, same as you." Carl's bald head bent around to eyeball Stu. "Landing without clearance is serious crap. Been over a month since he covered our butts. That's bad form, Ironman. And unload already, will you? Making me 'frimping' nervous, just standing there."

"Drinks stout. That's right." Stu walked forward, opening his fly, as if he meant to be there. "I'll get him a case."

Long minutes later, the break room provided little break. Stu's mind raced as he moved from one bulletin board to the next, sipping coffee, pretending to read. His upcoming debrief would likely get very ugly.

This year's scenario contained the simplest of *somethings*. A predictable, routine, manageable *something*, and yet he screwed up. While chasing a damn halo he lost the *here-and-now*. Fired outside the cockpit. And twenty minutes of internal debate had changed nothing. Zilch. Nada. If Gramps desired Stu's removal from the FFDO program, the grounds for his dismissal were solid as bedrock. He hated excuse-making anyway. What could he say? Hadn't slept well in months. Worried about his wife. Often dreaded going to sleep. That would just get his weapon yanked. Better to confess to sex with Martians than mention his dreams. What fifty-year-old man wakes with nightmares? What next, bedwetting?

Stu inspected a patriotic poster. Two jets in a dogfight. The artwork, a little off, wrong missile for that aircraft, and the trailing fighter's nose was way too high. It would never finish that turn. The caption, "Duty calls! Come join the fight for freedom" brought a memory and a grimace.

After the towers fell, he answered the call, volunteered for FFDO duty. How could he not? When he told Angie, she said she understood but the cleft between her eyebrows made an appearance. Probably just his imagination, but every year since, as his annual training approached, her cleft deepened.

Last year, Angie asked, "How much longer?"

"Until I quit," was his joking response.

Angie didn't laugh. Didn't smile. "Fine. When you're dead then," she said, her cleft cleaving a chasm between her eyebrows. Not his imagination.

She was right. He should quit. All this past year, he seriously considered quitting. Meant to. Yet here he was, doing his duty again.

Why?

What difference did one fifty-year-old man make? Especially a man of nightmares. And too little sleep. A man who stepped out of the cockpit and fired. The man who betrayed his wife's trust. A man without honor. Bedwetter.

Stu looked down at his bloodied wings. Rubbed them. Rubbed his shoulder, his temple, his eyes. He couldn't undo what was done, but he could do the honorable thing right now. He pulled out his cell phone, scrolled through the contact list and paused, thumb hanging above "Angie." What could a bedwetter accomplish in a two-minute phone call? Anger. Resentment. Argument. More crap to haul into debrief. Stu slipped the phone back into his pocket. He had already screwed up one *here-and-now*. Not going to screw up another. Focus— finish with Gramps, or more likely, the sharp-toothed Strickland.

Bedwetter? Stu removed four silky smooth blue pills from his pocket and tossed them into his mouth. Chewed and chewed, past chunks, beyond graininess until he achieved a creamy paste, thick and bitter. Swallowed. Chased it down with great gulps, draining the last of his coffee. The deluge of painkillers ought to provide an hour, maybe two, free of the throbbing ache. Bedwetter? So be it. He'd be the fiercest damn bedwetter anyone had ever met then.

Stu poked at the coffee machine's buttons, no sugar, extra strong, same attitude he'd take into debrief.

CHAPTER FIVE

When Angie was a girl she prayed for the light of God's truth. Later she wrote, "...perhaps the best truth is the one that kills the least, but only the end of history supplies the final tally."

Angie paced toward the back of the study, fuzzy slippers carrying her far from the merciless demands of the keyboard on her desk. Never had she fought so hard for the right words.

Her twelve muffled steps across the diamond-patterned carpet ended at the file cabinets. Fingers steepled over her nose, and thumbs dug into her jaw line, she tallied the heavy wooden drawers. Seven cabinets across, five handles tall, a total of thirty-five, all crammed with witness statements, photographs, and videos of flogging, amputation, ritual stoning, and worse.

Human trafficking. Women as chattel. Where was the common ground? What words sufficed when a woman's punishment for learning to read was acid in the eyes?

Angie rocked back and forth, heel and toe, hearing the testimony, and feeling the despair documented in every file. Her eyes settled on the base of the center cabinet, the dark and mottled panel. The drawer belonging to "The Bastard." The installer said the wood was rotten, the blackness of the stain soaking deep and uneven. He offered to replace it free of charge. She told him not to bother. Seemed right for what she hid there, the worst of The Bastard's emails and graphic photos of his atrocities.

Each time she posted a blog entry that resonated and swept the internet, The Bastard's file grew. The level of his agitation had

27

become her barometer of effectiveness. And wanting to know the instant her efforts raised his ire, she'd given him a special email aural alert to signal the arrival of his filth. Threatening his hellish world gave great hope to hers.

The grandfather clock chimed. Angie stopped rocking and turned. Its face depicted the balance of sun, earth, and moon using golden discs struck through their centers with silver lances. Today was special, lance of sun and earth aligned, the summer solstice, her self-imposed deadline. The day she promised the file cabinets she would find the words. Her letter was finished. The promise fulfilled. Only a click of the mouse needed. Instead, she planted her feet in the center of a diamond and wondered if her letter would read more powerfully in a bolder font. While she considered Gothic over Courier the sixth chime signaled another hour gone.

The files demanded action. Angie turned back toward her desk, a small cleft forming between her brows. From this distance the computer screen looked barren. Yet she knew each word written there, every vowel and consonant. The commas, colons, and periods all carefully selected to weave the sentences, bind the paragraphs, and capture not the letter, but the true spirit of God's law. Written more than three months ago and then rewritten dozens of times since, she'd honed and polished her plea. An open letter addressed to the women of The Realm, concerning the inequities of totalitarian governments, the right to vote, and the positive effects of inclusion. Replete with historical precedents and supported with quotes from the Qur'an, the truths she voiced were self-evident and undeniable. She was confident her letter presented a flawless argument that any court of appeals would uphold.

Then why did her computer monitor look like a window to the Arctic? Stark white and lifeless, the screen seemed to mock her with its cold emptiness.

Angie raised the collar of her pajamas, buttoned the top, then marched to her computer, sat down and pulled the chair forward until the arms thunked against the desk. She grabbed the mouse. Her index finger hovered above the button, then dropped to trace an eight on its surface.

A full minute later, Angie turned the eight sideways, scribing the symbol for infinity, acknowledging the truth—she'd never click. The computer screen was correct. The letter was cold and lifeless—

empty. Who was she to condemn a culture? What gave her the right to preach? She didn't know. She just wanted the killing to stop.

Angie's hand pulled away from the mouse, then pounced onto the keyboard, arrowing the cursor up and across to the middle of the black-lettered drivel polluting her screen. Pounding backspace and delete, she hammered at the keyboard, knocking down each letter until she forged a new pure white surface. File delete was easier. But this felt better.

Grabbing her purple pen, Angie clicked as she inhaled deep, clicked again and exhaled slow, and clicked once more to clear her mind. A ritual she developed during her first year of law school. A meditation. The purple color—her reminder of Sahasrara, the crown chakra, the seat of higher understanding, the seeking of renewed compassion, the understanding of others, and the way she learned to tolerate compromise.

Angie closed her eyes and, for the thousandth time, meditated on the burqa. She imagined the woman sitting across the desk, framed by the bay window, draped in fabric, with not a sliver of her humanity exposed to the world. No armor ever devised by man seemed harder to penetrate. In her mind, Angie reached out, trying again to lift that grille.

The seventh chime of the grandfather clock faded, the heels of her hands still resting on the base of the keyboard. Several times she caressed the letters, begging for inspiration as the space between her brows deepened. Her wrists ached. She massaged them, then reached up and rubbed out her cleft as Stu might have done. She felt his thumb, heard his chuckle, and breathed deep on his musky smell.

Angie turned toward her wall of family photos, her gaze settling on what she called Stu's hero shot. She'd caught him patting his aircraft's nose, black curly hair a mess, olive skin shining with the gleaming sweat of mock aerial combat, eyes serious and powerful. She needed those eyes right now to stop her chin from trembling.

And just beneath those eyes, her favorite family photo. Stu's arms wrapped around her shoulders, chuckling lips nuzzling her ear. She could still feel the soft heat. And their children, Maggie and Andrew, only toddlers back then, latching onto her best friend, Cheryl. Everyone crammed on the couch with tired happy faces, a litter of snuggling puppies—her family, her strength.

She lifted the cordless phone from its stand. Just a few words.

Any friendly voice would help.

But Cheryl already divided too little time between her redheaded twins and the grocery store. And Maggie crammed for finals at the language institute. Andrew maneuvered with his unit at Fort Bragg.

And Stu? His simulator session had ended long ago. Angie grabbed the thick file from the corner of her desk and fingered the sticky spot on the front flap. Pulling the caramel bag from the waste can, she checked inside one last time. Two facts were clearly in evidence. First, she was willing to take the witness stand and swear before God—"That bag wasn't empty." And second, Stu always called right after his simulator.

Angie set the phone back on its stand, circled the desk to the bay window and looked outside toward the lovers. Oak and maple, each with separate solid trunks, yet skyward their limbs entwined. And as Stu had joked, who knows what's going on below the ground where no one can see. Today Angie saw tired leaves from a too dry spring. The sky a pointless gray, no rain, only featureless clouds withholding the warm glow of a sinking sun.

Angie's back found the wall. Sliding down to a crouch, she hid behind her knees. The world has always warred. Those are ancient hatreds. One person can do nothing. The Bastard can't reach here. Husband safe. Children safe.

But Andrew would complete training soon, join his unit overseas and do his duty. Her little boy would end lives. He would kill. Angie choked her pen, jammed her thumb down to snap out another click, and threw. A throw so forceful that the pen left a mar of purple plastic on the printer as it glanced off and stuck into the drywall.

Angie banged her head onto her knees. Her child would kill or be killed. Children over there...wake every morning...and kill each other. "Children murder," she whispered. Her whisper became a bitter plea as she repeated the words again and again to the burqa, each repetition punctuated with Angie's forehead bouncing against her knees, her eyes letting go the frustration, her pajamas growing wet.

The burqa remained silent.

Angie snatched the black headdress from the chair. "Why won't you speak? Every day, dropping from the skies, blasting from beneath robes, the bombs. Yet the only protests I hear come after the metal rips through our children. Then how loudly your tongues wail."

The burqa's response was a black silence. A resounding quiet so loud Angie cried out against it. "Our children murder each other. Do you hear me? Our children murder." She twisted and wrung the black cloth, repeating over and over "Our children murder." But as her anger lessened, those three words became only two—"Our children." And then just one—"Our."

Angie rose from the floor and moved to her keyboard. She typed. "Our children wake each morning to kill." No, it wasn't right.

She inhaled, exhaled, and cleared her thoughts. Closed her eyes, and for the first time, donned the burqa. She felt the pain and the sorrow. She felt the fear.

Reaching up, she lowered the burqa's grille over her face. Felt its comfort and strength. Behind the grille her body seemed to fade away. Breasts, hips and curves vanished, leaving only mind. Angie was no longer body, she was spirit. No one could hurt her beneath the grille. Beneath the grille, she was love, she was mother.

Angie's eyes flashed open. She shuffled through the mess on her desk, found today's newspaper, and located the story that had bittered her morning coffee. She typed, copying nearly word for word, filling her blank white screen with the article, but changing each "she" to "I" and every "her" to "my." She hit print, yanked out the page and read the changes aloud. "I woke up this morning and saw in the paper that my son Achmed had strapped a bomb to his body and…." Angie pulled her purple pen from the wall and struck through the name Achmed. Above it she wrote "Andrew." She tried to read aloud again but faltered on "Andrew." After wiping her eyes, Angie pressed the page to her chest and thanked the burqa.

A somber tolling of church bells rang from her computer's speakers. The Bastard's aural alert. Good. She had an answer and wanted him to know. Angie did what she'd never done before. She punched reply. Nothing. She clicked reply again. Her screen went blank and the tower of servers next to her whirred with a clicking, manic noise. Her head snapped in their direction. Flashing lights signaled distress. Eyes wide, holding her breath, she tried the keyboard. Her monitor came alive.

And her face grew cold, the blood draining to leg muscles that demanded she flee, as photos flashed across the screen displaying a slide show of torture. The first few of a beautiful young woman dressed in faded blue jeans and a yellow tank top, posing with her boyfriend in front of the Washington monument. The next series, her capture and transport to the desert. There she was stripped naked in the sun and placed in a corral with horses. She was cut from the herd and tethered to a pole. Whipped as she ran in circles. They brought a saddle and bit, and Angie could take no more. She grabbed the power cord leading to her servers and tore it from the wall.

For the second time that day Angie locked the master bathroom door and entered the shower to wash away The Bastard's filth.

CHAPTER SIX

When Hosaam was a boy he demanded two things of Allah. First, that his mother be delivered from torment, and second, that he be the hand of her deliverance. His demands were met.

At the sound of the front door splintering from its hinges, Hosaam slithered out through a hole at the back of the bomb-cratered building. Keeping his belly to the dirt, he snaked through the deep rubble toward the outer edge of the Afghan village. After a few meters he stopped and pressed his hands over his ears. As expected, the flash-bang of a grenade preceded the charge of his pursuers into the entrance hall of the building he'd just vacated.

Yet those scampering inside didn't immediately concern him. The ones that might flank ahead did. Hosaam uncovered his ears, listening for boots running through the loose stone of the alleys left and right of his position. The trick was keeping the pursuit close enough, but not so close that he was captured or killed.

This wasn't the first chase he'd led them on. During each previous pursuit Hosaam had made himself a ghost, a lone gunshot visiting the night, running away at their approach, leaving only a set of footprints in the dust, then circling back to study their tactics. Before that first chase, Hosaam hadn't even known what to call them. He'd known that they weren't true believers—not really human. Yet, he had no fitting name for them. But as he watched them discussing his tracks, with their heads huddled low to the ground like they were sniffing at a fresh pile of scat, he suddenly knew them. They were scat-sniffers, mongrels, rabid dogs that needed to be put down. And Allah willing, this pursuit would be their last.

Tonight's chase had begun at the crotch-lick, as he'd designated their camp. The village was laid out like an armless corpse—head jammed east against the base of the mountains, torso squeezed between steep hills, two legs of road splaying out to the west. The dogs had chosen to bed down where the two roads merged, the crotch. After firing a shot into the crotch-lick, Hosaam had shown himself this time, bringing them snapping at his heels. Then he'd zigzagged across the torso, hopping crumbled walls and ducking in and out of deserted homes, creating sufficient separation before sprinting up the lone street at the village's narrow eastern neck, and entering the building at its head.

And now, came the most dangerous part of his plan. Inside the building, he'd left them a puzzle, closing every door, but locking only those two that led to his escape hole at the back wall. Hosaam smiled as he imagined them pondering that first locked door, their heads rolling left and right, sniffing, spooking, and padding in circles, as they wondered how to protect their backs while bashing into each succeeding room. This concern, he hoped, would draw every scat-sniffer inside, while he safely crossed the wide-open expanse of the abandoned garden ahead.

From inside the building came another splintering crash. Another flash-bang. Hosaam crawled faster, almost passing the camouflaged entrance to the tiny tunnel he'd prepared. Hidden by fragments of stone at the near end, the tunnel led to the remains of a fallen shed—a long strip of corrugated metal jutting out over the garden's edge. The perfect place to hole up waiting for the dogs to take down the last door.

While listening again for flanking boot steps, Hosaam quietly uncovered the tunnel's entrance. After slipping off his satchel, he rolled to his back and wriggled beneath. Fingers testing the metal's jagged edge, making sure his robe didn't catch, he scooted along one centimeter at a time.

Safe on the other side, he reached back under and eased his satchel through. Careful as he'd been, the satchel's drawstring had severed. The top lay open. He jammed his hand in, shoving aside the goatskin canteen and bundles of jerked lamb. Hosaam sought something far more important than water or food—a leather pouch, the size of a man's clenched fist. His mother's coin purse. His reason for living.

He tipped the backpack over, clattering pistol and spare ammo magazines to the stones. There, tangled among the ammo, he found the pouch and raised it to his lips, praising Allah. Only then did he consider the noise—and froze, listening.

After more than a full minute of silence, Hosaam repacked his satchel and crawled to the garden's perimeter to await the final flash-bang. In front of him lay fifty meters of open ground, then a winding footpath leading up and over the mountain ridge…to America…or to death, if the sniffers had already flanked ahead. Their night vision goggles would make him an easy kill, no matter how fast he ran. Hosaam studied the empty furrows for signs of recent passage—swirling dust, a boot track, trampled weeds.

All still. Not a footprint. Not a weed to be stomped in this parched soil. How long since water had flowed here? How many dead gardens in this dying land? Afghanistan had once overflowed with verdant farms. Like America, the people thrived, their faith strong, until decades of constant warfare made his country a wasteland. His homeland now produced just two things in abundance: opium and hardened young men, who witnessed little but death from infancy to manhood. He must leave this land.

Hosaam lifted his eyes skyward, toward the top of the mountain, to America. He sucked in a sharp breath. North and south, bright stars still littered the night sky, but due east, just above the ridgeline that he must cross, a faint light appeared. Hosaam silently cursed the twist of fate that had brought all his plans to fruition on the shortest night of the year.

He watched a star vanish. And another. Two more. Like shadows fading beneath the darker night, the stars disappeared, their light overwhelmed by the rising sun. Whispering aloud, Hosaam damned the coming day, and damned the ignorant dogs that trailed him. Perhaps the simple puzzle he'd left them wasn't simple enough.

Finally, the last explosion sounded, and like a flushed hare, Hosaam was out from beneath the crumpled metal and sprinting across the garden, zigzagging, a shower of dust spraying backward from his sandaled feet. If he survived the first few meters, then he might live to reach the footpath, draw the dogs over the ridgeline, and earn his way to America. His next ten steps would tell.

After twice that number, not a shot had rung out, and Hosaam reached the fissured bedrock at the mouth of the footpath unscathed. He peeked back. The rubble was empty, the alleys on either side deserted.

Minutes passed without pursuit. Certainly, they must have found his escape hole. Followed his tracks. Discovered the tunnel. Hosaam rechecked the eastern sky. A bloody glow had replaced the fading stars. He could wait no longer. Removing the pistol from his pack, he took careful aim and fired twice, sending the rounds through the building's remaining glass. After backing well into the fissure, he counted to ten, extended his hand high above his head, pulled the trigger once and dropped to the dirt.

A fusillade of bullets battered the bedrock around him. Four separate muzzle flashes inside the building, and one from each of the two alleys.

Six dogs. A good manageable number. Hosaam slid backward, snapped to his feet and raced up the mountain trail. For a while the fissure would shield him, and for a while longer, the boulders. After that, his chances of reaching America depended on distance and darkness.

Three hundred fifty meters was the tactical effective range of their goggles. Yet the path ahead was filled with dozens of switchbacks. Five minutes of running produced perhaps three hundred meters of separation as the vulture flew—or the bullets. Right now the mongrels were far too close.

But the six would move slowly until they spotted him. First splitting into pairs, left, right and center of the abandoned garden. Then the center pair would unleash another fusillade of bullets toward Hosaam's last known position, covering fire to shield the other four dogs as they raced across the barren furrows. After that, measured steps, two by two, leapfrogging, establishing a new firing position at every clump of boulders as they advanced up the mountain trail. Their caution took a lot of time. His desperation wasted none. Perhaps that difference was enough for him to move beyond the range of their goggles.

A loud torrent of covering fire came from below. The mongrels were already crossing the garden.

At best, he was three minutes ahead.

Hosaam ordered his tiring leg muscles to work harder, ignoring the ache by focusing on his dream for America. She was an oasis. A breadbasket. Mother to the western world. Her proud Lady stood tall, lifting high that flaming torch. During his worst sufferings and doubts, he imagined clutching hold of Lady Liberty, and his faith was renewed, his strength returned.

Her image vanished from his mind as daylight cut over the ridge and lit the valley below. Day, without a dawn. As sudden as a headman's sword, the first rays sliced clean through the village, bathing its body of broken homes in glittering white and leaving its head severed in utter black—absolute light against complete darkness. The difference was stark and final. Beautiful. But unlike the headsman, the sun didn't sheath its sword. By the time he reached the next switchback, another sliver of black had already dissolved, exposing the front of the building he'd just escaped.

Hosaam glanced up the mountain, remembering the many turns still ahead. The first goat herders had carved the safest way up this treacherous ridge, and the thousand generations that followed had respected their wisdom. Yet their path was born in a world where spear points wrought death rather than bullets. Right now, the silence of the dogs' rifles likely meant that he was outside the range of their night vision goggles. But in following the goat herders' path, the light would pare away his protective shadow long before he reached the top. What was the tactical effective range of a bullet in broad daylight? Five hundred meters. One thousand, if they had a sniper. He was no goat herder.

Hosaam ripped the satchel from his back, pulled out his mother's purse and tucked it beneath his robe. After heaving the satchel over the next cliff, he ignored the caution of his goat-herding ancestors and departed the ancient trail. Straight up the mountain he ran, cutting across the trail two and three times before following it long enough to recover his breath, and then off the trail and up again. But carving his own path forced his head low, on the lookout for loose rocks and exposed roots. Only the nearest stone, the next scrubby bush, mattered.

He spotted a switchback just above, and close beyond that, another. A chance to eliminate two loops of trail in quick succession. Stepping onto a boulder, he leapt. Where he expected to land a foot and leap again, his foot instead found air, and he recalled why these two switchbacks were so close together—a ravine dropping all the way to the village below.

One arm clutched air. The other caught stone. Fingers scraping at the near vertical slope, he managed a momentary halt before two fingernails ripped away and he plunged downward again. Clawing with both hands, he scratched for any hold.

Splayed against the mountain, cheek leaving a trail of skin, he slid until a thin ledge tore at each knee and smacked his jaw. Hands thrusting overhead, he caught the lip, stopping his slide, as the mountain continued to shed pieces into the valley beneath.

A burning fire replaced his missing fingernails. His jaw dripped blood. Below him, both feet scrambled to find nubs for support. Above, the ledge swarmed with ants hurrying across his fingers to repair their damaged home. And two black shiny beads stared down at him.

They were mounted on a puny gray and white head that jerked left, right, and then snatched an ant from his thumb, and two more from his wrist. Between pecks the bird seemed to puzzle Hosaam's predicament…then froze, staring down at the rock beneath its claws.

A second later, the puny head snapped up and jutted toward Hosaam's face, the bird letting out a piercing warble, then stabbing his hand one last time before dropping from the ledge, carrying both ant and skin. He watched the lark catch the updrafts and rise toward the morning glow, soaring up and over the crest without a single flap of its wings.

Hosaam's stomach muscles quivered, not from fatigue, but raw need. The day of his mother's passing taught him the difference. Then, as now, the muscular contractions signaled "the power" coming on, filling him. He needed to kill. Kill the ants crawling down his arms. Kill the mongrels that tracked him. Kill the lark that flew so free.

The whole mountain felt alive with his need, a low rumble radiating through the stone beneath his limbs. Echoes rose up the ridge. Vibrations loosed fresh rocks onto his head and shoulders. He melted flat against the bedrock, clutched bloody fingers to the centimeters-wide ledge, squeezed shut his eyes and prayed aloud, "Allah deliver me."

The reverberations teased free his mother's purse. His eyes flashed open to see it join the stones quaking past. Hosaam swung out full length, catching it on his instep, corralling the leather pouch until the shaking subsided and the echoes waned. Even then, he refused to move until a tiny roiling cloud appeared to rise up and surround her purse.

Rapture surged through Hosaam. Allah would speak to him again, as he'd spoken before. This same tiny cloud was present at the moment of his mother's ascension. Always did Allah answer the faithful. Easing his knee upward, he reached out and felt for the cloud, once more to touch the power, to feel the burning in his soul.

But this time, nothing. A trick of light. Hundreds of meters below, the sun shimmered across the billowing dust rising from the village, marking where the avalanche had come to rest. The tiny cloud was just an illusion.

The rapture left him.

Cursing the light, he grabbed the pouch and placed it between his bloodied teeth. Hand over hand, he worked sideways along the ledge toward a shallower section of slope. There, the hand and footholds proved plentiful. Still, he tested each one with a stiff tug before trusting his weight. One solid step after another, Hosaam struggled upward, grabbing brief moments of rest behind rocky outcroppings, then belly crawling over the lip and onto the path to avoid the dogs' unholy vision.

Sure that their goggled eyes searched the trail near the avalanche, he stayed low, scrambling around the next switchback and running stooped past the following two. Amidst a small thicket of scrub brush he knelt and prostrated toward Mecca, quickly praising Allah for deliverance.

He removed a knotted cord from his mother's purse. Tying each end to the purse's drawstring, he fashioned a necklace and slung it over his head. Then he renewed his attack on the mountain, this time sticking to the path.

But the path was long. Minutes passed, the grade steepening, the sun relentlessly rising. He again ordered his legs to work harder. They ignored him. His vision blurred, clouding with fleeting dots of gray. The trail seemed to come alive, shifting left and right. Twice he nearly tumbled over a cliff.

Hosaam plodded on, praying for strength, beseeching Allah to guide him.

A bright light lit one side of his face. He reeled toward it. The Lady had returned, brighter than ever before. But the earth itself seemed to fight his reaching her, the pebbles feeling like boulders, the dust quicksand. Yanking each leg forward, he slogged ahead, blind to all except her light. She was so close. His hands struck out, reaching for her. Blackness came. He toppled to the rocks below.

Feeling nothing, he sought Allah in the darkness. Finding nothing, he wondered if he'd entered hell. Yet, with the passing seconds, he realized that his lungs still gulped air. The sun warmed one side of his face. Dirt cooled the other. Pain registered at a cheek. He was alive. His strength would return. The struggle could renew. If Allah willed it, it would be so.

Lifting his head, Hosaam brushed away the dirt and pulled a small shard from his cheek. The light was all around him, his protective shadow gone.

Millimeters from his face, a long sharp fragment of stone spiked from the ground. Gleaming in the light and shedding the shortest of shadows, it confirmed a sun fully risen. He'd failed. He jammed his thumb down on the point, felt the stone pierce deep, and let out a loud cry, wishing his temple had impaled there. Better death, than never reach America.

A few meters away lay a vast bed of little spikes, any of which might have ended his life. Instead their many tiny shadows chorused his failure. He rolled onto his back to block their taunts. The sun met him squarely in the eyes. He sat up, inviting the dogs to shoot. No shots rang out. Why didn't they fire?

Hosaam sprang to his feet and spun away from the sun to face west. Before him was the crest. He'd already crossed over. Allah had delivered him.

He clambered back up the trail, lowered to belly, and snaked the remaining distance to the top. A large boulder shadowed his head as he waited for his eyes to adjust to the gray below.

Morning gusts struck at his back, rattling the scrub brush and blasting sand against the cliffs. The mountain winds also carried familiar grunts and hisses. Somewhere nearby, the griffon vultures fed. Yet he heard nothing that hinted of discovery.

Presently his eyes confirmed what his ears indicated. The mongrels still wound their way up the trail, moving in disciplined pairs, establishing a covering position at every switchback.

Caressing the pouch at his chest, he felt the power of Almighty Allah residing there. His plan would work. He would reach America.

See her cities in ruins. Fields barren, People in tears. Their tall proud Lady crumbled to her knees and ravaged, a headless torso holding a dark torch. He would bring Americans the constant fear of death. He would bring them Afghanistan.

Hosaam reveled a moment longer on the image of Lady Liberty's raped and broken body before slipping back out of sight. Rising from the dirt, he rushed down the trail. All six dogs followed. Judging from their position below, he might have fifteen minutes to prepare, probably less. But six was a good, manageable number for what he planned. Four or five to put down. One or two as pets.

CHAPTER SEVEN

"**W**ho'd you kill, Ironman?" Carl inclined his bald head toward the debriefing room door. "Looks like you've got good-cop, bad-cop waiting in there."

Stu forced his clenching jaw muscles to relax, then asked, "Gramps and who else?"

"Some big guy. But I've got to go. Just wanted to make sure we're still celebrating the Fourth of July at your place."

"What'd the guy look like?"

"Like I said, 'big.' Didn't see his face." Carl checked his watch. "My 'fricking' box time starts in two minutes." He hustled off toward the simulators. "What about the Fourth?"

Stu gave him a thumbs-up, then turned to face the debriefing room door. Two against one? Fine. He'd won plenty of those dogfights in the military. As always, the key was patience. Time it just right. Make the first missile launch a good one.

He gave his left shoulder a squeeze. Not bad. The deluge of painkillers had worked their temporary magic. "Bedwetters of the world unite," Stu said under his breath. "Fight's on."

Pulse slow and steady, Stu took a sip of "no sugar, extra strong" and opened a heavy windowless door into what looked more interrogation than debrief. Long bars of fluorescent lights fought to brighten gray, barren walls. The sterile odor of fresh wax, rising from a shiny chessboard of brown and yellow floor tiles, competed with the aroma of his coffee. Four black and chrome chairs sat opposing, two versus two, on either side of a long wood-grained laminate table. The only bit of warmth in this room came from Gramps, sitting legs crossed, hands encircling a steaming cup, small smile, no teeth.

A heavy thud sounded. The door sealing shut behind Stu.

Next to Gramps stood an unopened sports drink in front of an empty chair. A large figure filled up the back right corner of the room, stance wide and firm, hands loose at his side, face hidden in the shadow of a banged-up metal storage cabinet. Presumably, the bottle's owner.

Stu advanced toward the two empty chairs on his side of the table. Gramps or the shadow? He took another sip of coffee and pulled out the chair opposite the sports drink.

Gramps introduced their mystery guest. "Captain Pierce, you know Agent Mash from this morning's hand-to-hand combat exercise. He asked to sit in."

"Sure. Good to have you with us." Stu said, thinking precisely the opposite. "Didn't recognize you all cleaned up, coat and tie." He smiled and offered the dark corner a handshake. "Hope Ice's leg is okay."

Mash moved straight at him into the light, offered no return smile, shook hands and planted himself in the chair alongside Gramps. "He'll be fine, but that's not the point. You didn't freeze at the knock-it-off call." Like someone had just dumped a truckload of rocks, Mash's gravelly voice filled the room with a deep rumble, his words stirring up a dust cloud of rising questions.

Seemed this debrief concerned more than just his simulator performance. Stuart sat down on his side of the divide and mimicked Gramps's relaxed pose. "Some moves don't freeze well."

"Don't freeze well?" Mash glanced over at Gramps.

Like a fortune-teller reading tea leaves, Gramps gently swirled his cup and examined what lay at the bottom. Never lifting his eyes from the spiraling darkness, he shrugged.

Mash's eyes jumped back to Stu, his voice growing louder and rockier. "And the second time?"

"Second time?" Stu questioned, adding what he hoped only Mash could see as a barely perceptible smirk.

Mash's reply came fast, like a landslide. "Yes, Captain Pierce. You ignored the knock-it-off, not once, but three times. You hard of hearing, or just when it's about following orders?"

Before answering, Stu set down his coffee and took time to consider the small bit of white protruding between the dark blue fibers of his pant leg. "I wasn't the only one in the room who missed that call."

"Meaning what?" Mash leaned toward him.

Stu picked at what he thought was a piece of lint and found instead his good luck charm, the tip of one tiny wing poking through. "Meaning your man followed through on his attack after the knock-it-off call. I merely countered." Stu pinched off the wingtip and dropped it over the side of the table.

Mash's gaze followed the floating bit of white all the way down to a brown tile and then looked up to find Stu smirking at him. "Countered? That's a polite description for what you did, Captain. You countered him right into the clinic."

Odd, Stu observed, Mash's baritone lost most of its gravel when he was close to yelling. Sounded more like cracking ice. Perfect time to launch a missile. Stuart let out an exasperated exhale, the one that loudly declared "God, please grant me patience," then lowered his voice to just above a whisper and slowed his words to a condescending pace. "I was a tad aggressive...I admit...but defensive...not offensive. Your man was good...left me little choice."

"Little choice?" Mash's face came half over the table. "Listen up, Captain. You retain your FFDO status by passing this training, and right now I don't see—"

Gramps leaned into the fray. "Whoa now, gentlemen. Let's take a minute to catch our breath. Stu, how's your coffee? Agent Mash, you haven't touched your drink."

Stu broke eye contact, grabbed his cup and drank it dry. "Coffee's great. Wish I had more."

Mash didn't look away and didn't answer.

"Well, good then. Agent Mash, thanks for stopping by. I'll take it from here."

Mash uprooted, the front legs of his chair leaving the floor as it slid backward. He grabbed the unopened sports drink, nodded at his boss and exited, never looking back.

Gramps sighed and rubbed his bloodshot eyes, sending the glasses on his nose bobbing, then reached into his briefcase and pulled out a dark brown folder, plopping it down between them. The stuck-on label read "Pierce."

"Captain, I've reviewed your training summaries for the past eleven years. Overall, I'm impressed. Your performance? Exemplary.

Skills? Exceptional. No previous problems." He pulled the glasses from his face and tapped them on the folder. "But...."

The glasses dropped, rattling on the table. Agent Strickland's hands formed a divining rod pointing straight at Stu. "But now you and I have to deal with today. What's up, Captain? What's going on?" Strickland leaned backward, placed his hands behind his head, stiff, studying, waiting.

Below the table, Stu's hands squeezed the cold, chrome chair arms. He'd successfully reduced this fight to one versus one, but Strickland was no easy adversary. In his mind he recited, "no excuses, no bull crap," not with Agent Strickland. "Just a really bad day. I've screwed up three times. The last with Mash just now. I shouldn't have baited him. The man was right. A knock-it-off call was made and I didn't. Simple as that. No excuses."

Agent Strickland chewed the inside of his lower lip, looked away, looked back. His hands loosed from his head, opened the brown folder and pulled out a file marked with today's date. "Good enough for now."

Gramps returned the glasses to his nose. "Mash's boys tend toward showing off and—"

"Showing off...or getting even?" Stu looked Gramps straight in the eyes.

After several seconds of staring back, Gramps gave up an almost imperceptible shrug, conceding a "maybe." "From the power of the *mae geri* you delivered to them in the cockpit I'd say either one is a mistake with you. That was as fine a front snap kick as I've ever seen. Where'd you get the training?"

Stu's hands released the chair arms and moved to his lap. "Believe it or not, it started with my mother."

"She taught you?"

"Yep. She was a little different. Studied eastern religions. The woman actually took yoga seriously. Darn good at judo and could still kick my butt when I was fifteen. She thought the martial arts might center me, tame my wild streak."

"A unique woman, your mother. Did it work?"

"Not really." Stuart chuckled. "Took my wife to do that. But the self-discipline I learned was priceless."

"All right, enough about the hand-to-hand combat session. Let's move on to the cockpit scenario." Agent Strickland started chewing on his lower lip again. "Homeland Security Act of two thousand two, ring any bells?"

Stu's hands sought out the chrome. "Yes, I've read it."

"Maybe not well enough. It clearly states—"

"I know. It states that I have the world's smallest jurisdiction, that I cannot step past the cockpit door to discharge my weapon. I know."

"Yet, you did exactly that. Stepped past the door into the galley and fired until your gun was empty. Kept pulling after that too."

"I projected myself into the scenario. Just as we're supposed to do. Lost myself in the moment and—"

"Sort of looked to me like you were taken by surprise." Strickland smiled wide, lots of teeth.

And for the very first time Stu saw the Strickland everyone feared. The unsmiling smile. The vacant, unblinking eyes. Circling. The toothless first few words of his last comment—"Sort of looked to me"—sounding less an accusation, seeming more like an invitation…to share. One's thoughts. One's troubles. One's lame excuses. To share—weakness.

Instead, Stu concurred. "Yes, I was surprised."

For a moment Strickland's smile shrunk, his eyelids coming to life, lifting at the corners in what appeared an expression of amused approval. Then gone. "Look. We telegraph those scenarios. You knew something was about to happen. And yet, you weren't alert when the door cracked open. Something bothering you?"

Strickland would never quit circling without some small chunk of truth to chew on. Stu squeezed the cold chrome as he weighed his options. What could he safely share? His troubled sleep was likely the best choice. Everyone suffered that slight weakness from time to time. Admit to that shortcoming, but finish strong. "I haven't been at the top of my game, that's for sure. Flying lots of red-eyes. Throws my sleep off. Barely had any rest last night. But we've all got to manage those challenges. Don't know what else I can say, other than it won't happen again."

Long moments passed, Agent Strickland gnawing at his lip until music rose from his shirt pocket. Pulling out his cell, he checked the caller ID and then let the tune continue. "Okay…I'm going to exercise a little faith. We'll extend your evaluation. Run one more scenario tomorrow." Strickland held up an index finger, cutting off any response from Stu, and answered his phone.

Another scenario tomorrow meant Agent Strickland was tossing the proffered chunk of truth right back at him. Stu would get one more chance to demonstrate acceptable performance or lose his weapon. And Strickland got four more hours in the simulator and another entire debriefing to continue his incessant circling.

Strickland dropped the cell back into his pocket. "Maintenance said the throttle interface is fine." He grabbed Stu's performance report and held it up. "Keep focused. Don't leave the cockpit. And this little sheet finds its way into the circular file. Understand?"

Stu loosened his grip on the chair. "You bet, Gramps…." The old patriarch's nickname was out of Stu's mouth before he could stop it. "Thanks."

Gramps repacked his briefcase. "Do me a favor. Lighten up on the 'Gramps.' If my old eyes aren't deceiving me, I'm spotting a bit of late autumn on your head. Another decade or so and your hair will be as wintry as mine. Call me Tom?"

"I'm pretty sure it'll never be that white," Stu joked as he rose to leave. "But, Tom it is."

"One last thing." Gramps tossed a twice-folded sheet of paper on the table.

Stu unfolded. "My target qual. What about it?"

"Tightest cluster of bullets I've seen in a long time. Mom teach you that too?"

"Sure did. But her cluster would've been tighter."

"Of that, I'm sure," Gramps muttered.

"Come again? Did you know my—"

"So why empty your weapon, Captain? You'd already nailed each of them in the center of the chest—twice."

Stu relaxed for the first time since entering the simulator hours ago. Finally, a question with a simple answer. "If I'm ever forced to fire, I'll make darn sure they stay down, that's all."

"Well, I appreciate your attention to detail. But, take it from a man who's been there. If you want them good and dead, then remember this little ditty, 'Pop'em in the chest to drop'em, round to the head to make'em dead.' If you'd done that, they would've been just as dead and you'd still have two rounds in your gun. Got it?"

Stu ran the rhyme through his head, shortened it. "Pop'em—drop'em, head—dead. Got it. Thanks again, Tom."

Gramps stuck out his hand. "Make sure you get a good night's rest."

Stu put on his most confident face, shook hands, and departed down the hall wondering how a person made sure to get a good night's rest. Rest meant sleep, and sleep brought dreams. And of his recurring dream, he most feared...the fear.

CHAPTER EIGHT

The griffon vulture's hiss filled the whole of the mountaintop. Hosaam searched the eastern sky ahead. Above the trail, near the choke point for the ambush, enormous broad wings, half again as wide across as a man is tall, circled, blotting dark holes on the face of the sun. The griffons flew effortlessly—wings held in frozen arcs, catching the updrafts, long heads snaked low, casting about for the weak and the dead. His true brothers. Always beneath their swirling columns, he found nourishment. And like a brother, he only took what he needed to survive.

Several more vultures floated down from the peaks. A good omen. Soon he'd give them dog meat to feed on.

Six was a good number. Another kilometer would reunite Hosaam with a dozen of his countrymen, and counting him, that gave them more than a two-to-one advantage. Thirteen mujahedeen against a half dozen mongrels. Which still left Hosaam five men short of the ideal complement of eighteen. Three to one was textbook, the minimum number to force surrender. Yet the ambush he'd planned gave them a powerful force multiplier—surprise. Was that enough? Impossible to calculate. Though it must suffice. The Mullah wanted prisoners.

Delivering captives had so far proven impossible. The mujahedeen attacks always terminated by mongrel airstrikes. Ten of his bothers dead for every dog they put down. They never gained a prisoner, not even a corpse.

The difference this time was the pit. No bigger than a coffin, he'd dug it into the mountain weeks ago, leaving just two openings facing the trail, a tiny one to locate the target as it marched toward

49

him, the other, a little larger, through which to fire his AK-47. A small granite boulder disguised the entrance. Mere meters from the trail he'd watch them pass, searching for his target—the one that bore the radio—then empty his weapon into its back. If he could instantly eliminate that particular dog, no bombs would follow. Kill three animals, wound two more, and the last cur would come begging to heel—a pet for the Mullah.

Stooping for three stones, he tossed each against the boulder at the corner of the sharp turn ahead. A single stone, arcing back over top the same boulder, welcomed him. After beating the dirt from the front of his robe and adjusting his turban, Hosaam strode forward to greet his fellow mujahedeen.

But the stench of rotting flesh greeted him first. And around the corner, only three mujahedeen waited. His two most trusted brethren, and the pompous, black-turbaned Faiq. Below the trail lay the source of the stench, a dead horse, one foreleg buried to the shoulder in Hosaam's pit. Upon its haunch, a huge griffon vulture tore at the soft underbelly.

Only the pompous Faiq looked at him, arms folded, nose to the sky, looking down. The other two made great effort to avoid Hosaam's eyes. The young, beardless Kashif by sheepishly resuming his watch of the trail Hosaam had just traversed. And shaggy Abbud, perched upon a high rock like a mountain goat, his great graying beard dangling over the barrel of his sniper rifle, repeatedly blowing the dust from its scope.

"It's over." Faiq hopped down to the trail and pointed at the feeding vulture. "Allah does not favor your plan."

The griffon dropped a chunk of entrails from its beak, spread its wings wide and hissed at Faiq's hand stretched too near its prize. Faiq drew back his arm. "It's over," he repeated.

"Over?" The word left Hosaam's lips chopped in two, the second syllable drawn out in a breathy whisper as his mind struggled through the implications of Faiq's decree.

All these many months, he'd left no trace, not a track of his footfalls, not a fiber of fabric, nothing. Over? More than a year of his life, alone in these mountains, fighting starvation, studying enemy tactics, seeking any pattern to their maddening randomness. And now, so near his moment of triumph, this pompous jackass declared it over? "Our brothers?" Hosaam asked. "Where are they?"

"You were to reach us before the sun crossed. We delayed as long as—"

"Where are they?" Hosaam rasped.

Faiq's eyes flared wide. "I command here, Hosaam. You came to me, begging my help to convince the Mullah. The three of us waited for you, and now you screech at me like this creature." Faiq's finger jabbed toward the vulture, earning another bristling hiss. He slid his AK-47 from beneath his robe.

Stepping between Faiq and the vulture, Hosaam rested his fingertips on his knife, hoping Faiq would pull the trigger. How gladly he'd chance the wounds just to slit the jackass's throat. "Bullets are loud. Perhaps you'd like to try my blade?"

Faiq frowned, backed away and lifted his pack from the ground. "Kashif, Abbud, we go."

Hosaam's breathing slowed and deepened, his fists clenching as he watched them collect their gear. Faiq had never done without the warmth of fire, slept on hard stone, hid his waste beneath the rocks. Faiq didn't need captives. But without them, Hosaam would never earn the Mullah's favor. Never reach America. He swallowed hard, relaxing the anger from his throat. "Faiq, we still have surprise. Allah does show his favor. I was hidden as I crossed over and we can—"

"No. I stood high above the trail. Watched you stumble and fall. The sun hid you, not Allah."

"Allah took the darkness, but gave the sun to blind—"

"Enough foolishness. You sold your plan to the Mullah as protected beneath Allah's night. Now you claim Allah's sun." Faiq cinched up his pack. "We'll use your plan another time."

"But you know the dogs leave this area to the British. They won't return."

"So you will kill and capture British soldiers instead of American Marines."

"I can kill the British anytime. The Mullah wants dogs. Only six come toward—"

"We are but four," the jackass brayed. "They wear body armor and will radio for bombs so precise they can choose your left cheek instead of your right. You can't stop that now." Faiq turned his back. "Khashif, Abbud. Come."

"You choose to desert me? Betray me?"

Faiq answered without looking back. "Abandoning a fool is not betrayal. You make the choice, not us."

"And you, Abbud?" Hosaam asked.

The shaggy goat hefted his sniper rifle over his shoulder and turned away.

Hosaam grabbed Kashif's bicep. "You also? Afraid of dogs?"

"Look at your bloody cheek, your swollen chin," Kashif said. Still sheepish, he seemed to look everywhere except Hosaam's face. "Dying is not vengeance. Come with us."

"Go, little lamb. I stay with the griffon." The vulture tugged a string of intestines from the horse's swollen belly, tore off a chunk, raised its maw skyward and gulped. Hosaam stalked within centimeters of the ravenous creature, admiring its hunger, so unlike his so-called brethren.

Traitorous fools, all of them. Faiq by far the worst. Unfaithful, and a coward. Black turban? Hosaam snorted. As if the Prophet's blood could ever run so thin.

Hosaam scrambled up to Kashif's former lookout spot above the trail. Over his shoulder he watched the dust swirl about the feet of his retreating comrades. Jackass, goat, and lamb, all faithless animals, little better than the dogs they ran from. So be it. He conceived this plan without their help and would execute it without them. Working alone, he had total control. No mistakes. And the victory would be his alone. All glory to Allah, but the victory, only his.

Hosaam peered down the trail at the crest. The dogs hadn't yet crossed over. And when they did, what then? He still had surprise. But even if he managed to destroy the radio, how could he singlehandedly kill five rabid mongrels clad in body armor? What clever tactic created that miracle?

No! Those were Faiq's spineless thoughts polluting his. He didn't need a clever tactic. Nor body armor. Allah was the maker of miracles. He only needed faith. Almighty Allah had never forsaken him. As a boy, lost in rapturous prayer, Allah enlightened him to his mother's ascension. And for the past year, operating alone in these mountains, Allah had protected him. Mere minutes ago, Allah hid his crossing.

Hosaam's stomach muscles quivered as he lifted the pouch from his neck. Kneeling beside the collapsed pit, he placed it on the horse's rib cage, prostrating in submission. His entire body shook as the muscular contractions intensified, the power filling him, the raw need to kill consuming him. He prayed aloud, awaiting revelation.

From the stench it came. The horse was bloated, burst open at neck and rump, maggots eating the flesh. He'd seen this often. The small gap at the stomach, where the griffon fed, could easily be enlarged. Slipping the knife from his waist, he sliced the horse from barrel to bladder, sunk both arms past the elbows and scooped out mounds of entrails, pushing them toward the vulture. The griffon's face looked in awe, as if it too sensed the presence of Allah.

After wiping his bloody fingers clean, Hosaam snatched up the pouch with both hands, kissed the supple leather, raised it to heaven, lowered and kissed again. Removing his outer robe, he wrapped the pouch inside and stuffed it beneath the horse's fractured foreleg, deep into the wreckage of the pit.

Hosaam crawled between the flaps of rotting horseflesh, sliding in amongst the maggots. The wriggling worms knew little difference between him and the dead horse, probing his body for putrid flesh. Yet he barely felt them, his body surging with the almighty power of Allah. Sighting his weapon up the trail, he waited in quiet ecstasy to become the incarnation of his creator's vengeance.

More griffons alighted to nourish on the plenty Hosaam had provided. Squabbles broke out, challenges over the largest portions, hissing and flapping, scattering sand and pebbles in every direction as they fought for complete control of a carcass that could easily feed them all.

Good. His brothers' glorious hunger worked to mask his recent tracks.

With every passing minute, the maggots wriggled deeper, slipping through gaps in his clothing, reaching his groin, still searching for rotten flesh. One dropped into his ear and tested the soft wax. Hosaam trembled. Sweat poured off him, his breaths coming fast.

Still, he couldn't be wrong. The scat-sniffers had no choice. With a chasm to one side and a mountain peak to the other, they must cross this choke point or retreat. In all the many battles, he'd never seen them turn tail.

"Sergeant!" a voice yelled.

Dust poured into the horse's belly as a great flapping of wings rose around the dead horse. He fought the urge to cough, chomping down on his tongue.

"Sergeant, up here."

Hosaam heard boots scraping over stone. Sliding pebbles. Someone scrambling up to the voice. He bobbed his head, smirking. The dogs had strayed from the trail again. Of course, they had. Maddeningly random.

"Private, I just signaled Corporal Ramirez to take command. He's got our back."

Their hushed voices were only a few meters downhill. Hosaam's hand slid from his AK-47 onto the bandoleer across his chest.

"Why do you think I trust the Corporal?"

"Experience, Sergeant?"

"No, Private. Because his wife is five-foot-nothing with jet black hair and eyes so dark you think the entire universe is in there. And because his little boy can grip your finger tight enough to turn the tip purple. Now my little girl, Casey, she hugs the Corporal around the neck and calls him Uncle Amee. She can't get her Rs yet. Your girlfriend's name is Sandy, isn't it?"

"Uh…yes, Sergeant?"

Pulling gently to prevent a popping sound, Hosaam carefully unsnapped each of the bandoleer's pockets.

"I thought so. My wife's name is Sharon. Cute. You'd like her. Everyone does. Five-six, curly blond hair, green eyes, tiny bump on her nose. Your turn."

"Sergeant?"

"Tell me about Sandy. Go ahead."

With the snaps released, Hosaam slid out a grenade.

"Um…five-two…red hair, great body—"

"Does that red hair come with a short fuse?"

"No, Sergeant, that's what I thought, too. But she's real sweet."

Hosaam inserted his middle finger through the loop of the grenade's safety pin.

"Nice. I like your girlfriend already. Private, this morning in my briefing, what did I say was the most important key to survival out here?"

"Silence, Sergeant."

"Good…now what part of the word 'silence' don't you understand?"

Hosaam almost laughed as he pulled the pin.

"No part, Sergeant."

Holding the grenade's triggering lever down, he eased his hand forward.

"Are we being silent, Private?"

"No, Sergeant."

"Okay, one last thing before we stop talking. And listen close."

Hosaam released the lever and began a silent countdown.

"I'm not living here in these mountains, Private. And I need you to see where I live. See Sharon and Casey. Girlfriends, wives, kids, they're where we live. Silence gets us all back home. Total silence, Private…total."

"Sergeant, get down!"

Hosaam heard a muffled sound and quickly rolled out a second grenade. This one brought a deafening explosion and screams of pain. He lay still until he spotted the radio dog running the trail toward his fallen pack mates. He opened fire into the equipment on its back, crumpling the mongrel to the dirt.

The horse came to life around him, lifting, jerking, and then near flopping. Pops and cracks, fragments of bone spitting into his face and neck. Hosaam curled into a ball, offering his back to the onslaught, and his life to Allah.

The horse quieted. He felt along its ribs. Everywhere, little hard lumps of lead lay just beneath the flesh. A few sharp points protruded, nicking his fingers. At closer range he would already be dead. Hosaam reached for his last explosive.

A lifetime seemed to pass before a pebble skittered across the trail. Hosaam let loose the grenade. Deafened from the previous explosions he felt rather than heard bodies hit the ground. Then another detonation, and moments later bullets penetrated, one grazing his thigh, another, his chest. Pulling the trigger as he pushed his AK-47 out in front of him, Hosaam slid forth to die.

Weapon extended over his head, rolling and firing blind, he hunted for a target. Twelve o'clock—nothing. Ten and two o'clock—no one. He jammed up against something soft and wet, flipped to his back, slammed the weapon onto his stomach, and fired between spread-eagled legs. Still no one. Four and eight o'clock, the same. Not a single bullet impacted near him, yet the mountainside echoed with two familiar sounds. The staccato bursts of the M4A1 Carbine and the hammer-on-sheet-metal clang of the AK-47.

Hosaam stopped firing and pressed in alongside the dead body that had stopped his roll. The dog's forehead was decorated with a single red dot, the back of the skull missing. Sniper shot? Only Abbud killed this way.

After locating where the mongrels were pinned down, Hosaam maneuvered behind them and opened up. Sandwiched between rapid bursts of his AK-47 and the withering fire of his comrades, the two remaining dogs were put down. He continued unloading rounds into their bodies as he walked forward, finishing by pressing the end of his barrel into each eye socket and firing. Satisfied they would never rise again, he released the trigger and looked for his allies.

A bare thirty meters distant stood young Kashif, no longer looking the lamb, hands gripping stock and barrel, pumping his weapon toward Allah. Farther up the mountain, shaggy Abbud rose from his sniper position and raised a fist in victory. Well out of bullet range, high above them all, the jackass stared down.

Hosaam waved them in and set to work inspecting the fresh carrion. He yanked the nearest by an ear, pulled up its head, and snapped the dog tags from its neck. Releasing his grip, a pleasant little pop sounded as its head bounced on the rock. He snatched the next one, repeating the process, but no pop. Grabbing both ears, he slammed the head down. Still no pop. Hosaam frowned.

Kashif joined him. "Allah smiles on you today."

"And what of you?" Hosaam turned his frown toward Kashif. "Does Allah smile?"

"I didn't desert you, Hosaam. We vowed never to forsake each other. Our murdered mothers, forever our bond. I wanted to force you to—"

"Search the carcasses. Be quick. The dogs check in at regular intervals, as little as twenty minutes." Hosaam hustled toward the sniper kill.

Abbud crouched alongside his handiwork, tugging at his gray-streaked beard, staring down at the mongrel's face. "Why?" First left, then right, he thumbed the dog's eyes closed. "Why do they keep coming?"

"To receive Allah's justice." Hosaam pointed at the hole in its forehead, laughing. "Though a little left of center this time."

"I pull the trigger. Allah guides the bullet."

Bowing his head, Hosaam acknowledged Abbud's wisdom

before ordering him to the search effort. He snatched the mongrel's tags and moved on, propping the next carcass against its demolished radio pack. A comic sight, it leaned backward, arms limp in the dirt, chest proud, open-mouthed face pointing at the sky—a soulless poppy addict. But the neck was bare. Frantically searching the ground produced only bits of fractured radio. He kicked the mongrel in the stomach, snapping its head forward, straddled it, and tore the shirt open at the chest. Still finding nothing, he frisked from muzzle to hind legs. A lump and rattle at the crotch brought forth his knife. He stabbed and sliced, freeing his trophy, another set of tags, his fourth.

"Where are your captives, Hosaam?" Faiq strutted past.

Abbud's raised eyebrows and Kashif's gaping mouth told much. Both looked straight through Hosaam, staring at Faiq as if they'd sighted a spirit. They hadn't expected him to return. Hosaam's thumb tested the sharpness of his blade.

"America looks very far away, don't you think?" Faiq added.

Coward though he was, Faiq's questions cut true. Without captives for the Mullah, Hosaam would earn no place among the chosen. America, forever away. Stomach muscles quivering, Hosaam nodded in feigned agreement as he flipped his knife to hold the point between thumb and first two fingers, balancing, searching for the perfect grip. Setting a wide stance, he lowered the knife to a power-throwing position, and started a controlled spin to sight the target. A scream of pain halted him mid-execution.

"This one's still alive." Faiq stomped his full weight on the mongrel's bloodied shoulder, evoking another scream.

Hosaam sheathed his knife, and walked toward Faiq and the last two scat-sniffers. "Allah provides."

"Indeed, Hosaam, indeed."

One dog lay dead, an unnatural bend at the lowest part of its back, spinal vertebrae snapped clean apart, white and gleaming in the sun. Of course. This explained the muffled explosion of the first grenade. A good pup. Hosaam reached down and snapped off its tags. The other mongrel lay moaning, shrapnel holes dicing up its chest and face.

Faiq bent, snatching up the last set of tags, then straightened to his full height, forming a wall between Hosaam and the whimpering scat-sniffer. Not six centimeters separated their noses.

"Abbud, come bind my captive," Faiq commanded, a bit of

spittle spraying from his lips to hit Hosaam's cheek. "I will mention your efforts to the Mullah, Hosaam. Your role will be considered fairly."

Abbud hurried past, tending to his orders, as Hosaam's hands drew into tight fists, one choking the hilt of his knife.

"I'll even leave out how you refused to obey my orders," Faiq added.

Hosaam broke eye contact and cast his eyes to the sky above. He smiled at his circling brood of brothers, high overhead. "Thank you, Faiq. I am most grateful for any words you speak on my behalf." Wiping the spit from his face, he turned toward Kashif. "Let's dump this carrion into the chasm. The dogs can't get their helicopters down there." Hosaam's eyes found Faiq's again. "And the griffons still hunger."

CHAPTER NINE

Stu's index finger poked about the pile of pills on his hotel nightstand, touching the tops of some while flipping others to feel the bottom. What constituted a good enough reason? Gramps's departing words, "Make sure you get a good night's rest," was that reason enough?

Spilled from a single bottle, a jumble of three different drugs, legal and illegal, but every pill was the same shade of baby blue, all oval and small. He pinched one of the imposters between thumb and forefinger and appraised it beneath the lampshade, once again admiring the workmanship, identical in every visual detail, even the delicate script of the name "Allay." But the surfaces of the over-the-counter painkillers were silky smooth, while the *go* pills were slightly coarse across the embossed letters, and the *no-go* less velvety along their blank bottoms. Only a practiced touch could tell the difference. Stuart divvied them with ease.

As always, he made three groups, the biggest was the mound of painkillers. His shoulder throbbed mercilessly, but he'd already swallowed far too many painkillers today.

The next two mounds were much smaller. One he neatly arranged into the shape of an "N" for *no-go*. The other a "G" for *go*. Last June, both the "N" and the "G" were larger. Still, only three lapses in the past year—not so bad.

The first lapse in Seattle, must've been December—lots of snow on the roof, someone attacked and destroyed Angie's website. He swallowed a *no-go* to force a dreamless sleep, which necessitated a *go* to shed the morning grogginess.

And Baltimore, last month, a death threat in the mail. Angie

59

made light of it, said the world was full of harmless lunatics. Were all lunatics harmless? All those who intended harm insane? *No-go* and *go*.

Then Dallas, last week, she cried all night before he left—acid poured over a young Afghani woman's face for aiding one of Angie's clients. Stu carried the twin images all through the flight from Washington, D.C. to Dallas, the woman's face streaked red with burns, Angie's with tears. He entered his hotel room at five in the afternoon determined to sleep without swallowing a pill. But the phone call home didn't help, Angie still a mess. At one in the morning he finally dropped off. Woke an hour later, thrashing. At four, gave up and swallowed. Five hours later, swallowed again to fly home.

Seattle, Baltimore, and Dallas were his only failures of the past twelve months—each time for the only reason that mattered—Angie.

Stu rested his index finger atop a single *go* pill, the pill forming the flat hook of the "G," and rotated it ninety degrees to form an "O." He stared down at the "NO" and wished it were all that simple. Just say "NO."

Wished everything was that simple. Drive back home this morning? Just say no. Open Angie's file? No. His nightmares? No. But none of it was simple. One had to see the truth first. See the lucky angel wings already in his pocket. Or see the sticky caramel as he flattened the wrapper onto her file. See whatever damn truth his brain was trying to scream at him as he slept.

Stu rotated the pill to form a "G." Just one little *go* pill and he'd suffer no screams in his sleep tonight.

When did one become an addict? Surely, three uses in a year wasn't addiction. Not physically. Yet he couldn't deny the powerful desire. Which was harder to kill—physical or psychological addiction? Did it matter? Control desire or eventually die of it. That was the truth. And it really was that simple.

Yet, what then, of Angie? For her, he'd gladly die...or sadly...even kill. That was also truth. Stu kept rotating the pill between "G" and "O."

Angie was the ultimate drug, the adrenaline rush that made everything else not matter. On every flying trip he was bombarded with security bulletins highlighting the latest fear—suitcase bombs, tennis shoe bombs, underwear bombs—anniversary of 9/11, anniversary of the Iraq invasion, anniversary of Bin Laden's death.

America was very busy. Soon the government could save everyone some time and simply publish an annual fear *du jour* calendar. At the end of each trip he drove home with a brain stuffed full of random explosions and terrorist plots...and poof...all gone the moment he held her.

Suffering the occasional pill for Angie he could justify. But tomorrow's simulator—retaining his FFDO status? Was that worth a pill? Except for that demented fool in South America, no one had attempted to enter a cockpit since 9/11. Certainly, no attempt that Stu could take seriously.

Yet, this is how it starts, rationalizations always preceding the short trip to complacency. Pilots would find excuses to stop carrying weapons. The cockpit defense program would shrink. Then the government would shut it down and a patient Al Qaeda would strike. But what did all of that have to do with the pills? He'd swallowed a couple just last week in Dallas. If he used them up too fast he wouldn't have enough to shape a "NO." Enough strength in him to say no.

Holding the pill bottle along the top edge of the nightstand, he corralled the little blue ovals and coaxed them all back home. Snapping the lid tight, he tossed the bottle into his suitcase and fell backward onto the mattress.

Please. One solid night's sleep, free of bad dreams, eight hours, just once. Must be a couple of years since that happened without a *no-go*. Shortly after Angie began trying to change the world. Long time. And he was so damn tired.

G, B flat, A, and D stirred him from self-pity. "A Time for Us"—Angie's ringtone. He wasn't ready to talk. Not before mustering a convincing story about why he wouldn't be home until dinner tomorrow. Angie was even tougher to placate than Strickland. That prosecutor brain of hers came with a built-in lie detector.

He could tell her the simulator had mechanical problems? A kernel of truth there. He'd asked for more speed and the throttles went backwards, despite what maintenance claimed. Nice and simple. He could probably tell that sort of lie.

Stu got up and paced between window and bed. Nope—for over twenty-five years he'd never outright lied to Angie, stretched the truth maybe, but never a complete fabrication—not starting now.

As Romeo and Juliet expired, Stuart prepared for the thrashing to come, moving his suitcase to the coffee table, rummaging through his clothes, setting the Allay bottle to one side and grabbing his shaving kit. While listening for the message beep, he emptied his shaving gear onto the bathroom counter. The phone stayed silent.

Stu completed his bedtime ritual by clearing the lamps, clock, and hotel stationery from the nightstands. He rechecked his cell. Nothing. Not like her. At least not like the everything-out-in-the-open Angie of their first two decades together.

Plopping onto the couch, he shoved his feet between his suitcase and the bottle of pills to ponder the conundrum that was his wife. Except for her final year as a prosecutor, he'd never seen her so distant. Under the self-imposed pressures of her hobby-lawyering, she'd become a closed book, or at least only open to the pages she allowed him to read. Today was June twenty-first, her personal deadline. How can anyone take a self-made deadline so seriously?

After a few minutes, he chose the euphemism "rescheduled" as his stretch of the truth, willed cheerfulness into his voice, picked up his cell and tapped "Angie." On the sixth ring he heard her voice.

"There you are. I was worried something had gone wrong with your—"

"Hey, little darling. Saw you phoned." He had to cut off any discussion of his evaluation, but did he really just call her little darling?

"You couldn't answer?"

She was correct. Except when airborne or in the simulator, he always answered. "Had the ringer off." The lie spewed out quicker than a sneeze, and just as quick, nausea roiled his stomach.

Ignore it. Press on. Before she did. "No message for the man of your life." What was he, a country-western singer? The problem was, he'd no gift for lying.

"Message?" Angie's voice trailed off.

Her faltering reply reminded Stu of the many witnesses he'd seen wilt under Angie's cross-examinations. Knowing they were trapped, they sat silent, their minds reeling, searching for any answer that wouldn't sound false.

Stu heard the first click of her pen. Damn. He must keep pressing her. Don't let her think. Then he wouldn't need to lie. "Yes, a message. You always leave—"

"I just wondered how your training went?" Another click.

"Will you meet your deadline?" Stu shot back.

"Deadline? Not quite." Again, her voice trailed off.

Stu slung his feet from the coffee table, knocking the bottle of pills to the carpet. "Not quite...is the same as no, isn't it?"

After several seconds of silence her pen started clicking like a metronome. "It's my deadline and you never answered me about training."

"My training went well enough."

"I don't recall you ever saying your training went...well enough."

"Angie, you always leave a message and never miss a deadline. Something's rattling you." Stu snatched the bottle from the floor and rotated his wrist in rhythm with her clicks. Like a cracked hour glass whose contaminated sand had clumped together, the pills plunked up and down the plastic container while he waited. "Angie...you still there?"

"I...had another call. Hit call waiting to answer, that's all."

"Who called?"

"Stu, how did your training go?"

"They rescheduled the simulator. Won't be home until dinner tomorrow."

"Okay, eat around seven. That too early?"

Way too easy. Like she was relieved he'd be late. Didn't even question the schedule change. "Angie, something's happened. I can feel it."

"Nothing I can't handle."

"Your pen's clicking away." Stuart's wrist froze, registering a final unaccompanied plunk.

"It'll wait."

"I'd rather it not. Knowing you're hiding something doesn't help me in the...." No—not when he'd gotten her mind off the simulator. "Doesn't help me...at night."

"Fine. Instead of talking about me, let's discuss your thrashing in bed."

"That's not what I meant."

"Did you remove the lamps?"

Stu's jaw line bulged, his teeth gnashing as he squinted at the barren nightstands. "What I dream is worse than what you tell me." He slammed the bottle onto the coffee table. "Much worse."

"I'm not the only one keeping secrets. I'll share when you get back."

He unclenched his teeth and tried again. "I need something more specific than you'll share when—"

"Are you rubbing your scar?"

Stuart's hand jolted from kneading his left shoulder and became a fist. How could she know?

Carl was the only possibility. But he didn't participate in the morning hand-to-hand combat session. And if Carl had heard about Stu's encounter with Ice, his biggest question at the debriefing room door wouldn't have concerned the Fourth of July.

No. Angie said "scar." His old scar. He always rubbed it when he was tense. She sensed his jumpiness and struck. The woman knew his every quirk, each button to press.

"Stu?"

"Yeah, okay. When I get home...we talk."

"Stu, I...."

After the few awkward seconds felt like hours, Stu helped her out. "Yeah, me too." Those words of everlasting endearment, the ones other couples tossed about so freely, had become nearly impossible to say. He thumbed end call and flung the phone across the room onto the bed.

Damn it! Angie manipulated him like he was an opposing attorney. Stu snatched the pill bottle from the coffee table. His thumb popped off the cap.

He could land a jet in a blizzard. Best a CIA field operative in hand-to-hand combat. Yet, his own wife had him hamstrung. Stu felt for a rough bottom, tossed the *no-go* at the back of his throat and swallowed.

But none of this was Angie's fault. She was just being Angie. He needed to figure out how to be Stuart Pierce again.

CHAPTER TEN

When Kashif was a boy he asked himself, "If Allah's will is the answer, why does it never suffice?" Kashif answered, "It is Allah's will."

Young Kashif saluted the western sky, shielding his eyes while he scanned the treetops for aircraft. Sent ahead with Abbud to scout an unguarded pass into the safe haven of Waziristan, the two of them had repeatedly doubled back to avoid detection, tripling the distance and quadrupling the time it normally took to complete this trek. Now, so near the border, Kashif grew ever more wary.

"Again, we delay?" Abbud questioned, scratching at his shaggy gray-streaked beard and frowning.

Kashif held his tongue, instead pointing at the naked gap to the east. Once leaving the protection of the thick forest, they faced more than three hundred meters of open terrain. Even if they dropped all their gear and sprinted, exposure time approached a minute. Sixty long seconds without so much as a shrub to duck behind. The last seconds of their lives if an Apache helicopter bore down on them.

Loosening the pack from his shoulders, Kashif stepped off the trail onto a withered patch of yellow grass, and nodded at the dropping sun. "Asr."

"Asr? We're stopping for afternoon prayer?" A grimace spread across Abbud's parched lips. "Maybe you should consider a mullah's line of work." With a firm tug of the ties, he loosened his heavy load, picked out the largest tree within throwing range and slung the rucksack hard against its broad trunk, the ancient Persian walnut resounding with a loud thunk. "Verily. Let's pray for courage then."

Kashif set his pack alongside Abbud's. "I'll pray for patience."

Fear of death held no power over Kashif, but the French word "fléchette" did. His first attempt at the English pronunciation came out as "flesh-eat." This earned him a grim laugh and approving nod from his training instructor. He subsequently learned that a single fléchette rocket detonated into a shotgun blast of one thousand one hundred eighty hardened steel razors, all traveling at nearly two kilometers per second. Useless against anything armored, it was strictly an antipersonnel weapon designed to slice flesh from bone. Each Apache attack helicopter carried thirty-eight. More than forty-four thousand little flesh eaters.

Of the many American weapons Kashif had studied, only the fléchette rocket came to life in his mind, a waking nightmare as vivid as a Bollywood movie, including shredding sound effects and bloody Technicolor. He pictured the spinning razors slicing through the sky in slow motion, chasing him down, paring the skin from his face.

With a slight shudder, Kashif shook the paralyzing sequence of images from his head. "The shadows from the forest lengthen. Soon they will reach out and cover the first portion of the gap. Every meter helps our—"

"Faiq ordered speed."

"And Hosaam argued caution."

"I am new to this terrain, Kashif, so it is right that you lead here. But I'm old in battle. Speed wins."

Kashif spun to face him. "How fast is dead?"

Abbud checked the safety on his sniper rifle, collapsed buttocks to heels, and hugged the barrel between his chin and knees. "Dead is Faiq, if left too long alone with Hosaam."

Kashif let out an impatient exhale and squinted up at the jagged ridgeline to the north, imagining spinning rotor blades lurking just over the other side. Less than an hour after he and Hosaam finished dropping the dead Marines into the chasm, Apache attack helicopters cut through the mountains, carving an exact replica of the pattern Hosaam traced in the dirt. And every hour since had passed precisely as Hosaam foretold. After the Americans completed the initial search, discovery of the bodies sucked all of their helicopters into a tight blanketing of the area around the ambush point. With one Marine missing, a starburst followed, Apaches speeding overhead to block all known routes into Waziristan. Yet where were they now? Most of the afternoon had passed without sight of them.

Kashif knelt and rummaged through his pack, seeking a suitable cleansing cloth for ablution. "Understand me, Abbud. I know that Hosaam's manner is gruff, but his mastery of the American tactics has kept us alive. If Faiq felt threatened he would've ordered Hosaam to scout ahead, not the two of us. Why would he leave himself alone with—"

"Because Faiq imagines his lineage renders him immune."

"Immune?" Kashif frowned at the soiled scrap of cotton in his hand. "From what?"

"From those so low as...." Abbud clamped his mouth shut.

"Hosaam?" Kashif finished. "Is that how you see our brother?"

Abbud rose and inspected the damage his rucksack had done to the great walnut tree. "From those...Faiq deems...so low as Hosaam." He gave the grandfather walnut a gentle pat, then set the butt of his rifle atop a massive root and leaned the barrel into the deepest wrinkle of its gnarled face. "Faiq is a fool. It was murder I saw in Hosaam."

"Murder?" Kashif shook his canteen and sighed at the meager slosh before unscrewing the top and sprinkling a few drops onto the scrap of cotton. "You saw murder?" He reached up, offering the damp rag to Abbud. "And you call Faiq the fool."

Abbud shoved the rag aside. "Hosaam's eyes went wide...and froze...not a blink. Like this!" He stared at Kashif bug-eyed for several seconds. "I'm sure that except for the Marine's scream, he would've killed Faiq."

"You can know all of this from a man's eyes?" Kashif offered him the damp scrap again.

Abbud jerked the cloth from Kashif's hand. "Not just his eyes. Hosaam flipped his knife. You've seen him practice. It's always the same. A flip and a pause. Then a spin and throw."

"I've seen you blow the dust from the sight of your sniper rifle twenty times in a single day." Kashif removed another cleansing cloth from his pack. "How often do you pull the trigger?"

"It's not the same. And you know this," Abbud persisted.

Kashif spent half a minute moistening the second cloth and wringing the wetness through before starting on his nose. After cleansing each nostril, he folded the grime inward and went to work on his forehead. "More similar than you think, Abbud. You have practice rituals also. First you remove the dirt from your sight. Then steady the rifle stock against your cheek. Exhale halfway. Caress the trigger. One thousand meters distant, a melon explodes."

Abbud went quiet, hands wrenching the cleansing cloth into a tight spiral as he sank onto the roots. "Not the same," he muttered, removing his sandals.

"Might want to consider wiping your face before your feet." Kashif swabbed the grime from his beardless cheeks and neck, then rubbed his hair, arms and hands, easily lifting the dirt from his body, all the while unable to push the weight of Abbud's arguments from his mind. Yes, he'd seen Hosaam practice, dozens of times. And yes, Hosaam's throws were always the same. A flip of the knife from hilt to tip, whirl and fire, hitting the center circle each time, burying the blade to the handle. Kashif plunked down to wipe his feet. "Hosaam's no murderer."

Abbud finished wiping the dirt from his left elbow, then rubbed the dust from both feet. Uncapping his canteen, he started toward his mouth but instead jabbed the spout toward Kashif, carelessly sending water flying through the air. "You must've seen the blade in his fingertips as he spun?"

Kashif followed the precious fluid's arc to the ground and watched it vanish, swallowed in equal parts by dry leaves and withered grass. "I saw Hosaam cut free the tags from the dead Marine, sheath his knife, and talk to Faiq. Nothing more."

"Talk?" Abbud coughed out a mouthful of water. "The space between their noses was less than a hand's width. Snarling wolves talk that way." He shook his head, sending drops flying from his beard.

"The more you anger, the more you waste." With just a small sip, Kashif rinsed his mouth to complete the cleansing, then rose to face Mecca. After clearing his mind of all stray thought, he made the proper intentions in his heart.

"Please listen to me, Kashif. I know you feel a kinship toward Hosaam, both your mothers killed by the Americans. But open your eyes."

Raising his hands alongside his ears, palms forward, thumbs extended toward his jaw, Kashif ended the argument. "Allahu Akbar," he sang, opening the first Rak'ah.

Abbud relented, turned to face south, and chorused, "Allahu

Akbar."

With his Islamic brother aligned in equality alongside him, Kashif focused on the broad swath of yellow grass at his feet, the place of prostration. He stacked left hand above right, palms up, and raised both to his sternum, offering heart, life, and soul.

Throughout the Isteftah Dua, occasional sour notes held back their harmony. But Allah's almighty power soon quieted their discord, and by the Surah Al-Fatiha, with its long deep singsong tones, the resonance of each "een" and "eem" suffused, calmed, and comforted.

Around them, the aged timbers seemed to sway with their recitations. These last and oldest trees surviving in this corner of Afghanistan had doubtless heard and approved of such prayers for more than one thousand years. For they too were a majestic manifestation of Allah's divine will. In harmony with the rise and fall of the branches, Kashif and Abbud bowed and prostrated in unison. "Allahu Akbar," they intoned. And the thick cloaks of walnut leaves slipped one against the other, rustling a chorus of "Ahhk-bhharr."

Somewhere during the third of their four Rak'ahs, Kashif's prayerful meditation fused with the orange blaze of the western sky, the first cool breath of evening breeze, and the soft murmur of leaves. Washing, cleansing, soothing, until only He remained, Almighty Allah, the sole focus of Kashif's adoration.

She came to life then, as his mother so often did whenever Kashif wrapped himself in fervent prayer. Adorned in shimmering waves of blue, she knelt beside him, insisting he lead and that she follow, her voice at once melodic and strong.

With the memory of her at his side, he grew small. His reflections on her perfect love lighting his mind of her light. A soft and silver beam. Shining. Guiding. Slipping him back to his boyhood home, remembering.

Imitating her humble manner, her utter submission, at her side Kashif learned the purest love of Allah. After a time, he'd memorized every motion of the ritual, but still he watched her, marveling at her joyful faith instead of focusing on his prayers. Worried, he asked her if Allah grew angry at wandering thoughts, and might refuse to hear his prayers.

She smiled, and cupped his cheeks in warm hands. "Allah loves the good heart. He sees yours, my little one. He sees."

There, beneath the grandfather walnut, her spirit bent low to whisper in his ear. He waited to feel her cheek on his, inhale her sweet smell, and hear once more those favorite words.

The air above him pounded, battering her image from his thoughts. A thundering wop-wop-wop of slicing rotors flailed the treetops, cracking branches and snapping off twigs. Bits of bark and a shower of leaves rained down.

Kashif closed both eyes to shield them from the hurricane of debris and rolled, seeking the broad base of the mighty walnut. Instead he knocked heads with Abbud, who'd found the shelter of the trunk first.

"Does this void all of our prayers?" Abbud yelled above the thunder and grinned.

Instantly, the perfect answer flashed into Kashif's brain. He smiled, knowing that Abbud would not hear his words, but his mother's—his voice, but her love. Kashif pointed at the grandfather walnut above them. "No, Abbud. Long ago, Almighty Allah, knowing our eventual need, planted this great walnut in this precise spot to protect us. Allah heard the goodhearted prayer before the universe was made, before we ever thought to give Him praise."

The pounding moved west. Kashif leapt up and followed the receding noise, looking through tiny breaks in the dense canopy to determine the type of helicopter.

"Kashif," Abbud shouted after him. "What are you doing here?"

"I'm trying to determine the specific type. If it's a Blackhawk instead of an Apache then—"

"No." Abbud circled an index finger toward the canopy above. "No, my brother, what are you doing—" his finger poked at the ground, "—here? You've so many other paths. Just now, during the third Rak'ah, your song grew strong and became filled with a calm fire. Such a voice should cry from the tower, the muezzin's call to prayer. I was only half joking before, about a life as a mullah." Abbud grinned. "Or perhaps, become a star. A stone? What is it the Americans call their singers? Yes, become a stone star. That will get you to America."

Kashif burst out laughing. "Rock...rock star is what they call them. Abbud, you're like a kindly old uncle, always looking out for me, suggesting yet another fine path for me to walk. Even while we run these mountains, chased by the puppets of Shaitan, you look to my future." Kashif smiled. "I'll return the favor. I'm thinking comedian for you. I can see your name in lights. Abbud—the sniper's sniper. Showing America its decadence through cleverly concealed jokes. Using the scope of his wisdom to discern the unknowable. He can see a man's soul through his eyes."

Abbud's grin vanished. "My scope showed me where your bullets flew, Kashif. Have you ever taken a life?"

Kashif grabbed his pack, shook off the leafy debris and shouldered his burden. "My bullets kept the Americans shooting at me while Hosaam closed on them from behind."

"And what of Hosaam's training instructor? Should we give him credit for the dead Marines as well? While we're at it, let's throw in the mother that suckled him." Abbud shook his head, frowning. "You don't belong here."

"I fought and men died. What's the difference?"

Abbud stalked toward his rucksack. "I pull the trigger." He wrung the dust from his hands and reached down, pulling up his heavy load. "I see them drop. It matters."

"That helicopter was sleek like a wasp. Was it Apache or Blackhawk, Abbud? Did it carry ground troops or not?"

Abbud didn't answer.

"It was an Apache—no ground troops. Important to know if the Americans have landed troops, don't you think?" Kashif gave him a single stiff nod. "I belong."

Abbud grabbed his sniper rifle and blew the dust from the scope. "Yes, you're very bright, my young brother. But are you bright enough?"

Kashif flipped a small lichen-covered boulder, marking the route for Faiq and Hosaam. "I'm smart enough to know that the shadows from the trees are as long as they're going to get." He glanced back toward the spot of their prostration, the yellow grass at the base of the grandfather walnut, remembering her. Wondering if he'd soon be with her. Wondering if that was better.

"Time to run." Kashif nodded once at Abbud, then darted from the shelter of the forest, the show curtains opening wide, his very private terror playing in his mind while he sprinted across the gap: The distant wop-wop-wop of rotating blades pounded to a thunder as the helicopter drew near. Shrill whooshes of air signaled multiple rocket launches. The slapping sting of the first fléchettes cut into his cheek and spun him around. First his left ear slipped away, then his right. Turning his head against the rain of metal merely offered the profile of his nose to the onslaught, and like bits of chopped carrots, it fell away. Then his eyes and tongue departed. And, finally, a torrent of metal shards peeled all trace of skin and sinew, until nothing remained except a pristine skull mounted on a fully fleshed and clothed body.

Several seconds later Abbud caught up with him, crawled in among the dense boulders and sputtered between heaving gulps of air. "Kashif, forget about becoming a muezzin and calling the faithful to prayer. Olympics, consider the Olympics."

Kashif's trembling fingers tried to steady his quivering jaw. "Apaches," he stammered.

Abbud flattened against a boulder. "I saw none." His head twisted around to check behind them. "Where?"

"Gone now. Let's go." Kashif slipped off between the boulders, leaving Abbud still sitting there, searching the sky above the gap.

Several hundred meters later, Kashif knelt and crawled up to the crest to study the crossing into Waziristan—no man's land. Pakistan laid claim to the tribal territory, yet exercised little control other than keeping NATO troops out. This forced the American blocking teams here, along this narrow strip of valley, just prior to the border. Kashif strained through the growing gloom to locate their patrols before the twilight faded. American soldiers dominated the night, their goggles giving them the power of dealing death unseen. Maybe that was better. At least he wouldn't see his nose drop away in pieces.

Strong hands grabbed hold of his ankles, yanking him from the crest. Kashif flipped to his back, drawing his knife and slashing.

Abbud knelt over him, blocking Kashif's blade with one arm while stabbing at the sky with the other. "Vultures."

Kashif followed Abbud's pointing arm. To the west, a great column of griffons whirled in a vortex above the forest where they'd prayed. Twenty or more in a single spiral—a rare sight. He ripped the pack from his shoulders. "Stay here and locate the American positions." Slinging his AK-47 over his back, he sprinted toward the gap. Either his brethren had already fallen, or something deadly lay in wait. The vultures always knew.

CHAPTER ELEVEN

Kashif crouched behind a waist-high boulder. Ahead, the gap loomed. Americans also knew what circling griffons signaled.

Across the three hundred meters of open ground, the trees formed a near-solid wall. The only break was the well-worn mountain trail leading past the grandfather walnut, the yellow patch of grass, and her. Minutes earlier he'd prostrated and prayed beneath that forest's perfect cover. Now, unable to discern trunk from limb in the fading light, he imagined a battle-hardened soldier hidden in every shrub. The thought sent a shiver down his spine.

Three kilometers away, a pair of inky silhouettes slipped over the ridge, skimmed along the treetops and dove when they reached the far western edge of the woods. Dark paint, rectangular shaped, and quiet. Blackhawks ferrying an insertion team, the first boots hitting the ground before the helicopter's skids. Likely a full complement of twenty-two, armed with rifles, grenade launchers, carbines, and beefed up with a fire team carrying an M60 machine gun to rip through any stubborn spots of resistance.

Spots like Kashif. Yet, it wasn't their firepower that so frightened him. It was their hunger for vengeance. Like starving wolves, the combat troops would spread wide across the forest, trapping their prey in front of them. Safety locks clicked off, fingers on triggers, they'd strain at the leash, awaiting the pack leader's command to hunt.

A wave of their commander's hand and they were off, searching for Kashif's tracks, a broad line of barrels pointing left and right, up and down. Barrels that spewed seven hundred bullets per minute, every bullet capable of shattering his skull.

Still, Kashif's familiarity with the terrain made all of this firepower manageable for the next fifteen minutes. But as the twilight faded, each soldier would reach for night vision goggles, and the Americans would run through the dark forest like it was midday.

He'd hoped to salvage goggles from the dead Marines, but Hosaam got that detail very wrong. The six they'd ambushed had just two goggles between them, Faiq and Hosaam keeping those. Hosaam's bullet into their camp may have goaded the Marines to the chase ill-prepared. But these troops, landing at dusk to rescue their brother? They'd make no such mistake.

Kashif pounded his fist against the boulder. Moonrise was over an hour away. He'd suffer nearly sixty minutes of groping through the dark—a blind man against a score of hungry wolves. Enraged wolves. Sixty minutes or one-tenth of it made little difference. Any significant amount of time in the darkness and he was dead. He had the next fifteen minutes...or he had forever.

Every second he delayed decreased the odds of survival. But Americans never landed ground troops without adequate air support. Somewhere in that narrow strip of forest, or in the jagged ridgeline hugging its northern edge, attack helicopters hovered. Kashif scanned the treetops and located the grandfather walnut. Anchoring at the tree's crown, he followed each arc and twist of bough, searching nature's curves for the print of man—the rigid lines, right angles and boxes that melded to form Apache.

In the distance, their troop drop complete, the Blackhawks disappeared into the reddening sun. American domination of the forest would soon follow.

Hosaam often spoke of their training. Disciplined precision. Tactics swift and lethal. Their fire teams would slice through to this edge of the forest long before moonrise. And this was the least of his problems, crossing the gap alive his biggest.

Finding nothing south of the grandfather, he looked north, and with each passing moment his search for man-made lines among the rare arcs and singular sweeps of the individual limbs grew more pointless. The farther north he searched the less he saw, the treetops tangled in a background of broken mountains. If Apaches hovered there, he'd never see them. He tossed a handful of dirt to the wind. The tiny dust cloud blew toward the trees. He might not hear them either.

High above the treetops, the largest of the griffons detached from the bottom of the swirling column and spiraled downward. Something was dead.

Kashif turned his back to the tree line, searching the crest for Abbud. What sense to risk another run across the gap? What's dead is dead. What good for him to die also? He couldn't avoid what he couldn't find. Couldn't fight what he couldn't see.

The vulture aborted its approach, flapping hard to regain the column. Something lived.

He remembered his promise to Hosaam: never to desert him.

Kneeling to face the trees, Kashif cupped hands behind ears, closed both eyes and concentrated, straining for the sounds of rotors. But thoughts of rotating helicopter blades brought with them images of speeding fléchettes, slicing through his face. A loud pounding forced his eyes back open. His own pulse. Pleading for strength, Kashif looked toward heaven.

The deep blue sky had darkened to indigo, with the first sprinkling of stars just poking through. Allah's promise, his mother always called them. Embers to light a new dawn. To her, all the mysteries of the universe were simply elements of Allah's poetry to ponder. But right now those first stars meant that he had fewer than ten minutes to find Hosaam and escape. His only advantage lay in the gray dusk—not bright enough to highlight him against the rocks, yet too bright for night vision goggles, blinding whoever tried to use them. Placing both hands on top of the boulder, Kashif pulled himself to standing and sprinted for the woods.

Two hundred meters from cover he heard them. A pair of Apaches popped over the ridge. Their noses dipped. Targeting or accelerating? Probably both.

Kashif fought to control his legs—long, loose springs that ran out ahead of him, each foot laying a too-brief tap upon the ground before darting forward again. A sideways slip, a rock knocking one heel against the other, a slight stumble—every sensation reaching his brain too late. Hanging on, feeling as if his torso was attached to a loping gazelle, he shot across the gap.

At one hundred fifty meters the clear mountain sky clouded. White puffs of smoke pulsed from the rocket pods beneath each helicopter. In front of him, small spurts of dust sprang from the ground as if the first plump drops of a cooling rain spattered the dry soil. The illusion shattered as the sound caught up with the fléchettes. A roar like a passing train accompanied the torrent of metal shards tearing into the trail ahead, blasting countless tiny columns of dirt into the sky.

Kashif pushed straight into the storm. Rockets fired from a moving helicopter never impacted the ground in the same spot, or so he'd been trained. The survivors of such attacks taught that the safest place was the last point of impact. As Kashif escaped the dust cloud he remembered they also preached about never getting caught in the open. Too late. Two more explosions bracketed Kashif left and right. One instant he was running across clear terrain, the next between geysers of skyrocketing soil.

Still more than one hundred meters from the tree line, he lost sight of the helicopters. Closing on Kashif from the north had presented the Apaches with a two-axis targeting challenge, their first rockets missing because they led him too much, and the second volley sending one rocket long and leaving the other short. Patient and disciplined, the Americans now maneuvered to cut the odds of missing in half. The Apaches would roll out behind, spread to fly line abreast and hold down their triggers, walking a wide barrage of fléchettes and bullets up his back. Rather bullets than flesh eaters, he prayed.

As the wop-wop-wop of helicopter blades grew louder, Kashif tore his thoughts away from images of metal flesh eaters and concentrated on the trees ahead. He must exceed the Americans in both discipline and patience. Listening carefully to their beating rotors, he sprinted straight for the grandfather walnut.

When the pounding seemed equally loud to both ears, Kashif counted to three and cut hard right. On his left, the ground exploded. Ten strides later, he veered back left as another maelstrom erupted on his right. Again he changed direction, cutting back into the tempest, counting to five and reversing, exiting as more fléchettes entered.

Thirty meters from the forest's edge, Kashif crossed over the trail and spotted a black swath between the trees. Making each stride long and sure and quick, Kashif sprinted for the dark crevice. Downwash from the rotors pushed at his back. Chain gunfire echoed. Whooshes of air announced the launch of more fléchettes. Kashif dove.

In midair, time crawled. The sapling on his right vanished, most of the leaves fluttering toward the rocks below, a few defying gravity and floating higher in the wake of his passing. Bullets pummeled the entrance. A sharp burn stung his left shoulder. Kashif curled into a ball and rolled as he hit the ground. He slammed into a rock wall, the barrel of his AK-47 smacking against the back of his skull. Motionless, he waited for the steep waves of pain to recede as train after train seemed to roar past above.

Checking the back of his stinging shoulder, Kashif pulled away a warm wet hand. Pushing to all fours he tested the wound, arched catlike, then reached overhead. His arm functioned.

At eye level, everything was black. Higher up were glints of silver—receding twilight caught on bits of jutting stone. A jagged river of gray lit the crevice lips, narrowing as it flowed into the forest. Feeling along the rock wall, Kashif moved away from the air-thumping sound of the hovering Apaches, deeper into the crevice. The floor sloped down, every step dropping him farther from the forest above. He spread his arms wide. Right hand groping stone, left fingertips probing the air, he shuffled forward in the dark until he located the opposite wall. Grabbing a handhold on each side of the crevice, he pulled his feet from the floor, probed and tested the walls to find projections strong enough to support his weight. He worked his way higher.

Almost at the surface, a foothold broke and fell away. A section of wall followed, pinning his shoulders tight. Pivoting sideways, he freed his arms, but the wall tipped farther, pressing against his chest and forcing the air from his lungs. With his foot scratching for a new toehold, he worked his hands to chest level and shoved, moving the block far enough away to breathe. After several deep breaths, he heaved with all his strength. The heavy stone shifted, dropping a fraction and rocking back and forth before coming to rest.

Avoiding the teetering block, Kashif pushed his hand through the sod, grabbed a branch and drew himself upward. The bough snapped, and he slipped back below the turf. Again, he reached up and latched on, but still the dry bush would not cooperate. His head barely cleared the hole before he suffered another fall. Once more he pushed upward, this time snatching at the base of the bush and forcing his shoulders through as the undernourished roots released. Scratching and scraping, he clawed through the thin dirt, fingers hooking onto small fissures in the rock to drag himself free.

His vision blocked by the thick underbrush, he crawled to the edge of the bushes and searched the canopy for light. Five minutes of twilight, at most. Ahead was a patch of trampled yellow grass and an impossibly wide trunk. The grandfather walnut. Beyond it, the trail appeared as a lighter shade of black. Kashif climbed over the roots, stepped onto the trail and found the column of vultures circling less than one hundred meters to the west.

The path disappeared and reappeared as he ran. Three times, Kashif lost the trail. The fourth time sent him tumbling over a log, head filling with the laughter of his training instructor, admonishing his star pupil. The lesson came back. In low light, he must never look directly at what he wished to see. The center of the eye's retina contained the daylight-dependent cones. The night vision rods are located at the edges. At night, always look askance. Askance was key. Choose an object beside the actual target and focus there. Exercise patience. Out of the black will float the objective.

Kashif forced his focus onto the canopy. The path floated out of the dark. He hurried west toward the griffons.

With the swirling column nearly overhead, he paused at the lip of a small clearing. At the southern edge a huge griffon poked at something on the ground. A few meters beyond, a rifle-ready figure emerged from the woods to scan the clearing.

Kashif froze. Movement revealed position. The scan stopped, not on him, worse, beside him—askance.

Two choices. Both bad. Move and be seen, or remain frozen until the figure's peripheral vision floated Kashif's silhouette from the blackness.

On Kashif's left the trees were close, but too thin for adequate cover. To his right, he'd need more than ten long strides to reach the safety of a stout trunk. He held.

A quick shift from the figure and Kashif faced the long line of a rifle barrel.

Don't move, he coached himself. Not a muscle, not a twitch.

The figured edged closer.

Kashif stopped breathing. Remain still. Just another tree. If the figure were sure, he'd already be dead.

The griffon hissed and flapped its wings, lifting a few centimeters into the air, then resettling. Rocking back and forth, the raptor locked talons onto whatever dead thing lay beneath. The rifle barrel dipped, now aligned with Kashif's guts rather than his head. Another hiss followed by a hard peck sent a loud crack resounding through the forest. The rifle lowered. Stooping to one knee, the figure struggled with something on the ground.

Kashif slipped off-trail and bypassed two narrow trees to hide behind a thick walnut. The figure lumbered toward him with a slung rifle poking above one shoulder and a pair of legs dangling from the other.

A crunching of leaves sounded as the figure passed from the clearing onto the forest floor. Kashif performed a slow about-face. As the crunching grew louder, he pressed backward against the trunk. Not three meters distant the figure angled off between the trees. Kashif leaned forward to follow, snapping off a bit of bark. The load slammed to the ground as the figure whirled.

Kashif dove right. The air parted on his left, a light flutter brushing his cheek. The knife embedded into the tree behind him.

"Hosaam! It's Kashif."

Hosaam appeared beside him and yanked the knife from the tree. "Help me with our captive. The woods are infested with dogs."

"Where is Faiq?"

"Dead." Hosaam bent for his load.

"Dead? Where?"

"In the clearing, where the griffon feeds." Hosaam lifted the body back over his shoulder.

"Hosaam, forget the Marine. We must attend Faiq."

"This is what I...what we came for." Hosaam crunched off between the trees.

Kashif trailed behind, violent flashbacks assaulting his mind—the griffon feeding on the dead horse, sharp talons curling, clamping, puncturing the tough hide like it was thin paper. Beak tearing away strips of flesh. The vulture gulping.

Now gulping Faiq. "I can't leave him."

Hosaam didn't respond, disappearing into the darkness.

Retracing his steps, Kashif found the vulture ripping at Faiq's face. The griffon ignored him, tugging an eyeball from a socket. Faiq's head repeatedly lifted from the ground, bobbled about his neck and fell back to the dirt, the vulture his unwitting puppeteer, yanking at an eye still tethered by tendril strings.

Kashif rushed forward, feigning attack. But the creature held its ground, spread wings and hissed, dropping the morsel from its mouth. He reached over his shoulder for the AK-47, thought better of the noise and slid his knife from the sheath. At the sound of metal scraping from leather, the griffon hunkered and struck, snaring the loose eyeball. The vulture flapped hard, leaping backward, then backed farther still, neck snaked out, pulling, stretching the eyeball tendrils taut. A powerful jerk popped Faiq's head a half meter from the ground, his neck bending at an unnatural angle. The tendrils snapped and Faiq's head flopped down as the huge bird flapped away.

Above the trees, the column of vultures scattered. Kashif lunged out and grabbed Faiq's still-warm hands, dragging him beneath the canopy. A moment later spinning rotors pounded the air. Apaches hunted the clearing.

He crashed through the underbrush, heedless of the noise, seeking another deep crevice, a dense group of boulders, any solid cover. Far more effective than night vision goggles, the Apache's thermal targeting system would see right through the cool canopy of leaves, find his warmth, and fire its chain gun. Bullets, longer than his finger, thicker than his thumb, would sever the branches from the trees and the limbs from his body.

Kashif plunged headfirst into a gully, rolling, tangling up with Faiq, the corpse cushioning his impact at the bottom. Momentarily shielded by the steep walls, he quickly frisked Faiq's body. No satchel. No goggles. Only a bandoleer filled with grenades. Hefting Faiq to his back, he followed the gully, hurrying toward the path. Apaches at the clearing likely meant that the gap was open.

Where Kashif expected to find the trail, he climbed from the gully and focused on the trees above, waiting for his eyes to lift a pathway from the blackness. A dark gray strip floated from the forest floor. He followed.

Faiq's head bobbled oddly, bouncing again and again off Kashif's bloody back, repeatedly throwing him off balance. Under the burden of the constantly shifting dead weight, his gait slackened from broad strides to half steps to staggering. The smallest bump threatened to topple him down.

At the sight of the grandfather walnut, a surge of energy lengthened his stride. In another minute he'd gain the gap, and Allah willing, cross to safety as the Apaches searched the clearing behind. Eyes locked on the canopy, Kashif started to trot.

Helicopters passed over him. He felt a downwash of turbulent air as they landed close ahead. Blackhawks. More troops. The Americans no longer needed Apaches to guard the gap.

Strength left him. His legs buckled, tumbling him over the grandfather's roots to gasp for breath on the very spot where he'd prayed. Kashif lay unmoving, cradling left arm in right. But easing the pain of his wounded shoulder highlighted other hurts—aching legs, throbbing skull, torn fingers. His right kneecap burned as though he knelt on hot coals. He drew his legs into his chest and rubbed at the scrape.

Kashif searched the canopy. Everything was black except for the stars, their faint light winking off and on as a gentle breeze fluttered through the leaves. His breathing recovered. The Blackhawks lifted and flew west. It grew quiet.

Silently, he mouthed, "Wink of star, cool of night. Allah loves the martyr, death beauty in His sight." Not bad, Abbud would say. Become a poet, he'd add.

A snap of twig—south. Kashif nestled back among the roots and unslung his AK-47. A crack. Might be north. Hard to tell. Night played tricks with sound. His hand slid past the top three grenades to reach the bottom three. If he could draw them close enough, they would all die together.

The hammer-on-sheet-metal clang of an AK-47 rebounded through the forest, three bursts, followed by a barrage of staccato bursts in reply. American carbines. Was Hosaam firing blindly? No. He would never give away his position without a target. This had to mean that Hosaam could see. Yes, he had the captured Marine's equipment, and his night vision goggles.

Kashif slid from the grandfather's roots. Hosaam might have night vision, but Kashif had light. Grabbing the neck of Faiq's robe, he dragged the corpse across the grass, feeling for the bushes he knew were close.

He plucked a thermite grenade from Faiq's bandoleer, pulled the pin and heaved as far south as he could. Plucked a second, a third, and a fourth, throwing each in a cardinal direction, each of them clanging against a not too distant tree. Only the southern toss flew far. He never heard it hit.

With the sound of the explosions, the gunfire paused. As the forest ignited, the staccato bursts of the American carbines resumed and were answered by a continuous stream of AK-47 fire. Now everyone could see. Yet, soon the smoke would blind all.

Kashif pulled Faiq's body through the underbrush to the edge of the crevice. Grabbing the last thermite grenade, he muttered. "I kill the forest, Abbud. Do I belong now?" Pulling the pin, he threw it straight at the grandfather walnut. Bouncing off the massive trunk, the grenade came to rest in the patch of yellowed grass. No longer colored a dull, dying yellow, the withered blades instead lit gold in the firelight. And for a moment, she was standing there, a vibrant blue in the golden grass, then gone in the flash and bang of the explosion. "Do I belong?" he rasped.

Clutching Faiq's collar, Kashif pulled him toward the hole, the corpse's neck passing from shadow to light in the growing fire. Upon the throat, dark spots, four centimeters apart, a thin line connecting them. Kashif let go of the collar like it was a burning log and stared. Recalled the unnatural bend of Faiq's neck as the vulture tugged. Remembered the odd feel of Faiq's head bouncing against his back as he ran.

Kashif grabbed the front of Faiq's robe and yanked him up into the brightest firelight. His neck bore the raw, red ring of a strangulation cord. The dark spots? Knots in that cord.

The pounding thunder of the M60 opened up in the distance. Kashif looked up, waiting for a reply. No hammer-on-sheet-metal clang answered.

He dropped the corpse into the crevice and climbed down. Below ground he laid the body on its right side beneath the teetering wall and pressed the eyelids closed. As well as he could determine, he faced Faiq toward Mecca.

From his bandoleer, he pulled two concussion grenades, found gaps at the base of the wall and wedged them tight, leaving the pins exposed. He prayed a quick ayah, pulled the pins and strode out of the crevice into the smoke and flames.

CHAPTER TWELVE

The speedometer notched 114 mph, Stuart's 350SL a metallic blue bullet streaking along the highway, heading for Angie. She'd share her secrets. Not next week. Not tomorrow. Now.

The radar detector shrilled, its lights red and flashing manic. Stuart stomped on the brakes, slicing off fifty mph. His fighter pilot brain took over, scanning the clock positions for the radar that hunted him. Straight ahead—twelve o'clock—nothing. Three and nine o'clock—no threats. In the mirror—dead six o'clock—the road was empty. False alarm.

Stu checked the dashboard clock—6:15 p.m. He'd downed the *go* at nine this morning. That should give him at least five hours before he crashed. As long as he didn't get thrown in jail for reckless driving, plenty of time to hash things out, even with Angie. Stu set the cruise control at seven over the limit and tried to relax, reminding himself that patience is quicker, especially with Angie.

If he could just make tonight run as smoothly as this morning's evaluation. Four total shots on two assailants, a round to the chest and head for each, all delivered within the confines of his tiny cockpit, had alleviated any concerns still lingering beneath the patriarch's white hair.

Pop'em—drop'em, head—dead. Gramps praised Stu's perfect efficiency, adding that a good night's rest had worked wonders. Would his compliments have flowed so freely if he knew of the pills? And Angie, would the efficiency of his impeccable execution impress her?

Gramps offered Stu no little ditty of a rhyme to solve the Angie riddle. Still, he couldn't do this her way any longer. He wanted to know everything—as it happened. And not the PG-13 version. No more pills.

The radar detector flashed another warning. Stuart veered across the rumble strips, snagging the exit ramp, downshifted to third and then second, his right hand bouncing between gearshift and steering wheel. He checked six again. No police lights. No sirens. Stuart poked reset. The radar detector responded with beeps and chirps, and lights blinking green, yellow, and red, then several seconds of dark silence before a single clear tone signaled the device had completed a successful self-test.

Ten minutes later, Stuart drove down their long gravel driveway, reflecting on the simplicity of that test, wishing Angie were equally simple. Press a button and she'd confess all her secrets. They'd become a team again.

Ahead, the old stone farmhouse was mostly dark. Only a dim glow from the bay window of Angie's study struggled through the twilight to welcome him home. Even leaning over the steering wheel, Stuart couldn't distinguish the entry alcove from the front door. He turned on the headlights...and slammed on the brakes. In the door's archway stood Angie, looking as sad as he could remember.

For the third time his detector went off. Despite the stab of pain from his swollen shoulder, Stuart seized the power cord and yanked. Instead of the cord sliding from the cigarette lighter, the entire device flew from the dash, clipped his temple and broke open on the shift lever.

Angie's throaty laughter erupted. "I'm not buying you another one, Stu. No more sleeping at the wheel. You'll have to keep your eyes open."

Stu wiped at the warm, red wetness trickling down his cheek and gave up a faint chuckle.

The grandfather clock chimed nine. No matter how sad Angie looked, he shouldn't have waited until after dinner to confront her. "Wait in the library, I've a surprise," she said. Fifteen minutes had slipped away since then and more than once he'd closed his eyes just for the sheer pleasure of it. Perhaps too much wine, or maybe too much Mash and Ice and Gramps, but the *go* pill's power seemed nearly spent. Angie's library appeared fuzzy at the edges, like a fine fog lingered near the walls. Turning on the canned lights above the filing cabinets caused him to squint, worsening the illusion, the fuzzy fog creeping farther into the room. He whacked the switch back to off, sending a jolt of pain knifing along his collarbone and up into his head.

Where in hell did Angie keep this surprise? He'd give her another five minutes, then hunt her down. Stu rubbed at the knotted muscles in the back of his neck. Surprise? Only one thing would surprise him right now. Angie coming into the room, walking up to these file cabinets, pulling out the death threat and apologizing.

Actually, she could skip the damn apology. He'd settle for the ugly truth. Hell, even uglier than this rotted file drawer was fine with him. Stu tugged on the handle. Still stuck.

He'd warned Angie this drawer would be trouble. The dark, mottled stain a sure sign. Dropping to one knee, he dug a thumbnail into the drawer's edge, probing for softness and swelling. Although pitted and pocked, the wood was unyielding, hard as stone. Why hadn't she called the cabinetmaker?

Careful to leave his aching left arm completely out of the effort, Stu gripped the handle with his right hand, wedged a knee alongside the rotten drawer and leaned away. Didn't budge.

A swish of air and oncoming shadow drew his eyes away from the drawer toward Angie's desk. Big mistake. His nose and mouth caught the full impact of her purple pillow.

"Do I walk into your cockpit and start flipping switches, Captain?" Angie stepped back from her major league pitch, brushed imaginary dirt from her palms and laughed.

"Never should've shown you how to throw." Stu pinched the tip of his nose and moved it left and right. "Not broken." He removed a bit of black fringe from his tongue. "You'll run out of pillow someday."

"Not if you learn to mind your own business, Flyboy."

His own business? Heat bristled up Stuart Pierce's neck and face, and he rose with it. "Is that what we have here now, Angie?" Stu pointed at her long wall of family photos. "After all that? Now it's you do your thing…and I'll do mine. Confer once a week over lunch? That what you have in mind? A little business arrangement?"

"It's just a figure of speech." Angie lifted a decanter from the silvery tray on her desk and poured. "Sorry I took so long, but I had to let my surprise breathe. Cheryl found us a Chateau Lune. Remember Paris…the spilt wine?"

Angie had let down her hair since she'd asked him to wait in the study, her auburn waves now unfurled, rolling thick and lustrous across the black silk robe she'd changed into. And fresh perfume scented the fuzzy fog surrounding him. Apparently, she'd used the wine's breathing time to good advantage.

"No thanks," Stu replied. "Already had plenty. Think I'll pass on dessert too."

Angie swirled her wine, lifted the glass and watched the ruby rivulets trickle down. "My filing cabinets. I don't want…." Raising the glass still higher, she spoke from behind a liquid garnet veil. "I don't need you fixing things, Stu." Lowering the rim to her lips, she sipped and swallowed.

"More than twenty-five years we've shared a bed," Stu replied coldly. "Raised Maggie and Andrew. I've been there…through the very worst. I don't care where we're flying or landing, but I ought to damn well know who's shooting at us."

Angie's chin started to quiver. "No one," she said. Her little finger pressed a path from corner to corner beneath a lower lash. "Everyone." She rubbed at the black smudge on her fingertip. "Seems like the whole world."

Don't look at her, Stu told himself. He leaned back against the cabinets and counted the diamond shapes in the carpet. Verbal debate is her high ground. Silence wins this battle.

He stopped counting at forty-three. On the next diamond her painted toenails peeked through the open ends of black satin slippers. Sunset Red, she'd told him. And sparkling above her right instep, the anklet he'd given her on Valentine's Day—whisper thin threads of woven gold embedded with thirteen tiny heart-shaped rubies that accented the warm, red glow of her toenails.

Stu distinctly remembered white, closed-toed slippers warming her feet at the dinner table. No anklet.

Fresh perfume, let-down hair, satin slippers, and heart anklet. Angie had come well-armed—or perhaps, more precisely—well-legged to wage her own form of silent battle. In spite of her brazen ploy, Stu couldn't help but wonder what lay beneath that black silk robe. Maybe nothing.

He pulled his eyes from legs that still looked thirty and focused on the grandfather clock—almost five past nine. Now that the confrontation had begun he needed to employ patience. But patience took time, and time was running short. Judging by the fog still fuzzying the room, he had an hour, at most, until he crashed.

Fine. Sixty minutes playing mute if necessary. Seeing the long hand click five minutes past nine he counted the pendulum swings, predicting the click of six and seven and eight minutes past exactly.

"Stu, what's the difference? A single demon or a million faceless ones. How could it possibly affect your actions?"

Told him how much ammo—that's how. Pop'em—drop'em, head—dead. Two bullets were easy, two million, a lot tougher. "Look Angie, each month you assure me things will get better, that you'll soon take a break, get away from…your work…for a while and—"

"My work?" Angie plunked down her glass, a wave of red sloshing over the rim and washing across the tray. "It's quite a little bit more than just work." Lifting a thick file from her desk, she let it fall open to form a "V" in her palm, and then frisbeed eight-by-ten glossies to his feet one at a time. "These help your dreams?"

The photos floated down, covering the diamonds around Stu's feet beneath a photo-fall of sad truths. Ritual stoning of a fourteen-year-old girl for sex before marriage. Honor killing of a sister for shaming the family with adultery. Death by clitoridectomy bleed out. And on and on. "You showed me worse last year. But these photos don't excuse…don't account for…don't explain…." Stu stammered to a stop.

What didn't they explain? Her lips pressing too hard, lingering too long, burrowing her face too deep into his chest every time he came home from a trip—all of it, just too much? She'd shoot down all those "toos" the instant they flew from his mouth, probably joking that if he didn't like her affections she'd take them elsewhere.

"I know that it's more than just work to you," Stu said. "For me too. But these photos don't explain how you've been acting. I've seen you determined, resolute, even downright dogged, plenty of times…yet never obsessed like this…except maybe when you tried to get yourself fired from the D.A.'s office, chasing that rapist—"

"I've been shut down again." Angie pointed at the server stack. "Virus attack. The whole database is corrupted. Backup's fine, I think. But I'm afraid to bring it online until I get someone in here."

Stu glanced at the stack of servers. No fan noise. No lights. How did he miss all that? Maybe he was crashing earlier than he'd thought. He collapsed onto the couch.

"I met my deadline," Angie added. "I wish you could read it."

Using both hands this time, Stu kneaded at the back of his neck again. Shutting her down? Destroying her letter? Explained a lot, Stu thought.

"But it's trapped inside," Angie continued. "It's a good letter, Stu. Inclusive and tolerant and..."

He closed his eyes and tried to ignore her words. Angie was the master of plausible explanations. She sure hadn't spun the winking woman's battered face to his feet. No captions that read "PIERCE OF DEATH?" No smiley face. Where was that photo? Why not just tell him about the death threat? Yet he couldn't ask without taking the discussion in a whole other direction.

Stu's hands slid from rubbing his neck to massaging his temples. Then paused. He could drive their debate back toward the woman's photo, though, by simply mentioning previous death threats.

"...but personal makes it a powerful letter. Just what I wanted to front my website for the coming year, give it a fresh new—"

"I'm not buying it, Angie. Back in March, you took that death threat better than this. And now a virus attack has you spinning out of control...stuck in afterburner, engines flaming out. I thought we left that Angie behind ten years ago when you became obsessed with—"

"It's those pills. That's why you won't accept my explanation. You're popping again, aren't you?"

"I can't do this your way any longer," Stu said, much louder than he intended.

"Don't put your pills on me," Angie replied, even louder.

"I don't," Stu fired back. "I put...." He broke eye contact and started in on the diamonds again. What exactly did he put on her? He felt betrayed. So was it distrust? She'd certainly violated their agreement by hiding an obvious threat to her life. But it seemed much more than that.

He felt great shame. So did he also put his dishonor on her? No.

Opening her file was his choice. He'd dishonored himself.

Stu scratched hard at his scalp, digging his fingernails deep like he could somehow tear through hair and skin and bone and peel away layers of brain tissue to find the sore spot, the source of his...what? Anger? No, that didn't feel quite right either. He felt discouraged, disappointed, exhausted. Defeated. He had given his whole life to Angie, every last bit of himself, but for some reason that he couldn't begin to fathom, she still didn't...didn't.... Stu dug deeper, tearing past his distrust, and dishonor, and his not-quite-anger...and found...only sadness. He stopped scratching. Sadness? Why?

Stu's head slumped down, the question barely a conscious thought, yet the answer obvious. Angie didn't trust him. And just as obvious, some inner part of him had already known of her mistrust, had known it for many months. Because, he suddenly realized, his sadness had been there for many months. Beaten back, hidden beneath his not-quite-anger. Opening her file had simply made her lack of trust undeniable, his sadness palpable.

So what did he put on Angie? This answer, also obvious. Mostly, he laid on her his sadness. Stu's head slumped farther, the fuzzy fog drawing tight around him.

Angie seemed to interpret his sudden sadness as weakness, and pounced. "Okay, Stu. A hypothetical? Let's make it simple." She went into full cross-examination mode, arms folded, head tilted slightly downward, right slipper forward, pen magically appearing and clicking. "What if my whole problem were a single person? What would you do? Take a broken bottle to his throat?"

Stu's face went cold. Look at her—Angie, the prosecutor, staring down at him like he was some despicable murderer, grabbing any nasty weapon at hand to win her case. What bullshit...bringing up his past...using it against him. He felt angry now, and there was nothing "not-quite" about it. And anger felt a whole lot better than sadness. He wanted to yell, and did, a little, "Go ahead, Angie, fire away!" Stu clamped his lips together, his teeth grinding as he finished the sentence in his mind...use every last bullet, empty your weapon into the dead carcass of us.

He shook his head in disgust and started again, speaking in a dead, flat tone. "That's a cheap shot, Angie. You had a right...before you married me...to know my history. To know everything you were choosing."

A look of shock filled Angie's face. She reached out to embrace him. "Stu...I didn't mean—"

"So, tell me, Angie?" He pushed up from the couch and stared at her wide-open arms, his own remaining limp at his sides. "What am I choosing?"

With her brow furrowing and head tilting down, it was Angie's turn to stare at the carpet. Not a single click came from her pen.

Stu waited, watching the pendulum swing, but each completed arc sliced another second from the few minutes remaining before he crashed. He searched for something else to look at. Turning away, he found Angie's "snuggling puppies" photo on the wall, studied her happy face beaming from a pile of family and friends, and thought of that other photo again, the winking eye beneath the cruel crown. What crime? Stuart asked himself once more, and with the asking, all of his angry energy drained away.

"Forget it, Angie. You're correct. If your whole problem was one man? To keep you safe, I'd slit his damn throat. Because I'm not sure I could be sure, any other way."

"I know." Angie's hand rubbed along his back and started massaging his neck. "I know who you are."

Yeah...but did he really know her? The question seemed crazy. Paranoid. Ridiculous. Of course he knew her. Right here in front of him hung their entire lives, a wall of photos from childhood through courtship, marriage and children, right up to Andrew's graduation from West Point this past spring. Stu knew that bride, her proud grandfather escorting her down the aisle, and he knew that pregnant woman blossoming with Maggie, and he knew that passionate woman standing on the Supreme Court's steps. Yet somewhere, right around...there—Stu's eyes focused on a publicity photo snapped as she took the prosecutor's job—maybe he started not knowing her.

Could that be true? Again, the thought seemed crazy. Nonetheless, Stu felt an odd urge to stare at Angie as if he were a newborn presented with a stranger's face. Really study her. See her. Confirm that she was the woman he knew.

His shoulders started to turn, eyes almost following, but instead he forced his stare to remain on the wall of photos, blinking angrily at the unwelcome moisture forming in his eyes. The damn drugs, he told himself as he examined the photographs to his right—photos that depicted the years between her acceptance of the prosecutor's job and now.

Just one of those photos represented her entire six years in the D.A.'s office. Angie at a charity ball, gowned from pearled neck to heeled foot in elegant black, the only woman sandwiched between numerous male members of The Realm's Royal Family, all dressed in white. Stu never told her, but he always thought she looked like a fly that had landed on The Realm's cake. Angie, as always, gorgeous, but still. He never liked that photo much.

A half-dozen more photos portrayed the three years since she'd left the prosecutor's office. All of them, Angie at important functions, posed with powerful people common to her cause. His own face didn't appear in a single photograph from her acceptance of the D.A.'s job offer right up until today. He'd noticed this before, of course. Even joked about it with Angie. Didn't seem funny, at all, right now.

Stu looked back to the very beginning, far to his left, the first two photos, before they ever knew each other. Angie in her communion dress, and he, half a country away, skiing wild between the aspens—the first time his mother had let him ski the trees. "My first taste of God...and yours," Angie had said as she hung them on the wall.

She was right. No other experience in his life made him feel as spiritual, unfettered, as disconnected from all that the world preached. He never felt so calm, so at rest, as when he let himself loose in the deep snow.

In those mountains, alone and quiet, all nonsense gave way to sense. His skis slipping through the thigh-deep powder, winding a path between backcountry aspens, leaning, curling, swirling snow over shoulder and neck...and then an opening, a meadow, and he'd corner hard, darting into the wide open, chasing that chance to know again...closing his eyes, extending his legs and lifting, skis rising, floating, weightless, timeless, entering the void, the singularity before the first word, before there was a word, only oneness, and then open his eyes, and see...elk or deer at the edge of green, green pines, and bright, white snow layered along high chalky cliffs lifting the blue, blue sky, and high above, impossibly broad, gold-tipped wings soaring, and higher yet, a twilit moon and Venus rising, and at that moment he knew, he just knew, there is a purpose to all of this.

He'd fought to find the words and tried to explain it a few times. Got some polite laughs. But Angie hadn't laughed. She'd cried. And right now, her hand felt so warm on his neck, rubbing high, just behind his ears, precisely where his muscles always knotted up. Yes, Angie did know him. Seemed like she'd always known him. Knew him like no one else ever would, ever could.

"Okay, Angie, what do you want me to believe? Give me something. Anything to grab onto."

"I want you to have faith." She hugged him from behind, pressing her cheek into his shoulder blade. "I want you to believe…in me."

Stu made a second pass over Angie's many faces, stopping just before the D.A.'s handshake. "Okay." He hammered out another three "okays" punctuated with repeated snaps of his chin. "So how do we get your letter out of that computer?"

Angie squeezed tight, wouldn't let go. He tried to spin and kiss her, waited and tried again. The back of his shirt grew damp. Happy tears, he guessed. Stu caressed a hand and kissed, grabbed the other and kissed again, kissed himself free. Then he led her out the study door to the master bedroom.

Never releasing her, he reached inside his suitcase and hesitated, that seductive voice inside him whispering a promise of many peaceful, dreamless sleeps. But he'd pledged to himself no more pills. And if not now, when? Smiling at her confused look, he grabbed his shaving kit, drew her out of the bedroom to the great room fireplace and twisted the gas starter. The pre-stacked logs burst into flame. He lowered his bride of twenty-six years to the hearth rug.

Firelight flickered across her cheekbones, highlighting wide-open eyes and a tiny furrow—Angie's quizzical face. A face he knew. A face he liked. Stu bent down and kissed her furrow, then unzipped the black kit and removed a plastic bottle. "I'm in, Angie." Palm to lid, Stu rotated his wrist to open the bottle and spill the baby blue pills into the flames. "I'm all in."

She reached up, arms wide, furrow gone, surprise and happiness filling her face.

This was another face he knew. A face he didn't see much anymore. If only there was some way, any way, to freeze and frame this moment, keep the world out. Keep her safe.

But there wasn't. Lengthen these seconds to a few minutes,

maybe. He scooped Angie up and let her cry.

Despite the fogginess rolling through his every thought, Stu stood before the great room's wet bar, considering their drink choices. His last libation tonight, he was sure. "I've a new friend."

"Friend?"

"Yep. Ex-spook."

"Spook?" Angie's one-word question sounded more accusation than query.

"Your vocabulary's grown impressively monosyllabic. Yes, former CIA. Now he's director of the FFDO program." Stu searched the smoky mirrored tiles at the back wall of the bar for her reaction. "Probably got some killer contacts."

A cleft formed between Angie's eyebrows.

"Okay, bad word choice. Computer super-spooks to look at your system." The seam between the tiles cut her face in two, leaving one half misty Angie, the other half murky, or maybe it was just the fog in his brain. Neither face seemed to like what it heard. "I thought you'd be happy."

Angie noticed him studying her reflection and inclined her head, hair draping down to cover her face. "I am."

"Angie, I'm not…fixing things," Stu offered. "Just trying to contribute."

Her hair bobbed up and down. "Okay, but I work directly with them. Tell them exactly what I want."

"Wouldn't have it any other way." Stu reached to the top shelf, grabbed the single malt scotch and removed two crystal tumblers, pewter labeled, one engraved ANGIE, the other STU. He unscrewed the cap and inhaled twenty-one years of aging. "Our usual pour? To the bottom of the label?" He tilted the bottle toward her glass.

Angie's head snapped up. "No, Stu. The wine."

"It'll keep."

"Stu, please, it was expensive." She got up and rushed toward the study, heart anklet sparkling little flashes of red as she disappeared.

"But this is our tradition," Stu called after her. "We've toasted lesser things. What's more important than my trust, my faith in you?"

CHAPTER THIRTEEN

Moonlight, bright and cool, flooded through the library's bay window, shading silver all but the burqa. Angie pushed upward from her desk chair and slipped a tingling leg from beneath her black silk robe to the carpet below, the pricks of a thousand needles signaling the return of the blood to her toes. She removed the heart anklet from her other leg before folding it beneath her and settling back down.

After another sip of bourbon she dropped the grille over her face and resumed her argument with the burqa. "Stu's an honorable man. He deserves the truth."

"Honor is unforgiving." The burqa's reply was out of Angie's mouth so quick and clear, so alive, that she paused, considering the possibility that she was going insane. A passing stranger would think as much. Yet this was how she always prepared. Imagining the witness. Asking questions aloud. Voicing possible answers. Finding the loopholes and stitching them closed. After donning the black headdress yesterday she'd worn it every hour, even while sleeping, only raising the grille to eat and uncovering to shower, until Stu's car turned down their gravel drive.

No, she wasn't crazy. But with the burqa finally talking, each moment she spent beneath the grille was invaluable. And with the passing hours the burqa had become her confidante, her sister. To whom else could she speak so freely? No, she was fine, just fine. The burqa was only a sounding board, a soft and pliable worry stone sliding between her fingertips as she whispered her worst fears. There were no lies between them.

Angie eased a hand up under the grille to place another caramel in her mouth. "Stu forgives."

"Does he?" her dark sister argued.

"Yes. Stu is the most honorable man I've ever known. Ever could know." Yet did Stu forgive? Or merely tolerate?

Stu never got upset with those he couldn't trust. He simply grew cold, letting the relationship cool until it died. She rubbed at the goose pimples forming on her arms. "I am his wife. He will honor that. I must honor him with the truth."

"Honor is a man's game," the burqa said.

"In your culture, perhaps," Angie replied.

"Yes, for thousands of years I've born the cost of men's honor. They honor me with honorable sons and then honor me with their 'honorable' deaths."

Angie could think of no clever retort to challenge that truth. She pulled the burqa from her head, drained the bourbon and went to the bay window, setting the headdress onto the client's chair as she passed. The silvery light was fading. Inrushing storm clouds obscured the moon, darkening the lovers' limbs, the oaken arm lost in a tangle of black, as were her arguments.

"Your parents did the honorable thing," the burqa said. "Doctors without borders, working the jungles of Colombia, rewarded for their philanthropy with the hangman's rope around their necks. Honor took your parents before you ever knew them."

"Yes."

"And the grandfather that raised you was a highly honorable man."

"Right up there with Stu."

"And Andrew? Like father, like son?"

"No," Angie whispered.

"Honor will rend your son and—"

"No."

"...send him home in a bag."

"No."

"A roadside bomb."

"No."

"A closed casket."

"No," Angie rasped.

"No hands. No face. Your honorable son."

"You're a lying bitch." Angie swatted the burqa to the floor.

"A—" Lightning struck, flashing a reflection of her face onto the bay window and leaving the "lying bitch" hanging there, unspoken, filling the silence until the thunder came.

Maybe she was losing her mind. Her uncle had. Everyone said his was the most brilliant mind to ever enter the seminary. Photographic memory. On his eighteenth birthday he amazed all in attendance by quoting any verse of the Bible, then died in an institution screaming "God is alive" on his thirtieth.

And when her Irish grandfather discovered his last surviving progeny staring at empty palms, tiny fingers turning imaginary pages, reading *Jesus and the Little Lambs* word for word, he took all her stories away and gave her paints and brushes and canvases, and hammers and nails and wood, and brought home a piano. From age three to almost seven, Angie never saw another book. Instead, she played Beethoven for children, learned to drive nails, and made such a colorful mess of Granda's workshop that he relegated painting to only the sunny days, when he'd set her easel at the back edge of their tree-lined yard.

Seated at the foot of the great oaks, dressed in her dead mother's floppy hat to protect her from the sun, Angie first tried her hand at squirrels and chipmunks and the fat woodchuck that occasionally waddled past, but the painting of birds soon became her obsession. Initially drawn to jays and cardinals and orioles, her early messes were dominated by brilliant blue and blazing red and burning orange, all the bright colors that made Granda smile and say, "Ah, such grand colors for your old Granda." But during the final summer of her book-banned years, as she approached her seventh birthday, a crow alighted on her canvas, cocked its head and considered her, and she considered it, discerning that the great dark bird wasn't just black, but every imaginable shade of the darker blues.

Moving slowly so as not to frighten the crow, she repeatedly dabbed her brush into a splat of "midnight" and lightly stroked the center of the painting she'd just completed, coloring over the oriole's tangerine chest with her darkest shade of blue. The crow bent down as if to examine Angie's work, then squawked with what sounded like contempt and spread itself wide while turning around to face the oaks.

Shimmering within those feathered wings were blues of endless choice. Angie cast an angry look at the meager selection of colors on her painter's palette. Fearing the crow would soon fly off, she focused on those wings, then closed her eyes and pictured the myriad blues, reopened and saw the slight flaws painted in her mind, snapped her eyes shut again, over and over, until the picture in her mind was as flawless as the crow's wings.

Over the next several minutes she experimented, learning that only two colors could modify blue and still let blue remain truly blue. Then Angie went to work, closing her eyes and picturing the subtle hues, opening to mix in a bit of black or dab of white. She painted over the oriole's every feather and claw, until only its head still shone, then stuck her brush into jet black and stroked across beak and crown and nape until the oriole was no more.

As Granda called out for her to come and set the table for dinner, Angie stared at her portrait. The little bird before her wasn't a crow or an oriole. She didn't know what it was, yet it felt right. The blues so perfect, so deep that she wanted to fall into them. Angie started to cry.

Granda called out again, using his impatient voice this time, but she still didn't move. She couldn't stop crying and didn't know why.

The back door creaked open and slammed closed. Angie bent down, filled her palms with great gobs of black and white and splatted her portrait. She swirled her hands in hurried circles, rubbing away all her perfect blues, then smeared her arms and face and clothes.

As punishment, Granda locked away her paints for an entire week. Yet Angie didn't mind. In those seven days, he helped her build a birdhouse. A little A-frame with a thick sturdy perch and an entry hole Granda thought much too large.

"For the crows," she'd insisted, pounding her balled-up hand on the little hole he traced into the wood.

Granda gave in, cutting a hole much bigger than Angie's fist, the entire time mumbling that crows were nothing but flying rats without the manners to stay quietly hidden in the sewers.

And for Granda, she painted the front of her birdhouse bright red and the back a brilliant orange, and the roof golden with shining silver stars. When he saw her work his smile shone brighter than the sun and warmed Angie down to her toes.

The next day during breakfast, Sister Pauline, without so much as a quick courtesy knock, walked right through their front door and jutted her chin at Granda. "School started yesterday. She's already a year back. You can't keep her from the written word forever."

Granda's face got all long and he just nodded.

When Sister Pauline reached for Angie, she jumped from her chair and ran to hug Granda's leg.

He patted her head and said, "You go with the good Sister now."

"Three o'clock," Sister Pauline told Granda as she took Angie's hand.

Granda smiled down at Angie. "You listen for the church bell, child. When it chimes three times, I'll be there to bring you home. And you mind the Sister now. She's got the ear of God."

As they walked along toward the schoolhouse, Angie kept peeking up at Sister Pauline, searching for her ears, wondering what the ear of God looked like. But the Sister's ears were covered in white and draped with black. Angie gave up and inspected Sister Pauline's black robe for any hint of blue. Not a trace. Except for the silver cross dangling from her neck, everything concerning the Sister was either black or white.

The first few days of school were very cruel. All the other children had begun reading and writing the year prior in kindergarten. Angie was by far the oldest, and the dumbest, in her class. During lunch she sat apart. The outcast. Until Friday's art class. Then they saw her crow, and watched as she colored in her perfect shades of blue, and she made friends.

By the end of second grade, all the nuns called Angie brilliant and spoke in hushed tones of her photographic memory, with Granda scowling every time.

As a child, Angie never understood that scowl. In early grade school she thought it meant that Granda didn't like her smart. But when she pretended not to know an answer, Granda scowled even more. In the middle grades, she decided it meant he didn't believe the nuns, so she set out to prove that she was even smarter than they claimed. Straight As, three years winning the school's spelling bee, and national recognition for her sixth grade science project produced undeniable proof of her brilliance, and Granda's biggest scowls yet. By eighth grade, she concluded that his scowl just meant he was stupid and mean.

But in high school, she started to see him, see his worry. And in college she saw his fear. Granda had lost his only daughter, Angie's mother, to the hangman's noose. Lost his only son to madness. How could he bear also losing his only grandchild to that same madness?

At fifty, Angie now fully comprehended Granda's scowl. Even had her own version. With Andrew mere months from deploying to Afghanistan, every time she saw him, she literally had to raise her hands to her eyebrows and rub outward, trying to stop the feeling that her cleft was cleaving her head in two.

Realizing that she was rubbing her eyebrows at that very moment, Angie let out a long sigh. Maybe insanity had just taken longer to catch up with her. She'd gotten twenty more years of lucidity than her uncle. That was a blessing. And Granda wasn't here to see her go insane. Another blessing. Maybe she should be thankful? Maybe going insane before she buried a handless, faceless Andrew in a closed casket was a blessing too.

"I'm sorry," Angie apologized to the burqa as she lifted it from the carpet and gently untangled the grille. Returning the headdress to her desk, she wondered what Granda would think of her speaking to a piece of cloth like a best friend? The red flush of shame spread across Angie's face and she dropped her head like she was seven again. Granda would march her to the great room, throw the burqa into the flames and point at Stu sleeping on the hearth rug. "There's your friend, girly," he'd say.

More than twenty-six years ago, Stu pledged Angie his life. And when it came time in the ceremony for each of them to recite the special words they'd literally spent months preparing, Stu only said, "My honor is all I have. I give it to you, my bride." At the time, Angie felt a little disappointed. Thought his words sweet, but a bit too brief, and she wasn't quite sure what giving her his honor meant.

An inkling of understanding came weeks later as they moved into their first home. She found Stu in the garage, her childhood messes leaning against the walls, amazingly arranged in precise sequential order from messiest oriole to finest blue-hued crow. In the center of the floor—her birdhouse, the roof removed, and him sitting in a folding chair, elbow on knee, fist supporting a chin, staring at the blackness she'd painted where no one could see.

In childlike panic, she ran toward the tiny golden roof with the shining silver stars.

Stu intercepted her. "It's okay, Angie." His thumb rubbed out her cleft as he nodded down at her exposed birdhouse. "I married this too."

A few house moves later, after Wall Street, and children, and the prosecutor's office, after murderers and rapists consumed her life, after a three-year-old boy's torn rectum drove Angie to ask for the death penalty for the very first time...when Granda really didn't know her anymore...when she never really spoke to him anymore, Angie was reminded again what her husband's sweet words meant.

Stu brought them both into the garage. Had Granda walk the line of messes, and pull the roof from her birdhouse. Made him look inside.

Granda didn't scowl. He had trouble speaking. All he could manage was, "Why...why couldn't you tell me?"

And all Angie could force through her choked-up throat was, "I liked your smile."

Stu left them there, holding each other in the center of the garage, for a long while. When he returned, Granda hugged him like she'd never seen him hug anyone before, or ever after. Stu just standing there, not sure what to do, letting it happen. After all, to him, he'd simply done the honorable thing.

Over their many years together Angie eventually learned that Stu *was* his code. Honor was the very fabric that held him together, his cornerstone, his bedrock and his anchor, his everything. When life got confusing, honor left him with one simple reference frame, one question to ask. What is the right thing, the honorable thing, to do?

In giving her his honor, Stu was entrusting all of himself to her. Angie's eyebrows drew together. While exercising his code, Stu had proven that he always had her back. Now she stabbed him in his. No one signed on for that duty, no matter how honorable. She raised her hands toward her forehead, then forced them down to her thighs, some part of her wishing that her head really would cleave in two.

Angie shivered, grabbed both shoulders and hugged herself, trying to stave off the sudden chill. Stu was fast approaching the truth. She'd slowed him for a bit. Saw his eyes grow red, the crash coming on. Every time his words grew close to the subject of The Bastard Sala, she distracted him. First with computer problems, then his pills. He capitulated more from lack of sleep than anything she said. But he would wake refreshed. Then what? The man never quit.

Opening her desk drawer, Angie located the screwdriver beneath her caramel bag and marched to the file cabinets at the back of the library. Kneeling before the dark, mottled drawer, she slipped the screwdriver's flat head through an almost invisible slit just below the handle and gently twisted until the catch released and The Bastard's drawer slid free. A third of the way back lay a divider separating the files of the last twelve months from those of ten years past. Angie reached toward the very back, pulled out a dingy folder and flipped it open.

On top was Stu's thank you card—a reminder of the vow she'd sworn after she gave up her pursuit of The Bastard Sala. The front bore a charcoal sketch of a young woman dressed in bridal finery with head bowed, entitled "Thoughts of Oneness." Angie opened and read.

"Welcome back, Angie, my bride." To this very day—always his bride. She clamped hand over mouth and strained to stop the tears. "The kids missed you. I know it cost you to drop this case. It cost me too. I, the offspring of rape, best know its price. If it were only me, I'd let you pursue that monster to his grave. But Maggie and Andrew still need their mother. Without you, they'll never be complete. And the truth is, I missed you also. I tried not to, for you, but there's a big hole in me when you're gone. Thank you for letting go. Thank you for coming back to us. I am yours, forever, no matter what."

Angie pressed the folder to her chest. "Stu, I wasn't looking for him. He found me." How could she know defending her clients would lead back to The Bastard? And at the very moment she started making a real difference, he materialized. Taunting, arrogant, flaunting his untouchability. Was she supposed to run?

Returning to her desk, Angie stood the card upright and rifled through the file looking for the one man who could help her corner The Bastard Sala.

At the top of the material witness list, she found his name, Prince Uday Azwad. Next to it, the Royal House's unlisted contact number. Her hand hovered over the phone.

She should wait. Follow official channels. Write to The Realm's embassy. This case was closed and sealed by the court. Pulling a phone number from an official witness list she shouldn't even possess was not only unethical, but criminal. Yet she was out of time. Stu's mind wouldn't rest, working as he slept, ciphering as he flew, never stopping until he eliminated every possibility except the obvious. Hell, Stu wasn't fast approaching the truth, he already had the truth. Denied it because he couldn't connect the Angie he thought he knew—the one too principled to break a vow—with the Angie who could, for the right cause.

Angie's fingertips underlined the last three words on Stu's card—"no matter what."

After dialing the international prefix zero-one-one, she referenced the witness list for Uday's phone number, made the Sign of the Cross, and punched in the remaining digits. As she'd hoped, owning a nation meant your phone number never had to change. A voice stuffed full of formality answered.

She begged the universe for understanding, grabbed the purple pen and channeled her former self. "Hello, this is Assistant District Attorney Angela Pierce calling from Washington, D.C. I am in need of communication with the Royal Security Minister, Prince Azwad."

"One moment, Ms. Pierce."

Angie heard a shower of keyboard strokes as she clicked her pen and waited.

"I'm sorry, Madame. I show no one named Angela Pierce listed in the Washington, D.C. office. Are you new? If so, verification is requested."

"It's very late here in Washington," Angie offered.

Another rain of keystrokes. "Our security system shows your call originates from Virginia, not Washington, Ms. Pierce. If you could simply provide verification."

"There must be some error. Could you please check again?" Angie thumbed out half a dozen clicks, listening, hearing not a single keystroke in response to her request. "Is it possible you're making a mistake, Sir?"

"No mistake, Ms. Pierce. Verification is required."

"Perhaps I should delay my communication with Prince Azwad until the wheels of your personal bureaucracy have turned to your liking. Name and title, Sir?"

"Verification, Ms. Pierce." His tone dry as desert sand.

Angie nearly broke her pen crushing out another click. She was an idiot. In their culture, except for a royal spouse, a woman intimidating a man would never work. But what about rescuing her? "Please excuse my abrupt manner, Mr. ...?"

"Najjir, Madame."

"Mr. Najjir. Forgive my rudeness. I'm working against a deadline."

A slow exhale came across the phone. Sympathy?

"Prince Uday…excuse me, I mean Prince Azwad, is a friend and I need his assistance."

A tap of keys.

"And verification at this time of night is very difficult. I would wake important people."

"Madame Pierce, I apologize. However, you really should have mentioned your personal relationship. Your name appears on Prince Azwad's direct access list. Do you have a pen available?"

She copied the number, again begging the stars' forgiveness, thankful Prince Azwad's office was lax in updating lists. Angie hadn't spoken with him for nearly ten years. She glanced over at the photo on the wall—The Realm's annual charity ball. Uday wasn't in it. He was directing the photographer. Angie had no trouble picturing his chiseled features though. The constantly smiling Uday Azwad, former attaché to The Realm, now Minister of Security, a heartbeat or two from the throne.

Other than the Religious Ministry or the throne itself, no institution wielded more power for The Realm than Uday's office. Bribes, weapon sales, supporting foreign coups—all got done, yet never by the King. Inside The Realm, the policy was show the blood-drenched scimitar, but outside, layers of deniability were everything in the game of nations. The King delegated the execution of his secret whims to his second-born son, the Royal Security Minister, Prince Uday. If The Bastard Sala hid within The Realm, Uday's cooperation would quickly bring him to capture and trial, and if outside, could speed justice.

As Angie hung up the phone, heaviness washed over her—a disappointed sadness flowing from behind. She didn't need to turn around. It wasn't Stu. Instead, the heavy feeling came from the gift Stu had given her after Granda passed. A grandfather clock, the time marked by the movement of sun and moon and stars, all bonneted with a cross. Granda would've thought it marvelous, a perfect mix of pagan mystery and Catholic guilt. Sometimes she hated that clock.

"Now you've turned a mighty wrong, girly," the grandfather clock seemed to say. "Best turn back or there'll be hell to pay." Yet even as Granda chastised her, all Angie could think was that she'd gladly pay any price to see that worried scowl or hear the Irish hills rolling from his tongue one more time.

She picked up Stu's card. "I am yours forever, no matter what." He'd forgive. She just needed to bring him in. Tell him about involving Uday. She snatched up the burqa and pushed back from her desk. Give him honesty, complete and brutal. Angie rushed from the study, leaving her chair rattling against the couch.

She would open her confession with his card—the charcoal bride, and his promise written inside, "no matter what." Give him the ugly facts, but explain that her cause was greater than them both. Then burn the burqa just like he burned his pills, and ask forgiveness. Cinching her robe tight, Angie rounded the corner from the oaken hallway onto the great room carpet and stopped, her cold determination to give Stu the simple truth seeming so out of place with the warm, intricate beauty before her.

Fire filled the room, reflected flames, red and white and amber, bouncing from windows and sliding glass doors, crossing and re-crossing, layering shadow upon delicate shadow as they washed over sofa and lamp and chair. Angie had seen their great room colored by firelight many times before, but never like this. Tonight some rare combination of moon and cloud and flame had cast the room in a fiery magic.

Atop the granite bar, Stu's tumbler glowed. The smoky mirrored tiles acting like an observatory telescope, capturing the flames, concentrating the colors, then shooting the focused firelight straight into Stu's glass, tinting the bottom edge of the pewter label a molten red. Just above that gleaming crimson, his name shimmered, the once silvery letters now shining white as starlight.

Angie slid a finger back and forth across the cool metal, the individual letters of his name winking off and on. Christened at their wedding, confirmed at their decision to have children, and blessed by the births of Margaret and Andrew, the pouring of the scotch to the bottom of the label had become their sacrament—a ritual too sacred for her lies.

She opened the lower cabinet door and took up both tumblers. Pressing them first to her forehead and then her lips, Angie stepped up inside, gaining the inches needed to return scotch and untainted tumblers to the top shelf.

Peeking over the coffee table, she found Stu fast asleep on the hearth rug, arm stretched out, head on shoulder, tipped over wine glass moving in rhythm with his long, deep breaths. Strange…the fire lit none of his gray, only dark curls atop a shirt of blue. He looked so young. In many ways, still was. A hopeless romantic. "May he stay a boy forever," she quietly begged the universe.

Angie laid the burqa next to the flames, pulled the card from her robe and knelt to wake him. But he looked so peaceful, olive skin aglow, lips slightly parted, perfect for her teasing tongue. Angie lifted the tipped glass from his arm. Beneath, the wine had stained his shirt a darker shade of blue and pooled below his arm to purple the hearth rug. She pressed her fingertips into the rug. Almost dry. Probably too late to save his shirt.

Stained blue shirt, charcoal bride, and burqa, let them all wait. Leave him sleep beside the firelight.

Her fingers stroked his forearm, following thick veins over striations of sinewy muscle to knuckles and back across wrist, up and down, tracing and retracing the man as the fire's flames lessened and the darkness grew.

After a time, Angie tucked away the card and lay down next to him. She wiggled her hips snug into his lower stomach and opened her robe. Lifting his hand and lacing fingers through his, she snuck it under her nightgown to nestle between her breasts. Another tradition, and her favorite. She took a deep breath and sighed, "He's mine forever, no matter what."

Her confession could wait until the light, Uday until tomorrow, Sala's execution until…. Angie's eyes flashed open.

Alongside the dying flames, resting on stone, sat the burqa. "Yes, open your eyes, Ms. Pierce. Sala's execution? You'd pictured a clean extradition and a pristine trial before dispensing your justice?"

Angie raised a finger to her lips, before realizing the words were only in her head.

"All wrapped up nice and tidy," the burqa continued. "Sala in a wire bow, fifty-thousand volts dancing through his limbs." The burqa's words seemed to suck the last remnants of color from the room.

"Bitch," Angie whispered.

Still, the burqa was right. If Uday found Sala in Iran or Syria, what then? No chance of extradition from those countries. How far would she go?

"And what of the mountain warlords of Afghanistan? Do they extradite? Perhaps your honorable son can kill Sala for you."

"This is not about my son."

"Isn't it?"

Angie could almost see a sad smile beneath that grille.

"You'd kill every last man in Afghanistan to protect your son. And you'd kill Sala. Would Stu?"

"Yes. If I asked."

"Would you ask?"

Angie singled out the last lick of flame and watched it dart and weave. Stu already had one death on his hands. By mentioning the broken bottle, she'd used it against him tonight. Saw the ache in his eyes. Almost thirty years and he still wore the guilt. How could she involve him in...assassination? Wasn't one death on his hands already too much?

"You'll make yourself all alone, girly," Granda's voice cautioned. "With Stu, you stand strong against—"

"No," the burqa said. "She stands strong with us. Every woman who's gone before."

"You'd have her live a life of lies?" Granda argued.

The burqa laughed. "Women don't lie. Women survive."

Angie furrowed her brow and banished both voices from her thoughts. This was her fight, her broken bottle, her choice. Sala's neck was hers to slice.

Slipping from Stu's arm, she added several pieces of wood to the embers, held her hands to the renewed fire and closed her eyes. Felt the burn. Flames moving across her arms and face and body until she was so hot she could never be cold again. "I'm sorry. Granda." She withdrew Stu's card and read it one last time. Then tossed the charcoal bride to the flames and picked up the burqa.

"And what now, my little Aingeal?"

"I'll do what I must, Granda."

"And what then comes of you?"

"I'll survive."

"And Stu?"

"He'll be fine. He's strong as...as—"

"Iron?"

He didn't look like iron. Not in the soft firelight. He looked beautiful. Her honorable little boy blue, sleeping.

"Iron is strong, my little Aingeal. Yet brittle."

"Stu need never know. Must never know!"

"No matter what?"

Angie sank onto the stone hearth and shuddered. "No matter what."

CHAPTER FOURTEEN

"**A**llahu Akbar!" The muezzin's call to prayer echoed through the Afghan night.

But in Kashif's dream, the call became a great rustling of tree limbs. A resounding "Ahhh-luuu Ahhhk-bhhharrr" that rumbled through the canopy above and dropped down as a shimmering current of air, curling round the grandfather's broad trunk and sinking into the golden grass at Kashif's knees. Here, beneath the towering walnut, his mother lived again. Side by side they prostrated and prayed, her robe more blue, soul more pure, than sky.

She leaned to whisper in Kashif's ear. But high above, the grandfather's branches thrashed "Ahhh-luuu Ahhhk-bhhharrr," muzzling her words. She bent to try again. Kashif twisted toward her, rolled in his blanket and sucked sharp on the dry air, pain shooting from shoulder to thumb.

The final singsong iteration of the muezzin's call filled the air around him. Then other sounds. A barking dog. The recitations of the faithful. A shuffling of feet nearby. Kashif tugged the blanket from his head.

The prayers and the barking slid down from a dark square twinkling with pinpricks of light. Surrounding the square, a mass of gray extended up and down, left and right—mud walls framing a window of stars. The Mullah's walls.

"Skipping last prayer, Kashif?"

Searching the mass of gray, Kashif found Abbud's dark outline leaning next to the curtained doorway. "And you, Abbud?"

"The Mullah commanded I see to your needs. I obey."

"My need is to dream," Kashif said. "I keep waking. Can you see to that?"

"The Mullah will call for you soon."

"Yes," Kashif murmured. "And I will answer." Everything here was the Mullah's. Walls, ceilings, floors, food. Even the recitations of Isha. As the last adoration of the day, Isha had always received his mother's most fervent prayers, giving thanks for the day just passed, offering herself and her family to serve again on the morrow if Allah so willed it. Yet if the Mullah commanded the adoration to stop, it would.

Not for the muezzin, not for the Mullah, but for her, Kashif struggled to rise. Slowly pushing upward with his good arm, Kashif rolled to a sitting position. As his blanket fell away, the stench of ash and char—scorched earth—wafted from his clothes. The room spun and he pitched forward.

Abbud caught him around the waist and returned him to the cot. "Save what little strength you have. When Isha ends, the Mullah will order you brought before him. He's returned with yet another sheik."

"You mean another jetliner jihadist," Kashif corrected. "Dropping in like some fat goose migrating north for a little taste of jihad. He'll eat his fill of our struggle, crap some gold, and fly away before his robes gather any blood."

Abbud shrugged. "Black helicopters in the night. A bullet between your eyes while your wife looks on. Sheiks like Bin Laden are hard to find."

"Jihad's easy when it only costs a few barrels of oil."

"No, jihad's easy when you've nothing to lose. Is that what this is all about for you, Kashif? Jihad?"

"You know exactly what this is for me. And no matter how little I respect this sheik, if he leaves off enough gold to get us to America, then he'll have done more for us than Bin Laden ever did."

Abbud peered out the window, his head and shoulders blocking the starlight and muffling the recitations. "The Mullah will want a tale of heroic exploits. Something sure to enthrall our potential benefactor."

"Heroic?" Kashif snorted. "Hiding in the boulders across the gap. That's where I watched my heroic deed unfold. I burned the forest."

Abbud's shoulders slumped. He turned away from the window and slid down along the wall to his haunches. "I assumed Hosaam."

"No. Me." Kashif lay back on the cot, draping his forearm across his eyes. "Do I belong?"

An entire recitation of Isha passed before Abbud responded. "The trees will return."

"Will they?" Like photos Kashif had once seen of an atomic explosion, the smoke mushroomed high above the mountaintops. The fire quickly spreading, each tall walnut passing flames along its limbs to light the next until the entire forest blazed. "Every tree burned. They're not coming back."

"You cannot know that, my young brother. Stout trunks. Deep roots. Sometimes the strong ones sprout green again."

"Like the great walnut we prayed beneath?"

"Yes."

Kashif sighed and closed his eyes. For hours he'd watched the grandfather burn, the fire climbing upward, each successive limb suddenly crackling with a bright line of fire, as if it had snared a bolt of lightning. The vast crown soon became uncountable branches of white spider webbing across an immense cloud of billowing black smoke. Yet, unlike the surrounding trees, the grandfather's broad trunk seemed to deny the very existence of the fire, refusing to burn, a massive dark column, steadfast and intractable, indifferent to the blazing carnage all around.

But at the grandfather's base, fueled by grass and bush and falling limb, the fire raged, the flames heating from amber to gold to white hot. And at the core, a tiny gem of blue promised an even hotter burn to come. "He held strong for a long time."

"He?"

Grimacing through another jab of pain, Kashif sat up and peered through the gray at Abbud. "After I was sure the Americans had flown off, I made my way back toward the crest. By the time I reached the top, trees were exploding, casting limbs halfway across the gap. The heat so intense my face felt afire. But I couldn't stop watching." Kashif twisted the singed ends of his hair. "Every tree surrounding that great walnut...the grandfather walnut...burst apart. And every piece of shattered trunk and fractured limb was trapped beneath the broad reach of his branches. At his roots, the fire's color turned to sapphire, a brilliant blue like the hottest spot in a blacksmith's hearth. Then a great crack shook the air. And he tipped. Fell. Slowly. Into the gap."

Kashif rubbed his forehead, and then pinched his temples between fingers and thumb. "I wanted to...it makes no sense, I know...I wanted to run down and smother the flames. Stand the grandfather walnut upright. See him strong again. So yes, 'he'—the grandfather. Insane thoughts, are they not?"

Abbud shook his head. "No...I felt...." He glanced about the room as if he hoped to find the words he needed written on the walls. "When the helicopter hovered over us. Your words of Allah planting...protecting us—"

"Not mine. My mother's. She put those thoughts, those words in me."

Abbud nodded. "Righteous words. The grandfather. He. I accept this."

"He, then," Kashif nodded back. "I sat at the crest, watching him, the grandfather, die." He bit down on his tongue to stifle the rising vomit. "I recited the opening verse of every surah I could remember. But left them all unfinished. None brought comfort." Kashif dropped his eyes to the floor, wondering if prayers would ever comfort him again. Trees. Grass. Grandfather. All black now. All dead. "I burned it all, Abbud. Do I belong?"

Many minutes passed, his question never answered.

The recitations stopped. The barking continued.

Abbud left the window, nudged aside the doorway curtain and looked out. "Isha is over. They're coming. Time for you to regale the Mullah and his golden goose."

"You regale."

Abbud chuckled, short and guttural. "Mullahs don't like talking to men who can split a melon at a thousand meters. They like to pretend we don't exist."

"Hosaam then."

"He hasn't returned."

The vomit rose again. Hosaam gone? The man who walked the winter mountains alone. Ate carrion to survive. The warrior who carried his mother's coin purse. And crawled in amongst the maggots. Hosaam dead? The only mujahedeen who carried a knotted cord. Knots spaced the same distance as the red marks on Faiq's throat. "And what will I say of Faiq's death? The Mullah doesn't want that truth. Not in front of this sheik."

"The Mullah may not ask."

"Faiq's brother, Yusef, will ask. He's already demanded to question me twice. I've protested weakness from my wounds. But out there, before the fire, I must answer."

"Then you'll answer as you need."

"If I lie, then your silence is also a lie."

"There's no sword at your throat. You have a choice, Kashif. Either way, you can be sure of me." Abbud released the curtain and stepped away from the doorway.

"Why? We are not brothers, Abbud. Not by blood."

"I have asked myself this same question. Many times. But no answer has come to me. Yet, like the bullet that's already left my barrel, of this, I have no doubt."

"Abbud, if I could have chosen a brother—"

The room lit up as the doorway curtain parted. A head poked through. "Come. The Mullah will speak soon. Then call you forward. Be ready." The curtain dropped, turning the room gray again.

Rising, stretching, and walking all brought separate doses of hurt. Kashif finally stepped from the low hovel only to collide with a growling dog racing toward the darkness. Stifling a curse, he stumbled into the outmost fringes of the firelight.

Across the fire sat the Mullah. Next to him was a stranger, clothed in a simple white robe and turban. The robe looked a little too white for the mountains, and the turban bore not a speck of dust. The golden goose. Behind the sheik, his retinue stood guard, making sure the dirt never stuck.

Ringing the fire to Kashif's right were the mujahedeen, many conversing in low tones. While others, the most battle worn, sat each to themselves, stoic spots of silence dotting the quiet chatter. Abbud nodded at Kashif and wandered among them, all the warriors becoming silent as he passed.

At the base of the fire knelt Faiq's brother, Yusef, his eyes locked on the flames.

Completing the circle to the left, the sycophants babbled their careful mix of bravado and piety, always calling loudly for jihad. Yet whenever battle was joined, they were forever busy attending the Mullah.

All looked the same as most nights, but something felt very different. Perhaps it was the regaling expected of him, or the sheik, or maybe just the stray dog barking at the edge of the compound. Yet before this evening was through, he'd stand before the Mullah offering witness to the death of Faiq.

Across the fire sat Kashif's judgment. Looking up, he searched the night sky for comfort—the cool that warmed…the soft that strengthened…Allah's veiled light—the moon. His mother once told him that she believed the moon's full face so beautiful that Allah only let it show but once for every twenty-nine suns. But moonrise was still a long way off.

The Mullah rose. Gathering a lengthy portion of his robe from the dirt, he draped it over his forearm and swatted. A cloud of dust engulfed his face. The Mullah coughed, drawing the attention of those sitting closest. He rubbed the dirt from his eyes and swatted again. More dust. Another cough. More swats. With each eruption of dust, a few more heads turned and the babble from the crowd lessened.

When his swats brought forth no more dust, the Mullah stooped to examine the frayed hem and plucked away a few loose strands. He carefully scrutinized each strand before releasing it to float toward the ground. By now the crowd had grown so quiet that Kashif imagined he could hear the tattered flecks of white hem as they landed on the Mullah's sandals. Without uttering a single word, the Mullah had the fireside throng silent and waiting. After arranging the drape of his robe so that no part touched the ground, his eyes swept the heavens as he opened his arms wide.

Like a painting lifted from the forbidden pages of the Christian Bible, the Mullah's body seemed to gather onto him the firelight, the flickering flames alternately shading and highlighting his figure: one ankle dark beneath the hem, white robe angling upward across an even whiter knee, pleats of fabric fanning a bright arc between ribs and forearm, opalescent left palm cupped upward—offering to all who would listen, the teachings of the Prophet.

The Mullah's face glowed as he raised his right hand alongside his ear, the tip of a bent and gnarled index finger pointing to the stars. He looked like Moses, come to earth again. And as though he stood atop lightning-charged Mount Sinai, all eyes were fixed on him, waiting for the crash of his thunder. All except the sheik, who panned between the Mullah and the crowd, nodding his respect. The sheik leaned back and stroked at his beard as the Mullah spoke. "Jihad. Some die here in the lands of our fathers. Some will die afar.

All struggle. All die for Allah...."

The dog, growling at the night, competed with the Mullah's oratory. No matter. Kashif had heard these words before. Many times. They always started the wails resonating through his mind. One moment she sang as she made him breakfast. A bomb explosion later he tugged at her blue robe beneath the rubble. At night, he still tugged in his sleep.

The Americans apologized. Collateral damage, they called her. By nightfall she was buried. And to this day, it was not the lowering into the ground, nor the shovelfuls of dirt falling on her body, nor the parting prayers, but the ululations of the women, the terrible and glorious wailing of tongues, that never let him rest.

A loud yelping broke the Mullah's rhythm. He cleared his throat. "America, the Great..." A dog squeal finished his sentence. The Mullah signaled for water, gulped the goblet dry and resumed. "America..." He coughed. "...the Great...." The cough grew coarse, phlegm gagging his words. Bending over and grabbing his knees, he hacked.

The sheik lifted a finger and two of his men rushed forward, each grabbing an arm and slipping it over a shoulder, supporting the Mullah's weight until the coughing subsided. Another goblet was brought. The Mullah sucked at the contents, losing a portion out the corners of his mouth.

Kashif followed the escaping water. Little river-like fangs grew down the Mullah's long white beard. At the bottom, droplets formed and dripped off, one by one, dotting the sand. Kashif thought to rush forward and catch them. Foolishness. Water was always wasted.

"America, the Great Satan, fights his wars abroad, raping our lands. We must travel to America and rape his land."

The dog returned, limping by, right forepaw wet and pulsing red. From bloody teeth dangled a fleshy prize.

"Those of you selected to make this journey must don the camouflage of corruption, speak as they speak, whore as they whore. For in that decadence, your holy armor lies. Clothed in sinfulness you become invisible in the land of the Great Satan."

Kashif edged toward the darkness, tracing the dog's bloody paw prints backwards. After several steps they disappeared. He picked out a rock thirty degrees to the right of his line of travel and focused. Another mark of blood floated out of the dark. He stepped farther from the fire.

Each advance required a disciplined effort. Stop, look away—askance. Focus and wait. When it grew too dark for his night vision to find the bloody prints he halted, drew in a lungful of air and froze, listening. His ears picked up scuffing—leather over stone.

"Kashif, come forward," the Mullah commanded.

Something, a shadow, darker than the night, formed in the corner of his eye. A silhouette. Human. Maybe it was an American sniper. Perhaps about to squeeze the trigger and send a bullet through his brain. Providence. Give him a hero's death before he was forced to answer questions about Faiq.

"Kashif, our young brother, come and bear witness." The Mullah spoke louder this time.

The silhouette moved. Kashif's head snapped toward the motion. Gone. He clenched his fists. How many times must he repeat the same mistake? Never should he look directly at what he wished to see. Frowning, he backed to the firelight and weaved through the throng.

The Mullah waved him forward.

Kashif circled left, passing well wide of Faiq's brother, and entered the small gap separating the crowd from the fire. Nearing the Mullah, he paused mid-step. Beneath his foot lay the fallen water drops.

The Mullah's outstretched arms welcomed him closer.

Kashif broke eye contact, dropped chin to breastbone, dug his heels into the dirt and waited. For some reason he couldn't quite grasp, these drops deserved respect. Much like the tears that pooled on his mother's eyelashes whenever she'd stared at the moon...they mattered.

After an awkward few moments, the Mullah approached him. Kashif shuffled closer, setting his toes to the edge of the drops and leaning, hoping to preserve their short, evaporating lives. The Mullah patted Kashif's shoulder. "Our brothers have returned from battling the Great Satan. This young warrior has fought his fiercest minions. Kashif, our guest would hear of our struggle."

Kashif monitored the Mullah's right sandal, its tip overhanging a shrinking drop. They disappeared too quickly. Already, half as many drops remained. Another evaporated as he considered what to say.

"Come Kashif. We know that the Great Satan's forces died. Tell us how."

What was the truth? "They died…." Yes, he'd fired his weapon. And yes, Abbud had struck, sniping death from great distance. "They died…by Allah's will."

The Mullah squeezed Kashif's shoulder. "Yes Kashif. Allah willed it so. But his warriors. How did you achieve Allah's victory?"

Another droplet of water evaporated. "Allah's victory?" Faiq and Hosaam—both dead. An ancient forest burned. What victory? Kashif fought off the urge to spit out the question. "The Marines died because…Hosaam willed them dead. He crawled among the maggots. Hosaam led us to…that victory."

"No," a voice shouted from behind. "My brother led you. Faiq was in command." Yusef drew closer. "Where is he, Kashif?"

Another droplet vanished. "I buried him."

"How did he die?" Yusef stopped just behind Kashif.

Only two groups remained, six droplets in one, four in the other. "I found him dead."

"Yes, Kashif, you found Faiq and you buried him. You've already said as much." Yusef leaned in toward his ear. "But how did my brother die?"

Kashif watched another drop fade. "Your brother died—"

A severed head plopped to the ground and rolled to the edge of the fire. Six sets of dog tags hit the dirt next to it.

Striding forward into the firelight, Hosaam pointed at the Marine's head. "Faiq died saving me from that dog."

Hosaam looked as though he'd just escaped from hell. His feet were black. Half his robe was brown and shriveled, exposing a knee. Greasy fluid dripped from the charred skin sloughing from one hand. And his face, with beard singed short on one side, eyebrow absent from the other, seemed almost clown-like. Yet anything but funny. More like the hero of a comic tragedy, some dark madness propelling the walking corpse that was once Hosaam.

The Mullah backed away, eyes darting between the severed head and the walking dead. His mouth moved but no words came out.

Undeterred by the horrid spectacle, Yusef stepped nose to nose with Hosaam. "Faiq was a hero then?"

"Yes. He was mine." Hosaam smiled through cracked lips. "My hero."

"Faiq led you to victory?"

"Yes. He led and died. A victory."

Yusef smiled. "Then why does Kashif insist you led the battle? That you lay down with maggots."

Hosaam's hand moved to the hilt of his knife. "My friend Kashif does me honor. My role was despair. May Almighty Allah forgive me."

"Such modesty," Yusef smirked. "I think our guest would like to hear about you and your maggots."

For long moments Hosaam caressed the hilt of his knife, then recited in monotone. "I refused to leave a hopeless battle. Faiq sought to convince me by feigning abandonment. He returned to command our victory. Later our captive broke free and attacked. Faiq did not survive."

"Exactly how did my brother die?"

Leaving his knife sheathed, Hosaam's empty hand lunged at Yusef's stomach. Finishing the stabbing feint a centimeter from contact, he rotated his hand back and forth in a slow twisting motion. "He was knifed in the back."

Yusef didn't flinch, his eyes never leaving Hosaam's. "Kashif? Has Hosaam left anything unsaid?"

Kashif's eyes jerked up from the drops. "Unsaid?"

"Do you bear witness to this?"

"I was not there when Faiq died."

"You found his body. Was there blood on his back?"

Only a few water droplets remained. No one seemed to care. "It was too dark," Kashif offered.

"You buried him. Handled his body. His back...was it wet?" Yusef's voice grew loud. "Speak, Kashif."

A chuckle came from the sheik. "You've lost his other ear, Hosaam." He held the severed head by the hair, examining all sides. "And half a cheek."

Snickering filtered through the crowd.

"The dog was hungry."

Laughter erupted from the sycophants. The warriors remained silent.

The sheik dropped the head and picked up the dog tags. "Very resourceful." He dangled and jingled the metal tags, nodding approval at the Mullah. "Is Hosaam the measure of who you would have me support in America?"

The Mullah's face looked like he nursed a sore tooth as he considered the sheik's question. "Hosaam has proven our training methods effective."

"More importantly," the sheik added, "Hosaam's determination assures my assets would be well spent. Will he command in America?"

"Command?" The Mullah hesitated, studying the unblinking faces of Yusef and Hosaam, still nose to nose before him. He looked up at the stars and closed his eyes, then slowly lowered his head, a grimace spreading across his face. "Yes. He will command."

Yusef redirected his stare from Hosaam to the Mullah. "Kashif has not answered."

Sharp and hard, the Mullah nodded once. "Kashif, you must answer. Has Hosaam told us—"

"I will not go." Hosaam spoke past the Mullah, addressing the sheik. "I will not go to America."

"Not…not go?" the Mullah stammered.

"Not unless I choose my warriors." Hosaam stepped alongside Kashif. "I will only serve with the tested, those proven loyal and faithful."

Yusef shouted, "You'll not serve at all unless you're proven truthful."

The Mullah raised his hand skyward for silence. "Jihad is not a battle between brothers. It is the inward struggle to submit ourselves to Allah's will, and the outward struggle against the nonbeliever. This infighting must stop."

Stepping forward, the Mullah placed his hands on Kashif's shoulders, looking him in the eyes. "Will you end this? Do you bear witness to Hosaam?"

The answer was obvious. Say "yes" and go to America. Avenge his mother's murder. Yet something felt wrong. Changed. Different. The same strange feeling he'd felt when first stumbling into the firelight. The feeling he'd dismissed as mere angst caused by the impending questions of Faiq's death, or the pressure of impressing the sheik with tales of jihad, or even just the barking at the edge of the compound. But the dog no longer barked. And the regaling was over. Only answering the Mullah's question remained. So why was saying "yes" so difficult?

Sheik, Mullah, sycophants, mujahedeen—all eyes watched him.

Kashif searched their faces for the answer. Nothing. They all seemed the same as before.

To Kashif's immediate left, Hosaam remained oddly still, lifeless, empty. Like a corpse, Hosaam's presence emitted no warmth, no motion, not the blink of an eye nor a twitch of breath, only the cold promise of immutable permanence.

Softly, the Mullah repeated, "Do you bear witness?"

Lowering his chin, Kashif watched another droplet fade. Just one remained. He answered without looking up. "I do."

The Mullah squeezed Kashif's shoulder. "It is settled then. Hosaam, pick your warriors and lead them to America." He motioned the sheik forward and escorted him toward his lodgings, their feet trampling the last droplet as they passed.

Others filtered by, heading for sleep.

Abbud stood apart, silently mouthing two words at Kashif. "You belong."

Kashif shut his eyes against the rising ululations in his mind. He'd burned the forest. And lied for Hosaam. He belonged. Droplets formed and fell from his cheeks, re-dotting the sand below. But they too would soon disappear, just more wasted water. Abbud's "you belong" answered his nagging question. Nearly everything was the same. Only he...Kashif...was different.

CHAPTER FIFTEEN

When Uday was a young boy he prayed Allah show him a path to The Realm's throne. His older brother beat him unconscious.

The Royal Prince Uday Azwad basked a moment beneath the rays of The Realm's early sun, then descended marble steps to walk the garden among his many pretty things. "Begin with 'The Angel.' Anything new, Taamir?"

Three prescribed paces, Taamir trailed behind, poking at a tablet, his finger tapping a blur. "Yes, Excellency. Ms. Angela Pierce's latest fax begs audience during your next visit to America."

Uday paused beside a bed of purple irises. "Begs?" Reaching out, he selected a flawless specimen and followed the stem upward. With a fingertip he tested the sharp points of the sword-shaped leaves and stroked the velvet petals. "The Angela I knew would never deign to beg."

"My choice of words, Excellency."

The Prince bent to sample the flower's subtle fragrance. A tiny nose lifted from the Prince's forearm and edged toward the tasty flower. Uday tapped between its floppy ears and waggled a finger. The fat Cape hare drew back at the affront, sinking head between paws, its nose still twitching at the tantalizing scent mere centimeters away. "How many times has our Ms. Pierce attempted contact?"

"Twice by phone, five by fax, Excellency."

"And you've confirmed that in her first contact she represented herself as working for the District Attorney's office?"

"Yes, Excellency."

Uday pulled a few sprigs of ground cover from the flowerbed and offered them to the hare. The tiny nose sniffed at the sprigs and turned away, seeking instead the delicate blossom. The Prince dropped the greenery and tugged free a purple petal. He spoke to the hare as it nibbled. "The Angel thinks herself to fly so very high. Doesn't she, little one?" When the hare finished, Uday snapped blossom from stem and hid it beneath his robe, then attended to his first decision of the day.

Which route to the aviary? Left past irises, orchids, roses, and all manner of flower in between, or right under the shade of palm, date, and acacia trees? His garden awaited the choice, his path determining the watering. Outside these walls, nature dictated the cycles of life. Inside, an entire season's moisture came and went in the Prince's wake.

This morning he'd indulge himself, straight down the center to wander the labyrinth. As he moved amidst the forsythia shrubs an unseen hand turned spigots, releasing a misty spray, granting another day's life to flower and tree. But the parched bushes through which he strolled must wait their master's passing. "Her first attempt. How long ago?"

"Two weeks, Excellency."

Seven times in fourteen days. And why now? He'd done nothing truly different. Certainly nothing to inspire contact. He tapped the little black button nose nuzzling through the folds of his robe. "Soon, little one, soon." Uday stroked the long floppy ears.

Obviously, something had changed in The Angel's life. Some abrupt new pressure applied. And pressures came from only two directions—internal or external. She was reaching outward, toward him. So, external, Uday decided.

For Angela Pierce, external meant either work or family. Likely family, since she was retired. But both her children were fully grown and gone. Only her husband remained at home. Abrupt? New? Not Stuart Pierce. Steady as stone, that one. Puzzling.

A squawk from the aviary scolded Uday's tardiness. He measured the progress of the sun and frowned. "Taamir, let's move on. Oil?"

"Yes, Excellency." Taamir tapped once to reawaken his screen, then several times more. "Oil broke through recent support levels, hitting a six-month low."

"Signal our agents to accumulate up to one million contracts at three points lower." Uday walked the convoluted path, fingers testing the health and vibrancy of the hedges as he passed. "And what of gold?"

"Gold continues higher, climbing twenty percent above our most recent purchase."

"Let it climb another five percent, then liquidate our entire position." Uday fired off another dozen or so dictates, determining the day's disposition for much of the Royal Family's investments. He always manipulated the money markets with an easy precision. A great mass of people formed the markets. And people were simple. Lemmings. Whether oil, gold, or the next fad stock, they followed the crowd to their financial deaths. People comprised the simplest challenges of his long days.

But individuals? His father. His brother. Angela Pierce. Individuals were unpredictable. Dangerous. So far, he'd kept a safe distance from The Angel. Best keep it that way.

Uday delayed asking his next question, taking in the sky above, the trees below, and the hedges surrounding him, drawing strength from the untainted beauty. After several minutes, he sighed and forced out "And my appointments?"

"The Religious Minister demands audience today. Says we have done nothing to curb the spread of seditious materials throughout The Realm."

Uday stopped and grasped a bit of browning forsythia, repeatedly twisting it back and forth to fray the bark, then snapped the twig free. "Remind me again, Taamir, why I suffer this office."

"Because you follow the great path Allah has set before you, Excellency."

"Great path?" Uday rubbed a thumb along his spear-crested ring, then slowly rotated his hand until the star caught the sun and flashed a glint. A habit as old as the day his father first presented him the ring. "I've always thought of my life as following a star, Taamir. This star."

"Allah made all the heavens, Excellency. Path or star...it is the same."

"But three rings, Taamir, each bearing the same family star, yet each of us fated a different path. My star, determined not by my abilities, but by the arbitrary order of my birth."

"No man knows his path to Allah. When your ancestor—"

"Yes...yes, Taamir, I know...when the mighty Zuehb Azwad flew down the mountainside to singlehandedly slay a dozen marauders, he had nothing but selflessness in his heart, and his father rewarded him with the ruby-starred ring. And the mighty Zuehb, begot as second-son, became first, and his descendants were gifted all The Realm."

"Yes, Excellency."

"Then lay out this selfless path I must walk to earn the ruby-starred ring, and I will run it. Show me marauders, Taamir, and I will slay them. Tell me what feat will alter the moment in time that my mother saw fit to release me from the shackles of her womb, and I will perform it."

"Excellency, respect...please. I remind you that when you turned four, against the many warnings of your doctors and defying the royal command of your father, your mother went to you while you lay in hot fever, held you day and night while praying to Allah, took the fever herself, then smiled as your fever broke, and with her final breath lay a kiss upon your brow. You know this."

"I know what you tell me, Taamir. And I also know what my father tells me. You see my mother's actions as proof of her strength. My father sees them as her moment of foolish weakness. And he has missed no opportunity since her passing to single out the slightest weakness in me, to point out that my older brother slept alongside me and yet never took the fever, to remind me of my weak blood. I ask you, did my mother save me or curse me with what you call her strength?" Uday held up his hand. "Pay me no heed, Taamir. To this question, there is no answer."

"Allah answers all questions, in his time."

Uday sighed, shaking his head. "Your faith burns forever steady, Taamir, while mine has yet to flare. Perhaps you should meet with the Religious Minister in my stead. I have little patience for that zealot. He literally foams at the mouth like a rabid camel while he rants and raves, and threatens the throne. Sometimes I imagine that if my great ancestor had foreseen that fourteen centuries later our clan would still be living with the zealot-stink, he would have slid his silver knife across the throat of the first wild-eyed camel to stick its nose into our family's tent."

"Be careful, my Prince, the gardeners might overhear...word

could reach your brother's ears."

Uday nodded. Yes, his brother, the Royal Mullah, yet another one of the thousands of self-appointed experts on the Qur'an. The man had entwined himself within the Religious Ministry, the only autonomous institution among The Realm's governing bodies. And as first in line to the throne, his brother's rise within that fanatical ministry was meteoric. How long before those zealots appointed their future king as minister? And where would the Royal Mullah, as head of the Religious Ministry, lead The Realm once their father died? To jihad?

"Excellency?" Taamir's eyes were staring downward.

Following Taamir's gaze, Uday found his left hand white-knuckled around a frayed mess of ropelike fibers that minutes ago were a forsythia twig, his fingers brown and sticky with sap.

He threw the twig to the ground and motioned Taamir to continue. Fifteen minutes and twenty-three decisions later, the remainder of Uday's schedule was set, including an entire hour for the charming of the Religious Minister. He'd rather kill the man, but there was an endless supply of fools to take his place, and the idiot would likely thank him for a quick trip to Allah.

Uday opened the gate to the aviary. "Schedule a meeting with The Angel during the Finanthropic banquet in Washington."

"Excellency? Your table is full."

Removing the iris blossom from his robe, Uday tickled the hare's nose. "No, Taamir. I would not waste a decade's effort on her." He tossed the purple treat into the aviary and stroked the floppy ears one last time. "Whom would I subtract? The Fed Chief? The Secretary of the Treasury? Give Ms. Pierce audience with you. Time for her angelic feet to feel earth again." The Prince set the hare on the ground. "Off you go, little one." Though plump from captivity, the hare bounded through the gate, snatched up the blossom, and hopped beneath the shade of the aviary's lone tree as Uday sealed it safely inside.

At the sound of gushing sprinklers, the Prince turned to face his grand garden, watching the many tiny rainbows springing from the mists of his generosity. Tomorrow he would return to America and smile. As with every other long absence, the transformation would begin tonight. His personal barber would arrive, cut his hair, and shave his beard down to a thin chinstrap. Makeup would work its

125

magic, darkening the newly exposed skin to match his tan. The comfort of loose-flowing fabrics would be lost to tailored suits and choking neckties. None of these efforts bothered him. Only the incessant smiling. Here, he smiled when pleased. There, they always wanted a smiling Arab, and he always gave them what they wanted. In America, his winning smile was his trademark.

A loud screech drew his attention back toward the cage. The fat little hare froze as Uday's pride and joy, an enormous Martial eagle, swooped down and crushed its skull. Uday smiled.

CHAPTER SIXTEEN

Stu lifted the barbeque grill's lid and stepped back from a cloud of billowing smoke. "You going to help Angie or not, Tom?"

Gramps stood his ground, taking another sip of beer as the greasy cloud rolled up and over his face. "Question lacks a little eloquence, don't you think?"

"Eloquence?" Stu snatched a steak from the grill and eyeballed Gramps as he weighed the merits of various responses to the old patriarch's rhetorical question.

All of the responses Stu considered began eloquently enough, but more than a week had passed since Angie had asked Tom for help, and no matter how hard Stu tried, every reply he ran through his mind ended with the words "slow, bureaucratic ass." Insulting the old patriarch was probably not the best way to garner his cooperation.

Or maybe it was. Fast and lethal—"ballsy" was the reputation Gramps had earned while serving as the unofficial advisor to certain members of the Afghan Royal Family in the late nineteen sixties. But decades of shuffling paper at CIA headquarters separated that ballsy Gramps from the ponderous man Stu pleaded with now. The patriarch's little rhyme, "round to the head to make'em dead," implied that Gramps still carried "lethal," but it seemed like Washington politics had lopped off the old man's "fast." Maybe an insult would remind him of what he'd lost.

"I save the luxury of fancy talk for long simulator debriefs, Gramps. In the real world, things move a little faster." Stu flipped and slapped the steak back onto the grill, casting a shower of bloody drops to the coals. Spurts of hissing flame flared out.

Gramps shied away from the spitting fire. "And your grilling skills could use a bit of finesse."

Snatching up another steak, Stu flipped and slammed, sending Gramps back two more steps. Screw finesse, he thought. And screw eloquence. Finesse was for Washington bureaucrats, two-martini lunches, and thousand-dollar-a-plate political fundraisers. Zealots stoned little girls to death while the world's politicians searched for the soft, eloquent words to condemn them.

Stu pointed his dripping tongs toward the far corner of the house where Angie and their unexpected guest hovered over a scrawny bush. Both women looked down at a dirty white flower while shaking their heads side to side, Angie, no doubt, explaining her relentless pursuit of the true blue rose. "Eloquence? Finesse? Sorry, Gramps. Fresh out. Used them all up giving your young lady friend the nickel home tour. Seems like a sweet woman. I didn't think death threats made for a polite opening topic."

"Mary? Sweet? I'll have to tell her you said so. She'll get a kick out of that. Mary's a pro. Former CIA. Any topic's safe with her. You could tell Mary an hour-long story and she'd swear in court she didn't remember a word, and they'd believe her."

Stu flip-slammed another steak. "You're a little late with that information. This is the first chance we've had to talk privately and it's already over." Stu redirected his tongs toward the approaching Buzz and smiled a welcome.

Buzz flashed Stu a grin and offered Gramps a handshake. "Is this the spook? Don't look too scary."

Stu forced a laugh. "More like Casper. Tom, this is—"

"One of your two close friends." Gramps grabbed hold and shook. "Buzz, isn't it?"

Buzz's eyes narrowed as he searched Tom's face. "Have we—"

"You're a Washington National tower controller," Gramps continued. "Divorced. Shared custody of three kids. Served in Iraqi Freedom. Distinguished Service Cross for—" Gramps nodded over at Cheryl and her redheaded twins kicking a soccer ball across the yard. "—pulling her late husband from a burning jet. Drove all the way out to rural Virginia to help us celebrate our nation's birthday. You've got two cases of dark stout waiting for you in the study. I helped Stu carry them in."

Buzz finished shaking hands, then made an exaggerated display

128

of examining his shirt and jeans. "Just checking. Feel like I've been stripped naked." He held up his right hand and wiggled his fingers. "Everything's still here, though, including my class ring."

The patriarch smiled just a few teeth. "Yes, but keep it out of water. The microphone I planted can give a nasty shock."

Buzz laughed. "I take it back, Stu. He's a frightening man."

Across the patio, the great room's door slid open. Carl leaned out. "Hey Ironman, what's a Fourth of July without some flipping fireworks? Where you hiding the good booze?"

Before Stu could even finish processing Carl's question, Gramps interjected. "I'd stay away from that top shelf." With a wink, the patriarch's lips parted wide, shooting Stu columns of pearly white.

Gramps was showing off, letting Stu know he hadn't sat idle during the past week. He'd spoken of doing a little investigative research before giving Angie an answer, but he never mentioned that the two of them would be the target of his investigation. Only a week gone by and the old man already knew of their scotch tradition. Maybe he did plant a microphone in Buzz's ring. Stu's tiny crack of a smile answered the patriarch's broad grin. "Tom's right, Carl. Go near that bottle and the airline will be short a copilot."

"This ain't the frick…." Carl glanced over at the twins. "This isn't the stinking simulator. Who put Gramps in charge?" He turned away and shouted, "Hey, Angie, how about a wee nip of the single malt?"

She drew an index finger across her throat in a slicing motion. "I'll fertilize this bush with your remains," Angie shouted back.

Carl looked back at Stu, held up a hand and rubbed his thumb rapidly across his fingertips in the universal gesture for money. "You could buy another flipping bottle for your buddies." Carl disappeared back inside, mumbling "Cheap-ass captains."

Stu pointed after him. "Do me a favor, Buzz? Top of the wine fridge. My *Rebelion*. Little sipping tequila should shut him up."

"Sure thing. Pour myself a sip while I'm at it." Buzz gave his ring a twist. "Never shake that spook's hand, Ironman."

Stu waited until Buzz was out of earshot. "You've obviously done your homework. So what did all your research tell—"

"Told me Angie doesn't realize her position."

"Angie's got me to—"

"Nor do you." Gramps took a long draw on his beer, swished

129

and swallowed. "Here's how I see things. Angie takes her formidable skills and founds a legal website for what certain third-world dictators might call the great unwashed women of the planet. In the beginning, she mostly deals with human trafficking. Then she starts writing provocative open letters to foreign governments. Attracts like-minded voices. Together they stir the pot of discontent. That's all well and good. Make some people mad. Get herself an anonymous threat or two. And she probably shouldn't expect any invites to the camel jockey finals in The Realm's capital. But you start snatching children, you make real enemies."

"She didn't snatch anyone," Stu insisted.

"Doesn't matter. Last year, kid disappears from The Realm. Kid reappears in Rome. Angie helps win the kid's custody case. Angie's website documents every bit of this. Looks an awful lot like she snatched the kid. Or at the very least, she's the conductor, running an underground railroad for snatched kids."

"Kids?" Stu shook his head. "They're not goats. They've got names, Tom."

Gramps scratched hard at the back of his white head. "Are you hearing anything I'm saying, Stu?"

"That kid's name is Okeda." Stu poked the dripping tongs toward Gramps's chest. "And she has bright green eyes. Do you know how rare that is for her lineage? At twelve years old, she's already gorgeous. But she'll never have a normal relationship with a man because they tied her down and cut her. Cut the passion right out of her. And you'd suggest that Angie shouldn't let the world know?"

"Find some other way to let the world know," Gramps replied. "Get her out of the limelight."

"Have her cower while others die? She'll never go for that. Women have been stoned."

"Okay. Let me try this again. I'll rephrase in language more suited to you. Angie's set herself up as the lead fighter jet in these little rescue operations, and nothing quite disrupts a formation of aircraft like shooting down the lead airplane, now does it?"

A bouncing soccer ball ricocheted off the grill. Stu quickly stepped to intercept the redheaded twin chasing headlong after it. He scooped her up with his free arm, kicked the ball clear and sent her off giggling. "Stay away from the fire, girls."

Stu turned back to Gramps. "Lead airplanes don't get shot down if they have the right support—accurate intelligence reports, solid defense, and a good plan of attack. I was hoping you'd help us out there."

"Good. You're scared," Gramps said.

"I'm concerned," Stu corrected. "Want to be smart. Scared is too strong a word."

"You sure look scared. In fact, you look like someone who's hauled fear around so long they're about to drop."

Stu didn't respond, afraid that if he made up some story to explain his fatigue, Gramps would know it for a lie. After all, as Angie had always told him, he was a terrible liar. But if he answered truthfully, he might ruin any chance of Gramps helping Angie. He decided to ignore Gramps's comment, and knuckled the thinnest steak. Soft and squishy. "How do you like your meat?"

"You've got great big bags under your eyes, Stu." Gramps smiled that vacant shark smile, demanding some response to his comment, his eyes swimming circles around Stu's face, checking for any reactions to the undeniable fact he'd just floated.

Stu wanted to shout, "Because I don't sleep, that's why!" Instead, he knuckled the steaks again, stalling, searching for some truth he could tell. He wiped the juice onto his shoulder towel. "I stayed in a crappy hotel last night," he blurted. That was true enough.

Gramps just kept smiling, waiting patiently for some other chunk of truth to gnaw on.

Stu wondered what else the old man's research had discovered. His pills, perhaps? "Hotel had lousy beds—too soft. I didn't sleep well." There you go, Gramps, there's a couple morsels for those pearly whites. Chew on those. Of course, those two facts were unrelated. Truth was that without a pill, he never slept well anymore. But still, by themselves, both facts were absolute truth. Strung together they made a lie. The kind of lie he could bring himself to tell. "Now, how about your steak? I used to be a rare man. But as I got older I gravitated to medium rare."

"Got almost two decades on you. Prefer medium well." Gramps pointed his beer at Stu. "Two weeks ago, at lunch, Angie did all the talking. Nothing but yawns from you. Dinner out last week, bloodshot eyes. Shitty hotels the norm for your airline?" Gramps's smile got bigger and his eyes seemed even more void of emotion.

Stu shrugged. "Tough business, I'm in." That was true also.

"They've got pills to help a man sleep," Gramps said with a stone-cold tone.

Stu grabbed the spray bottle. Squirting at the coals, he created a wall of rising steam. "Not for me. Heard those can be addicting." Behind the mist it was easier to tell lies. He lowered the grill's lid. "This meat's so tender you can cut it with a fork. What do say about stopping at medium?"

"I say medium well. And I also say you'd sleep a whole lot better if Angie quit chasing after the devil."

Giggles closed in on Stu from behind. He spun, struck the ball mid-bounce and sent it high over the girls' heads. Where the hell was their mother? "Please keep the ball away from the grill, ladies. You'll get burned."

"Uncle Stu, can you play with us?" the twins chorused.

"After dinner, I'll whip both your butts." Scanning the yard, Stu found Cheryl standing between Angie and Mary, all three bent over, studying the thorny bush's lone drab rose.

"You want that woman—" Stu pointed his tongs at Angie. "—to stop chasing after the devil? I thought you CIA spooks were supposed to be good at reading people. You see anything that leads you to believe Angie would walk away from a fight?"

"You're her husband. The man that's supposed to—"

"Supposed to what? After 9/11, I volunteered for FFDO duty. Angie understood."

"Angie doesn't wear a uniform. Never swore an oath or pledged her life—"

"Exactly." Stu held up his hand. "You can stop right there. It's her life."

"But it's my help you're asking for." Gramps slammed his beer down on top of the hot grill lid. The jolt sent a column of foam up the neck and down the side of the bottle. Hissing steam from the burning hops rose between them. "My help...to end her life." No shark smile now, the old patriarch's mouth clamped so tight that his lips disappeared.

"I'm just trying to protect my wife, Tom."

"A man can set out determined to protect something and wind up doing just the opposite," Gramps fired back.

Stu pointed at Gramps's beer. "Getting hot."

"Yeah, it is," Gramps acknowledged, but left his beer sitting there.

A muffling of little girl laughter brought Stu around. "Freeze," he ordered.

Maryann, or was it Daryann, Stu couldn't tell, froze one step short of her twin's upraised foot. Mounted on top was the soccer ball, her sister looking like a mid nineteen fifties field goal holder, the ball suspended between big toe and index finger. An accurate kick would send the ball straight into Stu's gut. A slight miss to the right would crash into the grill.

"Might want to yell," Gramps recommended. "Put the fear of God into those girls before they get hurt."

Stu wanted to yell. Should yell. Haul them by the ears to the flames. Set the soccer ball onto the hot, black bars and burn grill lines into the leather. Let them see and feel the damage they would do to themselves and everyone around them. But that was a father's job. He was Uncle Stu, and not even a real uncle. Just their dead father's best friend. He would never yell at them. Never. His job was to protect them.

"Got a better idea." Setting down his tongs, Stu ran forward prepping for a kick. Instead, he grabbed the ball and laid a kiss on the holder's forehead.

"Yuck." She wiped away his kiss.

"Yuck? I was going to give it back, but wiping off my kiss means not 'til after I'm all done cooking, Daryann."

"I'm Maryann."

"Nice try. But Maryann likes my kisses. Only way I can tell you two apart."

Stu trotted back, wedged the ball under the grill's shelf and pointed at Gramps's heating beer. "Need to check those steaks."

"Bullheaded. Those twins," Gramps said. "Minute you turn your back…." He didn't bother finishing the sentence.

"Not if you help me keep an eye on them."

"My help, again?" Gramps asked.

"Fine. You agree to help Angie. I'll handle the twins. Just get your beer off—"

An outburst of laughter turned both of their heads toward the corner of the house.

The thorny bush at Angie's waist was now barren. She cupped

the bush's lone rose in both hands and lifted it toward the evening sun. Tilting her palms left and right, Angie examined each petal for any speck of blue as the sun's weakening rays poured down, flowing over her face and neck and arms like honey over cream, coloring her auburn hair some long forgotten shade of red, florid and deep. She looked like some ancient Angie, a temple maiden holding aloft an offering to the gods. And she was laughing.

"Do you really want to risk that?" Gramps asked.

"That?" Yeah. Gramps had it right—"that." That buttery brown warmth. That tangle of fiery locks. That laughter. That adventure. That joy. Stu watched...until Angie lowered her arms...until her laughter faded...until she turned away. "That? That's just a memory, Tom."

Stu couldn't see Angie's face. Didn't need to. He knew her cleft had returned. Seemed like the only thing that made it disappear anymore was laughter. "I gave her my word. There's no going back."

A little girl's scream pierced the air, followed by a crash and a cry. "Uncle Stu, you got me all bloody."

Stu spun around. One of the twins hugged a grease-spattered soccer ball to her chest. Neck and face and hair splotched with fat drops of greasy red. Scattered around her feet, the dripping tongs, a cracked spray bottle, and several sharp fragments of shattered steak platter.

"Freeze," Stu ordered. He lifted her from the mess and checked for cuts as she started to sob. "It's okay, sweetie. You're not cut."

"It's blood," she screamed.

"No, no, sweetie. Just the steaks." Stu hugged her close and wiped the splatters from her face. "There's no blood, sweetie. No blood."

"It is too blood," she cried.

Cheryl took her from his arms and headed for the sliding glass door.

"Uncle Stu got me all bloody," she screamed.

"No," Cheryl said. "He didn't, baby. It's not blood."

"He did too. He did...he did. It's blood." The argument continued as they disappeared into the house.

Gramps pointed at the smoking grill.

"Damn." Stu half-stumbled over the broken pieces and flipped open the lid.

Snatching the flying beer bottle midair, Gramps stoppered the top, the foam rising and choking off at his thumb.

Stu poked the thinnest steak—stiff. "Crap." He glanced down at the filthy tongs, decided his fingers were the cleaner choice and snatched the well-done steak from the fire, dropping it onto the warming rack. A quick knuckle to the others revealed all of them spanned a range from medium to well done.

Gramps licked the beer from his thumb. "Well, Uncle Stu, looks like your debriefing items consist of a bloody soccer ball and some not-so-bloody meat."

One after another, Stu yanked the steaks from the fire, burning his fingers in the process. He wiped the greasy blood from his hands. "You got something to say? Then say it. And please, get to the point this time."

Gramps took a swig of beer, made a sour face and poured the rest into the grass. "My point is that Uncle Stu can be determined to do one thing and wind up doing another."

"Damn it, Tom, stop calling me uncle. And I think I've had enough of your sage act too. This is about Angie. And I'm not her uncle. Hell, I'm not even the twins' uncle. But then, you already know that too, don't you?"

Gramps nodded. "Far as I can tell, the number of your close friends shrunk from three to two when Cheryl's husband died."

"What the hell kind of comment is that? More cryptic bullshit?" Stu challenged.

"No. Just that close friends tell you the truth. The less close friends a man has, the less truth he gets."

"We've known each other for…what's it been, two weeks? Is that what we are now, Tom? Close friends?"

"Nope. A close friend would tell you that you're in over your head. That Angie needs to shut down her website and get out of the kid snatching business. That you need to keep Angie well away from the devil. And keep kissing those twins. But I'm not telling you to do any of that. You two need to do exactly what you want to do. If you want to fight the devil, go right ahead. I'm just saying that if you do, there's a good chance you'll both wind up dead."

CHAPTER SEVENTEEN

Whenever the twins stayed the night, Stu spent the entire evening stirring them up, leaving Angie the challenging task of calming them down. A task she normally enjoyed, so full of little girl talk, all colors and stars, giggles and fresh-bath hugs. But tonight, two storybooks and several bedtime songs fell far short of the challenge, the after dinner soccer match and late night fireworks making for a particularly volatile mix.

Daryann complained that Uncle Stu got her all bloody and demanded endless repetitions of what she always called Granda's song.

"Until the day...." Angie's singing voice cracked and trembled to silence. She bent down and kissed the twins' foreheads like Granda had always kissed hers, and wondered if the girls were faking sleep just like she had learned to do.

Granda's whisker-rough goodnight kiss was the very best part of her little girl days. He often took a long time delivering that kiss. Once so long that Angie wondered if he'd forgotten and lifted her eyelids a fraction. Peeking through a fuzzy veil of entwined lashes, she discovered a Granda she'd never seen before. A face calm and soft. No big laugh. No scowl. Only the tiniest bit of a downturned smile. His big hazel eyes all wet and shiny.

At the time Angie had no idea what that face meant. She only knew the way it made her feel. Her blood rushed inward, sent her heart pounding, bursting forth warmth and strength. She felt like she could do anything, be everything, like she could throw off her covers and fly.

After that she'd never missed a goodnight kiss, sneaking peeks at

136

all of Granda's secret faces. And with one exception, years of motherhood had taught her what each face meant. She'd reveled in the painful pride of her own Granda-like, pressed-lips smile...and chewed the inside of her cheeks raw waiting for her baby's fever to break...and stared out the window, eyes growing scratchy and dry as she wondered what the future held for Margaret, her little girl so bold, or Andrew, her son, so very stubborn. And yes, of Granda's watery eyes, Angie had also learned. Sometimes the sight of her sleeping children, all quiet and warm and safe, was something too bright to look at, too beautiful to look away from, and she froze, her eyes welling.

But the meaning of Granda's long face was something she never wanted to know. With his eyebrows raised, eyes blinking and jaw slacking down, a slight quiver would take his lips, as his old worn fingers first caressed, and then kissed, a lock of Angie's hair. The same auburn shade as her mother's hair. His daughter's hair. Once, when Angie saw the long face appear, she stopped faking sleep and hugged him, but that just made him cry. No father should have to bury his daughter. No mother, her son.

Angie recited the last line of Granda's nightly lullaby. "Until the day...I die." And for a few moments she waited, as if Granda were there with her, waited for him to sing her favorite line—"Hush now, don't you cry." The words he first sang to comfort her as a child, but that over the passing years became so much more. Even in high school, college, and law school, Granda still used those same words to say all the things he couldn't. Each time she wished to quit, every time she wanted to retaliate, whenever she raged over a world she couldn't change, he touched her cheek, grasped her hand and looked into her eyes, and used those words to tell her she was better than that. In Granda's eyes, Angie saw reflected the most beautiful version of herself.

In Stu's eyes, she used to see the same. Was it still there? She didn't know. Hard to look him in the eyes anymore. Angie's lower lip began to quiver.

"Hush now, don't you cry," she whispered. But reciting Granda's line to herself didn't make her feel beautiful. Made her feel all alone. Angie bit down on her quivering lip, closed the bedroom door and headed down the hallway toward Tom.

He was the key to finding Sala. If the CIA had a fraction of its rumored capabilities and Tom's computer whiz contacts had even a fraction of that, then she could pinpoint The Bastard's location and provide that information to Prince Uday.

So far, communications with the Prince's office had brought her nothing but vague reassurances. She hadn't even spoken with Uday. The closest she'd gotten, a return phone call from his personal secretary, Taamir, pledging the Prince's full cooperation if Ms. Pierce would simply provide something more specific—a city, country, even a continent.

Angie had none of that. Only The Bastard's taunting emails. His trophy photos. The broken bodies with their piercing eyes. Eyes that even in death seemed to cling to hope. As if they never quite accepted that no one was ever coming, that no one would ever stop the stones, the whip, the sword. Eyes that stared straight through all of Angie's excuses and demanded an answer, a redress, justice.

Or maybe that's what she had to see in them—some rational argument for what she was doing, a *raison d'être* for her deceits. Perhaps instead the eyes were simply looking somewhere farther on, past the crushing impacts, beyond the burning lashes, to the far side of the severing sword...to God.

Angie halted halfway down the hall. She wasn't God. She wasn't even a prosecutor anymore. She was just a mother. And what sort of mother couldn't convince her own son not to volunteer for duty in Afghanistan? She had no power. All she had was lies.

The energy drained from Angie's limbs, forcing her hand to the wall for support. Minutes passed, Angie fighting the powerful feeling that she just wanted to go lie down—go back into the bedroom, crawl in with the twins and wait for Granda's kiss on her forehead. She wanted to lie down and never get up. "Oh, Granda," she whispered, "I miss you."

As if a window suddenly flew open, a rush of heat, like hot summer air, slid across the back of Angie's neck. But the hallway had no windows.

A chill ran down Angie's spine. She whipped her head around and looked behind. No one. Yet her senses flushed with a fleeting presence, like a shadow just faded, leaving behind an outdoor smell of wood and earth, a coarse warming at her cheek...and singing. "Hush now, don't you cry." Granda's voice loud in her mind. An illusion so real that she reached out into nothing, trying to find his whiskers…and look into his eyes…so that she could feel beautiful again.

Laughter filtered down the hall from the great room—Stu's deep chuckle, Mary's whistling wheeze, and Tom's laugh—loud and short and final, every bit as sharp as Granda's laughing bark. A laugh that brooked no argument, like an umpire calling a strike, making sure there was no doubt in the room, officially declaring this thing or that comment funny.

Tom's laugh was just one of several uncanny similarities affecting them all. Similarities that explained Stu's instant bond with a man he'd only recently met, and the twins climbing up onto Tom's lap every time he sat down, and her own mistrust melting away with the warmth of that initial handshake. The man was a spook, and Angie had been fully prepared to tell him exactly how she loathed the very concept of the CIA, until she saw his white hair, heard him laugh, and shook those old worn fingers.

A mere two weeks had passed since then. Only a lunch, a dinner, and today, the Fourth of July, spent in Tom's company. Yet Angie found herself envying the men who worked for him. Right now, more than anything, she wanted to call him Gramps. Beg his help. Ask for his protection. She wanted to fly.

But how? Angie edged toward the great room, hugging the wall opposite the mirror until she found the best angle to view the bantering trio.

Stu stood at the wet bar, rotating the cocktail shaker up and down, performing the role of mixologist. The diminutive Mary sat, feet folded beneath her thighs, on the center of their paisley love seat, one hand twirling her tight black curls ever tighter until she formed a twisted pointer. Poking it at Stu, she pelted him with one silly question after another between her wheezing laughs. Tom was opposite the bar, legs crossed on their leather sofa, smiling Granda's relaxed smile.

Stu's in-your-face honesty hadn't budged Tom from his decidedly undecided stance. Now it was her turn. Problem was she had no plan better than Stu's. How does a person force someone's help? This wasn't a courtroom where she could question witnesses, argue her case before a jury, and win a verdict.

Mary fired another mostly unintelligible question at Stu and burst into a fit of wheezing. Tom added his Granda bark, officially sanctioning her question as very humorous. Even Stu's usual deep chuckle escalated into outright laughter.

The woman had a knack for phrasing her questions in an amusing manner, any one of which, by itself, seemed quite harmless. Yet, each pulled out a tiny piece of the human puzzle. During the course of the afternoon, her little queries had drawn from Angie some of the most intimate details of her life, everything from her endless quest for the true blue rose to the horrific story of her embarrassing first kiss. Mary would've made a formidable litigator. Nothing more charming in the courtroom than asking humorous questions that made any reply other than the complete truth seem laughable. Charm was a powerful weapon.

Absent her purple pen, Angie's thumb snapped down onto her fisted index finger. That was it, the solution to her problem—charm. And why not use their great room as a courtroom? Mary was already playing the charming prosecutor, pleasantly pummeling Stu with amusing questions. Angie could enter the room as Stu's charming defender. And Tom comprised the entire jury.

The situation wasn't ideal. The pseudo courtroom had no judge to control the dialogue, and right now Mary's tight twist of pointed curls had the floor. But Angie could slowly alter that. Pick her spots. Steer the conversation. Gain control and convince the Tom-jury.

That viper pit they called a courtroom was where Angie had always thrived, her highly entertaining, often comical cross-examinations serving to defang witness, judge, and even the opposing attorney. At the end of a trial, she usually had them all swaying to the rhythms of her closing arguments as her summation charmed the jury to her way of thinking. Angie the Snake Charmer, her colleagues had dubbed her.

Well, if she could charm a pit of snakes, why not a single spook? But drawing a yes verdict from Tom would likely prove every bit as difficult as convincing twelve separate jurors.

Angie had discovered early in her career that the twelve always became one. They arrived at the viper pit of many different minds, most protesting the government's interruption of their lives, some glad to escape their boring jobs for a short while, and even a miraculous few with a dutiful sense of civic responsibility. But somewhere during the opening arguments, usually in the dead seconds just after the prosecutor said "murder," the jurors became one mind. It was then that they realized they were about to determine the fate of another human being. Their collective decision meant everything. Freedom. Incarceration. Even death. And under the pressure of that shared responsibility, through covered whispers and sideways glances across the jury box, they formed a single personality. The facts in evidence were of less importance. The key to winning became understanding each jury's unique personality and giving that jury-ego exactly what it wanted—what it needed—to trust her, agree with her interpretation of the facts, and deliver a favorable verdict.

So what did Tom want? What does a spook ego need? Angie crept to the end of the hallway and listened for the right moment to make a graceful, charming entry.

"No thanks, Stu." Mary reined in another wheezing laugh. "Any cocktail that has me asking, 'What brand of whisquilla is tits?' Well, I've already drunk too much, haven't I? How about answering a 'quersonal pestion' instead?"

"A 'quersonal pestion'?" Stu imitated, drawing an approving bark of laughter from Tom.

"Careful, Stu. She's got deadly aim," Tom declared.

"A drunk with deadly accuracy?" Stu chuckled. "Well, I've got to see this. Sure, Mary, fire away, as long as—"

Mary didn't hesitate, letting loose in two quick bursts. "Why Angie? Why did you pick her to marry?"

Tom belted out another loud, quick laugh. "I tried to warn you. Mary's a sharpshooter. You gave her a clear head shot and she popped you. First word out of your mouth should have been 'no.'"

Stu winked at Tom. "Hell, Mary, why not? Have you taken a good look at Angie?"

Stu's jest drew no laughing bark of approval from Tom.

And from Mary, not a trace of a smile. She just kept poking her twisted, curly pointer at Stu. "Why Angie?" she repeated.

Stu turned his back to Mary's poking pointer and popped off the top of the cocktail shaker. "Well, Angie seemed...." He filled his tumbler with a pale green fluid. "I mean she was...she is...." Taking too large a gulp, Stu started coughing.

Angie checked the mirror, wiped away a smudge of mascara, pasted on a charming smile and entered. "Give up, Mary. More than twenty-five years with the man and I've never gotten a satisfactory answer to that question. Besides, I trapped him. I wanted—"

"Oh, I get you picking him, Angie. That's easy—danger. Kurt Cobain with a jet instead of a guitar. A bad boy with ocean-like depth. I get it. But Stu, why her?"

Angie's brow furrowed at Mary's cutting her off, at the woman's quick dismissal of her as "Ms. Obvious." A sarcastic retort formed in her mind, but she reminded herself to remain charming. Pick her spots. Be funny.

Stu turned around, leaned against the granite bar top and swirled his drink, a devilish smirk pressing along his lips. "Well, like I tried to explain. And now you can look for yourself. Check out her figure at fifty. And in her mid-twenties? Wow!"

"So Mary, you were mentioning depth," Angie laughed. "He's really more like a mud puddle. His murk can fool you."

Mary's head visibly moved up and down as she searched over the length of Stu's entire body, top to bottom, and back. "He's covering. I see how he looks at you." She grabbed Angie's hand and pulled her down onto the love seat next to her. "He'd kill for you. Literally grab a broken bottle and slice and dice anyone so much as threatened you."

Angie jerked her hand away.

"You know it's true, Angie," Mary said.

It was true. But how could Mary know anything about a broken bottle? Or that Stu had used one to kill a rapist? That happened almost thirty years ago, and half a world away. Mary couldn't know. From what Stu had told her, no one could know. Could they?

Angie felt her eyebrows crushing one against the other. Spooks could.

She turned her cleft on Tom. It seemed impossible, but his bushy white brows appeared more jammed together than hers. Was that his look of confusion? Dismay? Tom's face looked like Granda's had always looked when he didn't quite follow or approve of something. But if not the spook, that left only…Angie's eyes flashed to Stu's.

As if he was reading her mind, Stu gave her an almost imperceptible headshake, signaling no, then redirected the conversation. "She ignored my birthday."

Mary slipped half off the love seat toward him. "I don't accept that. I'd be married a dozen times over if ignoring a man were the answer. This hooked you?"

Stu swirled and gulped. "No. It was more than that."

"More how?"

Twice again Stu lifted his tumbler, swallowing all of his drink. "Angie knew I wouldn't care."

"Wouldn't care?"

"Yes." Stu picked up the cocktail shaker and shook. Hearing only clinking ice cubes, he frowned and reached for the tequila. "She knew I'd approve."

"I don't follow." Mary spun toward Angie. "Can you explain him?"

"Explain Stu? No. Help you understand this particular point, maybe. My enigmatic husband thinks birthdays, holidays and such, are just ways people are managed. The cards and presents are…how do you say it, Stu?"

"Strokes along the back. Scratches behind the ears. Ways to keep a pet calm instead of taking the time to really see them."

"So not scratching or stroking, this is what hooked you?" Mary asked.

Stu poured himself two fingers of straight tequila and sipped. "Yep. Pretty much. That was all it took."

In a slow, deliberate manner, Mary lifted her twist of curls up alongside her nose, tilted her head slightly down, closed one eye, sighted down the length of her fingers and poked.

Angie found her actions so amusing that she couldn't fully suppress a laugh, a small giggle slipping out. Mary used that twist of hair like a symphony conductor's baton, sometimes using a tiny poke indicating that only a quick, simple response was desired, other times in more of a stabbing motion, letting Stu know that his next answer had better ring out with a lot more truth. Right now it was as if Mary was tossing a dart at Stu's big, hot air balloon of a lie, saying that his last answer was such a bad performance that he should just stand there and think about it until she chose to wave her truth baton at him again.

At the sound of Angie's muffled laughter, Mary turned toward her and waited.

The floor was Angie's if she wanted it, but Mary's face was drawn taut with a look of complete exasperation. She was much too intense, too intent on pursuing her line of questioning to accept any redirect of the conversation. Angie decided to play along, let the woman's intensity fade. She answered Mary's stare with a shrug. "This is where Stu's answers always start to get very confusing."

Mary pushed backward into the cushion, looped arms with Angie and poked her truth baton at Stu. "So that's what drives a man? That's your whole answer?"

Stu looked down, raised his glass, sipped, and sipped again. "You've come to the wrong place looking for answers. I don't know what drives a man."

Mary cocked her head to one side, tossed her twist of hair back over her shoulder, and just looked at him.

Yes, the woman would've made quite a prosecutor. The tossing of her truth baton telling the jury that she'd poked this witness's story so full of holes that he needed a few moments to recover.

Mary's intensity had faded a bit and it crossed Angie's mind to seize control of the conversation. Yet all of Mary's questions now bore an element of aggressive sarcasm, more like the cross-examination of a hostile witness. The humor gone. No more wheezing. Why?

Angie followed Mary's lead again, tilted her head sideways, slammed her eyebrows together and stared at Stu. Cleft and curls, they waited.

After half a minute, Stu started rubbing his forehead. A few rubs later, he started talking. "Look. All I know is that a couple months after she ignored my birthday, I was stuck struggling to learn a new airplane. Tons of useless numbers. Facts and figures they make you memorize. Not my talent. And Angie helped me."

"Funny, I took you for a natural-born star." Mary grabbed a handful of curls and poked.

"Star at what? Mainly the Air Force liked me because I could fly upside down, pull nine Gs and keep track of seven other aircraft in a dogfight. I'm pretty lousy at numbers. In college, history and philosophy was my thing—minus the dates, of course." Stu swirled and sipped. "Anyway, Angie and I go running and she picks up the pace until I'm winded. Then she starts firing questions at me about my new airplane."

Mary turned toward Angie. "You're not a pilot."

"I memorized a few facts and figures," Angie explained.

"Not true," Stu corrected her. "Angie memorized damn near all of it. And then she grilled me under the pressure of physical stress until I had it all cold."

"It wasn't all stress." Angie smiled at him.

"No." Stu smiled back. "But that was tougher yet."

Mary gave Angie's knee several firm taps. "Don't distract him."

Angie's smile disappeared. She wasn't some child to be tapped to silence. This was her damn house. She fixed a frown on the shushing hand and slid her eyes up the length of Mary's arm to deliver her best "back-off-bitch" look.

But Mary was busy studying Stu again. "So Angie played trick-or-treat. How original. First time a woman's ever done that." Mary punctuated the end of her sentence with a slow, stabbing poke.

Stu coughed down a swig of tequila. "It wasn't like…Angie didn't…." He took another swig.

A deep cleft replaced Angie's frown. Right here, with Stu tongue-tied and Mary awaiting his reply, was yet another opportunity to take control of the courtroom. But there was definitely some powerful undercurrent to this conversation that she wasn't following. And where had Mary's slur gone? The only one stumbling over words now was Stu. She stole another glance at Tom.

His eyes, like Mary's, were fixed on Stu, his smile wide and tall and clamped like he'd latched onto something and would never let go. This must be what Stu described as Tom's shark smile. She didn't remember Granda ever smiling like that.

Once more, Angie decided to wait. Only a fool tried to control what they didn't fully understand. She pulled Mary back onto the cushion alongside her. The two women became unwavering cleft and curl again.

"Look," Stu said, "fact was I knew the answers to all of the questions, from quarts of hydraulic fluid to the turn radius of every Soviet fighter. My instructors thought I was possessed and assignments came—"

"How romantic," Mary poked. "You picked Angie for career advancement." Poke, poke.

"Of course not." Stu poured two more fingers of tequila while spilling another. He pulled a towel from the drawer, dried the outside of his glass and wiped the bar top. "A month after making me look smart, we put flowers on my mother's grave."

Mary sighted down her fingers and threw a dart. "So she babysat your feelings."

"Babysat? Listen. She just fit me. She was my—"

"If you say soul mate, I'll throw up." Mary tossed her truth baton back over her shoulder.

Tom barked out a loud laugh. "Sorry Stu. Mary pairs a great bull crap detector with very little tact. And you did tell her to fire away."

Stu nodded, his jaw muscles bulging. "Fair enough." He took another swig of tequila, swished and swallowed. "A month later, with Angie's prodding, I visited an old college buddy addicted to pain killers. And soon after that I was volunteering out at Bethesda."

"Oh boy, now it's headed toward she made you a better man."

Stu pushed away from the granite bar top and turned head-on to face Mary. "Look. I don't put a convenient label on it."

"Don't want a label," Mary said. "I want to understand—"

"No. A label is exactly what you want. Something you can stick on me and file away. Pull me back out and dust me off when you need something taken care of. Well, pick the label that best fits your worldview. Label me soul mate, best friend, or funny valentine, whatever makes you feel good. I don't care. But the simple truth is Angie did fit me. She did make me better than I was. In less than a year she knew everything about me. Angie saw who I really was and stuck around." Stu tipped his tumbler upright and gulped. No cough. "She knew…and she wasn't afraid…of me."

Jaw dropping down, Angie's mouth opened wide. She lowered her head to hide the shock. Afraid? All these years. She'd never known. Afraid of Stu? He was never someone to be afraid of. How could he think that?

Angie's mind raced along their decades together. Saw the many times he was there with her, but gone, his eyes looking at her, his mind looking...where? Her "please tell me what you're thinking" always answered by Stu crushing her to his chest in a long bear hug. The kind of hug she never wanted to question because she never wanted it to end. A hug that made her feel so needed, desired, powerful.

Her mind flitted from one memory to the next, examining, collecting, connecting, until a nascent understanding evolved. What was it Stu had joked when he quit the military life? He'd been full time Air Force for over ten years and joined the Reserves for another seven. Then he just quit. It was shortly after she took the prosecutor's job. She'd questioned whether he wouldn't miss flying

146

fighters, and he replied, "One Batman in the family is plenty." Seemed really funny at the time. She'd laughed so hard that coffee almost came out her nose. But then he bear hugged her.

Was she the reason he could leave the military life behind? Because she fought the bad guys. She put them in jail. She stopped them from hurting anyone…ever again. And now she'd brought the bad guys right into their home. Was Stu afraid he'd have to kill again?

"No, Stu," she wanted to tell him, "Sala is mine." But she couldn't. Not until it was over. Then she'd tell him. Everything.

Angie looked up and surveyed the room. Everyone seemed content with silence. Stu searched the bottom of his empty tumbler. Mary's chin rested on her chest, her curls falling forward, hiding her expression. Tom's face was a broad frozen shark smile, yet he somehow looked more content, like he'd finally gotten something substantial to chew on.

Stu cleared his throat. "Sorry. Booze talking." His eyes found Angie's and started blinking rapidly. Looking embarrassed, he turned away and addressed Tom. "And, like I said, Angie came very well packaged."

Angie laughed loudly, trying to draw everyone in. "Mary, you see, he's nothing but a mud puddle."

Mary patted Angie's knee again. "Yes, you already said that. Now you're helping him to cover." Mary's eyes darted toward Tom. "Need to separate these…." She paused, her eyes shifting and settling on Angie. "Need to separate you two, I think."

And there it was—the undercurrent. But an undercurrent no more. Her ill-timed glance. The slight slip of tongue. What Mary had stopped herself from saying directly to Tom was, "Need to separate these two, I think."

None of this conversation was as casual, as innocent, as it seemed. And the only one suffering the effects of too much liquor was Stu. Tom and Mary? Both sober as the proverbial judge. Just two former spooks, playing some spook game.

This was the precise moment, while everyone's mind was still reeling from Stu's alcohol-induced outpouring and Mary's slip of tongue. Time for Angie to take control. And not with charm. Tom's frozen shark smile signaled that something had changed, that this wasn't the time for funny or charming. No one was laughing anymore.

CHAPTER EIGHTEEN

As a Washington, D.C. prosecutor, Angie had frequently peered through one-way mirrors and watched all manner of the interrogative dance. And after personally deposing hundreds of witnesses and suspects, she thought of herself as quite an accomplished interrogator. But these two? It was like having just graduated to toe shoes and finding herself on stage with Astaire and Rogers. No, this was far more embarrassing—as if unbeknownst to her, another set of curtains had opened behind Angie's first ballet recital, revealing Alessandra Ferri and Mikhail Baryshnikov performing the last dance of Giselle and Albrecht.

Quite the performance. Tom sitting back, mostly quiet, looking wise and grandfatherly, only sliding on stage to lift Mary high when her questions dragged the mood too low. "Mary's a sharp shooter," he'd said, and then laugh, laugh…and "Sorry, Stu, Mary pairs a great bull crap detector with very little tact," laugh, laugh. Hell, even Angie was drawn into their act, linking arms with Tom's little ballerina and pointing her interrogation-cleft at Stu.

Well, Angie thought, let's see how Tom did when she tossed his prima ballerina right into the orchestra pit. Angie snatched the patting hand from her knee, slid to the corner of the love seat and threw Mary's hand back into her lap. She directed her words at Tom. "Separating us? That will never happen."

As if nothing untoward had occurred, Tom just smiled Granda's patient smile. "A man will only take so much before—"

"I'm a woman."

Tom's smile vanished. "Yes, a woman hell-bent on dancing with the devil."

"But, surely you've noticed." She nodded toward Stu. "I've already got a dance partner."

"And if the devil cuts in?" Tom asked.

"God might be able to separate us, but never the devil," Angie replied.

"God and devil? You sure you can tell the difference?"

Stu stepped away from the bar. "Tom, Angie just wants—"

"I've got this, Stu," Angie said. Her witness was done. It was time for closing arguments. And this was between her and the Tom-jury.

"And just what is it that you think you've got, Angie?" Gramps asked.

Slow and deliberate, several times, Angie shifted her gaze back and forth between the two spooks, then settled her eyes on Tom's. "Why, I've got a couple of former spooks, sitting right here in my home, conducting some sort of spooky interview, all gods and devils and such. Did I pass?"

Tom's smile grew wide and tall and clamped tight. "You're getting real visible, Angie. You've already got a little cult following on the internet. Many of them calling you The Angel." Gramps looked to Stu. "She might as well fly a damn Fokker Triplane, paint it crimson, and call herself the Red Baron. Soon Angie will be every little Islamofascist's quickest ticket to fame."

Angie shook her head at Stu to remind him that this was her fight. "So now it's angels. I didn't know you spooks were so spiritual."

"Not me, counselor. Concerning God, my jury's still deliberating. But of devils?" He nodded several times, his eyes opening wide. "I'm a born-again believer."

"Well, let's leave God out of our conversation then. Restrict this interview to spooks and devils," Angie said.

"Can't. Your little internet cult? They claim you're doing the work of God. You run around doing God's work, Angie, and sooner or later the devil shows up. Doesn't get much more devilish than cutting the passion out of a twelve-year-old girl. Rescue her and the devil doesn't like it. Do that sort of thing too much and soon his dance card is filled with only one name."

"You keep forgetting, Tom. I'm a woman...not a little girl. The devil's going to find my passion a lot harder to cut out."

Tom's shark smile returned. "These custody cases. The children you represent. Are they vetted?"

"If you're referring to the legal custody chain, we never take on a case unless the plaintiff has a justifiable and clearly demonstrable argument."

"No, this is a far less kind question. I want to know if the children your organization represents are vetted for their familial relationships. Are they royal, distant cousins of royals or even close friends of royalty? The vetting I'm suggesting might lead you to eliminate helping a desperate child with an easily won case."

Angie bolted upright. "Refuse a child for fear of powerful enemies?"

Granda's patient smile reappeared on Tom's lips. "A dozen years ago some young princeling at Yale impregnated a coed. He was a distant cousin of a distant cousin but still royal. Two years pass, he grows a conscience and decides to retrieve his bloodline and spirit her home. The child's mother fought in the courts, and so far, has been rejected by every legal process." Tom paused, inviting Angie to comment.

She knew of the case, had strong opinions, even legal strategies in mind to employ, but she sensed a shark lurking just behind that patient Granda smile. There was more here. Something yet to be said. Tom smelled weakness, blood in the water. He was circling, ready to bite. Angie remained silent.

"That girl disappeared yesterday." Tom's shark smile flashed. "You know anything about that?"

"No."

"Good. That's one to stay away from."

"I can't promise that."

"They won't limit themselves to legal arguments, Angie."

"I'm not a fool."

"Kidnap? Torture?"

"I said. I am not a fool."

"They'll kill everything you love and let you live."

"They can kill God?"

"They killed him a long time ago. They wear white robes and the dirt never sticks to them. Been running their dark corner of the world since first they conceived to usurp the teachings of the Prophet. They know how to set examples."

"I know who they are."

"There's the devils you know, the devils you don't know, and the devils you think you know. You got everyone all figured out?"

Angie's right hand formed a fist, her thumbnail digging down into her curled index finger until she felt a sharp pain. What did this maddening Tom-jury want from her? "Look Tom, perhaps Stu and I should just turn this thing on its head. Invite the devil to dance with us. Then maybe God will show up."

Tom's shark smile flashed bigger than ever. "I didn't know prosecutors were so spiritual."

Yes, she deserved that comment, Angie thought. Tom had read her growing frustration accurately. Couldn't blame him for moving in for the kill. She'd have done the same. The only question now, how best to answer that sarcastic smile?

Angie parted her lips wide and clamped her teeth, mirroring Tom's smile right back at him. "The devil, I'm not so sure about. Jury's still out." She let a deep cleft form between her brows. "But of God, I have faith."

Tom's shark smile shrunk to something softer, but somehow even more rigid. "Faith? Or just hope?"

"You sure you can tell the difference, Tom?"

And for the second time in their debate she'd managed to wipe the smile from Tom's face. "All right, Angie, let's pretend it's faith. How deep? Joshua or Job?"

"I'm done reminding you, Tom," Angie said. "Try again."

"Sarah or Mary?"

"Mary."

"Virgin or harlot?"

"Oh, harlot, for sure."

"More faith?"

"No. We just have more in common. Both of us dancing with the devil until God shows up."

Tom's face grew long, not sad like Granda's, but something else, something more resolved. As if he were a defendant caught in a crucial lie, the fire of argument left his eyes, replaced by the cool certainty of knowing that a damning verdict was inevitable, that only the judge's sentencing remained. "And how long can you keep dancing...." His eyes left Angie's, his gaze lowering to the floor, his voice dropping with it. "Without my help?"

With that question, Angie knew the fight was over. She knew precisely what the Tom-jury wanted, what he needed. She felt slightly disappointed. The Tom-jury wanted what most juries wanted—absolution. Or more precisely, pre-absolution. Tom needed forgiveness for the sin he was about to commit. "Thou shalt not kill." Tom wanted pre-absolution for her death.

Angie knew exactly how to give it to him—Granda's song. Thank you, Daryann. She almost smiled, but this wasn't a moment for smiles. It was a moment for piercing eyes.

She pictured all of The Bastard's trophy photos, recalled their eyes, remembered how determined they looked in death—how sure. Yet she waited, remaining still and silent until Tom lifted his gaze from the floor.

Flexing her jaws and looking straight into Tom's eyes, she stared at him until he blinked, then stared right through him to meet the piercing eyes she visualized standing just behind him. She had to stop herself from singing the words. But still, they came out lilting, almost poetic, "Until the day I die…." The word "die" lingered long, a throaty vibrato escaping her lungs.

Tom pulled a cell phone from his pocket and looked at Stu.

For a moment, Angie was afraid that Stu hadn't followed all the convoluted debate, didn't know the preciseness, the totally committed, no-looking-back answer he must convey.

"When I'm dead," Stu said.

Angie's eyes welled at him. He never failed her. Not once. And with that thought the heat of shame washed over her. Soon, Stu. Soon, she silently promised.

Tom flipped open the cell and scrolled. Then held his thumb above the green button. "Last chance?"

"Just push it, Tom," Angie said.

Tom hit send and across the room Mary's phone rang.

She answered. "Bloodhound here."

"Bloodhound, I've got a job for you."

CHAPTER NINETEEN

Too-ra-loo-ra-loo-ral receded down the down the hall as Stu stuck out his hand, offering Gramps a shake. "Thank you, Tom."

"Buzz warned you about this," Gramps said with a shark smile. "Last chance," he added before grabbing hold.

Stu collapsed into the love seat, took a tiny sip of tequila and rolled it around his tongue as the song Angie was singing finished in his head.

> *Oh I can hear that music*
> *I can hear that song*
> *Filling me with memories*
> *Of a mother's love so strong*
> *Its melody still haunts me*
> *These many years gone bye*
> *Too ra loo ra loo ral*
> *Until the day I die*

"Some tough fencing lesson your wife just gave me," Gramps said. "Every time I nicked her with my foil, she clubbed me with the flat of her sabre."

"Yeah," Stu smiled. "That's the Angie I married. Really something."

"Quite a high she's on now, though. Will she sleep tonight?"

Unbelievable, Stu thought. Angie hadn't seen a psychiatrist since she'd needed help with Granda's passing. That was over four years ago. She hadn't taken a pill in at least three. He should go check the garage. Probably find Angie's crows, pulled from their storage boxes and lined up along the walls, Mary taking photos. "I think I'll start addressing you as Mr. Wizard."

"Medical records are easy to get, Stu."

"Is there anything you don't know?" Stu asked.

"There's always something I don't know. For instance, I have no idea why your mother took her own life."

What? What the hell? "That's some real shit you're talking, Tom."

"I just thought maybe you might know something about—"

"No, you didn't. That was just another bullshit spook move." Stu held his hand up, signaling he wasn't done while he calmed himself. "You know, Mr. Wizard, no matter your reputation for cutting people off at the knees who can't hack the FFDO program, I figured that you were a decent person. Deep down, actually a nice guy. More teeth than bite. But that move was just pure bullshit."

"That's the second time you've misjudged me today," Gramps replied. "For the record, all of my friends are dead—died in the field pursuing our nation's politics by other means. You and Angie don't need a friend, and trust me, you don't want a nice guy. I can be exceedingly pleasant, witty, even charming, but no one should believe me a nice guy. What I am is exactly what you two need, a powerful ally. Are you hearing me?"

"Loud and clear, Mr. Wizard. Now you listen to me. I don't like bullshit moves. My mother's death, I never talk about. I don't even think about it…except once a year when I put flowers on her grave. And this ain't that day. She raised me. She cared about me. And that's all you need to know. Got it?"

Gramps raised his glass, nodded and sipped.

Stu tossed the contents of his glass at the back of his throat and swallowed. Several minutes passed without a word. Angie came, gave him a quick peck on the cheek, grabbed two glasses of wine, and headed back to the study, "Too-ra-loo-ra-loo-ral, hush now, don't you cry," fading as she went.

Gramps finally spoke. "Angie's dreams are coming true. What about yours?"

"My dreams?" Stu looked down into his empty glass, then up at the tequila bottle. Decided he'd had way too much and set the tumbler down. "I don't sleep well, remember."

"You'd sleep better if you could keep tabs on Angie? Mary could give you a way in, a way to monitor your wife without her knowing."

"Gramps, anything I want to know, I'll ask Angie."

"No offense, but that's only if you know what questions to ask."

"None taken. I know all that stealing secrets stuff is first nature for spooks. But, it's not my style."

"Style? This is a war, Stu. Intel is everything. And just like you cozied up to 'Pop'em—Drop'em, Head—Dead.' You need to consider adjusting your style. Might offend your sense of honor, I know. Nevertheless, I'd recommend changing your tactics to fit the battlefield. A smart commander does that." Gramps sipped, then squinted over at Stu. "Next time you ride over to Bethesda, ask a legless soldier if he wants a smart commander or an honorable one."

For some reason Stu didn't quite understand, the dead rabbit popped into his mind. The image of a legless soldier reminding him of the rabbit's mangled leg, he guessed. He'd buried the rabbit beneath Angie's rosebushes. Deep, so the damn vulture wouldn't dig it up. Maybe that was it—he'd tossed the rabbit his apple, then mashed it beneath the tires of his car. What was it Gramps had said through those shark teeth? "Uncle Stu can be determined to do one thing and wind up doing another." Gramps was right about that. Stu rubbed at the dry fatigue in his eyes and wondered about his determination to protect Angie. Was he helping her, or helping to kill her? And the old patriarch was right about another thing too. Angie was manic right now. Bloodhound had her all spun up about making her website impregnable. Angie wouldn't sleep until tomorrow afternoon, and she'd wake as the sun set. Then what? Would the crows come calling in the middle of the night?

Quite the menagerie they had here, Stu mused. Gramps, the shark—Mary, the Bloodhound—Angie, the crow. And himself? Right now he felt all beat up. Dead tired. Guess that made him the rabbit.

CHAPTER TWENTY

With a dull thunk the knife sunk deep. From this angle only the handle was visible, well over fifteen centimeters of blade buried to the hilt. The slight downward tilt told Kashif that Hosaam was practicing an underhand delivery.

Each morning between sunrise and Dhuhr prayers, Kashif was required to sit in this room and pour over the Mullah's cache of weapons manuals, memorizing the details of both tactical operation and field maintenance. And every morning for the last two weeks, a few minutes after he sat down to study, the thunks began.

As the crunching of gravel announced Hosaam's approach, Kashif would slide his chair from the morning sunlight and disappear into the shadows, leaving only his hands and the weapons manual visible from outside.

But Hosaam never looked through the window. He'd walk past and lean a half-meter by two-meter board against the nearby rock wall. After slipping the top under a jutting stone and kicking the bottom until the wood was near vertical, he'd place a boulder against the base and roughly shake the thick pine. Starting with one heel touching the boulder he'd pace off out of sight. And then thunk. A knife handle appeared in the board.

Each day the sound seemed to amplify. Today the thunks were so loud that Kashif couldn't memorize a simple table of launch range parameters. He reduced his efforts to the top line. The Model 2 missile had a maximum range of 3,700 meters, and the Model 2M, 4,200 meters. But his mind kept changing "2M" to "2A." And for good reason—he didn't trust the translation. Why wouldn't the next model be "2A?" Who would leap from "2" all the way to "2M"? The worst translations came from old Russian manuals. And those were always the ones he was ordered to study. He slammed the book shut in rhythm with the next thunk and dropped it to the floor. Reciting the kill ranges, he moved among the shadows to the edge of the window.

Hosaam's blade had landed high on the target. The tip was a mere millimeter or two from the rock wall. Any higher and the knife would require hours of repair.

The barracks where Hosaam slept were at the other side of the Mullah's compound, half a kilometer away. Yet Hosaam selected this alley, behind this window, to lug his piece of pine. It was a good place to throw. But there were many good places to throw.

Hosaam marched by, left hand dripping blood. The bloody hand levered the knife handle up and down until the blade came free. After wiping the hilt, he sheathed the knife and paced back to throw again.

Kashif could never watch Hosaam practice without recalling the one time he saw the Americans play at their national sport. But baseball seemed no sport at all. Sport should mirror real life. Train men for the struggles ahead. Baseball seemed boring and pointless with artificial constraints and silly rules he couldn't follow.

Kashif slipped through the window and eased his feet to the gravel.

The Afghan national sport involved fighting on horseback for control of a goat carcass. While playing you mastered riding, maneuver and surprise. The reward symbolized a full belly. It made sense.

Five quiet steps took Kashif to the target. He leaned against the pine, resting a hand on the jutted stone at the top.

If baseball were Buzkashi, the batter would simply bat the pitcher into submission and take the ball. But then the batter would still go hungry. Baseball made no sense.

Hosaam finished twenty paces, took a deep breath and settled. He looked like a robed pitcher on an Afghan mound.

Yes, baseball was foolish, but one element had kept Kashif transfixed until the end—the pitcher trying to catch the thief. Now that made sense. Thieves were the scourge of honor. Kashif enjoyed the thief getting caught, approved of how the disgraced man ran from the field of battle, face held low in shame.

And everyone admired the pitcher. Trapped on the dirt mound, armed with only a ball, he must catch the thief. Catch him in the act by throwing the ball to his assistant who then slapped the thief.

Hosaam turned his head, focusing on the tall building that served as a makeshift mosque, his peripheral vision barely enough to sight the edge of the pine board. Hosaam's shoulders tensed. He was a precise copy of the pitcher on the mound of dirt, looking at the batter, but targeting the thief.

Yet he was an Afghan pitcher. The pine board, an American thief. A murderer. A stealer of mothers. And Hosaam needed an assistant. Someone to accompany him to America and punish the thieves.

Hosaam whirled.

The knifed thunked home and Kashif reached up to pull it free. "Your left hand is bleeding."

Hosaam walked forward, took the knife and spun, counting off twenty paces. "The fired skin is damaged. It cracks easily. You never visited the infirmary." He set, whirled and pitched.

Kashif yanked. "I asked. You were healing." He tested the tip, pricking his thumb with its sharpness before handing it back. "You could pull the knife with your right hand."

"I keep that hand pure." Two paces away, Hosaam paused and looked back over his shoulder. "Better my left hand bleed me out, than my right betray me." He resumed counting paces.

"Faiq didn't bleed much."

Hosaam halted. "Faiq's blood was thin. Said our hunger for vengeance made us weak. He proclaimed your mother a blasphemer who worshipped women, and mine a common whore. I called him out. He tried to pull his trigger, but I stuck him first. It was night, Kashif. The blood was there."

At the usual twenty paces Hosaam turned. "I've yet to pick my warriors." Then he counted off another ten and settled into his stance. "Be very careful, Kashif. This is a long throw."

"I'm not afraid of your knife."

Hosaam whirled.

"I fear the cord in your mother's purse."

Kashif heard a split and chip instead of a thunk. The handle was high on the pine board and still more than three centimeters from fully buried to the hilt. He examined the tip and found it bent against the rock. "You should fear that cord too." He walked back to the

158

window. "You'll pick me, Hosaam." Kashif climbed through and grabbed the weapons manual from the floor. Model 2, 3,700 meters. Model 2M, 4,200 meters.

Too late, Kashif woke, his hands darting toward his throat. The cord snapped taut, jerking his neck backward, suspending his head above the pillow.

"Lower your hands," Hosaam ordered, as the cord snugged tighter, sinking deeper into Kashif's windpipe.

Defying every screaming, defensive reflex in his body, Kashif dropped his shaking hands to the cot.

A knee jammed between his shoulder blades, pressing him flat against the canvas. The cord loosened a fraction. Kashif gulped in air.

"Always so clever, aren't you, Kashif? Threatening me with my own cord. Forcing me to select you. Yet now, weeks later, with all your training complete, and on the very eve of our departure for America, I have doubts. And questions." The cord yanked upward.

With the full weight of Hosaam's body on his spinal column and the knotted cord pulling his head back into the air, Kashif remained motionless. The slightest movement would snap his neck.

Hosaam's lips, wet and cold, pressed into his ear. "But a dead man can't threaten. So perfect, don't you think, for you to die by my cord?"

Another snugging of the rope silenced Kashif's attempt at screaming.

"How can I ever trust you?" Hosaam asked.

Kashif could only gurgle in response.

"How?" he growled.

The knots pressed tighter. "You're not answering me, Kashif." Hosaam's breath slid across Kashif's face in little excited puffs. "How can I ever trust you to follow my orders?"

Without air, Kashif couldn't answer this madman. Risking the snapping of his own neck, he forced his head slowly toward the pillow, biting the cord deeper, the knots pressing into his carotids, choking off the blood supply to his brain. Kashif's peripheral vision shrunk—from walls, down to canvas cot, to pillow, to just a coin-sized blurry tunnel.

Then he popped his head backward, drew in a quick breath and gasped, "Collateral damage."

The noose snapped tight again.

The room went black. Were his eyes shut? He wasn't sure. He tried to fight, but his arms and legs didn't respond. Instead, he felt his body relaxing. Was this death?

The cord loosened enough for him to suck in several deep breaths. The room returned to gray. "They called her 'collateral damage,'" he managed before the rope choked off his speech again.

Minutes passed, Kashif snatching gulps of air, fighting to remain alive as Hosaam pursued some internal debate, one moment tightening the noose and sniffing at Kashif's neck like a hungry animal, his pants quick and shallow, then loosening again, and taking long, deep breaths. Over and over, Hosaam seemed to hover at the edge of murder, like he couldn't let go, and couldn't go on. Or maybe he just wanted the murder to go on and on.

Finally, Hosaam spoke again. "Yes, Kashif, for the Americans, your mother was barely worth mentioning. She was simply 'collateral.' Something secondary. An unfortunate side effect. Not really even human. She was just 'damage'...like a broken window...or a pothole in the road."

"Collateral damage," Hosaam laughed, and slipped the noose from Kashif's neck. "You hate the Americans far more than you hate me, don't you?" Hosaam lifted his knee from Kashif's back. "Yes, I know you will follow my orders...because I am the only one who can unleash your hatred. Only I can give you vengeance."

CHAPTER TWENTY-ONE

Kashif had already finished most of his preparations as the first sirens closed in.

Normally the Washington, D.C. police were too busy chasing drug dealers and clearing crack addicts from the abandoned buildings across the street to bother with a shabby little safe house. Last month, Hosaam had stashed Kashif here, ordering "Never leave. Don't answer the door. Do nothing that draws attention."

Three weeks of peeking through window blinds taught Kashif that the police cars in this area of town were like mortar rounds in Afghanistan. Their deafening blares filled the air most every night. And just as one didn't duck at each whistling artillery shell, one needn't point a rifle at every approaching siren. Yet each time their wails drew close he still performed the basic preparations, lining the baseboards with phosphorus chips and placing jars of kerosene at each corner of the room. This time, with Abbud and Hosaam hours overdue, he'd also opened each jar and placed grenades at the midpoint along each wall.

With the safe house ready, he then readied himself, wetting a cleansing rag with clean water, and wiping his face and hands and feet, before prostrating and reciting a final short ayah. Prepared in both body and mind to face Allah, Kashif went to the front window, lifted a single blind and surveyed the dark streets outside. Initially dumped into the heart of America's capitol in the middle of the night, he awoke that first morning dismayed at the decay surrounding him. Sure, nothing here approached the squalor of the slums of Islamabad, but still, every building across the street was boarded up at the sidewalk level. All the top floor windows were cracked or

161

broken out with nothing to stop the wind and rain from pouring in. So weathered was the street sign at the edge of the yard that Kashif couldn't tell if their safe house was on the corner of "Rid" and "1st," or "Rig" and "17th," or "Rip" and any number in between.

A man sprinted past the sign and slammed into the boards across the street. The cycling wails drew closer, police lights pulsing the darkness with flashes of white and red. Spinning around, the man studied the safe house. He seemed to look directly at Kashif, then came running.

Chastising himself, Kashif dropped the blind, ran into the kitchen and slapped the light switch off. At the sound of loud knocking, he grabbed his AK-47, crouched behind the sofa and clicked the rifle's safety to off.

The knocking became pounding. Kashif aimed his barrel at the door. If the man burst through he'd but one option. Kill him, then grab his satchel, set fire to the house and run, hoping to escape in the chaos of explosions.

If Hosaam and Abbud were dead or captured, he'd call the emergency number, leave a message providing his new location, and await contact. The delay could be weeks or even months. Meanwhile, he'd follow his training and blend.

The local populace dictated the choices. At the Mullah's compound they'd taught him to observe and mimic. Yet what manner of dress afforded the best camouflage in America? For a stranger in Afghanistan, the decision was easy. Wear a beard, robe, and turban. Or accept the label of non-believer, and receive the predator stares—eyes that darted to and fro, searching for the non-believer's protectors while calculating his worth in ransom. In Afghanistan, every non-believer's life suffered the mercy of his protector's authority.

But America seemed all choice. No discernible pattern to their hair or clothing. He'd watched their television for countless hours, his confusion growing worse. Hundreds of channels. Most touting filth. A few were dedicated to news and religion. The former dominated by reporters commenting on the actions of their government, the latter displaying a chaos of clashing faiths, implying that mosques, synagogues, and Catholic cathedrals all coexisted peacefully in American cities. How was this possible?

One channel was solely devoted to what they called game shows.

And one of those shows had reduced the so-called game to simply choosing envelopes with various sums of money inside. Keep what you have, or choose again, each next choice a measure of the contestant's greed. The fat host even went to great lengths to explain the odds of each choice, as if the contestants were too ignorant to calculate their own. No skill, no knowledge required, just choose, and choose again, until no choice remained save one.

"Open the door, you fucking crack head." Done pounding, the man thrashed his entire body against the door. The top hinge snapped and fell away. As Abbud had taught him, Kashif lowered his chin to the rifle stock, laid his index finger on the trigger and applied a slight pressure. After drawing a lungful of air, he exhaled halfway and held his breath. The first bullet was the most important. A quick kill dramatically increased his chances of survival.

Searchlights simultaneously hit the rear and west sides of the house, shadowing vertical lines of black from the window's protective bars onto the opposite wall. Trapped between blinding lights and bars of black, a terror filled him. His finger trembled on the trigger.

The thrashing stopped. Running footsteps receded from the safe house.

"Stop or I'll shoot," someone commanded, gunshots ringing out while "shoot" still hung in the air. Then more sirens.

Kashif collapsed against the back of the sofa and waited for his hands to stop shaking before trusting them to safety his weapon.

An hour passed, filled with sirens and radio chatter and commands for the gawkers to stand back. Then another knock. "This is the police. If anyone's inside, it's safe to come out."

Kashif almost laughed. Yes, come out, it's safe. After years of training and fighting, almost dying, in the Afghan mountains. Weeks inside a cargo ship container. More weeks, hiking through Canada into Idaho. Days locked in the back of a moving van. Now, it's finally safe. Safe to come out of the safe house. Would they even trouble themselves with a command to stop if they knew? Knew who he was. Knew that they'd murdered his mother. Knew of his hatred. Knew what he'd come to America to do. Kashif wiped the tears from his cheeks.

Quietly, he lay flat on the floor and hugged the AK-47 to his chest. By the time Abbud shook Kashif's shoulder, daylight was seeping through the blinds.

"Why did you prepare the house for torching?" Hosaam questioned. "Even the kerosene jars are open."

"The front door." Kashif rubbed his eyes, trying to clear the sleep from his brain. "See the broken hinge. A man tried to break in. The police surrounded the house. But you're here. They must be gone."

"Down at the next corner," Abbud said. "Police cars and news trucks."

The television news supported Kashif's explanation. Every local channel was filled with reports of the shooting. Police had gunned down a fifteen-year-old Hispanic boy, the son of a city councilman. The D.C. police chief insisted it was justifiable homicide—the boy had in his possession half a kilo of crack and refused to surrender. The officers involved were removed from duty pending a full investigation. NNC, the National News Channel, interviewed a reverend who accused the police of murder and said the local community watch group would begin its own investigation by canvassing the neighborhood, searching for eyewitnesses to the incident. The anchorwoman questioned an expert who began quoting statistics. "People of color suffer a higher arrest rate, a much higher percentage of convictions, and receive longer prison sentences. DNA tests also prove a disproportionate amount of innocent—"

"We're no longer safe here," Hosaam declared. "Pack your things, Kashif. You did well. It's better that you move to the university." Hosaam tapped a number into his cell phone. "Abbud, you'll stay and sanitize. A task more suited to your skills." He walked into the kitchen, beginning to converse.

Kashif raised his eyebrows. "More suited to your skills?"

Abbud waved off Hosaam's comment. "I didn't kill who he ordered me to."

"Ordered you to what?" Kashif's mouth fell open.

Abbud shook his head. "It is of no importance." He looked over his shoulder toward the kitchen, then leaned toward Kashif. "Listen to me. I don't know when we can talk again. That night you stood before the Mullah and vouched for Hosaam, you asked me why I was willing to support your lie. I think I know. Yesterday, walking the street, a man looked me in the eyes and said hello. A woman saw me and smiled. Both times, I was…startled. In the Mullah's camp no one ever looked at me. I guess I'd grown used to—"

"That's not true. I looked at you."

"Yes, Kashif, you did," Abbud smiled. "You always did."

"Abbud, I think you're mistaken. Men respected you. That is why—"

"No, Kashif. Think back. During prayers. Only you and Hosaam drew near and prostrated alongside me. All the rest kept their distance. Only the two of you ever held my eyes. Hosaam, because he's impressed by...what I can do. And you, because...because I think that maybe you just see...everyone."

"I don't understand."

"Of course you don't, my brother." Abbud squeezed Kashif's forearm and stared into his eyes. "I was wrong when I said that I was the bullet that had already left the barrel. But hear me now." Abbud's voice grew raspy. "I am the bullet in the barrel. Your barrel. Your bullet. My life is yours, Kashif."

"What?" Kashif pulled away. "Abbud, you talk as if—"

Hosaam returned, interrupting, "I'm sorry, Kashif, but I must relocate our fearsome sniper first. Did Abbud tell you that he missed last night?"

Kashif's mouth fell open again. "You? Miss?"

"A gust of wind. My bullet flew high." Abbud winked at Kashif. "Did all your bullets hit their marks when we fought the Marines?"

"Come along, dishwasher," Hosaam ordered, heading for the back door. "I've got you a job in a restaurant."

The door slammed shut with Kashif's mouth still hanging open. Abbud had missed. Why? Abbud's wink suggested that he'd missed on purpose, and his question implied that Kashif had missed the Marines for the very same reason. Was that true? Had he wanted to miss? And pondering that question spawned another. Would he have shot that boy if he'd broken through the door? And all those questions took him to the floor, praying for the strength to do what he'd come to America to do.

After praying, Kashif resumed watching the news coverage of the shooting. The NNC reporter summarized all of the many experts' statistics, then commented, "Despite more than six years in office, the President has demonstrated little power to affect any real change." Next to her, the same reverend nodded sadly, and added, "The President is just a man. Only God can change the hearts of men."

A police spokesman issued an official statement explaining that their initial investigation revealed that the officers had followed proper procedures. They'd ordered the suspect to stop several times, and provided ample time for compliance, only firing their weapons when the suspect reached inside his pocket.

All lies, Kashif thought. The time between the command to stop and the gunshot was a split second. His mind reviewed the experts' statistics. He pictured the police chief, and the photos of the officers involved in the shooting—all white men, all with lighter shades of hair.

Kashif had his father's hair, more brown than black. That was lucky. He looked down at his hands, rushed to the window and opened the blinds. Rotating his arm, he scrutinized the color. His olive-brown skin had lightened over the past weeks. Good.

After rolling down his shirtsleeves, he buttoned them at the wrist, pulled up his collar, and decided to buy a baseball cap. Vowed to wear it every day. All day.

He'd become the whitest Afghani in America.

CHAPTER TWENTY-TWO

After more than a month, Mary's explanation of her "Bloodhound" nickname still visited Angie's thoughts. First the "good old boys" at the CIA had dubbed her with the too cute "Fair Mary." Then her initial successes at finding terrorists via the internet led to several quick deaths and the moniker "Bloody Mary." In the end, they settled on "Bloodhound" after she earned a reputation for finding anyone who'd been on the web, even if they'd spent only the briefest of moments online.

For the past several days Angie had pondered how best to ask, but there was simply no good way. So she just blurted, "Does it bother you, Mary? People dying because of what you do?"

"Nope," Mary answered.

And instantly, all of Angie's pent-up anxiety disappeared, replaced by utter dismay. She raced through her mental list of Mary's possible responses and her own well-rehearsed replies. If Mary pointed out that the life or death decision was never made until after she'd located the subject, then Angie would suggest that Mary's job was more like that of a police detective, letting the judge decide the criminal's fate. If instead, Mary expressed some measure of guilt over the bloodshed, then Angie would share her own worries there. But, from top to bottom, Angie's imagined list hadn't contained a single negative response, let alone a flippant "Nope."

Angie purged her list. "Nope?" she questioned, letting her dismay sound out loud and clear.

Entirely unperturbed by Angie's distressed tone, Mary casually responded "Not anymore," and set back to work.

With her darting fingers weaving a precise blur over Angie's keyboard, Bloodhound applied her art. She rarely needed the mouse, evidently knowing the shortcut keystroke combinations written by God. No key was safe. Even her thumbs joined in. Discontent with the mundane chores of space or click, they swung arcs from F8 to CTRL and everything in between, stroking at a speed that would put a texting teenager to shame. At times the monitor appeared more cluttered than Angie's desk. Files opened and closed, pages expanded and shrunk, and all the while Bloodhound continued to talk. "The last attack. How long ago?"

"Back in June," Angie replied as she ruffled through the mountains of documents littering her desk, still pondering Mary's flippant responses. Nope? Not anymore? Why the hell not anymore? Angie needed her purple pen. Just a click or two or three to help calm her thoughts. She pressed her hands down on each pile of paper, feeling for a lump.

"Angie, you're absolutely sure you didn't try to open an attachment?" With all four digits of her left hand already engaged, Bloodhound's thumb shot the gap between ring and little finger to tap the six key. The computer screen went dark. Power loss?

Puzzled, Angie backed away, examined the top of the monitor and the front of the server stack. All the power buttons still glowed green, yet that screen was completely dead. Mary's skills were a little frightening, Angie decided. "Yes, I'm certain. I only hit 'reply.'"

"Something embedded then." Bloodhound's fingers suddenly pulled up, hovering over the keyboard. "Sophisticated. Exotic. This might be fun."

Angie caught a glimpse of something purple peeking out from behind the desk leg. She snatched her pen from the floor and clicked. "You say the deaths don't bother you anymore. Why?"

Bloodhound's hands pounced. File upon file cascaded open.

Angie tried to follow as they stacked one upon the other. Some looked like her financial statements. One might have contained her password. She lifted a hand to protest.

Bloodhound ignored her and pointed at the electrical outlets along the wall. "Okay. About your power supply? Some of the hardware I brought along is best served by a few modifications to the usual wiring."

Angie lowered her protesting hand. Now the monitor only displayed her screensaver, a photograph of Maggie and Andrew as toddlers, running through the falling water, a sprinkler rainbow arcing over their giggling faces. Shaking her head at the futility of trying to keep up with the constantly morphing computer screen, Angie slid from hawking over Bloodhound's shoulder to the side of her desk to consider the outlets.

Bloodhound's right hand reached out again. "I see some good work down there." Her finger poked toward the baseboard. "Looks like separate lines to dedicated circuit breakers. Bulletproof power supply, I presume." Both hands returned to the keyboard. The screen came alive, this time filling with lines of scrolling code.

Angie looked at the tangle of wires drooping from the backs of her servers. At the floor they found neat order, all sorted and labeled before entering multiple wall outlets. "Bulletproof makes sense. Whenever I ask Stu for a favor, it arrives gift wrapped in armor plating. I requested an extra outlet. And two days later, he emerged from a cloud of dust saying something about no earthquake able to interrupt my power."

"Well, I have to interrupt it," Bloodhound declared.

"Stu's the electrician," Angie replied, pointing at the wires. "I'm interior design."

"Call him then. Put him on the speaker."

"No." Angie clicked her pen. "I hate to bother him at work."

"Bother him?" With a single tap of Mary's thumb, the scrolling lines of code froze. "Angie, I'd wager the large sum of cash you're paying me that Stu wouldn't be bothered a bit."

"I don't want to try the man's patience."

"We're talking about your husband, right?" Bloodhound looked over her shoulder at Angie. "Has he ever gotten impatient with you?"

Angie folded her arms and walked out of Bloodhound's view.

The scrolling lines of code resumed. "How did you trap the man, anyway?"

"I didn't trap him."

"That was your choice of words back on the Fourth. Change it to any polite euphemism you like."

"Besides, you're wrong," Angie insisted. "He's plenty impatient...about some things. And you're also incorrect about my wanting a bad boy with depth. Stu has a way of surrounding without smothering. Made me feel safe. I'd never had that. Felt I could go anywhere, do anything, and he'd always have my back."

Bloodhound stopped typing. "Stuart Pierce, the impenetrable force field protecting the good ship Angie." She spun the desk chair around. "Boldly going where no woman has gone before, are you? Going to find backward cultures and civilize them? Well, even the kindly Captain Kathryn Janeway of the starship Voyager left a goodly number of innocent bodies in her wake." Bloodhound resumed pounding keys. "I've done my homework and I don't know about you two. I'm taking Gramps's word, out of respect for him."

"I've done a little homework myself. Can't find a Mary Lacaunetailleur listed anywhere. Such an unusual last name, you have."

"Have you now? Well, good for you. Try searching the internet for Mary Wolfe, Fields Medal."

"Mary Wolfe?" Angie's mouth hung open for a long moment. "The frivolous lawsuit, Mary Wolfe?"

"You're entitled to an opinion."

Angie leaned over the keyboard to cock her head at Bloodhound. "You sued the Nobel committee."

"The fools awarded the prize in mathematics to a proven thief."

Angie lifted the pile of papers off the corner of her desk and tossed them into the center. "Mary, your case was dismissed with prejudice." She plopped down onto the clean spot and slid back, dangling her legs. "That means no appeals are possible. Judges don't do that every day. And then you disappeared."

"I really don't need a review of my history, Angie. Changing my name was part of the vanishing act."

"Okay. I'm just a little startled." Angie clicked her pen. "Odd choice of names."

"Seemed amusing at the time. Made it up when I started my hunting career with the agency. Lacaune is a type of French sheep and—"

"And 'tailleur' can be interpreted as a woman's suit," Angie finished. "A wolf in sheep's clothing," she smiled, then frowned. "But with all your talent. Countless opportunities. Why join the CIA?"

"Licking my wounds, mostly. Good place to hide. They had incredible computer facilities and unlimited budgets. Plus they encouraged unfettered research. Reach as far as you can, they told me. And I did. It was amazing. Intoxicating. Then came 9/11 and I wanted to help. The rest is cliché. After disillusionment came separation. The marriage passionate, but short. Now I personally vet the targets before I agree to pursuit. That's why the deaths don't bother me anymore. If I'm chasing, you're already proven inhuman." Bloodhound stroked and Angie's bank account popped open.

"Why do you need to see that?" Angie pointed just as the screen changed again, this time filling with archaic characters. An instant earlier, her seven-figure balance lay delicately scripted on the bank's tasteful parchment-colored background, but now, row upon unintelligible row of white code on black screen scrolled past.

"I assume you mean your bank account." Bloodhound's eyes darted, deciphering, searching.

"Yes. What've my finances to do with this?"

Bloodhound slammed a key and the scrolling stopped. "What are you little demons doing here?" A fraction from the glass, her pinky moved left to right, underlining the characters in question. Her finger dropped down three lines. "And you, Madame. What dark master do you serve?" She turned to Angie. "I didn't need to see your finances. I needed a pathway to find these little home wreckers."

Angie bent to study the ancient runes, searching for Bloodhound's so-called demons, but found nothing, not a single succubus, not even a voluptuous "m" or a curvaceous looking "s." Just a scramble of blocky letters, numbers, and symbols on a black background. She clicked her pen again.

"Angie, one of my clients once described what I do as a gynecological exam conducted by an IRS audit team. Are you sure you want to watch?"

Angie nodded. And twenty minutes later she decided the proffered description of Bloodhound's work lacked an ENT and a proctologist. Nothing was safe. Spammed emails returned. Deleted programs ran. Every website she'd ever visited reappeared. Even the interactive site "Erotic You," with Angie's avatar dressed in various skimpy outfits, flashed by. "That wasn't me. They have you import your photo so you can see how things look. I never...."

Bloodhound held up a hand. "I've seen much stranger." She tapped the bottom right pose. "Bet Stu liked that one."

Angie blushed. Yes, he had. Things had gotten a little crazy that evening.

And to her credit, Bloodhound never smirked or offered any

further commentary. She processed. After another two hours of rummaging through Angie's computer closets, Bloodhound spun around in the desk chair. Only Sala's emails were visible on the computer screen behind her.

"Okay, I have a handle on things. Someone either hates you, loves you, or maybe both."

"Hates, loves, both? Mary, I've just spent the last couple of hours with my skirt hiked up and I didn't enjoy a moment of it. As my favorite law school professor would say, dumb it down for the jury or quit talking."

"Well, the man doing this could do much worse. He simply chooses not to."

"You say 'he' like it's one person, one man. There've been numerous attacks, some successful, others not."

"Nevertheless, I believe we're talking a single 'he.' And you're correct. You only hit the reply key. You didn't need to open an attachment. He could have launched any message at any time, since he has complete and total access to your every keystroke. A control thing. Power. He probably took great pride in goading you into hitting reply. Everything smells male. Nothing subtle or elegant. All bold and aggressive. Yes, definitely 'he.' And the love-hate? There's some sick stuff here. Psychos have been known to confuse the two. Okay, time to talk to Stu about the power supply." Bloodhound hit the speakerphone button.

The buzz sounded. The red open line light illuminated. Angie reached out, silencing and extinguishing. "Just do whatever you need to do with the wiring."

"Not after what you described concerning Stu's armor-plated gifts." Bloodhound punched the speaker back on and pushed the button labeled "Stu."

Each ring jolted Angie like a dentist's drill nicking a nerve. She'd managed to keep Stu well away from anything to do with Sala. He didn't even know Bloodhound was here today. "I said no!" Pummeling the phone like a six-year-old in a tantrum, she managed to turn the speaker on and off several times before finally getting it to stay off. "No."

Bloodhound raised both hands as if Angie was pointing a gun at her. "Might keep in mind that it took over a month just to find an open day for you. Don't know when I can come back."

CHAPTER TWENTY-THREE

"**C**ome on, Kashif, take a swig," Todd encouraged. "I want to say I bought a man his first beer."

"Leave him alone." Tanngela smiled across the table and took a sip from her cup.

Kashif's task was simple. Drink. Just lift the cup and fill his belly, and the Mullah's "camouflage of corruption" would engulf him. Instead, he measured the progress of the tiny rivulets of foam sliding down the frosty mug. Halfway, they stalled, pooling along the pewter band decorating the side of the glass. From there, another eight centimeters would carry the intoxicant to the tabletop where it would waste away as it should. No, he corrected himself, he must think in inches. And he must speak the word inches correctly. The word was "inch-is," not "in-chez," as Tanngela had gently corrected him. First, of course, as always, she complimented him, saying that his English was, although very formal, nearly flawless. Yet, despite her efforts, the correct pronunciation of that simple word still eluded him.

"Would you like to try mine, Kashif?" Tanngela asked.

Todd made a face as if he'd stumbled upon a bloated corpse crawling with maggots. "You'll kill the man with that crap."

Intoxicants were decadence, the filthy works of Shaitan, forbidden by the Qur'an. Kashif lifted the mug, directed it toward Todd in what he hoped suggested a proper toast, then let it slip from his fingers.

As the beer crashed to the table the Mullah's oratory rushed through Kashif's mind. "For in that decadence lies your disguise, your holy armor." Like a flash flood from a mountain thunderstorm the words raged at the tenets of his faith, washing clean another layer

---

of Kashif's doubt.

Todd was up, out of the way and laughing as the alcohol spilled over his chair and onto the floor. "Holy crap, Kashif. You're not even drunk yet."

"Sorry, I'm not accustomed to the foam. It's slippery."

"No worries, my new friend. Plenty more where that came from." Todd signaled the waitress for cleanup and another beer. "Use the handle next time."

"No Todd, I've wasted enough of your money."

"Nonsense. Plenty more of that too."

Of course there was. This was the capital of America. Washington always supplied more of everything. Even its slums had more—more drugs—more crime—more lies.

And those who said the streets weren't paved with gold were fools. A man couldn't walk a kilometer...a half mile, he corrected himself...without crossing a stream. Even the dirt was rich, black as oil. And the trees and shrubs grew so vibrant that their leaves seemed cast in only two shades of green, the deep, dark green of old strength and the bright, quick green of young life—an Islamic green, the green of mosque and Qur'an, and the Prophet's Banner. "A fast-growing green," the Mullah had preached, "spreading to cover all of Allah's good, rich Earth." The green Kashif hoped was already sprouting from the ashes he'd left in Afghanistan.

A waitress arrived and cleaned up Kashif's mess. Another replaced his beer. Yes, gold was everywhere in America, including inside the dripping mug in his hand. Kashif set the fresh beer on the table and reached down, pretending his cell phone vibrated in his pocket. If only it would call him to battle. Send him to die before he lost his soul. He faked the motions of responding.

"Who's that? ISIS?"

Tanngela punched Todd in the arm. "You can be such a jerk."

"Come on, Tanngela. It was just a joke."

Tanngela was the reason Kashif had come. Dark and beautiful and kind, she kept inviting him every Friday after history class. Today he'd accepted. Not because she tempted him. No, he'd come to fulfill the Mullah's orders. Kashif must clothe himself in sinfulness to become invisible in the land of the Great Satan.

The Mullah's words had seemed unquestionable truth back at the compound. He'd heard them so many times during the past three years that he accepted their rightness, as he accepted removing his shoes to enter a mosque. The vile acts he so easily imagined committing as he completed his training in Afghanistan—drinking, gambling, cursing, forgoing prayer—now felt nearly impossible to perform. He needed help with the worst of them, and Todd seemed especially adept at sin.

"It's okay. Todd's right. Just a joke." Kashif raised his eyebrows and spread his lips into what he hoped was a devilish smile. "Besides, I prefer Al Qaeda." Then he slapped the table and mimicked Todd's loud laugh.

"There, you see, Tanngela, lighten up." Todd nudged the mug until the condensation wetted the back of Kashif's hand. "Now, drink up."

Tanngela pushed her white porcelain cup next to the golden beer. "It's not alcohol, Kashif, just tea."

"Don't do it," Todd begged. "If you drink her green shit instead of my golden elixir, I think I'll throw up."

"Speak as they speak," the Mullah had counseled, so Kashif did. "Golden elixir? Looks like urine to me."

Both Todd and Tanngela laughed. Todd's mouth wide, his loud howls aimed at Kashif, while Tanngela's quiet giggle came in tiny spurts, muffled between fingers.

"Nice try," Todd said, wiping the tears from his eyes. "But I think the word you're looking for is 'piss.' Yes, Kashif, piss is much funnier."

Kashif lifted the cup of tea and sniffed. Not pear, apricot or pomegranate, but still citrus of some kind—sweet, clean and fresh. Looking up, he found Tanngela smiling at him again. Liking the feel of her smile, he smiled back. "Not a simple green. Something more complex. I think I like your tea."

Todd slid his chair around toward Kashif and lowered his voice. "That's very risky, my friend."

Kashif set the cup down. "What's risky?"

"Your suspicious behavior." He waggled two fingers signaling Kashif close, wrapped an arm around his shoulders and whispered. "Extremely suspicious behavior—a college student not drinking a free beer. In all truth, I think it's grounds for dismissal from the university. And without that student visa, they'll stick you on the first plane out." He removed his arm and slapped himself on the forehead. "Wait...nope, I'm wrong. It'll have to be a ship. They don't trust teetotaling Muslims on airplanes these days." Todd burst out laughing again.

"Whore as they whore." The Mullah's stark vulgarity drowned the last of Kashif's resistance. He faked a laugh, took the mug by the handle and drained it.

"Beautiful! We'll make an American of you yet." Todd snapped his fingers, signaling the waitress for another round. "Next we'll get Tanngela trashed enough to marry you. Then get you a green card."

Kashif wiped foam from his lips. "What color green?"

They all burst out laughing this time.

Three beers later Kashif held Tanngela's hand to steady him as they walked to the auditorium. Inside, he plunked down in a seat and held his head, but the room kept spinning. The lights flashed and went dark. The lecture began with a slide of Rembrandt's "Moses Smashing the Tablets of the Law."

A kaleidoscope of memories, triggered by the color and texture of Moses's beard, whirled through Kashif's brain. A beard so like his father's—long and bushy, chestnut brown struck with strands of gray and white. The images spun faster than the room. Clutching his father's hand as they walked in the darkness toward the train station. A hug so tight that Kashif cried out from the pain. Puffs of steam and screeching metal as the train started west toward jihad. His father sitting atop the caboose, beard fired red by the sunrise, waving goodbye, never to return. His mother's voice calling him to breakfast just before the bomb struck. The crowded refugee train to Pakistan. Hunting rats in the alleys of Islamabad. The madrasa where he gained a scrap of food for each memorized surah. Hosaam reaching down to pull him aboard a train bound for the Hindu Kush. Jumping off and hiking days to find the Mullah's camp. And raging through them all, like he was trapped within the eye of a great firestorm—always the burning forest—limbs bursting, the grandfather tipping, and the acrid smell of ash. The lecture ended with his head still spinning.

"Last item for today. This painting. Anyone who can tell me its name and the artist who painted it can skip the next homework assignment."

A blue headdress filled nearly half the canvas. It adorned a delicate face that couldn't quite look at Kashif. Out of the Madonna's eyes poured a resolved sadness. As if she watched a cracking dam and couldn't bear to look downstream. In a moment a tear would slide down her cheek, the artist painting his last stroke just before it slid free.

"'Virgin Annunciate' by Messina," Kashif shouted and ran from the lecture hall.

Outside he fell to his knees and vomited, the beer tasting better to him coming up than going down.

"Careful, Kashif. You look like you're on a prayer rug," Todd laughed.

"Shut up, Todd. Just shut up." Tanngela knelt and rubbed his back. "Are you okay?"

Wiping the vomit from his chin, Kashif looked up, smiling his thanks. A gasp escaped his lips. Tanngela eclipsed the setting sun. Her face was shadowed, long hair draping loose like a burqa, the sun's corona anointing her head in a golden halo.

She was the Virgin Annunciate...robed now in ebony. She was his mother—her pure blue burned black.

Kashif started to wretch again. Water. He needed water to rinse the filth from his arms, wash the dirt from his face and hair, and cleanse the soil from his feet. The eastern sky called him. Face Mecca. Pray aloud the glory of Allah.

He laced his fingers into the grass, held fast facing west, and silently prayed for the strength to forgo prayer.

CHAPTER TWENTY-FOUR

"It's just a matter of time," Bloodhound had warned Angie. "Without installing special equipment, he will be back."

Turned out, "a matter of time," was precisely three weeks. Took another week of begging before Bloodhound came out to the house, and this time, she arrived with demands.

"Okay, Angie, your system's back up, but I'm not wasting my time searching endless lines of code unless we install the equipment first. Not doing that without talking to Stu. Why isn't he here?"

"Working," Angie answered.

Mary pointed at the phone. "If you want me to stop the fiend from sending you his latest torture-headshots, then dial."

"He's probably airborne."

Fingers and thumbs flying, uncountable keystrokes later, Mary pointed at the screen. "This says Stu's on the ground in Savannah, Georgia."

"Could still be too busy to answer." Mashing out a click of her pen, Angie hit speaker and speed dial two. "Might not even check to see who's calling."

"Doubt that." Mary twisted up a curl of hair and poked at Angie. "I bet he's even assigned you a special ringtone?"

Angie didn't reply, counting the rings, hoping to hear Stu's voicemail greeting.

"Of course he has," Mary poked. "What is it?"

Two rings. Angie ignored her question.

"Come on. Give over," Mary demanded with another poke.

Angie shook her head no. Three rings.

"Fine. Don't tell me. I'll guess."

Four rings. Angie tried to remember when Stu's voicemail picked up. Six or eight?

"'Harem Bare'm Bounce' by Sir Rap Sheik," Mary said, then started rapping, "'They might be drooping, but I keep snooping, love long breasts, cannot contest—'"

Angie burst out laughing. "Hey, I'm doing just fine for fifty years plus."

"Thought we could use some comic relief," Mary laughed.

Another ring. Was that five or six? Had to be six, Angie hoped. If Stu didn't pick up, maybe she could convince Bloodhound to install the equipment anyway. She leaned toward the speaker, hoping his voicemail answered.

"Angie...sorry I took so long. Out on the tarmac. A fuel problem."

Angie jerked upright at the sound of his voice.

Raising one eyebrow, Mary gave her a quizzical look and leaned in, replacing her. "Hello, Captain Stu. Mary, the Bloodhound, here...on the speakerphone with your lovely wife. She didn't want to bother you, but I forced her."

"Ignore her, honey," Angie jumped in. "She didn't force me."

"No, please don't, Captain. I already have an invisible woman complex when it comes to men."

"Bloodhound?"

"Yes, honey, Mary's here." Crap. The serious tone of his voice said he was already ciphering. She needed to end this call—quick. "Yes...yes, honey, she needs to install some equipment, but wanted your okay. I told her that wasn't—"

"I apologize, Stu," Mary interjected. "I could have called you last week, but I just assumed you'd be here."

"Last week?" Stu questioned.

Angie shoved her hand in front of Bloodhound's face and waved up and down. "Mary doesn't want to mess up all your hard work, honey." She placed an index finger over her lips in a shushing motion.

Raising both eyebrows, Mary returned to the keyboard, stroked a few keys and started scrolling through Sala's emails.

"Mary is a very considerate woman." Stu's voice was a monotone of distrust.

"Yes...yes, she is." Damn. Angie fought the rising panic in her voice. "So you want to just trust her?"

"Oh, I trust Mary." Stu said.

"Good...good, I really think this new equipment will keep hackers from—"

"Never mind what you think," Stu cut her off. "Let's ask the expert."

"Stu, she's already told me—"

"Mary? What do you think?" Stu asked.

"I think that this Sala fellow does some clever work. Pretty sure he's the man Angie is hunting for. Probably has some assistance, but it's him."

Angie's purple pen slipped from her fingers and rotated counterclockwise one full turn before striking vertical and bouncing from the diamond at her feet.

"Who does...clever...work?" Stu's voice faded.

And the truth was out there. Just like a courtroom. The jury had heard. Only deliberation and verdict remained. She could almost hear the commotion in the court of Stu's mind as the name "Sala" gaveled at his thoughts.

"Angie. Who did she say?"

He sounded so young. So hurt. Her hand stretched toward the phone.

"Angie?"

She pressed hold.

"Ang—"

The red light started to blink.

Stu pulled the phone from his ear. At one corner of the small liquid crystal window a tiny cell phone symbol threw out arc after wavy arc, confirming the good connection. Next to it the block letters "Angie's Study" verified the caller. Above her name, a length of call timer totaled the passing seconds.

"Angie, are you there?"

Did he hear that right—Sala does clever work? "Angie?" Not possible, Stu assured himself.

But what else could Bloodhound have said? Stu played her

words back through his mind. "...this Sala fellow does some clever work...he's the man Angie's hunting...has some assistance, but it's him." Maybe Bloodhound slurred her words—"this fellow" coming out "this's'a'fellow." Sounded kind of like Sala. But Bloodhound definitely said "hunting." When did Angie start hunting? And who the hell was she hunting?

From behind Stu came an answer. "She's hunting Sala..."

"What?" Stu whirled around.

The kid standing in front of him backed away. "I...I...just..."

"What did you say?"

"She's venting, is all...all I said." The kid took another step back, pointing at the wing. "The fuel. I was just trying to explain—"

"I know what venting is," Stu growled. The kid meant "she," referring to his aircraft, not Angie. In the flying world, jets were always "she." And he said "venting," not "hunting."

"I'm sorry, Captain. I didn't mean...." He offered Stu the fuel slip.

Snatching it from his hands, Stu confirmed the stick readings and nodded. "Looks good. Thanks. Now get that fuel truck out of here. I'm leaving soon."

Stu rechecked his cell. Four bars—good connection. "Angie!" he yelled into the phone.

"Captain, I...." The kid looked around like he was searching for someone. "I'm not..."

"You still here?" Stu gave an exaggerated shrug and shot him a look of dismay. "Son, your work's done. Get in. Drive," Stu ordered, then turned and walked under the wing to the landing gear. He hit the speaker button and set the phone on top of the tire.

Crap, he thought. Not the kid's fault. "Hey, son," Stu shouted, but the cranking truck engine drowned out his words. He gave the kid a thumbs-up when the engine started. Got a weak smile in return. The truck coughed and spit, first gear catching, grinding, and slipping out three separate times before holding long enough to shudder the fueler forward.

Stu returned his attention to the cell phone. The call timer finished counting out four minutes and started on a fifth. Didn't make any sense. If the connection was bad, she'd have hung up and tried again. No, she had him on hold. Why?

Bloodhound said, "...could have called you last week...assumed you'd be here." Which meant that for at least a week Angie had known about the appointment. And he was home right up until yesterday. Hell, he could've traded trips to be there. And after this trip he had the rest of the month off. She intentionally selected one of the few days he'd be gone. It all added up.

Angie needed to provide Bloodhound total access to her computer. Questions would arise. Some might prove difficult to answer with him underfoot. Stu took a firm hold on a dangling hydraulic line and squeezed—this would get worse—it always did. Sala was why Angie put him on hold. His heart pounded. Six beats louder, six softer, cycling up and down, each repetition hammering harder. He tried to focus on something else. Anything else.

The screech of metal on metal rang out as the kid struggled to find second gear. Stu embraced the noise, finding calm in the clash.

"Damn, Ironman, cover your ears." Three feet away, his copilot, Carl, was yelling above the din. "What're you holding on to?"

The truck's engine sputtered and quit, the fueler rolling to a stop.

Carl uncupped his ears. "If you found a leak, that's no way to fix it," he laughed. "You're going to get filthy."

Stu let go and brushed his hands together, smearing the grease. "You down here just to comment on my cleanliness?"

"Nope. If you're determined to get dirty, go right ahead. You're in charge. I'm down here because of that little frontal disturbance you noticed earlier. Got hold of Buzz. Not working today, but he called over to Reagan National. Freak storm hit the airport. Everything's a mess up in D.C."

"Looks like captain training time for you, Carl."

His copilot's head ratcheted down several notches, leaving only a tiny bit of his eyeballs visible. Above them, rows of forehead wrinkles extended back across his baldness in a rippling skin-over. Carl's vintage, "You can't be talking to me," look. "Pretty sure I'm misunderstanding you, Boss. Already been a captain. Circa 9/11. Back before Allah decided to screw with my frick'n paycheck."

"I've got something going on, Carl." He tapped his cell phone, leaving a smudge on the crystal. Now it read "Angie's S." Stu held back a groan. "How about you doing my captain's work and I'll spring for the refueling tonight."

Carl's head went shiny smooth. "A bribe? Free beer for your trusty copilot? Well, now we're frig'n communicating."

"Thanks, Carl. Tell the gate agent to hold off boarding for an hour. Then make an announcement explaining things to our customers."

"Consider it done, Ironman." He spun to leave.

Stu called after him. "And Carl, no F-words to our passengers."

"No flip'n problem, Boss."

As Carl moved off, thoughts of Sala moved right back in. Six beats up, the last two pounding loudly between his ears.

Over ten years since he'd heard that name, stopped cursing it when Angie had made her vow. Only two promises in Stu's life ever meant anything: "I do" and "It's over." Where he found the words to inspire the latter, he didn't know. Tell a woman like Angie that she was losing herself? Becoming something less, not something more. He'd treated her like she was a drug addict in need of intervention. Risked everything when he brought the kids into the study. Angie remained calm while Maggie and Andrew talked about the games she'd missed, the recitals, and the birthdays.

When the kids went to bed, she raged. Her accusations ranged from male chauvinism to lack of manhood. Each new attack bracketed by a loud "How dare you?" and a whispered "I'm a good mother." An hour later—he was speechless. Another hour and he'd gone numb.

She locked herself in the study for two days, then emerged to tell him she couldn't live without him. Told him that no one besides Granda had ever cared enough to give her that kind of hard truth. "It's over," she said. The best words he'd heard since "I do."

A week later, he gave her a thank you card. A charcoal sketch of a young bride. Said something nice underneath too. Couldn't remember what. It took days of writing and rewriting before he put his pen to the inside of the card. Didn't recall most of the words. Just the part that mattered. "I am yours, forever," he'd written. Stu reached up and covered his fast-blinking eyes.

She kept the card on her desk for over a year, then thanked him again and put it away. Perhaps that's when she'd put away "It's over," too. Stu's teeth ground as the hammering ramped up again.

He turned back to his phone. "Angie, you there?" he whispered. Dead quiet. He knew that she wasn't. Why ask? The timer showed more than five minutes elapsed, the seconds racing toward six. Utter madness, he thought. Madness back then. Madness now. Sala.

Crescendo and decrescendo, the loudest of the heartbeats so violent they forced his eyes closed, the softest, so quiet he thought his heart stopped. Stu crossed his arms, pressing against his chest, willing the waves to subside.

Reaching down, Stu grabbed his cell phone and rubbed at the grease smudge. Made things worse. Now it only read "Angie."

He could call Gramps. Confirm his suspicions. But he couldn't just ask. Maybe a friendly discussion. Casually mention Bloodhound's slip of tongue and Angie's reaction. He wasn't really spying if Gramps just offered information.

Stu snorted and patted the wing of his jet. "That's bullshit, isn't it? Yeah, we both know it is." No lying to an aircraft, he thought. Your hands were either true or she let you know, immediately. If the lie was big enough, you both died. She was completely objective, completely honest, completely true.

Ply Gramps for information without directly asking? Manipulation was still deceit. Still dishonest. Still just a lie. Still bullshit.

A man in a yellow vest came running up. Written across his chest, "Southeast Jet Fuels." Stumbling to a stop, he huffed, "Stupid kid. He's not trained to drive that fueler."

Stu searched for the fueling truck. Hadn't even noticed the kid getting the engine started again, Stu realized. In the distance, the fueler approached a stop sign. "All my fault," Stu told the man in the yellow vest. "He's a good kid. I ordered him to move it." The brake lights came on. Stu waited for the gear shifting havoc to renew but the kid only slowed, then rolled right on through. Couldn't blame him for breaking the law. Starting from a dead stop was the toughest part. He felt a touch of admiration as the truck disappeared behind the hangar. The young man was getting the job done, any way he could.

Stu looked down at his grease-covered hands. A gray mess also stained each bicep. A smear dulled his belt buckle. No doubt there was grease on his face and hair. Making a mess of everything he touched.

CHAPTER TWENTY-FIVE

Angie's racing pulse gradually slowed, matching the blinking cadence of the hold light. One beat—one blink. Each cycle of light and dark spoke to her, bright red insisting, "Pick up, talk to him," dark red contending, "Too late. He's gone." Which frightened her more?

At first, she kept reaching for the phone. Yet...to say what? Anything, counselor. Say any damn thing. Tell him that the phone was messed up, or that Bloodhound lost control of her thumbs. Hell, even claim that a rabid mouse had danced an Irish jig on the hold button. Anything was acceptable in those first few seconds. But after the blinks ran past thirty, she had to say something meaningful. Like, she was sorry...sorry she'd lied...sorry she'd asked him to trust her. Another thirty blinks required something more meaningful yet. Wish she could change the past...change herself. And now, after several minutes of flashing red, the only thing Angie could think to say that meant enough was that he deserved better, had earned better, was better, and that she cherished the man he was so much...that she wished they'd never met.

The light went dark. Stayed dark.

As if to emphasize the finality of the moment, the room grew gray. Clouds again. Distant thunderheads had threatened all morning. Hours ago she'd flipped the switch that turned on Stu's backup generator to safely isolate her study from the house's electrical system.

"Well, Captain Angie," Mary said. "Your impenetrable force field might need a bit of maintenance after that abuse."

Angie laid her pen next to the phone, reached down behind Bloodhound's lower back and yanked the purple pillow from the chair. Hugging it to her chest, she stared at the dark light.

"He won't call back. Will he?" Mary asked.

Unwrapping an arm from her pillow, Angie reached toward the phone. "No. He won't." Her fingers touched the handset and traced a slow path from top to bottom and back. "I married a romantic man, not a stupid one."

Fingers sliding from the handset, Angie pulled open the writing drawer and pointed at the printout taped onto the top right corner. "There's Stu's flying schedule. Save you a lot of keystrokes."

He was laying over in New York tonight, flying to D.C. early tomorrow, followed by a turnaround to Chicago. But blue handwriting obscured his arrival time back into Washington—Stu's blocky letters, barely legible in the darkening room. Angie looked away, glad of the inrushing clouds, not wanting to read his words.

Mary stood up, cocked her head sideways and bent over the drawer, squinting through the gloom. "It says 'In time to watch you shame another sunset.'" She fell backward into the chair, shaking her head at Angie. "You won't call him back either, will you?"

"No." Angie wiped at her eyes and grabbed her cell phone. "Perhaps because…I am stupid."

"And this works for you two?"

"No. It's what doesn't work." Angie tossed the pillow onto the couch and scrolled through the cell's contact list. No more dealing with the middleman. Her two conversations with Taamir had gained only excruciatingly polite reminders that His Excellency needed actionable intelligence. The smiling Prince Uday had been far more cooperative ten years ago. Always so willing to help, so concerned about Angie's needs, including countless inquiries about her dinner plans, repeatedly suggesting that she must get very lonely with Stu away so much.

Angie selected the Washington, D.C. District Attorney's office and pushed "send." Three phone calls and a handful of cashed-in IOUs later, she'd finagled a seat near Uday at the annual Finanthropic charity banquet. She turned to Mary. "I need to know where Sala is."

"Define 'where.' Continent, country, or city?"

"Where the fiend sleeps."

With a flash of four fingers and both thumbs Bloodhound made the screen black and blank. She swiveled the chair around. "Where the fiend sleeps? Now that gives me pause."

"You've seen my bank account balance, Mary. Write your own check."

Bloodhound rolled the chair backward and leaned away, propping her right elbow onto the edge of the desk, fingers dangling above the keyboard. "Just two keystrokes more." She poked F12.

A rapid series of clicks came from Angie's server stack. One by one, like jet engines shutting down, the high pitched whir of each cooling fan changed to a deep drone and silenced as the fan slowed and stopped. Whether green, yellow or red, every light on the face of each server lit steady. Whatever dark form Bloodhound's art had just taken, the result was a disturbingly quiet stillness.

"Captain Angie, the CIA may have given me the nickname Bloodhound, but I'm no one's bitch now." Mary's face mirrored the equipment surrounding her, frozen and silent. One finger hovered above the delete key, twitching.

Nice work, Angie scolded herself. Mary declares a personal moral line. Offer her money to cross it. A brilliant solution. Might as well call the woman a prostitute. Way to go, counselor. Angie looked away from Mary's twitching finger.

"I hit this key and everything goes," Mary threatened. "Stu's backup can't save you."

Wait, Angie cautioned herself. Think before you speak! After that dullard move, she needed to say something to lower Bloodhound's hackles. Angie studied the diamond-patterned carpet, searching for an answer. Like every bit of decor in the room, the pattern served a purpose. Granda's clock reminded her to respect all beliefs. Oak cabinets stored the hard results of beliefs run amuck. And the carpet? Diamonds—Mother Nature's toughest gem. And as she paced that pattern each day, the sharp points reminded her to cut through the pomp and ceremony of beliefs and, with great clarity and hardness, find the undeniable destruction. People responded to simple truth. "Mary, I need your help."

Bloodhound's finger stopped twitching.

"Please, Mary. I meant no insult."

"Where's this headed?" Bloodhound demanded.

"Wherever it goes," Angie replied.

Bloodhound leaned forward in her chair. "I vet my targets. Remember? I need a lot more."

"What's a lot more?"

"Everything."

"We don't have that kind of time. If we stop to discuss—"

"You don't have time, Angie. I've got plenty."

"Okay. But we've got—" Angie held up a hand, begging for a chance to correct herself. "—I mean…I've got…until lunch tomorrow. So you ask the questions and I'll answer until you're comfortable. Does that work for you?"

"Fine." Bloodhound snagged a fistful of hair, twisted and poked. "When did you first want Sala dead?"

"What?"

"You heard me."

Want him dead? No, she wanted him prosecuted. The courts would determine the punishment. "I want him caught and put on trial."

"For what?"

"Soliciting prostitution, rape and murder."

"Where was the murder committed?"

"Virginia."

"When?"

"Late summer, just before 9/11."

"Death penalty state. So you've wanted him dead for well over ten years."

"I resent that."

"Feigned outrage. Usually a sign of denial." Bloodhound shook her head and sighed. "But never mind. How did you get the case?"

"Get the case?"

"I don't need to tell you, counselor, repeating a question is usually the first step in formulating a lie. Gives the person time to think it through."

"Don't presume to lecture me. I've questioned a witness or two in my time."

"Second step is feigned insult," Bloodhound poked.

Angie literally felt her skin form a deep cleft between her eyebrows. Raising a hand to her hairline, she scratched a fictional itch and circled the desk away from Bloodhound to mask her growing irritation. "I got the case because I asked for it."

"With such an accommodating boss, it's a wonder you ever quit." Bloodhound said, her tone dripping sarcasm.

Lightning lit up the room. Several seconds later, a thunderclap shook the air. Angie reached for the open bay windows.

"Storm's still a long way off, Angie. Stalling for time? I always thought of lawyers as such accomplished liars."

Damn the woman! Yet, Bloodhound was correct. Admitting she'd asked for the case was, in point of fact, distorting the truth—one of the more effective lies. Truth was, she'd begged for the case. Angie tried to massage her cleft as Stu might have done. It deepened. "I asked for it because I knew one of the victims."

"That should've automatically eliminated you. Time is wasting, Angie."

Outside, the wind picked up. Roiling shades of gray filled the horizon. "Not necessarily. There were complicated legal statutes involved."

All the trees bent toward Angie. Fresh air, moist, cool and electric slipped between the window seams. First gust, Stu had taught her. Meant that somewhere nearby a thunderhead had cracked wide. Rain gushed down, pushing all the air out in a single huge gale. Windshear, pilots called the phenomenon. Feared it. The single biggest reason planes crashed. And Stu had cautioned, the stronger the first blow, the more fierce the storm to follow. Angie secured the window latches. "What do you know about the law anyway, Mary?"

"Why don't you skip all the crap?" Bloodhound poked.

A great rush of wind pelted the bay windows with bits of leaf and twig. Its roots too shallow, the young pine they'd planted this spring toppled and fell. Even the two lovers strained against the squall, the old maple and oak arching over her head and scraping their tangled limbs against the shingles above. "You want me to skip the crap? Fine. I didn't ask. I pushed my way onto the case. Okay?"

Bloodhound remained quiet, motionless. More lightning struck, each flash coloring Mary's face white as polished marble. Cold. Intolerant. Waiting. A face like Angie hadn't encountered since junior high—Sister Constance Ruth, the Mother Superior. Six feet tall with skin so white that the bleached cap and neckerchief surrounding her face paled in comparison. Contrary to the custom of all the other nuns, the cross hanging from her neck was not silver, but black. In her world, everything was either right or wrong. And just like Bloodhound right now, Sister Constance Ruth's terrible power was silence.

Angie recalled the Mother Superior stepping from her office, blocking Angie's path, waiting, wordless, until Angie stepped inside. The door closed. Taking the cool wood from the Mother Superior's hand, Angie laid it against her thigh. She slid the ruler up and down, not sure, back then, how to shape the good lie. Several times, she looked up about to speak, to try, but the stony face commanded, "Do not dare." In the end, Angie knelt on the hard tile, set the ruler's edge against the floor and reported the distance as too far. From beneath the folds of the Mother Superior's robes appeared a roll of masking tape. Angie added an inch of beige to her green plaid. Day after day she returned to school, defiantly wearing her measure of shame, until Granda discovered her stubbornness, tore off the tape and paid a woman to adjust the hem. "Lies kill" was all Sister Constance Ruth ever said.

So might the truth, Angie thought, and turned back to Bloodhound. "After obtaining control of the case I forced the direction of the investigation."

Still nothing. Bloodhound was Justitia unveiled, Lady Justice waiting for some final truth to tip her scales before she'd speak.

What damn truth? One person's truth was another's lie. A sound like falling pebbles poured onto the shingles. The roof shed a shimmering wall of water thick enough to blur the world outside.

Stu's fierce storm had arrived as predicted. Always the clever teacher, he'd once pointed to an approaching thunderstorm and asked her lawyer friends if it was good or bad. Recognizing one of his philosophical exercises, she cautioned everyone to wariness. Undeterred, they jumped at his question. Some argued that crops received water. Therefore the approaching storm was good. Unless flooding occurred, then bad. But forests too dry caused fires. Yet the lightning that accompanied storms started fires. Eventually the rain chased them inside where the arguments were summarized and presented to Stu for judgment. Who saw the truth? He took it under advisement and the arguments resumed.

An hour later, the sun broke through. Everyone rushed outside and stared open-mouthed. Stu pointed at the rainbow and said "Truth."

She was a much better lawyer from that moment. Had she ever told Stu that? Angie's cleft disappeared. The truth right now was just as obvious as that rainbow back then. She leaned over Bloodhound's chair until their faces were level. "I've wanted Sala dead from the moment I saw Nancy's broken body on the pavement below my daughter's dorm room window. Satisfied?"

Bloodhound's face thawed. "Almost. You forced the direction of the investigation? From suicide to murder?"

"Sala solicited girls. Good girls. Upped the money until they agreed to do unspeakable things. Got some sort of kick out of it. Nancy wasn't the only one killed."

"Committed suicide," Bloodhound corrected.

"Murdered."

"Debatable at best." Bloodhound waved off further argument. "Did you know Nancy needed money?"

"No. But I should have."

"So, absent your wealth, the broken body could have been your daughter's."

"Yes."

"Sorry counselor. I don't see murder here."

"Neither did the D.A. But he'd grown accustomed to me setting legal precedent and wanted Sala dead too. He let me pursue it a while."

"I'm not a D.A., Angie. Sala's either human or he isn't. Women sometimes kill themselves after abortions too, but I'm not helping bomb the clinics."

The grandfather clock chimed. One silver lance covered the other. Both pointed straight up, marking twenty-five hours until the charity luncheon. Angie yanked open her desk drawer and grabbed the screwdriver, strode to the back of the study and freed The Bastard's drawer. "Have a look in there." She stabbed the screwdriver down between the pages of Sala's fat file. "I know it's early, but I could use a drink—bourbon feels right. You?"

"Bourbon? No, thank you." With her chin lifted high, eyes fixated on the handle of Angie's screwdriver, Bloodhound approached the drawer. "I hate to see you drinking alone though, and I could use some caffeine. Irish coffee? I know it's a bit of an effort. Is it too much to ask?"

"I'll see what I can do." Angie headed down the hall, frowning.

In the kitchen, she dumped the morning leftovers into a cup, slammed the door on the microwave, selected two minutes, and headed for the wet bar. Not much effort at all, pushy bitch.

Returning to the study, Angie found Bloodhound sitting cross-legged on the carpet with a cell phone to her ear. Sala's graphic photos lay among the diamonds at her knees.

Bloodhound's phone hand jerked as Angie slid the cup and saucer in front of her. Clearly startled, she quickly composed herself, pointing with her phone at the photos. "I'm on board, Captain Angie." She placed a silencing finger across her lips. "But first, I've got to clear my schedule."

Angie mouthed a thank you before settling onto the couch to wait out the one-sided conversation.

"You should've asked me that earlier," Bloodhound said. "I'm with my client."

"I can't answer that right now." She rolled her eyes.

"No...no...a rush job location search." She sipped her coffee and smiled at Angie.

"Very specific."

"Around noon, but let me make sure." Bloodhound looked up for confirmation.

Angie flashed a single vertical index finger.

"One o'clock, tomorrow."

"Yes...I'll work straight through if I have to."

"All right. I'll call back when I'm free to speak...about that." Bloodhound pushed end call and took another sip. "Tastes a bit different. A person never gets exactly what they want from you, do they?"

Angie shrugged. "Instead of brown sugar and heavy cream, I just add Irish cream liqueur. It's quicker."

"Yeah. A lot quicker. But, I have to admit, nearly as tasty."

Angie shook her tumbler, clinking the ice cubes. "Your phone call?" She drank off the remainder of the bourbon. "I thought you didn't have a leash anymore?"

"Still have to take care of business." Bloodhound resumed her position at the desk, placing the coffee a safe distance from her thumbs. "Never completely free until you're dead." A stroke of the keys and the system whirred. Sala's emails reappeared on the screen. "Well, let's start at the end and work backwards."

The beautiful young woman in the yellow tank top returned as the slide show began. Angie made it three slides further this time. When the blood ran down the girl's legs, she turned away, only to find more blood among the diamonds of her carpet. Faces she'd studied hundreds of times. Lives she knew. Fates she couldn't alter. Angie busied herself collecting the faces from the diamonds, remembering, regretting.

"You could've just shown me this last photo, Angie. That's all I would have needed."

The slide show had ended. Angie's own face looked back at her from the computer monitor. Her head transposed onto the girl's broken body. Below the altered photo, the caption read, "The more beautiful and spirited the mare, the sharper the bit and the stronger the whip."

"One last question, Angie. When I find him for you. What then? Extradition requests and all that. Lots of legal mumbo jumbo."

"Legalities?" Angie faced Stu's photo. Reaching out, touching the glass, fingertips tracing his curls, she pretended to straighten the knotted oaken frame. "I want this over." She turned and considered the cabinets at the back of the room. "I already know Sala is inhuman."

"Then I'm here for as long as you want, for whatever you need. Forget about the money, Angie. This one's pure pleasure."

When the rain slackened, Angie went to survey the damage. Fallen pines and flooded rosebushes. Nothing that couldn't be mended. High above, the wind had untangled some of the lover's limbs. A cleft formed between her eyes.

CHAPTER TWENTY-SIX

Carl's cell phone slid across the table toward Stu. "Before you sit down, Ironman, call the company and tell them you're sick."

"Nice spot, you picked," Stu replied, ignoring the cell phone. He'd found Carl tucked away in the dreariest corner of the tiny, dimly-lit hotel bar. Two mugs sat in puddles on the lopsided table. Not the type of establishment to bother with coasters. One mug was half-filled with a golden fluid, the other overflowing and black. "Or we could grab something with a screwtop. Maybe a bottle of strawberry wine? Head for the alley. Sit in the dirt. Lean our tired backs against a dumpster and pass a brown paper bag back and forth." Stu sniffed the air and raised an eyebrow. "Guaranteed to have better smelling air next to that dumpster."

"Shitbag hotel's got no respect for smoking ordinances." Carl nodded at the portly man lighting a cigar at the opposite end of the room. "By the way…you look like shit. Call in sick."

"Yeah, been getting a lot of that lately." Stu shoved the cell phone back to Carl. "I'm not sick."

"Drop the Ironman act, already. Angie's got you all screwed up. Your head's not in the cockpit." Carl swigged his beer and wiped the foam from his upper lip. "Going to kill somebody. Might be me. Angie's amazing, but all this saving the world crap is exactly that—a big load of crap."

After checking the chair for spilt beer and brushing off the crumbs, Stu sat and grabbed the stout, watched the nitrogen bubbles swirl upward. "You've listened to all of my Angie problems for more than two years now." He lifted the mug and clinked glasses with Carl. "What if I told you that this very morning, beneath the wing, I discovered it was never about her rescuing the world." Stu drained the dark liquid in six huge gulps. "Nope. Saving the world never had anything to do with it." He held the empty mug a quarter inch from the tabletop and released. "It was all about Sala. What would you say?"

Carl looked down at his beer. His lips began to form a word and stopped. He took a swig, set the mug down and pushed away from the table. Drummed his fingers and almost spoke again. Nothing. He had nothing.

"Exactly, Carl." Stu nodded in slow motion. "Exactly."

While finishing his beer with one hand, Carl waved two fingers at the bartender with the other. Mugs filled with light and dark replaced the empties. They downed those. Two more mugs arrived. They sipped.

"Are you absolutely sure?" Carl finally asked.

"How can I be? I wasn't there. Bloodhound was."

Carl set his cell phone next to Stu's mug. "You need to go home."

"And what? Confront Angie? That worked so well back in June." Stu sighed in disgust and took a long draw from his mug. "Besides, you've seen our vice president's memo. He's seen a disturbing upward trend in pilot sickouts."

Carl frowned. "Yeah, your trend would rocket from never before all the way up to one. That little silver-spooned, Harvard-bred prick can't touch you, and you know it. At least skip the Chicago turnaround tomorrow."

Stu shook his head. "Might lose my nickname."

"If you bend a jet, or kill someone, they'll take a lot more than that, Ironman. I can't fly every trip with you."

"What?" Stu blurted, thinking back over the last couple months, trying to recall the last time he flew a rotation with a different copilot.

"Yep. You're too strung out to notice. Been trading trips with guys, and they're glad to give them to me. What did you think? That I was getting sweet on your ugly ass?"

A hand reached past Stu's shoulder and slid the extra chair from their table. "You guys don't need this. Thanks." The hand belonged to cowboy boots, giant gold buckle, and a tan sports jacket. He helped pumps, painted-on shirt, and big hair to navigate between the tables, and then held her chair as she sat down. His two replicas, silver buckle and gray buckle, grabbed two more chairs. The portly cigar smoker took the last.

Big-Hair sniffed. "My uncle used to smoke a big fat stogie. I like the smell. Like the size and shape a lot more," she giggled.

All three buckles chuckled. Gold-Buckle raised a hand and tried to attract the waitress. He pounded the table and held up a fifty-dollar bill. She weaved in his direction. Turning back he found Silver-Buckle caressing Big-Hair's hand and whispering in her ear.

"Charlie says he'll buy me a Screaming Orgasm."

Gold-Buckle laughed. "Charlie'd need to buy you that."

Charlie didn't laugh.

Three naïve fools who couldn't spot a pro, Stu reflected. He dug a thumb into his left shoulder and kneaded at the stiffness developing there. Everyone got worked by a pro at some point. He had a scar on his shoulder to remind him.

Cigar smoke wafted across the table between them. Stu waved it away from his face and followed it to the source. The rotund smoker stood next to Big-Hair. He held out the cheap cigar and joked, "I never cruise the bars without one." He poked it at her. "My bait."

"Compensating?" Big-Hair quipped, and they all howled.

A cigar-puffing fat man—three young idiots—and a pro. How many bad signs did he need? Carl was right. He was strung tighter than a high wire. About to snap. Thailand, all over again. Back then, it was his mother's suicide. Now, Angie's betrayal. Everything too similar. Last time, he'd killed a pimp and wound up in a Thai prison. "I'm out of here, Carl."

Stu scooted his chair backward and bumped into something. Glass shattered on the floor behind him. He was off the chair and spinning, knocking the waitress's tray, a wave of beer sloshing across his shirt.

"I'm so sorry, Sir." The waitress carefully set the tray on the table and dabbed his chest with her bar towel.

Stu held up both hands. "My fault. Thanks. I'm fine."

She apologized again and stooped to pick up the broken glass.

Bending to help, Stu knocked heads with her and set them both to laughing.

A cowboy boot kicked a piece of glass across the wood floor. "You frighten easy, old man." Gold-Buckle towered over him. "Jumping up like that. Looked like a dog popping out of a pond. Just as sloppy too. Got my boots wet." He launched three more shards from his gold pointed toe.

All three fragments bounced into Stu's left shoe. His heart thumped out the old cadence. He handed the shattered pieces to the waitress, winked and nodded her away.

She hurriedly excused herself to get a mop.

After straightening to his full height, Stuart assessed the situation. He gave up more than five inches and at least fifty pounds to Gold-Buckle in front of him. To the left, Silver-Buckle sat unsmiling. On the right, his vacant chair. Behind him, a table, two mugs of beer and Carl.

Stu pushed his chair under the table, sending out the false impression that he'd initially move in that direction. Truth was, if things didn't calm down he'd go left and low, yank the chair from under Silver-Buckle and come up hard into Gold-Buckle. A table separated him from Gray-Buckle. No immediate threat.

He smiled a friendly smile at Gold-Buckle. "Beer spilt all over your boots. That's troublesome. Could ruin your nap, young man."

Across the table, portly cigar man slapped the table and laughed.

Gold-Buckle's face turned darker. "My nap?"

Stu pointed at Gold-Buckle's boots. "Yes, your nap. Couldn't help but notice the suede. Beer might wreck the fluff."

Big-Hair giggled.

Gold-Buckle darkened another shade. "You're a real smart guy, aren't you?"

"No. Just concerned you'll ruin your boots. You said it yourself. I'm a cautious senior citizen."

"I said frightened old man."

Carl slid his chair back. "Doing okay, Boss?"

Big-Hair's pupils dilated with excitement. Hookers were good at reading people. Unlike Gold-Buckle, she seemed to sense how close the violence hovered.

Stu reached behind and with an easy downward wave of his hand encouraged Carl to remain seated, then nodded at Gold-Buckle. "Yes, you're correct, that's exactly what you said, and I appreciate the favor of your correcting my mistake. This frightened old man will do you a favor in return. Wish someone had done this for me a couple decades back." Stu pointed at Big-Hair. "Check your wallets, boys. She's a pro. And Cigar-Man here is probably her pimp."

All but the man with the cigar turned and stared at her.

Stu slipped away.

"It's barely dinner time," Carl yelled. "What're you going to do for the next four hours?"

"Figure out how to get a decent night's sleep," Stu shouted over his shoulder and kept moving.

Stu stumbled into his hotel room, letting the door slam shut. Except for the crack of sunlight slipping between the curtains the room was dark. He walked toward the sliver of light and bumped into a coffee table. Took a step back and collapsed on the edge of the bed.

Sala. His heart took off again, cycling up and down. But after the many intervening hours, it seemed a little less determined, like it wearied of urging him to battle.

He wasn't sure he'd ever been this tired. His eyes burned from the cigar smoke. And despite the heat wave rolling across New York, he felt a deep cold all through his body. Lying back, he pulled the coverlet across his legs and torso, and willed his heart to steady. Overhead, a fan spun. He should get up and turn it off. First, he'd rest his burning eyes. Just for a moment.

Cloaked by the thick underbrush, Stuart peered between tangles of branches to follow the woman's movements along the riverbank. Silent on the moss, her feet hidden beneath long tufts of white gown, she seemed to float over the ground. Starlight, reflecting from the placid water, played across the woman's august form, her skin glowing luminescent. She was living and breathing art. Chiseled alabaster. An incarnation wrought by the great sculptor's perfect hand.

She knelt on a massive rock that altered the river's path. A small pool of water, trapped by a jut of stone, lay before her. It formed a silvery mirror on which floated an exact replica of the moon above. Hands clasped before her, head bowed, eyes closed, she waited.

After a time, her right hand reached behind and retrieved a small turtle. She lifted the creature toward her face. It rested there, perched upon her palm, gazing up without hint of fear or struggle.

Whispering, the woman stroked its tiny head and kissed it, then released the turtle into the crescent moon's reflection. For a time her hand remained outstretched, trembling above the spot of release, then withdrew toward her heart. A tear slid from the woman's cheek, falling toward the moon. Water joined water, undisturbed.

Tear after tear, the woman repeated this process. And Stuart stood watch. As the long cool night wore its way toward dawn, she looked about her with concern. The more turtles she released, the more she glanced around, seeking something, perhaps anticipating something. Her eyes found him once. She warmed him with a smile.

The frequency of her glances increased, one for every tiny turtle she hurriedly released. Every glance directed toward a cypress grove. As Stuart strained to see among the ancient trees, he swore that shadows moved about their massive trunks. Yet how can shadows exist in such darkness? How can dark be darker than dark?

A fog formed over the river and slipped onto the land. The woman moved with a determined gait away from the water toward the early morning light. She followed a mossy trail that led off between walls of trees. The shadows pursued, paralleling her chosen path, but remaining within the forest.

The woman's white form blended with the swirling mist. Stuart strode forward to keep her in sight and became swathed in the flowery vines about his ankles. The more he struggled forward, the more enwrapped he became as the plants wound themselves around his shins and thighs.

She vanished. His last image was the white dress, flowing behind, leaving a glistening trail across the dewy moss.

Ripping flowers from stems, Stu pulled and kicked at the vines, but two replaced each one he managed to peel away. Through the fog he heard her voice, raised in anger.

Hunching down until his hamstrings touched his calves he thrashed upward against the bindings, his trousers tearing away.

Stu lunged forward, striking both his legs against an object hidden in the darkness, and crashed to the ground. He lay facedown on what must be the moss-covered path, but it felt dry and warm. His mind wrestled with that anomaly as he strove to orient himself in the blackness. A small band of light flickered to his left. He crawled toward it, shoving aside the strange hanging object blocking his vision.

Stuart threw up an arm to shield against the blinding light. The woman was gone. The mossy path, the trees, the vines, the shadows, all had disappeared. But the surface beneath him, its dryness and warmth, now made sense.

Twisting his head around, he found the object that had tripped him in the darkness. The coffee table made sense. The tangled coverlet made sense.

Why did the damned dreams always seem so real? That made no sense.

He closed his eyes, summoned an image of his home. The oak and maple at the bay window. Angie in her study. Andrew straight and tall in his lieutenant's uniform at the front archway. Maggie hugging her little brother, a proud smile on her face. But none of these images rivaled his dreams. There, the dark was more dark, the flowering vines more fragrant, the dew more moist. What did it mean that the woman at the water's edge occupied the top rung of his reality ladder?

Stu limped to the bathroom, removed his pants and propped one foot by the sink. He tested the colorful welts. They ranged from a raw pink near his ankle to a bright red at mid-shin. Stu grabbed the washcloth, warmed it with hot water and dabbed.

The mirror reflected a wreck. Felt worse. Carl had made several good points. Beat up, dead tired, and mentally drained, he really could hurt somebody. He should call in sick. What was he trying to prove? Or avoid?

Stu dropped one leg to the tile and raised the other. This shin looked worse. Tomorrow he'd call scheduling and tell them he was getting off in Washington.

What then? Go home and issue ultimatums? Everything else had failed. Ambush his wife of twenty-five years without any plan? He drew a bottle of peroxide from his shaving kit and started on his scrapes.

His shins tended to, he rinsed the beer from his shirt and grabbed his pants. Stu searched up one pant leg and down the other. Not a single tear. Yet, he'd heard the material rip.

Hobbling to the bed, Stu picked up the coverlet and followed the rent fibers and separating threads to a large tear. Month after month of the same nightmare, with never a change that mattered. But this time, he gave up prying at the vines and got angry. Yes, he'd stumbled and crashed to the ground. Yet this dream was different. The vines had snapped. He'd broken free.

So what? Nothing but a damn dream. Then why did this feel so important? Stu wasn't sure. Just listening to his gut. A gut didn't have thoughts. Only reactions. His gut liked breaking free.

With his shirt drying on the shower rod, legs bandaged as best he could, uniform readied, alarm set, and the decision to call in sick made, he faced the daunting prospect of trying to fall asleep. Damn near impossible with images of tomorrow's confrontation with Angie coursing through his brain.

Three choices, he figured. Find a *no-go* pill, get drunk, or call Gramps.

That last option was a new one. Gramps had Bloodhound, and she had evidence of Angie's guilt. And without Bloodhound's evidence, what did he have? A bloodletting.

Stu circled the bed preparing the room. He lifted the lamp from the nightstand and yanked the cord free. A push of his thumb straightened the bent plug. After setting the lamp on the carpet, he slid the coffee table toward a corner as he reconsidered his choices.

A *no-go* pill seemed appropriate. Angie's promises meant nothing. Why should his? Her addiction was far more destructive.

Yet draining a few tumblers of single malt scotch possessed a certain poetic justice. No wonder she didn't want to toast his capitulation back in June. Maybe he'd toast a solo vow or two—never trust her—never place his faith in her. At least he'd keep them.

Call Gramps? The white-haired patriarch was right, of course. In war, information was everything. And he was correct about changing your tactics to fit the battlefield too. But spy on Angie? How far was he willing to go?

Stu lifted the other lamp, yanked, straightened, and placed it against the wall.

Popping a *no-go* meant popping a *go* in the morning, and finding a supplier of both tonight. Getting plastered meant a hangover, dehydration, reduced reaction time, and compromising lives. Calling Gramps? Dishonor.

Stu plopped down on the bed, and examined the torn coverlet. Orange spirals on a red background interspersed with wavy black lines. Damn ugly thing. Nearly as ugly as his three choices.

Was Gramps right about Bethesda? Does a legless Marine want a smart commander, or an honorable one? Angie had changed this battlefield. What honor did he owe her?

Stuart Pierce followed each orange spiral inward, never finding its end before starting on another. Drugs? Alcohol? Gramps?

CHAPTER TWENTY-SEVEN

Like a master printer testing the quality of the paper, Stuart pinched the dangling parking stub between thumb and forefinger, and rubbed. Gramps was correct. Knowing things did make a difference. A bad one.

Gramps's information made Stu's situation perfectly clear. Angie had perpetrated a series of deceptions, if not outright lies. Two questions remained. Why? And for how long? The answers were inside the skyscraper towering above the parking garage in front of him. Inside was Angie.

But he'd reached for that parking stub at least a dozen times and left it dangling. It wasn't the hard truths he'd learned from Gramps that stayed his hand. Or the hellish prospect of confronting Angie with those truths. It was the truths he didn't know. Truths he felt gnawing at the farthest edges of his thoughts. Truths that, perhaps, he didn't want to know.

Next month would mark three years since Angie had retired. Thirty-five months of supporting her every desire, as she grew more distant. Over one hundred fifty weeks of waiting while she shut him out. What had he really accomplished? At what point did patience and understanding become enabling?

Stuart yanked the parking stub. A pop followed by a metallic hum preceded the first sliver of black appearing at the bottom of the garage door. He rolled forward a few feet and stopped, waiting while the grimy door crawled upward.

As he waited, Stu slipped the matching pen and pencil set from his right breast pocket and tossed them into his uniform cap on the passenger's seat. He lifted his left pocket flap and popped the fastener from each post of his nametag, pulled it free and pitched it in. A loud blare sounded from behind.

Stu checked the rearview mirror. Two upraised hands questioned his intelligence, asking what in the hell was his problem. Ahead, the entrance gaped tall and black. Shaded by the hotel's twin eighteen-story towers, not even the sun directly overhead shed much light into the garage below. What little sunshine reflected down between the buildings bounced from the hood into his eyes. Stu raised a hand to block the glare, relaxed a little pressure from the brake pedal and edged downward.

At the entrance, a row of four-inch high metal teeth protruded from the ground. A sign cautioned that backing up after crossing would result in severe damage. Stu turned on his headlights and crossed over.

The removal of his captain's wings always presented more of a challenge, especially with his shirt still on. Not a simple post and pin design like his nametag, the wings instead were attached with a long straight pin fastened by a wheel clasp, the safe removal of which was best accomplished with two hands. Normally he solved this problem by driving with his knees, but the old parking garage was dark and narrow. Tilting the wings with his fingers, he picked at the clasp with his thumb, successfully rotating the tiny wheel more than halfway around before it stuck. The speed bump did the rest, the sudden jolt setting the straight pin free and slipping it deep under his thumbnail. He jerked his hand away and licked at the blood.

Served him right. First time in his flying life he ever played hooky. But after speaking with the old patriarch last night, Stu reasoned that bold action, swift and decisive, was required.

Armed with Gramps's intel, he'd confront Angie in the act. War over. A grand plan.

Yet now Stu faced the dirty details of execution, the point where soldier met soldier in battle, the raw moments when the blood was spilt and the bodies were counted, while the politicians who'd started it all cried "Oh my." Except he was the politician this time, the man responsible for whatever resulted, the one who sought to end perpetual strife through open warfare. The possible body count—just two. Or rather—just one. Their marriage. The oneness. Yet, were they still one? She hid another life. Left him behind long ago.

He was trying to catch up. But in catching up, he paid a

shameful price. This morning, he called in sick, a despicable action that accomplished nothing unless he parked and went inside. But going in meant spying on Angie, a dishonorable act. More shameful yet, that dishonorable act seemed easier today than last night. Did calling Gramps make it easier to call in sick, and did calling in sick make it even easier to spy on Angie? Did the crossing of one moral line make it even easier to cross the next? Could he ever cross back?

Each concrete pillar had a fluorescent green square with a black "Sublevel 1" painted at its center. Just past the fourth pillar was a gold Lexus. The license plate read 2RUTH—Angie's car. Stu stopped. Truth for everybody but him, it seemed.

The horn blared again.

Stu edged far to the right, almost scraping Angie's bumper.

The car snuck past. "If you don't know where you're going, then go home!" the driver shouted, leaning on the horn as he accelerated down the ramp.

Stu chuckled a low growl. The man didn't know how close he was to the truth. Confronting Angie as she left the charity banquet would lead him…lead them…where?

Behind him the garage door squeezed shut, clamping off the last bit of reflected sunlight. He headed downward, looking for a parking spot. Two turns later the fluorescent squares turned blue, denoting Sublevel 2. Squinting through the gloom raised his hopes several times, but every spot he thought unoccupied was either filled with a motorcycle or labeled "Handicapped Only."

He stifled a yawn. Eight hours of sleep and he was still so damn tired. After speaking with Gramps, he'd crashed. A crash every bit as powerful as coming off a *go* pill. Worse really. Slept dream free yet woke more tired than when he dropped off. Wanted to lie there all day, and maybe the next. For the first time in his life he knew how Angie felt on those afternoons when he dragged her from their bed, bathed and dressed her, and drove through the hill country, talking softly about trees and grass and the hawk overhead, letting her know he was there, and that he cared. Stu rubbed at his blinking eyes.

The deeper Stu descended the more garbage he saw, and the colored squares seemed to warn against driving any lower, turning dingy yellow, muddy orange, and grimy red. Gramps said Angie'd already talked twice with Taamir. She'd never mentioned it. And if she'd spoken with Taamir, how far off was Uday? The damn guy resembled a Greek statue. Apollo with dark hair and a tan. Never liked how he looked at Angie. Not so much leering, as consuming.

The decay increased as Stu spiraled lower. Rusty beams and cracked concrete—mold and stench. Rot. Angie had intentionally scheduled Bloodhound's visits during his absence. No arguing that. And after begging him to believe in her, she immediately betrayed his trust. No other way to see it.

Stu reached bottom. Sublevel 6. Purple squares framed the first open slot. That figured. Turning the corner, he half expected to see Angie waving him in. Today she was supposed to meet with Taamir in person. Instead she'd spent twenty-five thousand dollars on a front row seat at this lousy banquet.

Stu shoved the gearshift lever into park. Gramps and devils? Damn right. The ones you know, the ones you don't know, and the worst—the ones you think you know. Twenty-five years, Angie. And now…we've come to this?

Keeping his bleeding thumb well away from his shirt, Stu unbuttoned the epaulette on his left shoulder and slipped off the captain's bars. After fumbling at the button on his right shoulder for a bit, he gave up and worked it with both hands, his thumb adding a bloody smear to the faint stain of spilt wine on his sleeve. Stu snorted. Angie'd said it would be tough to wash clean. Maybe she hadn't meant the shirt. He tossed the last piece of uniform into his hat. Now he was invisible. Just another guy in dark blue pants and a light blue shirt.

Across the ramp, an old man lugged a heavy coil of fire hose toward a doorway labeled "Stairs." Stu got out of his car and jogged over, pain shooting up his bruised shins. He ignored it.

Everything about the man said ancient. The leather of his work boots was dry and cracked. Once-white coveralls now matched the dingy gray of his hair. His gloves were more hole than cloth.

Stu held the door open and followed him through into a room that made the old man look young. Dank dripping water, oily pools, moldy peeling paint.

"Where you going?" the old one said.

"Up."

The old man studied the ceiling and shook his head. "Up's a tough direction from here."

Stu looked around. Only one set of stairs, leading down.

The old man's gaze left the ceiling and shifted to Stu's shoes, panned slowly upward, lingered at his chest, and finished at what Stu assumed were his very bloodshot eyes. "Nothing but heat and steam down this way, youngster. Maintenance tunnels." He shifted the weight on his shoulder. "You look more wore out than me. Let me guess. You're lost. Need to find your car and go home."

"No." Stu smiled. "Tired, but not lost. Just trying to find my way up."

"Nope. You're definitely lost." The old man opened the door and pointed.

Stu stepped through. Past his car, beyond three purple-squared concrete pillars, was a yellow flickering wall sconce. Beneath the dying light, an oily puddle and a doorway.

"Got no airplanes down here," the old man cackled.

Airplanes? Stu turned to question the strange comment but the door pounded shut. The old fellow had vanished. Lucky he'd gone the wrong way, though. The Mercedes's headlights still shone.

Flipping off the switch, Stu caught a sparkle from the windshield, an odd hint of light. Seemed familiar somehow, but the time for chasing hints was long past. Time to act. Stu mashed down the lock and slammed the door. Only ten minutes until the banquet was scheduled to let out.

He jogged to the doorway, hopped the puddle and pushed the only button: "Up." The sparkle must have come from his uniform cap, he decided. Should have tucked it under the seat. Classic car like his, all it took was a wire coat hanger. Funny how quick a person's identity could disappear.

Angie marveled at the man's charm. More than ten years since she'd witnessed Uday's smile in action. Soon after Prince Azwad's arrival on the Washington scene, his disarming dazzle had gained him the ear of many a congressman, and if the rumors bore truth, the earlobes of more than a few of their wives. Now she watched Uday woo the most powerful moneychangers in human history.

Angie skewered a single, small piece of shrimp and scraped away any trace of sauce with her knife. Thumbing her nose at Sister

Constance Ruth and twelve years of Catholic etiquette, she lifted her fork and conveyed the dripless morsel across a full three inches of spotless white tablecloth, over chiffoned thighs, up past her scoop neckline and into her mouth. Odd way to eat, but any lean toward the plate drew her face from the shadows of the column next to her.

She'd spent a pretty penny in IOUs and hard cash to get this cheap seat. Twenty-five thousand dollars had bought her a ticket at a front row table, and left the astonished woman she'd traded for this half-price seat to wonder what subterfuge she plotted. But a quick allusion to an old lover and the woman winked.

Trade complete, Angie sat comfortably anonymous in the dark, just behind a pillar, observing.

"Ms. Pierce, what brings you out of retirement today? From the look of your plate, it certainly isn't the food." The man across the table had been eyeballing her for the past hour.

So far, Angie had avoided anything more than a polite rejoinder by feigning a keen interest in the charitable cause of whatever celebrity currently occupied the stage. Tougher, now that lunch was complete and all in attendance awaited the appearance of the annual surprise speaker. "I heard rumors of a big guest this year, perhaps the biggest," Angie answered.

He leaned across the table toward her. "Too bad. I was hoping you were rethinking retirement?"

Angie looked him over for the first time. Meticulous haircut, manicured nails, dark suit, white shirt and red power tie. Even the recent near collapse of the nation's banking system couldn't change the uniform. "Do I know you?"

"No, but my wife, a lawyer at Founding Mothers Legal, practically worships you. She'd faint if I told her I'd signed you up. New Millennium Wealth has a place for you, Ms. Pierce."

Laughter erupted at Uday's table. With his head tilted down and a slight cock to one side, he smiled at the Madame Secretary of the Treasury, his dark eyes suggesting the woman was still desirable. And the Madame Secretary could believe it true. Although eminently qualified for her position, many an insider had quipped that the President was no fool when he submitted the nomination, selecting her for both form and function. And Uday's almost imperceptible flirt worked like magic.

Angie studied Elizabeth Crowell's reaction to that gentle Uday smile. First, a comically winsome pout appeared, the Madame Secretary pretending she was insulted by the Prince's comment, which caused everyone to laugh again. But she followed that up with a nod even more imperceptible than Uday's smile. A nod that said we'll have to find a way for you to make it up to me. Uday was the master of the understated flirt, the type of flirtation that lingered for days, leaving one's mind wondering if it was really a flirt at all.

Angie moved her chair a few inches left and rotated it a little to the right. Still shaded by the pole, she faced the banker while studying Uday. "Really. And just what would a mutual fund company want with an old has-been attorney?"

"Don't underestimate your power, Ms. Pierce. Investors flock to someone trustworthy, especially now. We'd build a whole line of funds around you. And you'd be doing something good, helping to bolster the financial markets by drawing capital to conservative investments." He frowned and wagged his index finger. "And shame on you. Never use the word 'old.'" His frown turned smile, eyebrows lifting. "I'd sure pick up any brochure with your face on the cover."

Angie smiled back, surprised that she enjoyed the compliment. Yet, by comparison, the banker's strokes of flattery were like a first grader finger painting next to Van Gogh, bright and cute versus Uday's smoldering masterpiece. "Tell me more."

"Well, our brochures would feature your bio and…"

Angie listened just enough to provide polite nods when appropriate, flash a smile or two, and even threw in the occasional "very interesting" as she observed Uday wielding his charm.

Stu checked the time. Five minutes. The up button was lit. He'd pressed it a dozen times. Maybe the old man was right. He was lost. Angie would emerge from the banquet room and he'd do what? Confront her? She'd just be Angie, all heat and passion in private, absolute calm and cool in public. Rattle her? Make her see she was killing them both? The idea now seemed silly. Stu tried to imagine how he'd begin. What could he say to open her up?

"You getting on or not, flyboy?" The woman held her finger against the OPEN button. "I had to ride all the way down to go back up."

"What?" Stu mumbled.

The man next to her dropped his briefcase and leaned against the brass rail. "I'm running late, pal."

"Last chance." She released the button and the doors raced toward each other.

Stu leapt through the narrowing crack. "Sorry. Asleep on my feet." The doors sealed shut. Did she say "flyboy"?

The elevator rumbled and jerked downward.

"I hate this old box," the woman complained. "Always one more shot in the gut before heading up."

After several stops, Stu understood why she had to ride all the way down to go back up. They stopped at every floor, people fighting their way off between those wanting on. Perhaps he'd get to the banquet too late. Perhaps he should. The doors opened again. This time, more people got off than on. Another two stops left him all alone. His floor was next.

The whole day had seemed to work against him. Hotel van broke down—he paid for a cab. Numerous maintenance issues with the jet—much to Carl's disgust, he agreed to fly it anyway. Dangerous winds for landing—not that dangerous, he decided. No parking space—sure there was, if you drove yourself far enough down. And then, to top it all off, some cryptic old man telling him he should just get in his car and go. How many signs did he need? Yeah...maybe he'd just ride the elevator back down and drive home.

As the elevator opened, a sparkle of gold reflected from the aluminum doors—just above his heart. Stu looked down and found his wings, loose, but still clinging to his shirt. A spot of blood coppered the golden wreath surrounding his star. He felt again the needle sliding beneath his nail. Remembered the blaring horn. Recalled the old man's disturbing comment, "Got no airplanes down here," and his more disturbing, "You're lost. Need to find your car and go home." Stu snatched the wings from his chest. The old man's comments weren't some cryptic warning. Nope, he was just a clever old man demonstrating that his wit was still intact, having some fun with the youngster.

Stu knifed through as the doors closed, spilling into the chest of a human roadblock.

The man's feet were spread wide, hands low behind his back.

Military parade rest position. He wore a dark suit and flesh-toned earpiece. Didn't look hard of hearing. Looked more like an NFL linebacker. Secret Service for sure.

"Step back, Sir."

Stu stepped back. Except for the linebacker's four clones at the banquet room doors, the area behind the man was empty.

To Stu's right, stretching down the hallway, was what looked to be the hotel's cart brigade. Lots of carts. Two men per cart. The first four were filled with bar-height tables. Behind them, carts full of white tablecloths, vases stuffed with tasteful arrangements, desserts, cheeses and fruits. At the rear of this entourage was a baby grand piano flanked by seven-foot-high wine racks. Stu spotted a parchment-labeled bottle with burnished accents. If it was adorned with a big scripted "G," then Angie's twenty-five thousand seemed reasonable. The "G" stood for Godly, the sommeliers claimed, and Stu agreed, but it also came with a godawful price, over four hundred dollars a bottle.

The linebacker placed a finger against his earpiece. His already stiff manner stiffened more. He spoke into his wrist and the four clones behind him moved to parade rest, one in front of each set of double doors leading to the banquet room. Though he flashed a smile, he didn't look happy.

Stu matched his smile and waited. In his pocket, his thumb rubbed at the dried blood on his laurel wreath.

Uday turned his charm on the Fed Chief, brandishing confidence, strength, friendship, and trust. The Federal Reserve Chairman responded with a litany of the nation's financial challenges.

A waiter clipped Uday's chair. The sympathetic interest in his eyes flashed to fire and back. And Angie remembered. The Realm's embassy. A decade ago. A cleaning woman spilled a bucket, dousing the royal Prince's shoes. First the brief flash of fire and then the kingly smile, one instant anger, the next stooping to help the woman right her bucket. If Angie could just turn that fire on Sala and keep it there?

"...So, you can see Ms. Pierce, New Millennium has both you

and your nation's best interests at heart." The banker leaned back, satisfied he'd made the sale.

Someone tapped the microphone and introduced the Vice President of the United States. The only one who didn't look surprised was Uday. He winked at the Madame Secretary, who smiled. Pointing at the Fed Chief, he rubbed his thumb over fore and middle fingers. The head of the U.S. banking system laughed, pounded the table, and reached for his wallet. Out came twenty dollars, which he slid over to Uday. Everyone stood and clapped for the nation's second in command.

The Vice President spoke briefly. Staying on message, he touted the benefits of the administration's plans for fiscal recovery, hitting each of the obligatory buzzwords: jobs, responsible lending, affordable housing, health care, and back to jobs again. He left amidst a standing ovation from his fawning adulators.

Stu checked the time. Twenty minutes past three. The banquet ran long. Longer than his resolve. He pushed the elevator's "Down" button, breaking his chain of dishonorable acts.

The Secret Service agent lifted a hand to his ear and listened. His plastered-on smile cracked and vanished, but now he actually looked happy. Probably meant that his mission was complete, the banquet over.

Stu tapped "Down" several more times.

Speaking to no one in particular, the linebacker droned "Thank you for your patience. Have a nice day." It sounded like the agency's version of the obligatory postgame pleasantries. Might as well be saying…good game…good game…but the Vice President is still alive…too bad you lost. And like he'd just heard the ref's last whistle in his earpiece, he did an about-face and walked off the field of battle.

Stepping inside the empty foyer, Stu scanned the room for a staircase.

The cart brigade rushed past. Bar-height tables sprouted in groups of three across the lobby. No chairs. A woman laid a white tablecloth over each. Another woman followed behind placing a vase of flowers on top.

212

Stu circled, checking behind each door as he went. From the other side of the foyer he saw people filing into the elevator and ran, yelling, "Hold please!" They didn't.

The baby grand piano rolled past over to the corner. Cheese, fruit and desserts were placed against the wall below the windows. The twin wine racks wheeled by filled with rows of ports, cognacs and brandies. Stu spotted his favorite extravagance. The tawny port with the scripted "G." Waiters opened a few of each. In minutes, the place was transformed from a long barren room into a hall of plenty.

Stu pounded the "Down" button.

A tuxedoed man sat and played bits and pieces, starting and stopping, testing key and pedal. He moved his fingers across the breadth and depth of the implement, tuning himself to the instrument. His hands became still.

Stu tapped a passing waiter's shoulder. "Where's the staircase?"

"No hablo Inglés." He smiled, and hurried his cart forward.

Crap. Too complicated. "Stairs?" Stu called after him, but the first soft notes from the piano muffled his question.

The music gained momentum, filling the room. Stu's head whipped around. From the waist, the pianist's torso made a slight sway. His sway grew larger, filtering up through neck and chin, as the music seemed to move through him. His head lifted. His eyes closed. And Stuart saw. Closed his own eyes and waited. Warm and sad, the exposition floated from the keys.

Twice in their marriage, Stu had returned from a trip to hear that music. Both times, Cheryl had the kids and Angie sat alone in her study, door closed and curtains drawn, rocking in her desk chair. Just rocking, not speaking. Hours they sat, listening, Beethoven's *Moonlight Sonata* playing over and over.

No. This was all wrong. He had to get out of here. Right now. Stu grabbed hold of a waiter and shouted, "Stairs? Door?"

Angie outmaneuvered the trailing banker and joined the crowd lingering near the stage. Hovering behind Prince Azwad's back, she listened to the conversation.

Uday leaned toward the Madame Secretary. "My country's

wealth is at your disposal. Your Congress need only reconsider the walls they've built. Thinking to protect your banks from foreign interests, they've constructed a prison where your nation's people languish. Your banking laws prevent the free flow of commerce to the detriment of all."

The Madame Secretary nodded. "Perhaps. But what guarantees? There is flow in and flow out, Prince Azwad. How long will you stay?"

Perfect. Angie stepped past Uday, while intentionally bumping his shoulder. When he turned, she ignored him and greeted the Madame Secretary.

"My God, it's Angela Pierce. I'd heard you'd gone to pasture. Are you back in town? Working?" The Madame Secretary hugged Angie.

"Not exactly, Madame Secretary. I've—"

"Angie, if you call me Madame Secretary one more time I'll have the Secret Service arrest you. And never mind why you're here. I'm being rude. Prince Azwad, may I introduce…"

"No need, Elizabeth. Uday and I are old friends."

"Really?" Elizabeth gave Angie an eyebrow flash. "How old and how friendly? Maybe you can help me out. The Prince seems to have a devilish side. Can I trust him?"

Angie gave her old friend an emphatic nod yes. "Prince Azwad was instrumental in a rape investigation years ago. The fiend fled the country and disappeared. My greatest regret from my years working for the D.A. But new information just surfaced and His Royal Highness has pledged his nation's assets in support. I'm counting on him."

"Well, Angie's vote of confidence is a big jewel in your crown, Prince Azwad."

"Yes, Ms. Pierce's passion for this man is no greater than my own."

Perfect. She had Uday cornered. Angie smiled and said, "That's wonderful to hear, Your Highness, because I have news. Actionable intelligence. Proof that Sala is in The Realm."

The Madame Secretary squeezed Angie's arm and looked at Uday.

Uday slipped a cell phone from his suit, scrolled, pressed, paused, and then started giving orders. "Taamir, Ms. Pierce has information indicating that Sala resides in The Realm. Have our office set up a special unit to find him. They'll work directly with Ms. Pierce. Failing her is failing me. Make that clear." Uday tucked away his phone and smiled. "Ms. Pierce, I will not rest. Count on my full support until Sala is arrested."

Someone tapped the microphone and announced, "The Vice President's motorcade has departed. Please join us for wine and dessert in the foyer."

The banquet room doors flew open. Not twenty feet away— Angie. Stu ducked behind a cart.

Beside Angie, the tanned Apollo. Behind them, the Madame Secretary of the Treasury and the Chairman of the Federal Reserve. Two dark suits closed in on either side of Uday. Their confident stride and darting eyes labeled them bodyguards.

Uday signaled for wine. "Oh, I have my special ways, Madame Secretary."

"But I've heard that Arabians are both spirited and jealous, Prince Azwad," the Madame Secretary retorted. "How do you handle them?"

"With diamonds, Elizabeth, lots of diamonds," Uday winked. "We speak of Arab women, do we not?"

All but Angie burst into laughter, and the tan god segued straight into a grand story of the quiet desert and the stars, his favorite gray and white mare adorned with the great Zuehb Azwad's ornate tack, the saddle's silver horn lustrous in the moonlight. With Beethoven accompanying his words, both the Fed Chair and the Madame Secretary appeared enthralled. Angie, however, seemed all business— probably the *Moonlight Sonata*. Pulling the cell phone from her purse, she excused herself and stepped toward the wine cart.

Stu crouched behind the bottles, stealing hopeful glances at the elevator doors behind him.

Angie scrolled, tapped the surface, put the cell to her ear and listened, then shook the phone and tried again.

A waiter offered her a glass of wine. "Give it another minute or two, Ma'am. Worst kept secret around here is that the Secret Service jams the airwaves whenever somebody important shows up."

Angie put her phone away, reached for the glass and stopped, her hand suspended in midair. "Excuse me. Did I hear you correctly? They jam the phones. For how long?"

"Yes, Ma'am. For the President, Vice President, anybody important they're protecting. It's supposed to prevent remote bomb signals or something. Always starts well before they arrive and…"

Angie's standard ringtone sounded.

"There, you see, Ma'am. I told you it would end soon."

Waving off the wine, she answered. "Yes, Mary, it's me. I'm sorry, but the Secret Service was jamming for the Vice President." Angie bent her head and pressed the phone tight against her ear. "There are no seats to sit down on. Just tell me what you found."

Angie circled right, staring at Uday.

Stu did the same, peering between the wine shelves at Angie, the *Moonlight Sonata* swirling around them. God, he could smell her. Her perfume drifted over the bottles and engulfed him. Stu's eyes darted around the room, searching for escape. The elevator arrived, but Angie now stood between him and the opening doors.

As the doors closed, a wave of disorientation swept through him like he was in an aircraft spinning out of control. But just as if he were at the controls of that aircraft, Stu took a deep breath and told himself to remain calm, that there had to be a way out of this. Rash decisions had brought him here. Poor choices. Patience would see him out.

But Beethoven seemed to mock Stu's thought, each subsequent note of the sonata more inevitable than the last, demanding he play out his choices, insisting that a rash fool he'd come, and a rash fool he'd leave.

"Mary…Mary, you're breaking up. Did you say he's operating out of The Realm's capital?" Angie bent her head and stuck a finger into her exposed ear. "That can't be possible. Sala's emails come from Uday's palace?"

With Angie voicing Sala's name aloud, Stuart Pierce's heart slammed in his chest. The pounding cycle erupted. Six vicious beats louder, the last coursing through his brain.

Raucous laughter burst from Uday. "No, Madame Secretary. I always say…" He smiled and poked his finger toward her nose. "…the more beautiful and spirited the mare, the sharper the bit and the stronger the whip."

A crack and hollow pop drew Stu's eyes toward the floor. He followed a little black rectangle as it skittered over the granite tiles and slipped between a pair of golden high heels to bounce off his shoe. He recognized the shape, a cell phone's battery pack just like his own. And Angie's.

Again, everything seemed to spin around him—Angie, Uday, Sala, Beethoven, loud laughter, fragments of phone. His heart hammering in his chest, Stu tried to catch up, to process.

Low and angry, Angie's voice penetrated Stu's swirling disorientation. "Elizabeth, did you know the Secret Service was blocking all phone signals? I finally received an important call. This man, His Royal Highness, Prince Uday Azwad, is a pedophile, a rapist and a murderer."

A loud slap echoed through the room as the sonata's somber recapitulation began.

Stuart stepped from behind the wine cart to see Angie's hand scraping down Uday's neck.

A bodyguard grabbed each of her arms. The back of Uday's hand swung toward her face and connected with a dull thud. Her head flew sideways.

Stu's heartbeat steadied. Everything outside him slowed down as his mind sped up. Stuart reached for a bottle of the scripted "G."

Grabbing the hair at the top of Angie's head, Uday rotated her face forward as he leaned all of his weight into a powerful forehand slap.

Uday's ribs snapped as Stu's roundhouse kick pushed past bone, driving toward lung. Then a swish of air as the "G" swept a downward arc to impact the skull of the man holding Angie's right arm. It shattered. But the bottle held together, so Stuart swung it hard against the other man's pistoled hand. The bottle survived this cracking sound also. Stu spun a complete circle and extended his heel. The formerly pistoled man's left knee collapsed in loud pops, bending in a way nature never intended. Stuart caught Angie and lowered her unconscious body to the floor.

He somehow sensed rather than felt an attack and ducked lower, something hard brushing his hair and glancing across his shoulder blades. A vase smashed to the floor, scattering the flowers into the blood pooling on the granite. In a single fluid motion, Stuart sat, rolled to one hip and swung a quick leg whip.

Uday's legs were cut from beneath him and he crashed head and shoulders to the tiles.

Stuart was on him. He raised the scripted "G" and smashed it to the floor. It shattered and the thin tawny fluid melded with the thick crimson already flowing from the bodyguard's cracked skull. The bitter smell of iron blended with the sweetness of the wine, together making an unholy odor.

The jagged edge of the broken bottle penetrated Uday's throat and sliced toward his jugular. Another smell wafted up, the sharp and sour ammonia of urine.

"Stu. No!" Angie's voice.

Stuart's hand paused, then cut a fraction closer to its goal.

"Stu, please." Her voice, a shallow cry. "Don't. You said…never again."

"So did you," Stu rasped.

Angie held his gaze a moment, faltered and looked away. She tried again, her eyes glancing over his, and then settling on his chin. "Please. Don't do this. It's murder."

The man beneath Stu was everything wrong. Powerful, charming, intelligent—by birthright, a leader of men. Yet he used those attributes, used his position, to toy with lives, corrupt innocence, rape women. He made Stuart embarrassed to be a man. Yet, Angie was right. If he pushed the glass farther, it was murder.

Stu slid the glass from Uday's throat.

Angie began to tear up.

The tanned Apollo winked and pursed his lips in a kiss to Angie.

Stuart sank the broken glass back home. Dug it deep into Uday's left cheek and twisted, carving great gashes toward his lips, then shoved it between the teeth to muffle the screams. He rose and wiped the blood from his hands onto his pants.

Uday pulled the glass from his jaw and gurgled. "She's next."

Stuart kicked, his shoe snapping the blood-red god's nose with a crack. And kicked again, this time to Uday's stomach. When the Prince curled into a ball, Stu aimed for the back of his head.

"No," Angie kept repeating as each of Stu's kicks landed.

Stuart kicked until he finally realized that all defensive movements had ceased. Backing away, Stu had the strangest feeling he'd lost something.

Collapsing under the combined weight of three security guards, Stu fell amidst the smell of defecation. The man with the shattered skull, he supposed. Three feet away, a golden straight pin poked up from the pool of blood and wine and urine. His wings.

Stuart Pierce's heart beat slow and steady as they cuffed him. And the world around him returned to normal speed. He wondered when the music had stopped. Beethoven was right, he thought. No escaping his rash choices.

CHAPTER TWENTY-EIGHT

Uday felt a cold wetness slide across his forehead and slip down along his left temple and cheek. The right half of his face felt neither cold nor hot—nothing, dead. Perchance, Mr. Pierce had sliced it clean away. Uday struggled to lift his eyelids, but they felt as though they were mired in a thick muck, maybe a pool of his own coagulating blood.

Or was he dead? Perhaps this puzzling combination of cool and numb was merely the first stirrings of a consciousness in hell.

"What have they done to you?" someone whispered.

The cool soothing moisture reversed, sliding back above Uday's eyes.

Another whisper. "My eagle…my fierce little eagle."

So he wasn't dead after all. A pity. "No need to speak so softly, Tama." Pain shot through the tip of Uday's swollen tongue. A slur tagged each of his words.

"Yes, Excellency. My…my apologies." Taamir cleared his throat.

Uday forced his eyelids open. The old, bearded, praying mantis of a man had never looked so good. "Don't stop the cool cloth, Tama."

"Yes, Your Highness." Taamir rinsed the towel in water and leaned across the hospital bedrail. "I didn't mean to wake you, Excellency. And I…I meant no disrespect."

Uday tried to lift his left hand but found it tangled with tubing. With his right he squeezed Taamir's elbow. "It's okay, my old friend. Nice to feel six again."

"Long time since you've called me Tama, Excellency." He laid the cloth on Uday's forehead, kneading it across and down.

"Maybe too long. You've always been here, Tama."

"Not always, my Prince." Taamir slipped the rag from Uday's face and dropped his eyes to the floor. "Not always."

"Nonsense." Uday patted Taamir's hand. "Only at my orders have you ever left my side."

Taamir wrung at the cloth, wetting the floor. "But your troubles return whenever…"

Three knocks on the anteroom's open doorway, and a nurse entered.

"His Highness sent for no one," Taamir challenged her.

"The monitors brought me." She was all business. After changing out one IV bag, adjusting the delivery rate on two others, and mopping up Taamir's drips, she paused in the anteroom. "Royal or not, I've never let a patient prevent me from doing what's good for him." The outer door swung closed behind her.

"How long have I slept, Taamir?"

"Almost twenty hours, Your Highness."

"I was dreaming."

"I'm sorry, Excellency. Again, I only sought—"

"Of my father, Taamir."

"Oh, I see, Your Highness."

"In my dream I was twelve. My father asked me to pass judgment on an American guilty of consorting with an Arab woman. I boldly recommended removal of the offending organ. He told me I was by far the smartest of his boys and I beamed up at him. He slid the Great Zuehb Azwad's silver knife from his waist sheath, handed it to the guards, and directed them to carry out my sentence. 'But Father,' I protested, 'our ancestor's knife is sacred.' He laughed, saying, 'Don't be a fool, Uday. It's merely a shiny bauble for the peasants to worship. Now study the man's eyes. See how his hatred grows.' After the man's screams subsided, my father passed judgment on me. 'The proper punishment was beheading. Hatred now lives in this man. Hatred breeds vengeance. But no man can avenge his own death. The throne requires more than just superior intellect, Uday. Your mother's line thins your blood.'"

"It's the drugs, Excellency." Again Taamir dipped the rag into the water bowl. "They muddle the mind. This dream is not…it isn't…. Excellency…another time, we can discuss—"

"I know, Tama. An unpleasant memory. Not just a bad dream."

221

Uday waved away the rag. "But, for a moment, it was," he sighed. Just one of many unpleasant memories—his father's lessons. The application of surgical violence. When to make a show to the masses. When to quietly eliminate. How to make people do things they never imagined doing. How to teach them to crave the humiliation. And the hardest lesson of all—how to manage one's own cravings. Something he'd never fully mastered. "I'm sure this incident will inspire another of my father's fine lessons. He'll use it to teach my future sons of weakness, no doubt."

"Ice water, Excellency?" From a dripping pitcher Taamir filled a cup, inserted a straw and offered the tip. "Keep the water to this side, Your Highness."

"Yes, of course. Mr. Pierce has opened up the other." Uday tilted his head left and sipped, the cold water soothing his swollen tongue. He sipped again. "What have you found of him?"

Taamir tapped, awakening his tablet. Seconds later, he began pecking away. "Little at this moment, Your Highness. Mr. Pierce was born in Colorado. Bachelor's degree in history. Master's in philosophy. Air Force pilot. Airline captain. The most personal detail we have so far is his nickname. Fellow pilots call him Ironman."

"Yes. I felt his iron boot on my head." Uday pressed his fingers past the top of his bandaged right cheek and moved across his skull, feeling the numerous spongy lumps hidden beneath his hair. "As I grew dizzy, it seemed as though he was my brother, kicking me senseless again. Perhaps why I woke thinking of my father. Did I ever tell you the two incidents were linked, Taamir? After my father's disappointment, I prayed daily that Allah would show me a path to The Realm's throne. Like most exuberant children, I felt that greater fervor would make Allah hear me. I began praying aloud. Naturally, my brother took exception. This thrashing makes twice that I've been beaten unconscious. My dear brother Sadeem, my very own blood, paid the price with his legs. What bill, then, would my father say is due Mr. Pierce?"

"Excellency, blood has soaked through the bandages on your cheek. Perhaps you should lie quiet."

"What hurts us most, Taamir?"

"Excellency?"

"The most pain for a man?"

Taamir leaned over the hospital bedrail and checked the

bandages. His hand came away red and wet.

"When Mr. Pierce pushed the jagged glass through my flesh it was very painful."

"Excellency, talking increases the flow of blood." He pushed the red call light.

"I could feel the glass slice through my gums, wedge between my teeth. One would think I'd avoid the sharp point. But, I couldn't stop myself. As if chasing after a festering canker sore, my tongue kept pushing at the shard, shredding the tip."

"Excellency, that is done. Gone. We should turn our eyes forward. I've already placed calls to the Fed Chief and the Secretary of the Treasury. I'll schedule meetings for..."

"There won't be any meetings, Taamir. The Angel's eyes bore the fire of conviction. Her voice held such contempt. No one has spoken to me like that since my father questioned my blood. The Madame Secretary saw it too—her hand leaping from my forearm like she'd suddenly learned I was a leper. And the Fed Chief, stepping back and regarding me with revulsion."

"Your Highness. I placed the calls but an hour ago. I think we should wait to see—"

"The Angel's slap was perfectly timed. Her blow landing precisely with my realization that she had completely destroyed a decade's worth of delicate negotiations. All of my work ruined, in an instant, by a brood mare. I'd never struck a woman before, Taamir." Uday studied his hand like he examined a foreign spy whose story was filled with lies. "Nor even a horse, for that matter. But any chance I had for such meetings ended when I backhanded The Angel."

After three quick raps, the nurse hurried to the bed.

"His Highness is bleeding." Taamir pointed at Uday's bandages.

The woman bent over the rail to examine him.

A salty taste filled Uday's mouth. "These women, the ones The Angel holds me responsible for. Never once did I force. Money is not a gun to the head. Merely an excuse. A reason to do what they wanted. Commit the sins already living in their souls." Wet warmth coated his lips. "How well I know the truth of this. Gold is not the craving, only the means."

"Majesty...Majesty...silence." Taamir reached around the nurse to squeeze Uday's shoulder. "Lie quiet while the nurse tends your wounds."

The nurse reached up and increased the drip rate on one of the bags. "He's delirious. Try to get him to stop talking while I get the doctor."

"Yes, delirious. His Majesty raves," Taamir agreed.

"Mr. Pierce fell on us like the Archangel Azrael carrying the full wrath of Allah's judgments. And then the pain began." Hot wetness dribbled down Uday's chin.

"Please, my Prince. The nurse asked you to lie silent." Taamir wiped at Uday's lips.

"The Qur'an says '…Whoever kills himself with an iron weapon, will be carrying that weapon in his hand and stabbing his abdomen with it in the Hell Fire wherein he will abide eternally forever.'"

Taamir folded the blood-soaked section of the cloth under itself and dabbed.

"What if The Angel died, Taamir? How would this Ironman weather his pain? Worse yet. What if he witnessed the one he cared for most in all the world…the mother of his children…the woman he holds each night…commit suicide? Would he then kill himself? Both of them sentenced to suffer for all eternity, the agony of repeated suicides, watching each other's pain."

Taamir blotted up the blood. "My young eagle, you must stop this. Your wounds will worsen. Infection may set in. Scarring."

Uday grabbed Taamir's hand. "Let it flow. The plastic surgeons will soon make it all go away. And don't worry, Tama, the words you hear me speak are my father's counsel. There reside other voices within me."

"Yes, my Prince. Your mother's bloodline is not thin. Listen to her voice."

"No, Tama. Your voice. My brother's beating of me was unjust and he has paid. But the Ironman merely defended his Angel. If she were mine, I'd have killed him. Very slowly."

A single knock preceded three doctors filing into the room.

Uday halted them with a raised hand and the look of command. "Taamir, leave me now. As for Mr. Pierce, make this all go away. And don't waste time with the Madame Secretary or the Fed Chief. Call my old friend, Mr. Walters at Metro World Bank. Get him down here. I need someone to play chess with."

"Right now?"

"Yes. Let Roger know that I'm shopping my certificates, thinking of dumping every last share of Metro stock. He'll take the first flight down."

CHAPTER TWENTY-NINE

A hissing static crackled from the overhead speakers. "Your lawyer just entered security screening, Mr. Pierce."

Stu waved at the ceiling camera hanging in the opposite corner of the interrogation room, faking a smile to the guards who monitored his every action. Days of pondering had winnowed a vast field of questions down to the same crucial two. How long had she lied to him? And why? But now, with Angie seconds from entering the room, he discarded them both and asked himself the one question that mattered. How could he ever trust her again?

Lowering his hand, Stu stepped away from the corner and stopped. He glanced at the locked door beside him, then frowned at the knee-to-ceiling mirror extending all the way to the next wall. Stepping backward, he leaned his shoulders against the cinderblock, returning to the only privacy available in this damn box.

There was little doubt that faces devoid of all sympathy were stationed behind that mirrored glass. His isolation over the past few days proved that whoever ran this operation had no respect for the constitution. After granting him a one-minute phone call to Angie— nothing. No charges brought. No questions answered. Not a single word spoken. Food slid through a slot. The lights went off for a number of hours, then came back on. Nighttime, he assumed. When he needed solace from his long list of unanswered questions, he filled his mind with the same memory that had sustained him so many times before—skis slipping through the thigh-deep powder, winding a path between backcountry aspens, leaning, curling, swirling snow over shoulder and neck…and then an opening, a meadow, and he'd corner hard, darting into the wide open…closing his eyes, extending his legs and lifting, skis rising, floating, weightless, timeless, entering the void…. And then opened his eyes and saw…his prison cell…and wondered, is there some purpose to this too? A crazy thought, but he clung to it.

His only human contact, a handwritten note from someone named Mr. Rudy. It accompanied each meal, always demanding an answer to the same question. "Are you a payer or a player?"

Stu jammed his shoulders deeper into the corner, lowered his head and stared at the floor tiles. Always the same decorator, he thought. No matter whether an after-combat report, a simulator debrief, or jail, if someone had you by the gonads, they always chatted up your future while juggling your balls over a chessboard of black and white squares. Hell, even in a Thai prison, where every inch of cell wall, floor and roof was formed of a damp crumbling concrete, the interrogation room was tiled with bloodstained dark and light stones.

He understood the logic of Angie visiting as his attorney rather than his wife. But didn't shutting off the cameras and microphones simply spawn more lurkers behind the mirror? Unknown foes that considered privacy laws a mere annoyance. Something to circumnavigate by citing safety concerns. Anyone could stand there, leering and judging, leaving him without a clue as to whom or what or why. How could he fight that?

At least in Thailand Stu could see the shadows moving beyond the bright lights shining in his eyes. Could blank his face. Mask his reactions. He knew when each chess match began and when it ended. But here, his only choice was to assume that the contest was always underway—Big Brother perpetually watching. Fine. If he kept himself crammed into this corner of the room, then Big Brother had two choices. Accept a camera shot of the top of his head, or press their lurking faces against the back of the glass and squint past the doorframe just to see half his profile.

Another crackle preceded the voice. "Please take a seat, Sir."

He nodded at the camera, then lifted both arms above his head and folded forward at the waist. He stretched his sore legs. His fight with Uday had multiplied the coffee table's damage many times over. Twenty years ago he'd have already been on the mend. At fifty, the intervening days just meant more swelling.

Stu much preferred the cameras to the mirror. Everyone in the interrogation room got recorded fair and square, the images grainy and impersonal, the custody chain clear. And any review of the tapes? Restricted by law, all the names recorded as part of the court's official documents.

Raising a pant leg, he provided the camera a clear view of his shin as his fingers measured the lumps. The performance sent the air sucking through his teeth in a grimace, but anything that delayed parading before the lurkers was worth the pain.

The speaker crackled again. "Door opening, Mr. Pierce, you must take a chair."

Stu limped from his corner and assumed the required position—seated, feet flat, hands on the chair arms, table separating him from the door.

Angie glided across alternating black and white tiles to stop, feet centered, on a white square. The briefcase at her side slid in front as she grasped the handle with both hands and squeezed. "They shouldn't have put you here." She dropped her head and spoke to the black tile just beyond her toes. "Not in this place."

The door sealed shut with a magnetic click and the speaker crackled again. "Door secure. You may leave the chair." The red record light beneath each camera lens extinguished.

Stu remained seated and silent, searching what little he could see of her face. Angie's hair dangled along one cheek, the swollen side. Should've killed Uday.

"I used to threaten suspects with incarceration here." Angie's eyes left the tile and flitted over his hands and arms and face. "You look okay." Her hands turned white on the handle as she returned her gaze to the floor. "Please...tell me you're okay, Stu."

His move. Stu eased around the corner of the table, determined to hide any hint of pain. He crossed three tiles, stepping onto the black square in front of her. After several moments, he slipped his fingers beneath her chin and coaxed it upward. "Hi."

Angie closed her eyes, drew a deep breath and reopened. "Hi."

"I missed you." He pinched a lock of stray hair and wove it back in place. Beneath was heavy makeup. Careful of her bruises, he cupped her cheeks in his hands. "I miss...us." His thumbs smoothed out the crease between her eyes. "I'm okay, Angie."

She raised a shoulder and tilted her head, trapping his hand against her cheek. "I'm so...." Her voice broke with a sob.

Stu wrapped her up and folded her in. "I know, Angie. And it's all okay." He buried his face in her auburn waves. Breathed her deep. "Everything's okay."

She melted in stages. First her arms and shoulders went limp on his chest. Then her cheek fell against his collarbone, briefcase clunking to the floor. Her back arched and softened. She bent at the knees as her breathing went deep and rhythmic, each inhale matching his, her breasts pressing into his ribs.

Stu slid his feet wide to support her weight and relaxed to the rhythm of their lungs. There was so much good in Angie. He'd seen it. It was real. Trust could be regained. All his pain drained away. Even his shins stopped throbbing. He knew who they were fighting and why. Had a good wingman he could count on again. Flying side by side, checking six, they'd watch each other's backs. "No more secrets, Angie."

Her legs straightened as she shifted to support her own weight.

He lost the sensation of her breathing. Regretted speaking. But for the first time, in a long time, Stu felt whole and wanted Angie to know. "Feels good, doesn't it?" He kissed her hair. "We're on the same team now. We've got him."

Angie lifted her head. "It's not that simple."

Stu hugged her tight, sought to regain the rhythm. But each time he thought to inhale, she exhaled. "Angie, you called him a pedophile, a rapist, and a murderer."

Her body stiffened as if a drill sergeant had given an order.

Stuart slid his hands to Angie's shoulders and held her at arm's length. "We can end this…end him…get our lives back."

Slipping from his grasp, Angie picked up her briefcase and laid it on the table. "Stu, you nearly killed one bodyguard and crippled the other. Beat unconscious a prince of The Realm's Royal Family."

"I was rescuing my wife from a killer."

Angie opened her briefcase. "A jury decides what you were doing." She dropped a stack of papers on the table. "There's the list of charges."

"Angie, you have his DNA on the floor, and on the wine bottle. It's all over my clothes, for God's sake. Match them with the crimes."

"I already had his DNA under my fingernails."

"Angie, don't pretend your slap was some clever plan."

"Don't you pretend that a DNA sample fixes everything you

did."

All Stu's aches and pains came rushing back. He gave in to the throbbing, hobbled over black and white and black again. Used his hands on the corner of the table to help him around to the chair. "What about the damn computer attacks?" He slid his chair sideways to align Angie's body between him and the mirror. "And Bloodhound's research?"

"Mary's work isn't proof. More art than science. It's not like fingerprints. There's no formal precedence established."

"What about his threats?"

"They weren't all his."

"The emails and photographs. The letters. We'll dissect them with Bloodhound. There's got to be something there."

"Please, Stu, just leave it be. They're not fools." Angie tapped the stack of papers. "These charges are carefully crafted. The jury will never see, or hear anything…of Uday's threats…at your trial."

Stu picked up the papers and skimmed the litany of his crimes. "Fine." He tossed them back into her briefcase. "I get charged. You still go after him."

"They're offering a deal. Both sides drop everything. Blanket immunity for everyone."

"That's because they're scared. I can do time. Can Uday?"

"A couple months in a Thai prison isn't the kind of time we're talking about."

"Some things are worth the price, Angie."

"And you'll pay it for us both?" Angie slammed her briefcase closed and leaned over the table. "When did all our sins become yours, Stu?"

He glared up at her.

She didn't look away. For the first time since entering the room her eyes were steady.

All of their sins…his? Yes…she was right. He had claimed all their sins as his. But when? That was the puzzling part of her question, her accusation. When had he taken responsibility for everything? Not at "I do." That's when you agreed to share your sins. Not when she'd battled depression. They'd searched her childhood for the answers. And he certainly hadn't felt this way when he'd given her the charcoal bride. So when?

"You can't do this, Stu. It isn't fair."

"Open your eyes and look around you." Stu pointed over Angie's shoulder at the wall of glass. In the mirror, the black tiles appeared to float above the white. And a very squat Angie was perched atop a dark column while he was trapped on a white square one level down. "I believe we can agree that you're not some dwarf queen standing on a three-dimensional chessboard. So that means we're having a confidential legal discussion in front of a one-way mirror. I think we've left the great land of right and wrong far behind. And you can punish them for this, Angie. You can punish Uday. You're the lawyer. Not me. This...." Stu lifted both hands toward the ceiling, then swung an arc at the surrounding walls and finished by pointing at the floor. "This is what I can do."

"Stu, it took me two full days of fighting the system just to get in here. Both of our esteemed senators were unavailable. And our congressman insisted on meeting with the oil lobbyists before he'd talk with me. We didn't speak long. Everyone wants this to go away."

"The man committed crimes, Angie. He can get away with them only if the D.A. allows it."

"It's all rolling down from above, Stu. The Realm appointed Prince Azwad to a diplomatic post and the Administration asked the State Department to expedite his paperwork. The D.A. has bowed out. Said he would concede to the desires of the presiding judge."

Stu worked his jaw muscles, grinding his teeth audibly. "And what does 'His Honor' desire?"

"Judge Price wants..."

"Price...Judge Price? You're joking?"

"No, I'm not." Angie looked at the floor. "He wants what most judges do. A chance to right the wrongs, fix broken laws, make history. Judge Price wants a nomination to a higher court."

Stu shook his head. "And the Administration nominates."

"And Congress appoints." Angie nodded.

"Separate but equal, huh Angie? Do you suppose the founding fathers would approve?" Stu eyeballed the mirror. "'My country, 'tis of thee...sweet land of liberty'...as long as you're singing the right song."

"Judge Price wants an answer today," Angie responded.

Stu rubbed his temples. "And what do you want, Angie?"

"If you buck the judge," Angie tapped her briefcase, "and are convicted of these charges, do you think he'll be lenient?"

"And what about all those girls, and their families?"

"I can't change what happened to those girls."

"And our daughter? She still mentions Nancy sometimes. Would Maggie be proud of us, Angie?"

"I can only help women who are still alive."

"You twist our lives around, risk everything and everyone, to chase this madman. Then you want to pretend it doesn't matter."

Angie rested her hands on the handle of her briefcase. "So you'll make a life here. Conjugal visits? Is that what you have in mind?"

"I'm willing to stay here and finish him, but you want me out. Everything...always...the way you want it. When did all our dreams become only yours, Angie?"

She drummed the leather beneath her fingers. "I want you out of prison."

"No, Angie, you want me in yours."

She picked up her briefcase and walked to the door, pushed the buzzer for exit. "What should I tell the judge?"

"Tell him...I'll think it over."

Angie pounded on the door, "I just want you home, Stu," and buzzed again. "I miss us too."

The speaker crackled. "Door opening."

Stu listened for the magnetic click before he limped back to his corner. He stared at the chessboard floor. Administration, Congress, courts. Every powerful piece had moved against him. What were the rules to three-dimensional chess?

CHAPTER THIRTY

With her toes set six inches from the glass wall, Angie leaned forward, kneecaps pinning her briefcase against the back of the mirror. Like a confessor awaiting penance, she bowed her head. Her forehead touched the glass. Cool and smooth, it felt good, drawing the heat from her skin.

Stu's parting words. A prison? Was that what she'd made of their life? Championing the burqa was her choice. Sala, her deceit. Even moving to a country home was her idea, not his.

The move placed Stu twenty minutes farther from the airport. Yet he never complained. At the beginning of each month he gave her a detailed copy of his schedule. When was the last time she'd picked a trip and gone along to explore a new city together and lie with him at night, seeing and feeling his world?

"Come away from the mirror, Angie."

Her fingers whitened on the handle of her briefcase. "Why?"

"Your body introduces heat…inconsistent backlight. You change the reflectivity. He'll see a shadow."

"He's not an idiot, Tom. He knows someone's watching." Angie rolled her forehead over the glass, cooling temple, then cheek. She peered through the one-way mirror and down the length of the wall. Only Stu's feet and elbows were visible. "No worries, Tom. I've backed him into the corner."

"He put himself there, Angie. Long before you ever walked into that room."

"All by himself, did he?" Angie turned from the mirror to face Gramps. "No help from us?"

"Us?" Gramps raised his eyebrows. "All I did was answer his

questions."

Angie marched straight at him, stopping inches from his face. "Then I can do the same."

"You needn't answer what he never asked," Gramps replied.

"Do you really think I need you explaining how to nuance truth?" Stepping past him, she stopped at the observation room's exit. Six steps down the checkered hallway would take her to a closed door leading back through security. Immediately on her left was the locked door that led to Stu.

"Go ahead then. Push the buzzer. Let Stu know you're suspicious that Uday has bought everyone from judge to congressman."

"I've got much more than simple suspicions, Tom."

"And for what? Do you really see your husband, Angie? A man like Stuart Pierce doesn't happily honor shades of gray. Tell him what you've discovered and he'll never take the deal."

"He's not a suspect to manipulate. I can't play games with him anymore. I won't."

"Before you embrace this...born-again honesty, ask yourself what Uday's wealth can buy in this prison. Too many people with nothing to lose. You'd be killing Stu."

"And what am I doing now, Tom?"

"Slowing things down, buying time."

"At what price? I'm torturing him."

"Time is hope," Gramps offered.

She lowered her head toward the black and white tiles. They looked like a hopscotch court. Sister Constance Ruth would demand that Angie's feet touch only the white. "Tom. Stu's phone call...his questions. Why didn't you come to me?"

Gramps placed a hand on her shoulder. "Why didn't he, Angie?"

She spun from beneath his grasp and swung her hand, stopping a fraction from his face.

Gramps didn't flinch. "Why, Angie?" His eyes shifted from examining her upraised hand to staring into her eyes. "Why couldn't Stu come to you?"

Her shaking hand formed a fist and dropped.

"You're saving his life," Tom said.

"Am I?" Angie unclenched her hand. "Is that what I'm doing? Because it feels like I'm just lying to him. Again."

"What about Andrew?" Tom asked. "The offer to keep him out of Afghanistan…turn that around and…"

"I know…it's not just an offer." Angie waited for her chin to stop quivering. "It's also a veiled threat." Uday had offered to send word to the country of Angie's choosing. Within twenty-four hours a request would arrive at U.S. Army headquarters requesting Second Lieutenant Andrew Pierce as special military attaché to that country. Turn down the offer and what word would Uday send to Afghanistan?

"You could tell Stu about the offer," Tom suggested.

"It wouldn't matter. Stu would insist on talking to Andrew. In the end, they'd settle on honor."

"But the boy could save his father's life."

"Andrew would see it as killing Stu's honor, killing Stu. Honor is life to those two."

"Your son would choose to go into Afghanistan with a bounty on his head?"

"Yes."

"Just like his father," Gramps said.

"No," Angie sighed. "That part's more me."

"Well then, Angie, the only way for you to save them both is to keep to the plan."

"You mean lie."

"Yes."

A tapping sound came from the mirror. Stu seemed to stare straight at them through the glass. "So we let a murderer walk free?" Stu asked, his jaw muscles bulging like Angie had never seen before. He walked around the table and picked up a chair. "Uday makes us all worse than we are." Stu hurled it at the mirror. "Makes us worse, because we let him."

Angie shielded her eyes as the chair bounced off.

Gramps reached out and lowered her arm. "It's an inch thick. Special glass. Like you said, Stu's not an idiot. He knows he can't break it."

The overhead speaker crackled. "Please take a seat, Mr. Pierce."

Stuart laughed. "I'll need my chair then." He picked up the chair and swung it hard against the mirror.

Another crackle. "Mr. Pierce, unless you take a seat, we'll be forced to restrain you."

Stu slammed the chair into the mirror.

Angie pressed her hand against the glass and felt the impact of Stu's rage. "Promise me, Tom. Give me your word that someday Stu will see Uday receive justice."

The chair slammed against the mirror again.

"Uday...is my only mission, Angie."

She looked at Gramps and nodded, then turned and, stepping on both black and white tiles, she slipped past the inrushing guards.

CHAPTER THIRTY-ONE

"**A**re you a payer…or a player? Either way, you've got to make Mr. Rudy happy."

Stu swallowed a bite of well-chewed cornbread and washed it down with milk. "You're a cryptic fellow, Mr.…?" Stu waited for the refrigerator-sized man to fill in the blank, but got only a frown. "Does this cafeteria always serve rock-hard cornbread?"

"Mr. Rudy sent me for an answer."

"How about a trade? You answer my question and I'll answer yours." Stu set down his milk. "How many boards do they stack in three-dimensional chess?"

Clearly, the Refrigerator was confused. He shifted from left leg to right and back.

Something wrong with the big man's left leg, Stu observed. Ankle, knee, or hip? Needing more information, he quickly spun around in his chair.

The Refrigerator stepped back and set a wide stance, his hands forming fists, his weight mostly on his right leg.

That left ankle should bend more, Stu decided. It either couldn't or was injured. Either way—vulnerable. Stu raised his open palms in surrender. "Relax. Here's an easier one. What do you make of the floor?"

"The floor? That's a stupid question."

"No, it just seems stupid because you have no idea what aspect I'm referencing. I could mean the concrete, the brown stain, or the polyurethane finish. Heck, I might be asking if it's level, or too slippery, or too cold, and so forth and so on. The trouble is my question's ill defined. One might say cryptic. Just like yours."

"Not my question. It's Mr. Rudy's."

"Well, let's go talk to Rudy then."

"That's Mr. Rudy to you. And Mr. Rudy doesn't ask his questions. I do."

"Seems like a needlessly cumbersome arrangement fraught with potential misunderstanding."

The Refrigerator shifted back and forth. "Mr. Rudy wants his answer today."

Stu scratched his forehead and smirked. "Your Mr. Rudy will have to wait in line. He's not the first to demand an answer from me today."

The Refrigerator's eyes flashed to the far end of the room and back. "Who? Was he a tall skinny guy, most of his right ear missing?"

"Calm down. I'm talking about my wife. But like your Mr. Rudy, she sees only one correct answer to her question. She's not always right, though." Stu rubbed his temples. Angie was dead wrong about one thing. Surviving a few months in a Thai prison had thoroughly educated him about inmate psychology. Like receiving a PhD in canine behavior. Stu looked up at the Refrigerator. "Does Mr. Rudy play chess? Maybe he knows the three-dimensional rules."

The Refrigerator spoke through bared teeth. "Last time I'm asking."

"Okay. Take it easy." Stu thumbed over his shoulder at the far end of the room. "Tell Mr. Rudy that old One-Ear back there wants to know what he makes of the floor."

"What's that supposed to mean?"

"I don't know, but it doesn't sound like 'Mr. One-Ear' is respecting Mr. Rudy. Nope. Sounds pretty damn insulting to me."

Stu scanned the room as the Refrigerator returned to Mr. Rudy for further guidance. Out of the four guards who walked the catwalk above, only one focused on Stu's unfolding drama. The same guard whose face expressed such disappointment after rushing into the interrogation room and discovering Stu seated, feet flat on the floor, hands open and palms up on top of the table. The guard had raised his baton above Stu's head, then glanced at the cameras and scowled. He was scowling right now as he watched the Refrigerator walk back to the corner and converse with Mr. Rudy. So did that make him Mr. Rudy's man, or just a guard with an attitude?

More three-dimensional chess, Stu thought. Damn hard to keep track of the pieces. Or follow all the moves. Today was his first exposed to the general prison populace. Same day he received the offer. A good move—here's the carrot-offer, and now here's the Mr. Rudy-stick. So how should he counter that move?

Skull tattoos proliferated on Mr. Rudy's side of the room. Some sort of flag tattoo dominated One-Ear's side. Both types of body art thinned out toward the middle where Stu sat.

Good place to play Switzerland—too much trouble for too little gain. He just needed to show some hackles and teeth for a day or so until he figured things out. This deal of Angie's made no more sense now than an hour ago. Judges wanting appointments to higher courts was expected. And district attorneys always worked to smooth their path to a political office. Every congressman lived and breathed for campaign funds. But Uday? Why would he agree? Uday could return to The Realm and ignore the pleas for extradition forever.

Over in the corner, Mr. Rudy looked irritated. Like a dog on the hunt, he had his nose in the air, pointed across the room at One-Ear. He rose, and two others went to heel on each side of him.

Just like Thailand, Stu labeled each by his dominant features. Mr. Rudy, sleek and well groomed, definitely a Doberman. On his right, stocky with a squished-in face, a Bulldog. To Rudy's left, a solid man with a big smile, a Rottweiler. And bringing up the rear, the man simply too big for any label but Refrigerator. They looked like the typical prison pack coming to piss on their territory.

Mr. Rudy stopped to mark Stu. "My associate says you want to know the color of the floor."

Stu ignored Mr. Rudy, addressing the Refrigerator instead. "Just as I thought. You see what I mean about cumbersome and fraught with misunderstanding?" Stu made an exaggerated frown and slowly shook his head. "Now tell Rudy that's not what I said."

Mr. Rudy stepped between Stu and the Refrigerator. "People around here speak of me as Mr. Rudy, or they soon have trouble speaking at all. Now, why don't you just tell me what O'Donnell said?"

Stu pointed at the Refrigerator. "Well, O'Donnell here said something about playing you. So I asked him if you knew the rules to three-dimensional chess. Then…"

Mr. Rudy raised his voice. "I don't give a shit what this idiot behind me said. I want to know—"

"If you think O'Donnell's an idiot, why do you care what he says?"

Mr. Rudy nearly shouted as he jabbed his thumb back toward the Refrigerator. "He's not O'Donnell. The one-eared son of a bitch is O'Donnell."

Behind him, Stu heard several chairs scraping the concrete. A quick glance showed that at least three flag tattoos had swung around from their tables and moved to the edge of their seats.

Mr. Rudy lowered his head and stared each of them down.

"Look, Mr. Rudy, perhaps we've gotten off on the wrong foot here. Introductions might help." Stu offered a handshake. "I'm Stuart Pierce."

Mr. Rudy sneered at Stu's hand and bent forward until he was a bare three inches from his face. "No, you're not."

"I'm not?"

"No, you're a smart ass. And the only thing I want you to understand is if you don't pay, then I sell you for play. Protection money from that juicy little piece of meat came to visit you today, or from a rich uncle. I don't give a shit. But you pay me every week, or I rent out your ass. And that ain't no tricky use of the word, smart guy." Mr. Rudy pointed at Stu's chair seat. "I mean rent out your ass, just like I'm your pimp. Except you don't get no cut of the money."

Stu raised his voice. "I'll pay. Pay plenty. Do I pay you or Mr. O'Donnell?"

Mr. Rudy smiled over at the flags collecting along the tables. "You think I don't know you're considering a deal, Mr. Pierce. That you could be out of here in a day or two. You want to rile up the flags. Stall for time. You misread my world. I'm not King Rudy. I'm Mr. Rudy. More like the President. This room is mostly like Democrats and Republicans with a few Independents that pay for protection." Mr. Rudy looked at the catwalk above. "Up there. Well, that's my judicial branch. New man. But he's real smart. I just hired him yesterday. And we're all saying you've got to pay or play."

Stu's heart pounded six beats up and six down. "So...you see this as my new country, and your whole system of government is stacked against me." He checked the position of the nearest ceiling camera. Scooted his chair back a few inches to afford the lens a clear view. "I see it different, Rudy." Like a hitchhiker, Stu poked his thumb back over his shoulder. "The flags see it different, too." Stu put his feet flat on the floor, placed hands on knees and rotated palms open and facing up toward the camera. When this thing went down, the tape would show him completely innocent. "I've been screwing you ever since you walked up. You're just too stupid to see it. You're my bitch, Rudy. But you're a lousy lay. So, go fuck yourself."

Rudy lunged for Stu's throat, but fell to the floor choking.

Stuart let the momentum from his knuckled stroke to Rudy's Adam's apple carry him forward. Sliding from the chair, he jammed his heel into the Refrigerator's left ankle.

A pop, and the Refrigerator crashed beneath his own enormous weight. Rottweiler produced a shank and stuck it into Stu's left shoulder as Bulldog charged.

The charge was a godsend, pushing Stu backward and pulling the shank from his shoulder. He rolled backward to the ground and kicked, and kept rolling a complete somersault, finally returning to his feet.

The flags joined in from the left and the skulls from the right. Alarms blared. Canisters of tear gas popped open on the floor.

From the back of the room, where Stu retreated, he looked up at the catwalk.

Rudy's judicial branch stared down at him, shaking his head.

Stu cupped his hands around his mouth and yelled above the din, "Tell the Prince I'll keep his cell warm."

Still moving his head side to side, Rudy's man set his weapon down, tossed his cap to the floor below and departed. Real guards don't do that.

Stu was willing to bet that the man started working here the day they tossed him into his cell. And that Rudy was surprised when he'd been bought for so little. So who did that guard really work for? The D.A.? Judge Price? Really didn't matter. Everyone worked for Uday. Three-dimensional chess might be easier than it first appeared. A phone call to Angie wasn't necessary. Everyone would soon hear he'd rejected the deal.

More guards arrived and shot another round of canisters into the fray.

Coughing began near Stu. He hacked at the gas entering his lungs. As his eyes started watering, he wondered if he'd look better wearing a flag or a skull.

Stu wiped the blood flowing down his arm. Either way, he'd have to pick the meanest dog in the pack and kick his ass, or become a gang play toy. Damn shoulder better heal fast.

CHAPTER THIRTY-TWO

Taamir circled the foot of Uday's hospital bed, placing himself directly behind Roger Walters's chair and pointing at his computer tablet.

"Excuse the interruption, Roger. But evidently Taamir has information he feels can't wait."

Roger's eyes remained locked on the chessboard. "You haven't come this close to beating me since college." He slid a bishop forward to block Uday's queen. "I think you and Taamir are attempting to distract me."

Uday plucked the queen's rook from its corner and reached across the board.

Roger held up his hand, signaling stop. "This is why you always lose to me. Take a little time to consider your moves. Just like pulling out of my bank—such a rash act."

"Not rash at all. I gave you several options for keeping my money."

"Yes, each of them ethically unpalatable if not outright illegal."

"Legal. Illegal. Quaintly nationalistic notions in a world dominated by multinational corporations, don't you think? Perhaps your bank should employ lawyers with more global vision." With a wave of the rook, Uday motioned Taamir to speak and stretched his hand toward the far side of the chessboard.

"Excellency, our representative reports that your generous offer was rejected."

In the air above the board, Uday's hand froze. "Rejected?"

"The report is detailed, Excellency. I'd characterize the manner of his rejection as utter disdain." Taamir laid his tablet at the base of the chessboard.

Uday skimmed the half-page summary, retracted his arm and plunked the rook back down in its corner. "Well, Roger. I must admit to feeling more than a little rash right at this very moment." He pressed his head against the pillows supporting him. "You're the chairman of one of the world's most powerful banks, a captain of the business world. What's your advice?"

Roger's index finger drew lines through the air, tracing out the rook's potential lines of attack before answering. "Annihilation."

"Now who's rash? Such finality, without knowing a single detail?"

"In this case, the details don't matter. Your expression at hearing Taamir's news indicates you were taken by surprise. Very rare for you, my old friend. Your opponent is obviously unpredictable. That's dangerous. I assume you offered a prize."

"Yes."

"And made clear the consequences of rejecting that prize."

"He is well aware."

"Then annihilate him…or he'll cost you."

"I'm reminded of my father. You and he are kindred spirits, Roger. I think he'd advise the same."

"Kindred? He never seemed to like me much."

"Well enough, Roger. He liked you well enough. America is what he didn't like. My father cares only for sand…and annihilation." Uday snatched up his rook and set the piece six squares down its file. "Here's your big chance, Roger. Explain how you'd handle my problem. Perhaps that will restore my confidence in your bank."

Roger looked up from the chessboard. "The strategy's always the same. Find out what a man craves most and give it to him. Then give him more." He slid a pawn two squares forward, threatening Uday's rook, then leaned back and folded his hands in his lap. "Here's a simple example. If a factory worker wants a quiet little home, lend him enough to buy a mansion. More than he can handle. Soon you'll own both him and the mansion. Works the same for entire companies. Even small nations. I assure you, this tactic works."

"Sounds like what almost caused your entire banking system to collapse," Uday said.

"We did fine," Roger smiled.

"You mean, you did fine. Your bank didn't." Uday bypassed the pawn. "Check."

"I can't believe I fell for that. You're the devil, Uday. Tempting me with your riches." One by one, Roger lifted and considered a rook, a knight, and his queen, rejecting them all and finally committing his bishop to a blocking position.

Uday attacked with a knight. "Check."

"Damn. Who's been coaching you?"

"What do you think of Mr. Walters's advice, Taamir? What does our man crave?"

"Right now, I would've thought his free...." Taamir's eyes darted a glance at Roger. "The freedom to determine his own future, Excellency. But his response to your offer indicates otherwise."

"Yes, it's obviously much more than freedom." Uday lowered his head in thought. The Ironman had shown no fear. Why? Probably the same reason any man is fearless. He feels powerful. Again, the same question—why? Trapped in prison, awaiting prosecution, assailed on all sides and yet still unbowed. The man was an enigma.

Roger knocked over Uday's knight, replacing it with his queen. "Your move."

Following Roger's recommendation meant reinforcing the Ironman's illusion of power. Then crushing him with it. "You've provided sound advice, Roger. Thank you." From the end of the board Uday sliced his bishop diagonally and captured Roger's queen. "And thank you again. Check."

"Giving you advice seems to have cost me everything." Roger stood up, leaning low over the board.

"Not yet. The game's not over."

"I can read a chessboard. How about restoring your confidence in my bank? How am I doing there?" Roger castled, altering the positions of both king and rook.

Uday pointed at the door. "Taamir, please give us a few minutes. And let's take Roger's advice. Give our man what he craves. Begin by calling our associates and have all the legal issues dropped. Make it clear. I want him released from any...constraints. Immediately."

"Yes, Excellency." Taamir bowed his head and disappeared.

"Your bank lacks reserves, Roger. And I own far too many shares of America's Airways. The airline's future is lackluster, my money languishes. Selling all my shares at once would collapse the stock price, unless a determined buyer emerged. What if I arranged for a major infusion to your capital reserves in exchange for your bank supporting my exit from the airline? Buy the stock as I sell?"

"Again, Uday, what you suggest is…questionable. How big an infusion?"

Greed is such an amazing motivator, Uday reflected. Wonder how greedy? Two billion, maybe three? "How much do you want?" he asked, retreating his bishop.

"Five billion. No paper trail. Handshake agreement."

Impressively greedy. Roger's bank must be in more trouble than Uday had suspected. "Let's make it ten billion. You'll need a lot of cash reserves to support my stock sale." Uday stuck out his hand.

Roger's hand shot out and grasped hold. "Pleasure, my old friend." He stepped back from the board and bent at the waist, eyeballing each piece. "Now how do I get myself out of this mess?"

When Taamir returned, Roger was still bent over, studying his predicament. "Mr. Walters's advice is fully implemented, Excellency. All constraints lifted within the next hour."

"Thank you, Taamir. Our business here went well also. Now, what do you think of Mr. Walters's position?"

"Very precarious, Excellency."

Roger straightened and pushed his rook the length of the board, sliding right through the spot vacated by Uday's bishop. "Check."

Uday castled.

Roger pounced, hopping a knight to the attack. "Checkmate! Taamir, I'd have thought you better at spotting traps."

Uday clapped.

Roger wagged his finger in admonition. "As I said, my old friend, you're impetuous and rash. Not good qualities in a forty-year-old."

Uday tried smiling, but the result was more a sneer, only half his face responding due to the numbing anesthetics. "Taamir, now that Roger and I have settled our business in such fine fashion, it's time to sever our Afghan connections. We must take control of…those assets. Put them to work here in America."

"Yes, Excellency."

"Selling all your airline stock, Uday?" Roger interjected. "Putting Afghani assets to work in America? Sounds like you're pooling your resources for something big. My bank would love to play a role."

"You will, my friend. I promise."

"What area? Energy? Tech?"

"Call it...." Uday searched his mind for a playful way to describe destroying the Mullah and seizing direct control of his terrorist cells. "Telecom."

"Telecom covers a lot of ground, most of it heavily regulated," Roger commented. "Your every move scrutinized by some government. There are safer plays to make."

"No, telecom it is," Uday replied. "But more specifically...."

"Cellular networks, Excellency?" Taamir suggested.

"Yes, Taamir, cellular networks. Perfect. But there's a troubling old man in the way, Roger."

"A hostile takeover then." Roger smiled.

"Very," Uday nodded his head. "Taamir, pass the specific objectives to our contact here in Washington. Let him handle the...what was your term, Roger?"

"Annihilation?"

"Yes, have Washington handle the annihilation."

"Smart move, Uday, keep your hands clean."

"Thank you, Roger." Uday sneered a smile.

CHAPTER THIRTY-THREE

She plied her trade as whores do. The stroll, the pose, the promise. A shake of her head and the Cadillac drove off.

Hosaam lifted his foot from the brake and rolled forward to keep her in sight.

A hand slapped the hood of his cab. "Hey! Ali Baba." The man glared through the windshield. "Keep it out of the crosswalk, will you, buddy?"

Hosaam resisted the temptation to glare back and instead forced a submissive nod. He backed up a few meters, snugged the tires against the curb, and shifted the gear lever into park. Straight ahead, across the street, was the alley where she took most of her clients. To the right, the city block she always walked and the pristine tree-lined avenue she never crossed. The Washington police didn't bother women who walked the dirty streets, the streets tourists didn't frequent.

The rear door opened. A bearded man slid onto the backseat.

"I'm off duty, Sir."

"Then you should extinguish your light, Hosaam."

Hosaam's eyes flashed to the mirror. The man's face was gaunt. So thin his thick beard and bushy eyebrows were all Hosaam could clearly make out. "My name is Yusef," Hosaam countered, smacking the toggle switch that turned off the cab available light.

The man pecked like a starving chicken upon his tablet. "Ah yes, I thought so. Yusef is poor dead Faiq's little brother, my report says. Hard to leave it all back at home, isn't it, Hosaam?" The man rapped at the clear plastic divide and held up a large envelope.

Sliding aside a small window, Hosaam pulled it through. The

envelope was sealed in ancient fashion, twine coiled about a thin button and dripped in wax, impressed with a signet stamp.

"Open it."

Hosaam studied the signet impression: crossed spears above a five-pointed star.

"Take your time. Trace it if you wish. The symbols are old, Hosaam. Long ago, their meaning lost to all but a select few. Long before the Prophet walked the earth."

Hosaam pulled the end of the twine. The wax cracked and crumbled to his lap. Inside were three small slips of paper stapled to an aerial photo. Each slip bore an address written in Arabic. The photo depicted the Mullah's compound, bomb cratered, the buildings reduced to rubble.

Hosaam tried to ignore the photo. "Where can I take you?" His hand shook as he pointed at the addresses.

"A better question is where can your benefactor take you? The Mullah is dead. You're alone."

Hosaam reached for the handle and threw open the door.

"Such cowardice from a man so fond of feeding dogs to dogs?"

Hosaam paused, hand still on the door.

"Your benefactor said I should tell you he has no desire to limit the number of heads you might sever."

Hosaam closed the door. "And who is my benefactor?"

"The man who lifted the severed head beside the Mullah's fire. The man who will support you here in America. A man with a task for you."

"Why should I believe the Mullah is dead?"

"When did you last receive any communication from him?"

"We were told contact would be sparse."

"Call your contact number, if you like, but an automated voice will answer, informing you that the number you are trying to reach has been disconnected."

Hosaam reached for his cell.

"And while you're calling, look at these." Another envelope fell onto the seat next to him.

Inside were close up photos of the Mullah and several members of his inner circle. All wore the familiar mantle of blood and gray. All quite dead.

"And how would my benefactor come upon such evidence?"

"He has vast resources at his disposal." The man pulled a wad of cash from his suit pocket. "Resources at your disposal, as long as you understand that he's your mullah now."

"And what does my new mullah desire of me?"

"Much the same as the old one."

"The death of America?"

"Your new mullah's wants are more modest, more attainable in the near term, a mere humbling. He desires Americans see themselves as they truly are. Much like young A'shadieeyah standing over there, the one you watch with such vigor. Dressed in her colorful clothes and smelling of exotic perfumes, she still knows what she is."

"My benefactor seems to know everything about me. Shouldn't I know of him?"

"You need only know how to mete death and destruction."

"Blind trust?"

The man stroked his beard. "Perhaps Kashif or Abbud would need less information?"

Hosaam twisted around and nodded.

The man reached through the window and dropped various denominations onto the seat. "Five thousand dollars. Plenty of phantom fare money. Much more than you'll need." He glanced at A'shadieeyah. "Take the night off and scout the addresses. Return here, if you like. She's from Pakistan. Along the Indian border, the city of Lahore, I believe." He opened his door.

"She prostitutes," Hosaam growled.

"Visit with her or not, Hosaam. But don't stalk her so often. Makes you predictable." The bearded one slammed the door and disappeared toward the cleaner avenues.

Across the street another car slowed. A'shadieeyah turned and stared into the windshield. The car stopped. They all did, that first time. For A'shadieeyah's stare startled. Her pupils—broad black pools swirling. Her irises—bold blue waves raging. Her whites—thin low banks constricting. A'shadieeyah's eyes begged, "Unleash my storm."

Around those eyes she wore a veil of many colors draped in proper desert fashion. Yet below her headdress was a robe too sheer, wrapped too tight. Her curves were rich and full, soft mounds sculpting the gown with the tease of flesh. Jasmine, she called herself.

Hosaam called her lost. And America was much the same. Masked in a finery of verdant green lawns and shimmering white stone, it lied. There were no riches here, only fool's gold, freedoms that led to chaos, tolerance that corrupted the soul.

Their National Mall was mere blocks away. Bracketed by a bearded giant on the west and a phallic tower on the east, the lawns between were lined with the graven images of conquering crusaders. False idols for the followers of Shaitan. Washington was filthy, vulgar, a blasphemy.

A'shadieeyah shook her head and the car sped away.

What was she saying no to? What wouldn't she do? In America, even whores seemed to have a choice.

Hosaam studied the slips of paper. The first address was a mystery. The next was in the Virginia countryside, a long drive. The last was Daingerfield Island, just south of Washington Reagan International Airport. If his benefactor sought to humble America, it was a good place to start.

A black Mercedes stopped. There was always a steady supply of cars. And Hosaam knew why. She invited pleasure without pain, connection without commitment, fulfillment without judgment. Some only came to talk of their deceits, confess their worst sins to one who could forgive. A'shadieeyah forgave everyone, everything. How could she not?

She entered the black Mercedes. Maybe this was someone who just wanted to talk. The car rolled forward and turned into the alley. Some time in the next half hour, the car would leave, and five minutes after that, A'shadieeyah would walk from the alley, adjust and tighten her veil.

The car's rear bumper commenced a gentle bounce. Hosaam dropped the slips of paper. He grabbed his mother's purse from the glove compartment and pulled out the cord.

How long could he watch A'shadieeyah drown in this cesspool of the Great Satan? She needed someone strong. A person who cared. Hosaam could rescue her right now. Meet her in the alley after the car departed and save her soul. He wound the knotted cord around his hands and snapped it taut.

It was quick. The grind, the sweat, the spew finished, the car bumper grew still. White reverse lights illuminated. The black Mercedes backed up and drove away.

Minutes later, A'shadieeyah walked from the alley, securing her headdress.

Hosaam's hands paralleled her movements. She lifted the loose fabric—he lifted a loose bit of cord, wrapping it round his hand. She draped the cloth over her shoulder—Hosaam draped the rope over his other hand and wound it tight. She adjusted the veil to cover her nose and reached behind her head, pulling it snug. In perfect timing with her pull, Hosaam jerked his hands apart, the knotted cord popping with a twang, a twang strong enough to snap her neck and free her soul. Next time.

A'shadieeyah waved away two more cars.

Hosaam flung the knotted cord to the floor. He had fewer choices than a whore. Picking up the addresses, he shifted into drive, and drove off to pursue his new mullah's biddings.

CHAPTER THIRTY-FOUR

Stu drummed his fingers on the police inspector's desk. Where was the man? He'd promised good news by the time he moved offices. Well, the walls were barren but for empty nails, the desktop deserted except for a few skittering balls of dust and the inspector's wooden name block—Kennedy.

After rubbing his dry eyes raw, and then stifling another yawn, Stu went back to drumming. More than three weeks of hard work had passed since he'd demanded Angie drive him straight from prison to the police station. Inside, he filed an official complaint against Uday Azwad for assault and battery. And with the first of his retaliatory strikes completed, he pushed out through the police station's doors, stopped beneath the gray lamplight and checked his watch. Five minutes before midnight. Not bad. A successful attack launched within four hours of his prison release.

Of course, released was a polite way to think of it. Hell, he'd been kicked out. They couldn't process him fast enough. He was taken straight from the blood-washed cafeteria floor to the infirmary. A man in a white lab coat flushed his eyes of tear gas, checked his lungs, stitched up the stab wound, injected him full of antibiotics and stuffed a ten-day supply of pills into his pocket. Never even introduced himself as a doctor. Thirty minutes later, the gates shut behind him. He waited for over an hour in the cold night air before Angie drove up.

But he was plenty warm, basking in the afterglow of his triumph. Forced Uday's game from chess to poker. Called his bluff. Went all in with the only chip he had to wager—his life.

And Uday folded. Each time Stu grew fatigued over the past few weeks, recalling those victorious moments sent his blood surging, as it surged right now. Uday Azwad was not untouchable.

Inspector Kennedy had proved himself the perfect man to ensure Uday got touched. Initially cool and distant, he'd grown focused and fervent after concluding his preliminary investigation. Called back day after day as Stu laid out all he knew of Uday. The inspector was thorough, pumping Stu for how he'd uncovered so many obscure details about The Realm's Prince. He wanted to know the specific source of each of Stu's facts. Kept repeating that in order to land the big one you needed lots of bait.

Unfortunately, Stu'd had to mislead the inspector. Couldn't give up anything on Gramps or Bloodhound. Instead, he insisted the computer skills were his. And since Kennedy kept coming back to this same topic, Stu spent every free hour pursuing a crash course in computer hacking. With Bloodhound's guidance, he was gaining quite a knowledge base. Each time he spoke with Kennedy, he hit him with a new piece of hacking lingo. Today, Stu brought along "quadruple bucky." Simply meant pressing all four of the shift keys on Bloodhound's custom keyboard while still typing...

"Mr. Pierce, is it?"

Stu's drumming fingers snapped straight out, knocking Kennedy's name block to the floor.

"Hello, I'm Patrolman Malloy." The young patrolman retrieved the block from the black and white tiles and stuck out a hand. "Good to meet you."

Stu grabbed and shook.

Patrolman Malloy tried out Kennedy's chair as he examined the wooden block. "I wonder why Kennedy left his name plate behind?" He pulled open the center drawer and found it empty. Then opened each of the others. "Guy didn't leave me so much as a stub of a pencil or a scrap of paper. Just this piece of wood." After tossing the nameplate into the top drawer, he slammed them all shut. "Sorry, Mr. Pierce. I just need to grab something to take your statement."

"My statement?"

"Yeah. You're the guy got in a bar fight, right? Some coward smacked your wife around?"

Stu snapped to his feet. "Where's he at?" Leaning over the desk, he jabbed his finger down at the drawer containing the inspector's name block. "Where's Kennedy?"

The patrolman leaned away from him. "Take it easy, Mr. Pierce. I thought the situation had already been explained. Some sort of screw up by IT. Whenever someone leaves the department, files are transferred, passwords are changed, lots of security procedures. Apparently, your case was accidently deleted. But don't worry, the department's going to make it right. I've been assigned to you exclusively. We'll get this guy."

"Where…is…Kennedy?" Stu growled.

"He's gone. Landed a job at some international security company. More than twice the pay, I heard. Can't blame him. Heck, that's more than the chief makes."

Stu placed both hands on the front edge of the desk and slowly lowered himself to the chair.

"Mr. Pierce. Are you okay?"

"The seal."

"Excuse me?"

Stu pointed at the desk drawer again. "Kennedy's name block bears the D.C. Police emblem. He left it behind because he's through using it."

"Yeah, but you'd think he'd take it with. You know, as a memento."

"Kennedy took what he wanted."

The patrolman shrugged. "Guess you're right."

"Officer Malloy. Do patrolmen usually get assigned detective work?"

"Sorry…didn't mean to confuse you, Mr. Pierce. Just didn't feel right about jumping ahead. I officially take off the blues and don the sport coat at midnight tonight. Kennedy's good fortune is my ticket up."

Stu tilted his head back, closed his eyes and started massaging the back of his neck. The fatigue was overwhelming, felt like he could just collapse in the corner and not move for days. Too many restless nights, plagued by ill-defined dreams…starts and stops, snippets of images hinted at, but not yet fully formed. He'd broken free of one nightmare only to find himself trapped in another. Maybe that's what this new dream had tried to presage, some part of his subconscious trying to tell him that all of Kennedy's dutiful enthusiasm had come way too easy. The manipulative prick simply needed lots of bait to land a high-paying job.

So Uday had struck back. What did he expect? Deal with it, he scolded himself. He still had two more meetings today and...

"Mr. Pierce, you sure you don't want a cup of coffee...an aspirin, maybe?"

Stu opened his eyes. "No...I'm fine. Just tired. And congratulations on your promotion."

"Thanks. Now sit tight while I find something to take notes with." Malloy hustled off.

Stu waited until he disappeared down the hall, then headed for the stairs.

Outside the police station, he found the nearest diner and stepped inside. "Coffee. Black." The waitress slid over a cup and saucer. Slopped in some coffee. Steam rose toward Stu's face. He stuck his nose close above the cup's rim and filled his nostrils.

Okay, he'd acted the naïve fool. A smart man would have expected a counterattack. After all, the elaborate deal he'd been offered in prison meant that Uday's money had wound up in countless pockets, everyone from senators to prison guards.

Stu sipped the coffee. "Got anything a little fresher?" he asked the waitress.

"Just made it," she replied and turned away.

Stu added a spoonful of sugar and stirred. Obviously, calling Uday's bluff had only thrown the Prince off his game for a few moments. This was chess again. And for every move Stu made, Uday seemed to make eight. Battling him was like playing three-dimensional chess against a gilded octopus, the Prince's golden tentacles stretching out and curling around several pieces at once, Kennedy just a cheaply-bought pawn. Stu took another sip of coffee. Still harsh. He reached for the cream.

Doubtless, the inspector had sold Uday every last bit of information he gathered during his long conversations with Stu. And when it became clear that Stu wouldn't give up his sources, Kennedy destroyed all the files and moved to Uday's side of the chessboard. The man probably thought himself very clever, telling Stu to come in on Monday for some "good news." Gave him plenty of time to clear out. Stu sipped and frowned at the bitter taste.

Hell, Stu thought, the truth was that someone had likely followed him from the moment he'd stepped free of prison. Probably sat across the street in a nice, warm car, watching Stu, the proud peacock, strutting about as he waited for Angie to pick him up.

Stu began searching the mirrored wall behind the counter, studying each new patron's reflection. Any or all of the four people who'd entered since he'd sat down could be a tail.

Three full weeks of wasted effort. Now what, start over? A month or more of bringing a rookie detective up to speed. Then what? Malloy goes to work as Kennedy's assistant?

Stu downed the remainder of the nasty brew, threw a five on the counter, and exited out back into the alley. He jogged to the front corner of the building and watched the entrance. No one hurried out. After several minutes watching, he hailed a cab.

Arriving at the law offices of Wilcox, Henderson, and Braxton nearly an hour before for his scheduled appointment, Stu approached the receptionist's desk. "Hi Jenny, I'm early for my—"

"Mr. Wilcox said I was to send you in the moment you arrived, Mr. Pierce." The secretary pushed a buzzer.

Stu walked into Wilcox's office and five minutes later, he appreciated just how long was the reach of Uday's golden tentacles, how deft was his touch.

"The police report, Stu. Without that, our law firm can't go forward."

"But I'm paying you. If my civil suit fails, you still bank the billable hours. If I win, your share of the punitive damages will lock in a good year's profit for your law firm."

"It's our reputation, Stu. We're not ambulance chasers. And where's Mrs. Pierce?"

"This is my money, Mr. Wilcox, my lawsuit. Angie has nothing to do with it."

"Well, I just think Angie's voice might help lend you some understanding of our delicate position in this unfortunate situation. Our law firm simply can't risk—"

Stu held up a hand, signaling Wilcox to stop. Shaking his head, he rose from the chair and left. An hour later, he plopped down in a booth inside the Lincoln Avenue Starbucks and stared at the door, awaiting the arrival of an old friend, Ben Turpin. Ben was the lead investigative reporter for the *Washington Sentinel Dispatch*, and Stu's last hope.

A solid hope, Stu reassured himself. Ben was incorruptible. Congressmen had threatened his career, the mafia his life, but he never quit until the full story got told.

Yet, as the minutes slipped by, the bitter taste of the diner's coffee rose back up Stu's throat, reminding him of all that had seemed so sure last night, and gone so wrong this morning. Stu slumped in his seat and thought about ordering something sweet to wash away the acrid taste.

The door swung open. Stu popped up from his seat. "Thank God for the free press. Ben, you've no idea how glad I am that you—"

"My editor shut this down, Stu."

Stu searched Ben's face, neck, and arms for golden sucker marks. "I serve you up a prince of The Realm. The complete inside story of the 'Playboy Sheik's' filth…and your editor opts out. Bullshit! Go freelance then."

"No one wants this story. You've got no police report. No civil suit. What am I supposed to write, Stu?"

"Write that a murdering degenerate is using his billions to laugh in the face of American justice. Try reporting the truth."

"Have you seen today's issue of the *Dispatch*?" Ben held up a copy.

"I don't want to read the damn paper, Ben."

"I'm sorry, Stu. But I have to go. Deadlines to meet." He held out the newspaper.

Stu just looked at it, shaking his head in disgust.

"Recommend you read the business section, page two, far right column, then page three, local business updates. Finish up with the front of the society section." Ben tossed the newspaper and headed for the door.

The paper landed square in front of Stu. On the front page Ben had jotted a note with the same reading recommendations and an apology, "Sorry, but I just don't know how to fight this."

Stu opened to the business section. Ben's first recommendation was an article about sovereign wealth funds. He skimmed through. The recent proliferation of oil-rich countries using their massive national funds to invest in companies around the world had some governments worried. Unnamed sources speculated on the undue influences on their nations' economies.

Stu stopped skimming when he saw the words "The Realm," and started reading every word. "Communications Holding Group announced an infusion of capital from The Realm today. In exchange for three seats on the board of directors, the Royal Azwad Family has provided sufficient funds to secure the company's expansion plans throughout the next decade. CHG stock shot up seven percent on the news. CHG, the world's largest media conglomerate, has a controlling interest in several major newspapers, including the *Washington Sentinel Dispatch*, as well as magazines, and radio and television stations."

Flipping over to page four, Stu raced through the local business updates. "The law firm of Wilcox, Henderson, and Braxton announced their selection as The Realm's legal counsel in North America."

He rifled to the society section. Centered on the first page was a color photo of Uday in his hospital bed surrounded by physicians. The caption read, "Don't worry, ladies, the 'Playboy Sheik's' smile will return." Stu crumpled the edges of the newspaper as he read the article. "Billionaire playboy Uday Azwad will be up and running soon. Three weeks ago, in a case of mistaken identity, The Realm's Prince was savagely attacked, suffering severe facial lacerations. A team of top plastic surgeons assured this reporter that the Sheik's surgery was a complete success. Not a scar will show."

Stu felt dizzy with fatigue. He cast the newspaper to the floor and lowered his head to his palms. The memory of calling Uday's bluff, the victory that had sustained him over these past three weeks, came flooding back, viewed in a new light. It drained what little energy he had left.

"Quad venti latte...single squirt of caramel?" an accented voice asked—an Arab accent.

Stu's head snapped up.

A tall man, all lank and bone, slid into the booth across from Stu. His pointed beard added another layer of gaunt to his slender, almost emaciated appearance.

"I believe it's your preferred drink when you're completely exhausted." He pushed the paper cup toward Stu. "There's no dishonor in a defeat well fought."

Stu's heart pounded six beats up and six beats down.

"Your son, Andrew, is bright and talented. Requests from foreign nations for his assistance as a military liaison would look nice on his service record. He'll make a fine general, someday."

Along with the pounding, Stu's jaw began to grind.

"Now, concerning your beautiful daughter, Margaret. You call her Magpie. Delightful nickname. She's an Arab speaker. A rising star in little need of our assistance. But the sky's no limit for her. With a helpful hand up the State Department's ladder, Secretary of State someday?"

Stu's hands crushed the cushion beneath him.

"NOAA is predicting deep snow out west this winter." One of the man's vein-ridden hands slipped under his lapel and pulled out an envelope. He placed it next to Stu's untouched caramel latte. "Open it."

After half a minute, the man gave up, retrieved the envelope and broke the wax seal himself. From inside he pulled out a photo and dropped it down in front of Stu. The photograph depicted a mountain chalet next to a ski lift. Multiple pages followed. "Just a simple set of closing documents, Mr. Pierce. Sign where indicated and it's yours. Aspen. You skied competitively in college. How long has it been?"

At least a full minute passed in silence.

"Your wife is free to pursue her rescues. We'll even help, quietly. But, from time to time a child will be declared off limits. Can't change that." The man shook the envelope and a miniature duplicate envelope fell out, the wax seal covering almost half of one side. Below the seal he wrote something in Arabic. "Here's the first of those names. This girl is forbidden." He slid the tiny envelope back toward Stu. "Why don't you—"

"Why don't I reach across this table, tie your skinny ass into a jumbled ball of knots, and drop you into a toilet. See if your bottom-feeding master snakes out a tentacle and rescues you."

The man frowned and stood. "Why don't you open that little envelope and trust to luck?"

"The only reason you're not already lying dead on this floor is that you didn't directly threaten my children's lives."

"I know that, Mr. Pierce. I know you very well." The man turned and vanished out the door.

Ten minutes later, the pounding in Stu's chest finally subsided enough for him to push the murderous thoughts from his head. Instantly replacing them—two questions. Could he ever accept Uday's offer? Could Angie?

His answer—never. Hers? He wasn't sure.

Last month, Stu would've answered "never" for Angie also. But since then, she'd begged him to spare Uday's life at the charity banquet, encouraged him to accept Uday's offer in prison, and shown little interest in Stu's plan to punish the murdering monster. And if Angie could bring herself to accept Uday's terms, where did that leave him?

He tried to imagine accepting Uday's offer. But that essentially meant trusting Uday. Stu tried looking past recent history, beyond the man's depravity, long before Angie had met him, to see if anything could serve as a foundation for trust. But all Stu could see was a royal life of whim and fancy. A snap of a finger and Uday's every desire fulfilled. What did that do to one's view of everyone else's life? If a simple nod of one's head could cause another person to lose theirs, then what were other humans to Uday? Sheep? Tend them, shear them, butcher them? All of humanity divided into just two groups, Azwads and chattel? Was this Uday's view of the world? That would explain a lot. But it sure wasn't a foundation for trust. No, Stu decided, he could never trust Uday.

What if he never told Angie of the offer? The question immediately triggered a feeling of self-loathing. Stu rubbed his temples. What was happening to him? A few months ago, that sort of thought would never have crossed his mind. Now it seemed he constantly beat such thoughts back. And each battle brought fatigue like he'd never before known. A deep tired that made him want to rent a room in some back street hotel and hide away. And what kind of man did that?

Stu rested his head on the table and closed his eyes. Uday's offer didn't even make any sense. The Prince played a chessboard of queens against Stu's pawns, effortlessly blocked every possible avenue of retribution. So why offer a draw? The only explanation— some vulnerability existed that Stu hadn't yet figured out. But what?

Maybe Gramps could help. Wasn't that precisely what the best CIA agents did, spot weakness and vulnerability, and turn those observations into opportunities? And in his new capacity with the NSA, wouldn't Gramps have access to the latest intelligence on the Azwad family?

Stu searched the table for his cell phone and found it next to the tiny envelope the skinny old Arab had directed him to open. What was it the old man had said, "…open that little envelope and trust to luck." What the hell did that mean?

Cracking the tiny wax seal, Stu tipped the envelope and shook. Twisted wings fell out and floated toward the table. Before they even landed, Stu's hand clutched at his left front pants pocket. Nothing. He turned his pockets inside out. All were empty.

Reaching out with a single finger, he tested the candy wrapper. Felt the familiar sticky residue. He pinched it between thumb and forefinger, raising it to his nose. Caramel. The wings were real. Stu twirled the twisted wrapper back and forth.

Trust to luck? Stu ran his fingers into his hair and yanked until the skin pulled away from his skull. Uday was mocking him. Telling Stu that there was nowhere to run, no way to win, nothing he could do, but exactly what he was told to do. When Uday said a little child's name was off limits, it was. When Uday said that Stu should go ski, he'd go ski. When he wanted Andrew or Maggie promoted, up the ladder they'd go. Or, if Uday wanted them dead, they'd die. And if he and Angie agreed to this offer, Uday would own them for the rest of their lives.

They would never beat Uday at his game. Ever. How do you beat a man whose whole life was the game? Even Stu's heart seemed to recognize the futility. Where normally he'd expect to have trouble stifling the raging cycles, there was only the apathy of a slow, dull beat that somehow felt very far away. The self-loathing returned. Fatigue with it. And the murderous thoughts.

Stu pulled out his cell phone, searched the contact list and pressed the entry labeled "DREAMS."

After six rings, a man answered. "Who's bothering me?"

"It's Stu."

"Been a long time, Ironman."

Stu's jaw bulged, his teeth grinding.

"You need pills?"

"Yeah...that, and a lot more," Stu forced out. "We need to meet...now."

"Don't like the sound of this, Ironman. You've never been that sort. I don't deal with that sort. You been sampling elsewhere? Got yourself a problem? Because, if you need that kind of help, it only comes from inside—"

"Cut the philosophical crap, Squid. Remember Iraq? You owe me."

CHAPTER THIRTY-FIVE

Uday woke to a face throbbing with pain, his hospital room silent and dark. Too dark, it seemed. He squeezed his eyelids together and reopened. Utter blackness. Where were the green glowing digits of the table clock? And no light seeped from beneath the door where his bodyguards stood watch.

A brief rattling noise came from the blackness.

Uday froze. Like a startled deer, only his ears moved, shifting back and forth, straining to reacquire the sound and comprehend its source.

Again, the rattling. But this time, less like a rattle, more of a slight sliding sound followed by a dull plunk. Then silence.

"Taamir?" Uday's left hand shot out for the control pad, moving only a mere centimeter before jerking to a halt. He reached with his right hand, but that leash was even shorter. Attempting to roll over, he found both ankles lashed to the bedrails. He went still again, listening for another slide and plunk.

Straining against the lashings, stretching out his fingers, he located the control pad and pushed. Not sure which button, he pushed and pushed again. Any button. All the buttons.

A click sounded and a beam of light shone down on his pecking fingers.

"His Royal Highness...poking for an alarm like a night cashier at the corner gas station."

"Sadeem?" Was that odd sliding and plunking actually the sound of his brother's wheelchair? The manner of speech was certainly similar. Biting sarcasm. A condescending tone. But no, that was not Sadeem's voice. And not their father's either.

An American accent. A hired gun, then. Perhaps someone paid to kill him. By whom—the Mullah? Retribution from the grave? But those were American bombs. No one could connect him with the Mullah's annihilation. Uday closed his eyes and willed his racing thoughts to slow. "Whatever baubles they paid you pale next to the treasure I can place at your feet."

The light clicked off.

"You're American, correct?" Uday inquired.

Silence, except for another slide and plunk.

"Women? Any you desire, for whatever you desire. Trained in pleasure or pain. Virgins? Unspoiled…young or old. I can make it all happen. Can your employer?"

After each question, Uday paused, but the only response was slide and plunk.

"Fame. I can get you that too. Set up a corporation. Make you CEO. Your photograph on the front of business magazines. I'll make you legitimate."

The flashlight clicked on, the beam shining straight into Uday's eyes. "Could've snatched the life right out of you."

Uday dropped his head and twisted away from the light, aggravating the throbbing in his face. "Yes, you could have...but you didn't...and you needn't," Uday forced out between the throbs. As if someone were repeatedly jabbing Mr. Pierce's broken bottle into his jaw, each throb became a sharp pang.

"I stopped the morphine drip. Gave you pain. Just as easy to let your painkiller flow like a river until your lungs simply stop moving."

"What about vengeance? Is there anyone you wish dead?"

"Anyone?"

"Name the target, and they will die. I promise you."

"How about if I untie your hands? Will you reach up and choke yourself to death?"

Uday raised his chin and squinted into the blinding light. "What do you want? Speak, and it shall be yours."

The light clicked off. "I already have the first part of what I came for. I wanted to see you fear."

Such vitriol and contempt in that voice, Uday thought. Even hate. This was not some paid assassin. What American loathed him so? "Mr. Pierce?"

"I should've sliced your jugular straight through."

The man was an impulsive fool. "Acting the cowboy...again, Mr. Pierce?"

"Should've cut you down before you curled your tentacles around a cop...and a lawyer...and a damn fine reporter."

"I only gave them what they already longed for. And for the record, your reporter friend remained very loyal. So we went over his head. The Realm now owns a controlling interest in the world's largest media company. Very American solution, don't you think? Everybody's a winner! Isn't that what you Americans teach your children?" Uday rotated both his hands palms up and waggled his fingers. "Now, as for this silliness, we both know you're not here to harm me, Mr. Pierce. So why not take care of these restraints before I grow impatient."

"As you desire, Your Royal Highness." Mr. Pierce switched on the flashlight and, grabbing hold of a hospital restraint, gave the end a stiff jerk, pinning Uday's hand tight against the cold metal rail.

"Am I supposed to cry out and beg for my life?"

Tugging three more times, Mr. Pierce circled the bed and then reversed direction, pulling and testing each arm and leg for any hint of slack.

"I've never met a man so determined to have me kill him."

Mr. Pierce ignored him, flipping the light switch next to the bed. A faint flicker first sputtered and then steadied, coloring Uday's head and chest in pasty white. "Are the restraints to your liking, Your Royal Highness?"

"Before you die, I'll kill everything you've ever loved."

"Good." Mr. Pierce pulled a chair forward into the pale light. "Very good. Now we're playing poker again." He sat and stared at Uday, clinically, like a surgeon deciding where to cut. No, more like a coroner pondering a corpse.

A shiver rippled the length of Uday's body.

The Ironman slouched against the backrest, then slid the chair backward until the shadows hid his face. "The dark hides my eyes, puts you at ease, lets me study your face for poker tells."

"Poker?" Desperate to stifle the growing pain, Uday tucked his jaw against his collarbone, which only served to replace the sharp pangs with a hot burning sensation across the full length of his cheek.

"Hurts a bit, doesn't it, Your Royal Highness? I'll turn the drip back on if you can tell me how many boards they play in three-dimensional chess."

"Chess…poker? Are you insane?"

The Ironman pulled a small plastic bottle from his pocket. Suspended between thumb and index finger, he rotated the bottle clockwise until the pills slid and plunked against the cap, and then counterclockwise, stopping when they tumbled to the bottom again. "The pain will only get worse, Your Royal Majesty."

"You cannot hope to get away with this, Mr. Pierce. Fingerprints. DNA from a fallen hair. Security cameras taping the storefronts in every direction for miles surrounding this hospital. You're not a professional criminal. And even a—"

"No, but I've a friend that's very professional, Your Royal Highness. Or he was. He's very disillusioned now. Wouldn't dream of killing you, or anyone else. But he's quite philosophical about the process, and quite good at assisting. Guarantees me that none of those cameras will record a thing. Even supplied the nurse's code to your morphine drip, and showed me how to bypass your vital signs alarm." The Ironman reached into his jacket pocket. He pulled out a pair of latex gloves, a small spray bottle and a scrap of white cloth, setting them on the floor. "Supplied these too. No fingerprints, Your Majesty."

"But you're the obvious suspect, Mr. Pierce," Uday hissed through the burning pain.

"Yes, that's true, if they suspect murder. But the image of His Royal Highness pissing himself as he dies is worth the prison time. In fact, the isolation of a quiet jail cell will allow me to savor the memory without interruption. Now, what about that pain in your cheek? Those chessboards, Your Royal Majesty…how many?"

Another tremor ran through Uday's entire body. Maybe questioning the Ironman's sanity wasn't so rhetorical. "Three. They play three boards."

"I just knew you were a chess player." The Ironman typed the numbers one, three, five, and seven into the panel controlling the liquids dripping into Uday's arm, then pressed the up arrow several times before leaning back into the dark. He recommenced tumbling his pills. "Now here's something I've pondered all day. How can an amateur chess player, like me, ever beat a grandmaster, like you?"

Uday strained to study him through the gloom. But the man was mostly shadow, just one rock steady hand extending from darkness into the dim light, sliding and plunking his drugs. "Have you swallowed one too many of your special pills, Mr. Pierce?"

"No, Your Royal Majesty. But your bodyguards did. Fortunately they like their coffee strong. Hides the bitterness."

"If the old one dies, you'll learn that a man can live an eternity with most of his skin peeled away."

"Chess, Your Royal Highness. Stick to chess. Calling me a cowboy, questioning my sanity, and casually mentioning my little pills, all subtle, understated chess moves. Very nice. But threatening my life while strapped to a hospital bed is a real bad poker bluff."

"If Taamir dies, you'd better kill me too."

"Concern for someone besides yourself? I'm astonished. But don't worry. The gentleman who provided the drugs is an expert. He assures me that no one will die but you, Uday. Forgive me...I mean...Your Most Royal Highness."

"Spare me your acid-dripping honorifics, Mr. Pierce. Is this about my lineage? I didn't choose my parents."

"But you choose now, Uday. All choices are yours alone. Not your father's, or his father before—"

"And what do you know of fathers, Mr. Pierce? You carry the bastard's chip on your shoulder. Don't visit your demons on me. Isn't it well past time for you to move beyond the unfortunate manner of your conception?"

Uday breathed a sigh of relief as the pain in his jaw lessened. "Besides, aren't all Americans bastards? How does your Statue of Liberty poem go? 'Give me your tired, your poor...the wretched refuse....' In other words, those their mother-whore-nation didn't ever want begot. Aren't you all more like the spew that dribbled down her thigh, ragged away and tossed out to find a new home in America?"

Despite the restraints, with the pain nearly gone, Uday felt calm, relaxed, giddy. "But then, you're a bit more of a bastard, aren't you? Your mother was raped, wasn't she?" Uday chuckled. "With no claim of his own to a throne, has the bastard come to topple mine?"

The Ironman clapped twice. "Bravo, Uday. Shouldn't you proudly announce 'check' after that move? Tossing out my innermost secrets—knowledge no one could know. Your nonchalance hinting that there's no place on God's earth safe from your tentacles." The Ironman reached out of the darkness and zeroed the drip rate. "But a little too much happy juice, I think. Because right now you're all mine…your throne…your crown, and….." Using a single knuckle, he rapped Uday on the forehead. "Your miserable life."

Uday jerked his head away. "I'll have your guts….." He bit back another bad poker bluff. Perhaps the Ironman was correct. Too much morphine. "Why are you here, Mr. Pierce? Kill or untie me. I grow bored."

The Ironman leaned back into the shadows. "I've come to acquire."

"I've already offered you the American dream—money, sex, fame and—"

"Understanding. I want to get to know you, Uday. After all, you know me so very well. Electronic invasions of my home. Catwalk prison guards following my every move. Your little fairies flitting about, placing sugarplums beneath the pillows of police officers and lawyers and corporations until only the most extreme option remained. Well, here I am. Right here, right now…no fairies…no money…just you and I getting to know each other, Your Most Royal Highness. Most Royal? What does that mean? Most ruthless? Most narcissistic? What?"

Uday exhaled in disgust. "Americans. You believe because the sky has no clouds, it's blue. The water is clear, it must be clean. The winds are calm, so the sand must lie still. But it creeps. It always creeps, covering, seeping, grinding until everything but the Great Pyramid is worn away. And even it will vanish beneath the sands someday. My royal ancestors were there to hear the Prophet's first words. Saw the power residing there. Prostrated their way to the top. We'll be here long after America is dead and time has sanded away Mohammed's words. Such arrogance. First Greek, then Roman, now American. You'll choke on your freedoms. And an Azwad will set your headstone and smile."

"You truly believe that crap, don't you?"

"In my forty years I've seen nothing to dispute these truths."

The Ironman's bottle tipped and the pills plunked, over and over.

Uday counted one hundred plunks. And lost count after a few dozen more. "Mr. Pierce, you can still salvage…"

"Your whole life is isolation, isn't it, Uday? No truth but Azwad truth. No road but your father's. Your first sex…administered, wasn't it? You expressed curiosity and a woman was brought. Taught you how and how not. Grabbed you by the testicles and said now."

"Western views of morality don't interest me, Mr. Pierce."

"And what if the fires inside you had burned a slightly different shade, Uday? Non-Arab, let's say? The blonde, the redhead, the Asian or the African? What then? Suppose the young strapping Uday had fallen in love with a black woman. Would the royal Azwad line grant admission to her blood? Did the young Uday need to prove that all the other colorful souls were unworthy—too tainted to mingle with Azwad blood? Is that why?"

"Why what?"

"Was it sport? You grew bored with polo ponies? Your appetite tired of the tastes of mature women who went willingly to your bed to play your tortured games. So you fed on the innocence of girls?"

"Innocence? I hear Diogenes chuckling through the centuries. They did what we all do—what they wanted to do. I freed them."

"My daughter's roommate leapt from the fourth floor. Is that the freedom you offer?"

"The jumper." Uday cocked his head, thinking back. Yes, such a sweet young thing. The investigation eventually led the police to The Realm's embassy. But politics dictated that the D.A. handle such a delicate inquiry. "I'd forgotten. That's how I met your Angel. Your daughter's roommate. A Francine, or was it Irene?"

"Nancy."

"That's it, Nancy. A fragile girl. But she isn't why you've lashed me to the bed, is it? No. You're wondering if your little 'Magpie' has some dark secrets. Maybe, you should—"

"Save your breath, Uday. I know my daughter's character better than I know my own. This is about Nancy. And all the other 'Nancys.' The girls you killed inside."

"Suicide, Mr. Pierce. Check the police reports. Nancy's death was never my intent. Just bad luck."

The Ironman placed a finger on the up arrow. "How fast do you suppose this can this drip? Perhaps we should set you free. Like to trust your luck with Allah?"

"You're not here to kill me, Mr. Pierce. Americans don't kill up close. You prefer bombs. Americans conduct business. And nothing too personal there either. So what's your business?"

Pulling out a tiny envelope, The Ironman reached across the

bedrail, tipped and shook. The lucky angel wings landed on Uday's chest.

Uday laughed. "Very clumsy move, Mr. Pierce. I was beginning to think you were a grandmaster yourself. But, we're finally to the truth of it, aren't we? This is why you risk all—for your Angel. You want to know. Did she play with me? Did Angie take the horse's bit between her teeth, bite down, and enjoy what I did to her. Did your Angel learn to cherish the pain?"

The Ironman's face vanished in the shadows. His hand extended out of the dark and rotated. The pills slid and plunked. "The slap? Out of all that has happened these past weeks, the thing that won't leave my mind is that slap. A prince of The Realm, slapping a woman in public. Why would—"

"Your Angel slapped me. Remember?"

The Ironman's fist rotated clockwise, then counterclockwise.

"She destroyed years of delicate negotiations."

One slide and plunk followed another, endlessly.

"I snapped."

"Doesn't make sense, Uday. You rub shoulders with the heads of governments while toying with their wives. I've subdued your bodyguards, lashed you to the bedrails, dialed your pain up and down, and rapped you right between the eyes. Yet you lie there and calmly threaten my life. You never lose control."

"Any man can be pushed too far, Mr. Pierce."

"But you weren't. You did the pushing. You were the Sala that wouldn't go away. Emails of torture. Death threat letters. Why?"

"She was arrogant. Looked down on everyone."

"No. Angie looked down on Sala. She was very fond of Uday."

"Angie liked the Uday that wore a suit and tie. The one who shaved his desert beard smooth. Tanned his face and charmed the Westerners." Jerking at his bindings, Uday succeeded at rolling the bed a few centimeters from the wall. "Angie liked me...." Uday turned away to stare at the wall. "When I smiled."

The crack of plastic on tile preceded a rolling, then a rocking, as the pills settled to one side of the fallen bottle. "I never considered the impossible. But your concern for an old man's life, Uday. The genuine affection. In your own perverted manner you're...capable of...." The Ironman rose and grabbed Uday's chin with a vise-like grip and wrenched his face around. "Are you...in love with my wife?"

"Love your wife?" Uday repeated in dismay. Love? The Angel? Insanity. He was a prince of The Realm. The woman barely qualified as a brood mare. She needed a bit between her teeth. Needed someone to teach her what she truly was. Yes, he'd enjoy that. But love? Uday laughed, and then spit into the Ironman's face. "Your wife is a common whore."

The Ironman's fist swung.

A searing pain flashed through Uday's right jaw followed by a numbing deadness. He smiled through the fresh blood dribbling over his lips. "Did your Angel share her toils? Came home all worn out and told you how I tempted her?" Coughing and hacking, splattering his white bed sheets with splotches of red, he gave the Ironman the truth he didn't want to hear. "I'd received all the right signals. Her sideways looks and soft, wet smiles. Did your Angel tell you of my helping hand on her back? My body a little too close to hers. Our shoulders touching. Hips grazing. Does Angie talk in her sleep, Mr. Ironman? Whisper aloud the dark desires haunting her soul. Didn't Jesus teach that anyone who looks lustfully has already committed adultery in her heart? I don't love whores, Mr. Pierce. I give them what they crave. Pain."

The Ironman picked up his pill bottle. "Time to die, Your Royal Highness." He tapped the up arrow until a constant stream of painkillers filled the tube. "Your private nurse isn't scheduled to check in on you for almost two hours."

"You won't kill me. You'd sentence your whole family to death."

"No, Your Royal Highness. Not unless you made preparations. And I'm betting you didn't. We're playing poker here tonight, not chess, and I'm wagering that you never predicted me." The Ironman searched Uday's face. "Did you, Your Royal Highness? Did you leave orders to have us all killed if you died under suspicious circumstances?"

"I didn't need to. I…"

"There…right there." The Ironman pointed at Uday's eyes. "The dilation of your pupils. It happens every time you voice your idle threats. I wonder…do you think your bodyguards will admit to falling asleep when you're found dead? And there it is again, the brief flash of dilation."

"You have no bomb to drop. This is too personal. You

won't…"

"I told you earlier. All day I gnawed on a single question. How does an amateur defeat a grandmaster? I thought up numerous plans, but your golden tentacles are everywhere, twisted and turned and wrapped so tightly about everything that I soon realized all my ideas to unravel them were nonsense. I felt like Alexander pondering the Gordian knot."

The Ironman slouched and rested his head against the back of the chair. "Your research must have uncovered my prison time in Thailand—the bar fight? Three men pushed a woman into a back room. She screamed. I put two down and killed the one forcing himself into her."

"You're not frightening me, Mr. Pierce. A moment of passion defending the damsel in distress. Nothing more."

"The woman stuck me in the shoulder with a broken bottle. Turns out, the dead man was her pimp. Imagine that, protecting the man raping you." The Ironman started his pills tipping. "Anyway, after months of interrogation, I'm released. All charges dropped. Sound familiar?"

Uday fought his drooping eyelids. Managed to keep them half open. "There's no one here to rescue, Mr. Pierce. No cowboy heroics to perform." A thickening of his tongue slowed and slurred his words.

"But there's one thing interrogations can't reveal. And your investigators couldn't report." The Ironman stood and bent within a centimeter of Uday's face. "I liked it. I watched the life leave that rapist's body and felt joy. Wanted to find every rapist on earth and kill them all."

Uday shouted for help, but the words left his mouth soft and fading.

"Go ahead. Cry out, Uday. Your money bought this very private room…and absolute isolation. Scream louder. Your voice must carry past the door and through the outer room where your bodyguards sleep, past yet another door and down your private hallway…and still more doors. Your Gordian knot, Uday. And my solution—just like Alexander, I cleave your tangled tentacles in two."

Uday's loins grew warm and wet.

"Don't worry, Uday. The bowels always release when a person dies. No one will ever know yours released a little early. How does an amateur defeat a grandmaster? He kills him. A very American solution, don't you think, Your Royal Highness? Or perhaps it's Greek. After all, as you pointed out, I'm a bastard of rape."

Uday's eyelids fluttered and closed. One after another his senses shut down. The salty taste of his blood, the wetness of his loins, and the ammonia odor of his urine, all faded. Only his hearing remained. Slide and plunk, the only sound.

CHAPTER THIRTY-SIX

Reaching through the blackness, Stuart's hand slid across the cold wood to bump against the doorjamb and then down to the keyhole. He slipped his house key home and twisted counterclockwise one cautious degree after another. A low click signaled the deadbolt clear.

"Still can't follow orders, Captain Pierce?"

Ducking low, Stu swept out with a kick before his mind registered the gravelly voice. Pulling up short gave his hamstring a sharp twinge. "Mash?"

"I should put a bullet in your leg just to teach you a lesson."

Stu rose, grimacing. "Some lady, without identifying herself, orders me to—"

"Wait at the end of your driveway until contacted. Was that so hard to obey, Pierce?"

"Gramps guaranteed he'd take care of Angie. I call him back, and after a bunch of beeps and clicks, like my call was getting transferred to Mars, Bloodhound answers, barks an order and hangs up. Am I supposed to trust—"

"You kill the car's headlights turning into the driveway, ease to a stop thirty yards from the house, and creep to the front door. The only reason you're not spitting up blood is because Bloodhound identified you driving past her position. Ordered us to stand down. Are you carrying, Pierce?"

"No. I—"

"Don't know how long we can dedicate resources here."

"Gramps told me—"

"This isn't simulator training, Captain Pierce. You don't splash a few red paint balls, talk your way into a passing grade, and go home.

Do you need a weapon?"

"Mine's inside."

"Then dust the damn thing off and check the ammo—real rounds. Fail now, and someone dies. Not a great loss in your case, but your wife's a class act."

"Agent Mash, you're one uncompromising prick. But the truth is, there's no one I'd rather have here right now."

"Love you, too, Captain Pierce. But I'm not here. And neither is the barking Bloodhound in charge of this operation, nor Ice, whose leg you nearly broke in training, nor the other two agents flanking your home east and west. None of us are here. But if we were, we'd report your wife safe and everything nice and quiet. No one's visited except a certain white-haired gentleman who grew very disturbed at your long absence. He rushed out a couple hours ago." Mash pulled something from his pocket. "Left this for you. Said he's tired of cleaning up your messes."

Stu felt the pointed ends of cool metal—his wings. "Thought these were lost forever. How in hell did he get them?"

"How does the man do a lot of things?"

Stu stuck out his hand. "Agent Mash, thanks."

"Just collecting a paycheck, Pierce." He shook, and like some two-legged panther, padded off silently over the leaves.

Stu lost sight as soon as Mash slipped between the lovers' trunks. Could've saved himself a hamstring pull. His kick would never have landed. Not on Mash. A smile started, then faded as Stu faced the door.

He pressed an ear against the wood and listened. All quiet. Stu eased the door inward a few inches and a gray pall of light oozed forth. Backing away, he rechecked the bay windows. Angie's study was still black as the moonless sky above.

Stu pushed the door just far enough to sight down the hall. A dim glow filtered from the great room. Slipping through, he eased the door closed and removed his shoes.

At the top of the hall he peeked around the corner. The end table's lamp was lit, and beneath the shade, encircled in stark white, were Angie's face and chest, her shoulders propped by cushions, head resting across the love seat's arm—her usual late night reading pose.

Stu strained to read their anniversary clock on the mantle. Above the twirling balls, the minute hand was lost in shadow. The stubby arrow pointed southeast—well before five. Much too early to talk.

Three steps brought him to the back of the love seat. He looked down and frowned. Strewn all about Angie—evidence of troubled hours. The coffee table's candle and wreath lay tumbled onto the hearth rug. Replacing them, an ice bucket and empty liquor bottle. Beneath the coffee table was a glass, marred with fingerprints, and dozens of caramel wrappers.

The bottle, he noted, was bourbon, not scotch. Even the best of Grandfathers taught the worst habits—bourbon and caramels. Stu nodded and whispered, "Good choice, Angie. Nothing 'scotch' about tonight."

Angie stirred and settled, her breasts rising and falling in a deep steady rhythm. She was a clash of colors and textures. Her hair cascaded down across a short white robe. Ratty purple slippers covered her feet. Between the white and purple she wore black silk pajamas, crumpled tissues polka-dotting her thighs.

A photograph lay facedown on her stomach. One hand held a rosary, the other, *Tales of the Arabian Nights*—the twin pillars of her childhood. Stress often drove a person back in time, and Angie was no different. But few found solace mixing east with west. And only Angie saw no contradiction in clutching to both "veil" and "habit." Only Angie seemed able to see the sameness of Middle Eastern woman and Catholic nun.

Her eyelids were red and swollen. Smeared mascara darkened her temples. And even while she slept the crease between her brows furrowed long and deep. Stu's thumb rubbed gently at a crease in the love seat's leather, his lips mouthing a silent apology. "I wish I could promise everything would be okay."

From Angie's study the grandfather clock chimed a warning—the tolling of the hour to come. Angie stirred and mumbled. Stu quickly reversed his path off the carpet onto hardwood and around the corner. Four bells, then silence. He watched her breathe for several minutes, then tore his eyes away and headed for the study.

A small hop carried him over the creaking planks at the threshold and onto the diamond-patterned carpet. He closed the door, flipped on the light, and reached up behind the grandfather clock's bonnet, retrieving his gun case. At Angie's desk, he dialed in the combination and opened. Inside were his pistol and three full ammo magazines. No paintballs. He slammed home a magazine, racked a round, and set the pistol on the desk. "Okay, Mash, you principled prick. I'm ready."

Stu tossed his coat over Angie's chair and plopped down, the armrest bumping against her desk and knocking an empty picture frame to the floor. Swiveling to face the wall, he located the vacant spot, the photo currently rising and falling with Angie's every breath—her "snuggling puppies." Stu nodded—yeah, Angie, that was a good moment. Hold on to that.

Just below the vacant spot, his "hero shot" hung crooked. He half rose from the chair, then settled back down. Straightening the photo seemed wrong. Back then, standing alongside his F-15, everything was crystal clear, all his choices sure. Now, a gut-twisting uncertainty accompanied his every thought. Stu snorted. He'd leave the "hero" be. Crooked felt right.

He grabbed the empty frame from the floor. Stuck to the wood…what else…a caramel wrapper. He almost smiled. Stu twisted it into the usual set of wings, but they looked funny. When had they last looked right? He unfolded and tried again, recalling the happy faces that normally lived in that picture frame—a day when a bowl of ice cream and a hug fixed any problem. "Those were good days, Angie. I don't know what happened, either."

Stu examined the refolded wings. His worst yet. He blinked rapidly, then covered his eyes.

Too bright. Stu flipped off the light, felt his way to the bay window's curtains, drew them aside and waited for his vision to adjust to the starlight. After a few minutes, the lovers floated out of the dark. Stu searched for Mash between their trunks, but true to his profession, the man couldn't be seen.

Stu rubbed his aching neck. Another hour of waiting lay ahead. Returning to the chair, he slouched, leaned his head back and felt a lump. Pulling the pill bottle from his coat pocket, he tossed it on the desk and closed his eyes, seeking the disconnection, the leaving behind of all that was senseless. Meditating, one deep breath after another, he relaxed into his skis, chasing that chance to know again, some purpose.

Slipping through the swirling snow…thigh-deep powder…floating weightless…timeless…winding a path between backcountry aspens…entering the void…the singularity…and then, a meadow....

In the center, standing upon a great stump, was the woman in white. Around her, all manner of men fought and fell, a mass of shadows cutting them down. She reached out toward Stu, beckoning.

Sword in hand, hacking through the shifting darkness, he went to her. The woman placed a hand on his shoulder and stepped toward the ground, but Stu pushed her back up to safety. She tried again, and again he pushed her back up. Tears formed at the corners of her eyes and slid down her cheeks. She turned her palms up, pleading.

Stu helped her to the ground. The woman pulled a sword from a fallen warrior. The shadows came at them. Back to back they fought.

After a time, the shadows thinned, the darkness fading away. But the woman was no longer white, her dress torn and splattered with mud. From her womb, blood flowed. She fell.

Stu knelt beside her.

She placed a bright red hand on his cheek.

Stu slid it to his lips and kissed.

"Am I still your hero?" the woman asked.

"Hero?" Stu pondered as he watched her life fade.

With a stab of lightning and a crack of thunder the clouds burst open, the sky pouring blood-red rain. Hard droplets struck his nose and chin and cheek. Stu's hand held a single large red drop. Two more fell onto the diamonds at his feet.

Angie leaned over him, dribbling pills onto his lap. "I don't see a doctor's name here." She dropped the empty bottle into his hand.

Stu let bottle and pills fall to the carpet. "What time is it?"

"Almost five. So does that mean a handful of *go*, or is it time for *no-go*?"

"Is it fair to lecture me on empty promises?" He grabbed his pistol and headed for the shower. "Before you do, make sure you know which one I've broken."

In the bathroom, Stu set his pistol by the sink and pulled the two extra magazines from his pocket. Sandwiched between them came the tiny envelope. He stared at the Arabic letters. Who was she? How young—how damaged? His heart pounded six beats up and six down. Had she been strapped to a cot, the passion cut from her loins? He gripped the countertop until the hammering subsided.

Stripping, he entered the stall, rotated the spigot to full hot and let the water flow. Almost time…almost. With the water scalding his face and chest, Stu squeezed the showerhead with both hands and let it burn. Until a man actually takes a life he can't appreciate how perfect the phraseology.

Dropping bombs wasn't taking lives. People died, but you didn't take their lives.

He knew. He'd seen a last convulsive shiver, a final gasp. The letting go. Stu had taken a life. And he'd retained every vivid detail. The whimpered cries of fear. Weakened hands falling from his forearms. Skin grown gray. The foul odors and acrid taste in his mouth.

And the body didn't grow cold over hours. That was a lie. The instant the life departed, a chill spread from the dead man to Stu, seeming to fill the entire room. Taking a life meant exactly that. Stu had taken it. And he would keep it. These final moments were his…forever.

"Stu?"

He let go of the showerhead. The whole front of his body was bright pink. He rotated the handle toward cooler.

"These pills are red, not blue."

Stu scrubbed and rinsed.

"What's going on?" Angie asked, her face inches from the shower wall.

He cleared a hole through the fogged glass. "What time is it?"

"A few minutes later than the last time you asked."

Stu stepped from the shower. "The nurses will have checked in on him by now, Angie."

"Nurses?"

"Uday was right."

"Stu, what have you—?"

"I held his nose and covered his mouth. But each time the gray colored his face, I let go. The last time he was very weak. Hands didn't even struggle against the bindings."

"He's dead?"

"In Thailand, the rape was right there in front of me. Uday was helpless, strapped to a bed, his crimes hard to visualize. I tried to picture him raping, butchering. But I never saw him cut the passion from a woman. I tried to see him pushing Nancy. But he wasn't even there when she jumped."

"Is he alive, Stu?"

"I don't know. Probably not. I left the morphine streaming."

"Then you've got to go back there, right now."

"It's too late. The nurse made her rounds at five."

"It doesn't matter. Barge in. Contaminate the scene. Create reasonable doubt and—"

"Stop, Angie. Just stop it. Damn the half-truths, tiny deceptions, misinformation. All the clever, dirty lies."

He felt like a man cut in threes, his mind arguing that she was right, his heart pounding—demanding action, his gut feeling reckless.

His gut won. "If Uday is dead, then he's dead. And I did it."

"They'll find evidence. Stray fingerprints. A fallen hair. They'll link his death to you."

Stu shrugged. "In a few days, I'll pack. For work or prison, I'll be ready."

"And if it's a life sentence. Or the Azwads...end your life. What will I do?"

"You'll go on living," his gut answered.

"Without you?" She shook her head. "I'm not sure I remember how."

"Sure you do," Stu's gut said. "You began living without me the moment you started lying to me."

Angie wrapped her arms around herself and stared at the floor.

Long moments passed, the mad cycles of his heart thumping louder and louder in his ears, demanding that he ask. "Why...?" Stu started, his mind recoiling at the question, his mouth clamping shut.

"Why what?" Angie sighed.

Stu's gut forced the question out. "Why did you slap him, Angie?"

"You're dripping wet," she said, her head sinking to her chest.

He tried to lift her chin.

She twisted away. "You should put on a robe."

"Why?" he asked again, his voice harsh in his ears.

"You're so cold," she whispered, sounding almost frightened.

Stu's gut told him to press her, show no mercy. But his mind railed at him to walk away, calling him a beast, an animal no better than Uday. Yet his heartbeats steadied. There was another way.

Stepping forward, he kissed her forehead, gently unwound her arms and lowered them to her side. "I'm not cold, Angie."

He tugged the tie at her waist. The ends fell loose. Her robe opened. "Feels good—naked." Underneath was another tie. He pulled and the black silk fell from her hips, piling about her purple slippers.

Angie gathered up the right side of her robe, wiped the beads of water from his chest, and patted his still-healing shoulder wound. "You feel...so cold."

He pushed the fluffy white from Angie's shoulders. The robe slid toward the floor, catching on her arm. "Just the skin. Beneath, I'm warm."

Angie lowered her hand and the white robe fell, collecting atop black and purple.

Stu undid four buttons, shoved the last of her black to the floor and pulled her to him. Her slippers catching up in the tangle of cloth, he lifted her naked from the pile of colors and set her bare feet alongside his.

She rested her head on his shoulder.

"Ten years ago," he began, his heart beating a strong, steady cadence.

Angie cringed in his arms, part of Stu's mind seeming to cringe with her.

"Before you knew what he was," Stu continued, each word bracketed by a heartbeat.

Angie's whole body trembled.

So did Stu's, his mind crying no, but his heart still pounding steady. "Did you fall in love with him, Angie?"

Her chin moved slowly left and right. "I don't think so."

Stu felt wetness on his shoulder, then itching as the salt from her tears soaked into his mending skin. "Did you sleep with him?"

Her chin moved left and right again. Faster this time. "No."

"But...." He faltered, his mind trying to shut him down again. "But you wanted to?"

Her chin bobbed up and down, driving the salt deeper, burning. "Yes," she said.

He went numb. Couldn't think. Couldn't feel her. Could barely feel himself. Only his heart. Still beating. Steady. Strong. He focused on that.

A minute. Another. Silent.

Her tears stopped. She hugged him. Fierce. The tears started again.

Wetness. Burning. Feeling. Thinking. Yes, she'd nearly fallen in love with Uday. Probably had, Stu reasoned. She just couldn't admit it to herself. And yes, he'd known. Some part of him had always known. He just couldn't admit it to himself.

And she'd wanted to sleep with Uday. Sleep with a monster. What had that realization done to her? "Hurts to give yourself to someone like that, doesn't it?"

Angie pressed her forehead into his chest and nodded. "Yes," she sobbed.

Stu forced her chin up. Looked into her eyes. "You are not a monster." He picked Angie up and carried her to their bed.

CHAPTER THIRTY-SEVEN

Uday scribbled across the hospital stationery in big, black, capital letters, "HE WAS HERE," and glared at Taamir, then shifted his grip, holding the pen like a toddler to gouge a deep vertical line alongside his words. He dotted his exclamation point by plunging a hole through the paper.

"Excellency, the forensics team found nothing."

Uday pointed at the four men examining his window and scribbled, "FOOLS! THIS IS 9TH FLOOR." With his jaw wired shut, he couldn't scream, "He's Ironman, not Batman!"

"My Prince, you were twelve hours in surgery and twelve more unconscious. The investigators have dusted and swept. They've examined every surveillance tape within a five-block radius. The only fingerprints were nurses, doctors, and ours. Not a fiber of fabric is unaccounted for. And the Ironman appears on not a single video recording."

"YOU? FALL ASLEEP? NEVER BEFORE."

"I need little reason to nap these days. The older I grow, Excellency, it seems the faster I grow older."

"AND MORE FOOLISH. THINK, TAAMIR!"

The room suddenly darkened. At the window, the men finished covering the glass with a heavy mesh screen, then fanned out to the four corners of the room. Each man detached from his belt what seemed a large cell phone with a long antenna. After connecting an earpiece they swept every square centimeter of wall, and then started on the ceiling.

If Uday could smile, he would. The drugs must have slowed his wits. This was a security team. Taamir was playing the fool for the purposes of anyone listening.

Uday scratched on his pad, "NOT SO OLD," and nodded.

Taamir smiled. "Yes, Excellency, the investigation was thorough. All of this, an unfortunate accident. You should rest now."

All too familiar with the process, Uday leaned back against his pillow and waited. The mesh screen was his addition to The Realm's security procedures. Using lasers to read the speech vibrations from the glass of his predecessor's office window, he'd uncovered a plot to overthrow the monarchy. Over the ensuing six months, several powerful mullahs suffered untimely "natural" deaths. A few of the less well connected were put on trial and executed. The hundreds of low-level conspirators simply disappeared into the sand. His father had joyfully run that part of the reprisal. Now every important meeting included mesh screens, thorough sweeps, and jammers.

After the communications team repeated the sweep with two identical-looking, but functionally different handheld devices, they set up and tested the audio and video jammers, pronounced the room secure, and departed.

"Please forgive my caution, Excellency, but the forensic team's report was exactly as I stated. They detected no trace of the photographers from the newspaper nor our financial advisors. Roger spent days with you, eating meals, discussing business, and scratching his head over his next chess move, yet not a fingerprint or a hair was found. Nothing from anyone other than the hospital staff and our men. The room is too clean."

"IRONMAN? IMPOSSIBLE?"

"Yes, Excellency, I agree. This level of cleansing would require experts."

"CIA? NSA?"

"Yes, Your Highness."

"DID YOU RESEARCH?"

"Yes," Taamir frowned. "No direct connections, Excellency. Nevertheless, few in the world could accomplish this feat. We must have opponents that we do not see. Should we postpone our operation against Roger's bank?"

Uday rapidly shook his head, wincing as an aching throb surged through one side of his face.

"Excellency?" Taamir reached for him. "I will call the doctors."

Uday clutched Taamir's hand as another throbbing wave rolled across half his face. "PAIN ALL HERE." He rubbed his temple and slid a finger below his right eye to the bridge of his nose. "BUT HERE, NOTHING." He indicated his right jaw.

Taamir looked toward the door. "I'll call the doctors, my Prince."

"INJECTIONS?"

With his free hand, Taamir reached toward the call button.

Uday shook his head again, bringing more pain. "WHEN WILL I SPEAK?"

"Several days, at least, my Prince."

"FEEL?" He tapped his right jaw.

"My brave eagle…" Taamir's voice cracked.

Uday glared.

"The doctors should explain."

"NO. YOU EXPLAIN."

"The doctors can tell you better than I, my Prince."

Uday grasped the old man's hands in both of his, squeezed, and waited.

Seeming to draw strength from their linked fingers, Taamir spoke in starts and stops. "The nerves? Crushed. Blood pressure? Too low—too long. There was nothing the doctors could do. The nerves…already dead."

Uday patted the old man's cheek.

Taamir refused to lift his eyes from the one hand he still held. "You'll never regain control, Your Highness."

"MY FACE, HALF FROZEN?"

"Don't think of this."

"HALF A SMILE."

"These thoughts…do no good."

"FOREVER."

"No, my Prince."

"GROTESQUE."

"No."

"A MONSTER."

Taamir's eyes watered as he shook his head.

Uday tried to picture his new face. Would it ever appear normal? Maybe as he sat at his desk, expressionless, thinking on nothing—not the thrill of an eagle's strike, nor the lust of a woman's hips—no thought that inspired his mouth to mirror the feelings inside him.

Maybe sand. Just think about endless sand. Or would half his face still droop. Drool spilling from one corner. Perhaps he could hire a staff of royal dabbers, holding hand towels, stepping forward whenever the slightest glisten reflected from his lip. If any woman ever thought to kiss him, would she first need to wipe the royal spittle from his chin?

How much delight would visit The Angel's face when she learned of his disfigurement? How broad her smile need be to reflect her utter joy? Uday's hands trembled with rage.

"Excellency, please talk with the doctors. They know how best to handle…the change."

"ROGER'S BANK?"

"Yes." Taamir's face brightened. "Yes, Your Highness. Business." He tapped the face of his tablet.

"NO NOTES." Uday waited for him to set the tablet down.

"INCREASE SHORT POSITION AMERICA AIRWAYS TWENTYFOLD."

"Excellency, you've only a tenth of the assets required."

"MARGIN."

"Borrow money to short? If the stock rises significantly, you'll be wiped out."

"THINK ME A FOOL?"

"No, Excellency, Please forgive me. I meant nothing. But the—"

Uday patted Taamir's hand. The old man was correct. Technically, "shorting" was borrowing someone's stock and selling it at today's price with the financial obligation to replace the shares later. Of course, the trick was to sell high and buy back low. A rising stock price meant lost money. If the price doubled overnight, big losses. Borrowing money to short was exponentially worse. Shorting was like selling the extra sandbags and betting the spring floodwaters wouldn't rise. Borrowing money to short was selling all the sandbags and stopping payments on the home insurance. A person could wake up to find a dam built and a reservoir where his home used to stand. Uday scribbled, "STOCK WILL FALL."

"Excellency, even margining, you've not a fifth of what you'd need."

"SOVEREIGN WEALTH FUND."

"You have no authority."

"FATHER'S PASSCODE: ENDLESSSAND." One, two and

three words at a time Uday outlined dramatic changes to his original plan. First, using several dozen investment firms scattered across the globe, Taamir would direct a twentyfold increase in the short position of America Airways stock. Second, order the immediate shipment of one missile from Chicago and one from New York to Washington. Third, learn the flight schedule of the Ironman.

"Yes, Excellency. But there are easier paths to retribution."

"MY WAY!"

"Your father will soon discover that vast amounts of money—"

"DO IT!"

"But your brother will learn of the missile movements—"

"YES."

"My Prince, you risk your nation and your life."

"DOMINOES! FOUR MISSILES ENSURE AIRLINER CRASH...STOCK WILL CRASH...ROGER'S BANK INSOLVENT...COVER SHORT POSITION...BUY CONTROL OF BANK...FATHER GETS MORE SAND...BROTHER GETS MORE MARTYRS...DEAD IRONMAN SENDS MESSAGE TO THOSE WHO HELPED HIM."

"And what do you get, my Prince?"

"I GET TO WIPE THE SMILE FROM THE ANGEL'S FACE." And The Angel gets endless pain. Beneath the bandages, half of Uday's face smiled.

CHAPTER THIRTY-EIGHT

Angie sat at her desk, cradling her "snuggling puppies" photo, seeking some thought, some word, to represent how she felt. Almost a week had passed since Stu had lifted her naked from the robe tangled about her feet and carried her to their bed. And still, she lingered in the haze of that next morning—unsure of whom she'd been—frightened of who she was now. Somehow, she was new, but she didn't yet know how to function. She was—broken. Yes, Stu had broken her.

Yet Angie found herself wishing he'd broken through long ago. They'd made something? Made love? No. This was too raw. Too true. She hadn't felt like this since…since…hell, she'd never felt like this. And the releasing? No. It was a letting go. A letting go of everything. To something beyond. From neck through thighs, her muscles were still tender from the violent waves. "*La petite mort?*" Maybe? If dying were the letting go of everything, and a person could die again and again and again, then yes.

At first she'd thought it was because he was somehow different. How he had cradled her. Letting her cry. Then came the magic of his thumb between her eyebrows. She never wanted it to stop. And his kiss. Gentle like his thumb. His eyes grabbing hers. Peeling away all her shame. Without speaking a word, telling her that she was good— so very good.

Then the thought of losing him came and she opened herself in a way she'd never done before. At that moment, nothing mattered. Not the next hour, minute, or second. Nothing but the feel of him— right then. His eyes so open, so accepting, had opened hers, and her opening somehow ignited him, each in turn, seeing, feeling

288

something different, something new, something so alive, building and building…no…no…shrinking and shrinking. Intimate. Small. A collapse of everything they were into the tightest oblivion. And she didn't care about anything. But him.

He wasn't different. He was the same. Like living a lifetime on an iceberg, never knowing that most of it lay below. She'd finally let go and dove, and seen all of him for the very first time. And she broke.

But she still hadn't let him see all of her.

The courtroom witness oath echoed through Angie's mind. "Tell the truth, the whole truth, and nothing but the truth…." She'd told Stu the truth, and nothing but the truth. It was that middle part, the whole truth, where she'd come up short.

Angie ran her fingers along the photo's frame, looked at the man chuckling there, his arm curling about her shoulders. He'd always been there. Marriage, depression, children, career, more depression. Always there. For her. Was she? For him?

Stu had once told her that all the lies people tell are for themselves. No exceptions. A person either sought to gain something or to avoid something by lying. And every lie was a cheat. Ultimate narcissism. Each lie denied someone else the information they needed to decide the paths of their lives. Writ small, fibbing that a dress looked nice denies a woman the chance to change clothes. Writ large, asserting that God wants nonbelievers to die denies life itself. But what about the lie never voiced? So very clever—that lie.

Right now, Stu thought he'd seen the worst of her truths, and yet he remained steadfast at her side. If she told him her real worst truth, would he understand? Would his eyes burn away the rest of her ugliness? Would she still be good?

Or would he leave—forever? Couldn't fault him that. But Stu…gone? That meant the end of them. And the end of her, she knew. Yet, she also knew this as the moment. The only moment. Tell him now, or tell him never.

Never meant that she would remain the faithful wife. Become that lie. Forever. And that lie would never lay low. Not after the breaking of her. That lie would hover. Shrinking her every smile. Muffling his every touch. Smothering her. Until there was no her. No them.

No, she had to tell him. Every morning, she watched Stu wrestle with the truths he already knew. Saw the frozen moments. Two stirs of his coffee. A spoon suspended above the cup, dark fluid spiraling, slowing, stopping. Eye blinks, rapid and jerked, half a minute or more. A violent shake of the head. Eyes crushing shut. The blinks cease. Another spoonful of sugar. A taste. A frown. Down the drain. Grabs the pot and pours. Empty. Stares at the bottom. A minute passes. And another, Stu frozen.

And frozen he'd stay, pondering in circles, because even after all he now knew, he still couldn't let her down from that lofty place he kept her, that place she didn't deserve.

Even now, standing at the bay window, Stu was frozen, watching the lovers sway. Was he even aware that the silence between them had stretched to several minutes?

Initially Stu's mood had brightened a little. Gramps had cleaned up his mess, stopped the streaming morphine and brought in a team to sanitize the hospital room. In saving Uday's life, saving Stu's as well. For the few hours Gramps stayed, Stu's smiles were relaxed, natural.

But that was days ago. Now his smiles were forced. The lips parting, the teeth showing, but the eyes darting away. And he hadn't uttered a chuckle in days. Not even at the sight of their neighbor, Mr. Culinn, twirled up in ten feet of retractable dog leash and yanked to the ground, his affable Labrador nuzzling the old man free. Stu had only smiled and turned away.

And if she told him? Would she ever hear his chuckle again? Told him the whole, ugly truth. Would Stu ever smooth her cleft again?

Damn it! Angie scolded herself. This wasn't about her. Stu deserved the truth. Now!

"Stu?"

He turned and studied her.

She wished he'd study something, anything else. Angie returned to the photo—the happy faces. United, strong, they were. And they would be again—family. She focused on the Stu chuckling there. "Ten years ago, I went to him."

Angie glanced up. Stu was frozen stiff, except for his rapidly blinking eyes. Eyes she couldn't hold. She looked back to the photo and couldn't hold his eyes there either. For long moments she faltered, until the witness oath again echoed through her mind—

"...the whole truth, so help you, God." Yes, please, dear God, help, Angie silently prayed.

She forced her mouth to open. Willed herself to speak. As if she were someone else. A court recorder, reading aloud the convicted's allocution of her crime.

Angie confessed, the disembodied words falling in little clusters on her ears. "It was a Friday. You were on a layover in Seattle. I put on my black dress. Makeup. Perfume. And went. I went to where I knew he'd be. To where it could happen."

Stu made not a sound.

"I sat in the bar across the street. Watched the restaurant...the table he used every Friday night...all evening. He never showed."

Angie forced herself to look up.

Stu blinked and stared.

The whole truth! All of it, she screamed inside. "I wish...wish I could tell you...that if he'd showed up...that at the last...I would have turned away. But that doesn't feel true. Not for who I was back then." Angie shook off a shiver. "No. It isn't true. But I wish...I so do wish."

Without the violent shake of his head, without first crushing his eyes shut, the blinks just stopped, and Stu walked toward the study door.

Angie intercepted him, grabbing his arm. "Where are you going?" Did the question sound as hollow as it seemed? "Please stay," she begged.

"I'm going to pack for work tomorrow."

"Call and tell them—"

"Tell them what?" Stu snatched her fingers from his arm and pulled them to his cheek. "You feel a fever?" He shoved her hand away. "You want me to call and say I'm sick? Lie? And cheat?"

Angie fell back into her chair and shook her head. "No."

"When, Angie? When did you—"

"Ten years ago."

"No. When did you start therapy? Before or after you went to him?"

"After."

"You took up horseback riding back then. I encouraged you. Thought it might help your depression. Was it because he loved horses?"

The whole truth, she thought. He deserves the whole truth. "Probably. Yes."

"You first started working with the Women's Center for Mideast Issues ten years ago. Him again?"

She dropped her head and nodded. "Yes."

"Your depression. The private sessions with your therapist. The subject? Always Uday?"

"Yes, mostly." Dear God, the truth was unbearable. It burned and burned. Angie started rocking in her chair and couldn't stop herself.

"What did the therapist recommend?" Stu asked.

"She said what's done is done. No good could come of confessing something no one could ever know."

Stu shook his head. "No one believes in God anymore, do they? Was there ever mention of me?"

"She said it wasn't about you."

"Not about me?" Stu snorted. "Well, it sure as hell was done to me. I would've made any effort for you, Angie. Moved to the Mideast and opened a girls' school. Anything."

"Stu, this was my failure, not yours."

"You're right. But I'm not some colleague you disappointed with an inadequate legal brief. I'm the man who pledged his life to you. Not a day passed during those hard years that I didn't wonder how best to help you. But it seems that the only way I might have helped was by not being there. I always thought your reasons for depression were noble and lofty, but it turns out they were of the lowest order, the most common."

"Stu, it was all so long ago. I'm not that person any—"

"Not for me, Angie. It just happened. Right now. I haven't been working on it for a decade. Haven't seen a psychologist who forgave me my sins. I haven't had time to rehearse my lines. I see it all happening…right now."

"Stu, please—"

"Please what, Angie? I'm not Granda. You didn't get caught with your hand in the candy dish. I'm the man who never gave up on you. The man you made a fool of."

Angie looked into his eyes, but couldn't find him there. Her forehead ached where she knew her eyebrows knitted to form a chasm. "I don't know who I was back then."

"What do you want from me, Angie? Should I show my passion like Uday? Slap you."

"Yes." She grabbed his hand. "If that's what you need."

Stu jerked his hand free, grabbed the "snuggling puppies" and threw. The frame smashed into his "hero shot." Shattered glass littered the couch. Pieces of the frames fell toward the diamonds. The photos followed, one landing amidst broken glass, the other on splinters of wood. "You want passion? Sorry, Angie, that's the best I can do."

Tears collected on Angie's chin. Soon they formed a steady stream. The space between her eyes ached.

Stu just stared, his jaw muscles flexing in and out. Then he walked from the study, the hallway floorboards creaking as he disappeared.

Stu had broken her. Now she had broken him. Angie dug her fingernails into her cheeks. "The truth, the whole truth, and nothing but the truth," she whispered. "So help me, God."

CHAPTER THIRTY-NINE

His face an ashen mask, young Kashif peered out his dorm room window, listening to the tolling of the hour. When the bell tower's last knell sounded, he jerked the window cord downward, snapping the blinds shut, then laid his phone on the desk and stared at the text message. "Clean up nice. Eating some place special. One hour."

He'd endured years of training for this day. Languished for months awaiting this message. Yet now he wasn't sure what he felt. Not the fervid anticipation of righteous vengeance. Not the calm satisfaction of imminent justice. Mostly, he wanted to throw up.

Where was the anger? The hatred? Kashif thought back, seeking the fury that sustained him so often in the past, and found instead the ululations. He closed his eyes and released himself to the memories.

Still numb from the explosions, he'd walked the village streets beside his mother's shrouded body. Forbidden to cry, lest his tears demonstrate a lack of faith, he'd focused on hate and let the wailing tongues voice his hurt. Over the many years, the wails had come to resound throughout all of the memories he held close.

In the madrasas of Pakistan, the ululations wailed as he rocked manically back and forth, memorizing the Imam's careful selection of surahs—in exchange for food. The Imam's choice of Qur'anic passages differed greatly from his mother's, yet perfectly suited his pain.

Lost amidst the barren peaks of the Hindu Kush, the tongues wailed loudly when at last he stumbled, starving, into the Mullah's camp. There he learned to channel pain to action—hate to vengeance.

And how loudly the tongues howled when he discovered

someone who shared his loss. A man whose mother was also murdered by the Americans. Hosaam understood.

The ululations had even slipped backward in time, their low wails now lending a soft chorus to the memory of his mother's final song. With the luscious morning smells of spiced meats and sweetened breads curling into his room, she called to him from the kitchen. As he rolled away from her voice to sleep a little more, the wails grew louder. She entered his bedroom and kissed his cheek. His stomach growled with hunger. She laughed, and hugged him tight. "Allah has blessed us with another day. Let us sing his praises before we eat." He pulled the blanket over his head, the wails surging higher. She rubbed his back. "Come soon, my little one. Only a single night has passed, and already I miss you so." She left the room, singing her favorite surah. The ululations screamed.

Kashif's anger returned, his hatred rebounding.

The phone rang, its crystal screen illuminating with "Tanngela." Kashif let it ring.

Tanngela was everything wrong. The product of a Chinese father who worshipped a smiling, bald fat man, and a Jamaican mother whose voice hushed with reverence when she spoke of the tree spirits. Both were college professors in New York City, free to spread their chaos. Tanngela was raised in a house of shame.

The phone stopped ringing. Kashif cleared the missed call. Hosaam's text reappeared.

"Clean up nice." He left his desk to carry out Hosaam's order.

Kashif bolted the door and grabbed a stashed-away jug of water. He poured most of the contents into a pitcher, reserving a small portion at the bottom to rinse his mouth. Then he soaked a washrag and wiped his face and head.

Once more, the phone rang. Tanngela again. Half a minute later, a message beeped its presence. He listened. "Hi Kashif. Guess you're running late. Hope you're not mad at me. And don't forget to bring your history notes."

History? Kashif sneered. More like some unholy concoction of fact and fancy, carefully contrived, he was sure, to deaden the appetite for truth. Western history books accurately reported the brutal atrocities committed by Christian Crusaders but told utter lies about the Spanish Moors. Yet Tanngela took it all in stride, arguing that earning an "A" was easy. She merely had to spit back their facts.

Not believe them. Her mother's silvery blue eyes flashed wide as she emphasized the word "spit."

Kashif refreshed the rag and wiped his forearms. Tanngela's skin was a shade darker than his own, a warm olive that glowed shiny and golden in the sun, but grew dark and mysterious at night, leaving her silky black hair framing copper lips and silver eyes. Always at night she spoke of Allah, her parents, and her seemingly endless choice of paths. She was a mess.

After dipping and wringing, Kashif thoroughly cleansed his feet. A rinse of his mouth and he was ready. He turned to face Mecca, raised both hands and intoned, "Allahu Akbar." So long, without prayer. The feeling, so glorious. Tears of joy ran down his cheeks.

Again, Tanngela called. Another message beeped.

With his intentions clear and his prayers pure, the salutations flew by, all his sins seeming to vanish as he prayed. Cleansed in body and mind, he picked up the phone and listened. "Kashif. I didn't mean to preach. Please call me." He pressed delete.

Only twenty minutes remained until rendezvous. Kashif surveyed the room. "Clean up nice" meant he might never return here. Yet with Hosaam in command it was difficult to know. The words of the text were those specifically designated to confirm an actual attack. But Hosaam had once used them in a practice drill, chastising Kashif for arriving three minutes late at the pickup point, and then severely rebuking him for leaving behind a personal item.

Kashif stuffed a complete change of clothes, including fresh sneakers, into his backpack, and then retrieved the object of his rebuke. From beneath his mattress, he pulled a large manila envelope containing the last remaining link to his past.

Tanngela was the only living person, other than Abbud and Hosaam, who'd ever seen the photo inside. Showing her was his way of explaining the panicked flight from the lecture hall—and the vomit. Embarrassed and drunk, he'd presented her, his Virgin Annunciate.

She'd stammered and agreed, "My God, Kashif, your mother could have sat for the painting."

Kashif slid the photo out. With it came the memories of her final minutes, and the wails. That morning, a bomb interrupted her song. The blast leveled their entire home, except the two walls cornering his bed. Barely visible through the settling dust, a bit of blue hung from the rubble. He ran toward her, but stumbled in the loose stone. Crawling, he reached her side and pulled at the broken wall. His child's body lacking the strength, he tugged at the blue robe and prayed aloud to her beautiful Allah.

A second bomb demolished the home across the street, the concussion tossing him far from her body. Disoriented and coughing, he struggled up through a cloud of thick dust.

The screech came first, then the shadow. A jet sliced through the sky over his head and performed what he later learned was a victory roll.

His mother was gone. In his hand, he still clutched a piece of her bloodied blue robe.

Kashif reached back into the envelope, pulled out the bloodstained scrap and laid it on the photograph. After aligning blue upon blue, he slid the back of his fingers over the silk that now framed one side of her face. "I'm sorry I didn't get up for breakfast, Madar."

He swallowed hard. "Today I finally take the battle to the Great Satan's homeland. I know what I'm supposed to feel. Elation. Power. Greatness. I feel none of these. I might get to see you soon. That brings me comfort. But mostly, I feel a strange fear. Not when I was nine and abandoned on the Pakistani border, nor when I was surrounded by enemies beneath the grandfather walnut, did I suffer such fear as I fight now."

A bleak wailing of tongues rose in Kashif's mind. His heart thumped, a great pressure falling upon his chest. A dull ache extended from his sternum outward into his right shoulder and jaw. He rubbed his ribs, breathing slow and deep. As the ache subsided, the wailing fell away. When this day was through, would he still hear the wails?

"Kashif?" Tanngela knocked at the door. "Open up."

Startled, he gasped, and then held his breath.

"I hear you, Kashif. Are you okay? Please open the door." She twisted the handle back and forth. "I'm sorry about last night. My parents taught me better. If you don't believe in God, I respect that. I'll never bug you again about going to mosque with me."

Kashif lifted his phone from the desk and checked the time. Less than ten minutes until he must meet Hosaam. He could yell at Tanngela. Be loud and angry. Tell her to go, and she'd go. He could do that. Instead, he slid the phone into his jeans and waited.

A slip of paper slid beneath the door. Tanngela's footsteps receded down the hall.

He padded over and picked up her note. "Kashif. You have such a good heart. Please use it to forgive me."

A tiny wail accompanied his head dipping onto his chest. Tanngela saw the world through his mother's eyes. Raised in a land of chaos, she had still found the beauty of Allah. All she wanted was to share that beauty with him. Tanngela wasn't everything wrong. She was everything right. Rushing to the window, Kashif cracked open the blinds.

Head bent, Tanngela walked toward the coffee shop. Kashif found himself hoping that this was another of Hosaam's drills, and that just like before, Hosaam would drive around Washington and Virginia for hours only to drop him back on campus.

Perhaps he would go to mosque with Tanngela. Pretend to learn. Let her teach him of the beauty of Allah. That thought evoked a broad smile. Seeming to sense his eyes upon her back, she stopped and spun. Saw him at the window and came running.

He jerked the blinds closed and raced for the door. Stooping, he snatched up his backpack and stuffed both her note and his mother's photo inside. Turning away from the sound of her climbing footsteps, he hurried to the opposite end of the hall and took the back stairs, two at a time.

At the bottom, Kashif crashed through the doors and ran. The wails ran with him.

Sweating and out of breath, Kashif reached the parking lot at the edge of campus. A quick scan found four white Chevrolet panel vans, three with silhouettes behind the wheel. Almost two months had passed since he'd last seen Hosaam. How would he recognize him?

Despite his tardiness, Kashif reversed direction, stepping back between the buildings. Although Hosaam had seemed reluctant to practice the techniques taught in the Mullah's camp, seven weeks was plenty long enough for him to drastically alter his appearance. Adopt new clothing. Shave his head bald or grow his hair shoulder length, as

Kashif had done. What was he supposed to do, rap on each van's window?

Well, why not? After all, he was just a college kid. He could pretend he needed directions.

Kashif tugged a ball cap from his pack and slipped it onto his head, using the elastic band to keep his hair back from his face. A quick glance at the coffee shop's window brought a nod of satisfaction. The black onyx decorating his earlobe and the peace symbol on his t-shirt were each a good touch.

Sneakering through the traffic, he hurried toward the driver's window of the first van. Thirty yards away he recognized Hosaam, who hadn't bothered to blend at all.

Kashif knocked on the window but was waved off. He tapped repeatedly, pointing at his face.

The window cracked. "Get in."

He climbed onto the passenger's seat. "Hosaam, it's good to see you."

Hosaam released the parking brake, shifted into drive, and accelerated onto the street. "Peace be to you, Kashif."

"Peace to you...." He started responding, but Hosaam's glare, his eyes moving up and down Kashif's body with a look of disgust, stopped him mid-sentence.

Kashif removed his baseball cap and answered with precise formality. "And to you be peace together with Allah's mercy, Hosaam." He tucked his hair behind his ears.

"Allah? You would speak of Allah?" Hosaam flicked Kashif's earring. "Do you whore with the Americans also?"

Kashif pulled the magnet from behind his lobe, dropping the onyx from his ear. "Fake." He stuffed the earring into the front pocket of his blue jeans and pointed at the stars tattooed across the back of his hand. "Henna." Grabbing a handful of his curls, he shook them at Hosaam. "This...scissors."

"Put your earring back on, Kashif. Suits you. Back to your roots. The pampered baby. Gardeners, tutors and all. You're weak. I shouldn't have pulled you up onto that train. Should have let you starve to death in those mountains. The Mullah would never have accepted you, trained you, except for your English."

Kashif pulled the baseball cap back over his head. "And what good did the Mullah's training do you? Camel among a herd of horses, that's what you appear—"

"I remember who I am. But you?" Hosaam smiled. "You look very natural here with the Great Satan."

"And you look like a fool. An FBI terrorist wanted poster."

Hosaam pulled over. "You forget yourself. Abbud is an able backup."

"The Mullah trained us as three-man teams. And taught us to blend. Look in the mirror."

Hosaam pointed at the glove compartment. "Look inside. Our latest communication from the Mullah."

Kashif opened the latch. Inside were photographs. Bomb blasts of rubble and ruin. He searched the dead faces, tossed the photos back into the glove compartment, and slammed it closed.

"Maybe you shouldn't put so much faith in the Mullah's teachings," Hosaam said.

Kashif fingered his cell phone, trying to decide whether to call the emergency number. Yet, what if the Mullah's entire organization was compromised? Were men waiting to trace any calls?

"Go ahead," Hosaam urged. "It's disconnected." He accelerated back onto the road. "Save your faith for Allah. And your respect for me."

They departed Washington Avenue. The roads quickly became unfamiliar, the buildings worn and the graffiti thick. More than four years ago, Kashif had attached himself to Hosaam's star. Seemed there was no way to let go. "Despite what you see as my objectionable appearance, Hosaam, I am cleansed in both body and soul. I've prepared as if this was my last day on earth. My dorm room is sanitized. My mother's photo here." He patted his breast pocket. "Nothing back there can point to you or to Abbud. I've carried out my duties precisely as my training instructor taught. I will be as dutiful to you."

Hosaam stared at him for several seconds and nodded.

The pain in Kashif's chest renewed. He rubbed his ribs, leaned his head back and listened to the soft wails. Once more, Kashif found himself hoping that this was another practice drill.

For twenty minutes they drove southeast, Hosaam never mentioning a plan nor a target. Snatching glances at the back of the van, Kashif checked the seats and cargo area. Nothing. No weapons or crates. Only their two satchels. The tightness left Kashif's chest, his thoughts returning to Tanngela, remembering their first…their only kiss…and smiling.

At a bus stop alongside the Potomac River Abbud waited, satchel slung over his shoulder. His manner of dress was halfway between Kashif and Hosaam. Hair cropped short, clean shaven, leather jacket, blue jeans and boots. He could pass for an off-duty campus police officer. What a team they made—hippie, cop, and Hosaam, the beggar.

Abbud gave Kashif a thrice-over look, and scrambled in. "I see you've fully embraced the Mullah's advice."

"And you, Abbud. What inspires such tidiness?"

"I'm a cook, remember? The owner demands either this, or a hairnet."

Kashif laughed. "I remember. And how many have you sickened with your food?"

"None that I know of. Mostly, they eat and smile. And how goes your studies?"

"Well enough so that I don't get thrown out." Kashif smiled.

"Pretty girls at this university?"

Kashif blushed. "The Mullah ordered us to blend."

"Yes, I see there's at least one. For the Mullah, of course," Abbud laughed.

"The Mullah is dead," Hosaam declared. "The camp destroyed. All of them…dead."

"Well, peace be to you, Hosaam."

Hosaam glared straight ahead and pointed. "We cross the Potomac into Virginia. It is time."

The wails erupted in unison with the sudden pressure in Kashif's chest. He took a deep breath. And several more. But each time he thought of Tanngela, thought of never seeing her again, the pressure returned, and the wails.

Thirty minutes later they stopped alongside a railway underpass. "Fry cook, guard the van," Hosaam ordered. "Kashif, those bushes." He pointed at the clump near the river's edge. "I dug a hole at the center. Hide our satchels there. Cover them well. Dirt and leaves. Without them, we don't escape." Hosaam tossed Kashif the keys. "You will drive from here." He pulled out his cell phone and scrambled up onto the railroad tracks.

Pushing through the thick underbrush, Kashif located the

clearing. Seemed much bigger than necessary to hole up for a few hours, or to hide their backpacks. Every twig, leaf and rock cleared. Imprints in the dirt indicated two sets of shoes, one large, the other small. Tracks trailed off toward the riverbank. Perhaps this wasn't the safe hideaway Hosaam imagined.

Following the tracks brought Kashif quickly to the water's edge. Only the large tracks reversed, returning toward the bushes. Had the smaller person entered the river? He searched the ground a few meters to the south. No footprints came back out of the water. He checked the ground to the north and found the same. Turning back, he noticed three vultures circling the shore fifty meters upriver. Below them, something colorful.

Kashif trotted toward the pile of colors. Stopped well away. A woman. Dead. Wrapped in a robe of many colors. A matching veil covered one half of her bloated face. Her neck looked marred or slashed? The ululations filled his mind.

As he stepped closer, a hand grabbed his arm and spun him around. "Leave her, Kashif. We must hurry. First to pick up our equipment, then to the launch site." Hosaam yanked him back toward the bushes. "American vultures. Such scrawny things. How hungry they must be? But soon, they'll have much to feed on." He smacked Kashif between the shoulder blades. "Your vengeance is at hand. You will kill many today, Kashif, and it will feel…glorious."

CHAPTER FORTY

Angie first checked the caller ID and then pressed the speakerphone button. "Carl?"

"Good news, Angie. Buzz swapped tower shifts. He'll be working. It's all arranged. He's already left your name with security. TSA is expecting you."

Angie hugged her purple pillow. "Thank you, Carl. I can't tell you...I don't know how.... It just means so much."

"No worries, Angie. Be fun to see the flipp'n look...sorry. I can't wait for the expression on Ironman's face. Anything else? Because I've got to go. That asshole, Koleshat, the one who thinks being a corporate vice president makes him God, is on our flight this morning. I want to personally greet His Holiness. Politely suggest that he give his first class seat to a paying customer, and sit in coach, preferably by the toilets."

"Nope. Got everything I need. Thank you, Carl." Angie punched off the speakerphone and consulted Stu's flight schedule. After landing in Washington this morning, he was flying to New York and returning, then up to Boston for a long hotel layover.

From the control tower, she'd wish him "Godspeed" to New York, and then greet him upon his return. Fly with him to Boston. Walk the streets. Kiss him. Hold him. She would fix things. Fix everything.

She dropped her purple pillow onto the chair. With ratty-slippered feet sliding around the corners, Angie rushed to the master bedroom, flung open the closet door and pulled out her lingerie. Red lace or black? Threw both into the suitcase.

Angie backed out of the garage onto the circular turnaround.

Leaves, brilliant orange and deep red, floated down, landing on the car's hood. She looked up at the lovers. Despite the storm's damage, most of their branches were still entwined, colors blending together. That's what they could be, she and Stu, what they should be. That's what she'd make them be. Even if it took the rest of her life.

At the end of the driveway sat a police car, both doors open, County Sheriff's star emblazoned on each. One officer was behind the wheel. Another was stooped over, examining the edge of the road.

Angie stopped well short of the car. If Uday could buy a Washington, D.C. police detective, a major law firm, and a media conglomerate, what challenge a County Sheriff? She lowered her window and leaned out. "Can I help you?"

The officer straightened from examining the roadside. "Yes, Ma'am." He pointed behind her. "Do you live there?"

"Have I violated some law?"

He walked toward her, shutting the patrol car's passenger door as he passed. "I'm Sergeant Collins from the County Sheriff's Office."

"And what brings you off our public highways, Sergeant Collins, and onto private property?" She tapped the door lock switch.

"County easement rights, Ma'am. Don't think I'm quite on private property yet."

"Did they teach you the intricacies of property case law at the police academy, Sergeant?" While awaiting an answer, Angie gauged his distance. Could she raise the window before he got to her? "If they didn't, I suggest you stop right there." She put her finger on the window button. "And explain why you're here."

He slowed. "Just a few questions, Ma'am."

"I know you're trained to take control, Sergeant. But unless I'm a suspect, you can ask your questions from right where you're at. Private property statutes aren't my specialty, yet I'd happily wager my knowledge against yours."

The other police officer stepped out from behind the driver's wheel. "Chuck, the car she's driving is registered to an Angela Pierce who resides at this address."

The Sergeant stopped, looked back at the patrol car blocking the driveway and then scanned the emptiness all around them. He took two steps back. "I think maybe I've gotten off to a bad start with

304

you…Ms. Pierce, is it? I don't mean to alarm you. But over the past few weeks, one of your neighbors has been calling our office. Reported a suspicious white van parked in this area late at night. There are some pretty distinctive tire tracks along the road here. I just wanted to see if they matched yours. Might explain things."

"Explain what? I'm driving a gold Lexus."

"Do you know a Mr. Culinn? Lives just up the road. He has a good view of this end of your driveway."

"Not really, met him when we first moved in. Since then, it's only been the occasional neighborly wave. Seems nice enough."

"Please don't misunderstand, Ma'am. He's harmless, but kind of a kook. Become a more frequent caller since his wife passed away. Reports an awful lot of…." The officer raised his hands displaying twin peace signs, fingertips flexing, bracketing his next two words with quotation marks. "Suspicious stuff."

"Probably just lonely." Angie's forehead wrinkled. "But if Mr. Culinn isn't to be taken too seriously, I'm confused about why you're preventing me from leaving my driveway."

Sergeant Collins pointed across the road and up the hill, toward the large log house that overlooked their home. "The owner of that estate returned after several weeks in Europe and reported a burglary. When we consider that break-in along with Mr. Culinn's suspicious vehicle report, well, perhaps we should take him a little more seriously. Have you seen anything out of the ordinary, Ma'am?"

"Just the two of you. And unless you have something else, I'd like to get going."

"Well, yes Ma'am. Funny thing about the break-in. Nothing was stolen. Appeared as if someone was simply using the place. Had a chair pulled up close to the big picture windows. A rug too, like they slept on it. Weird, unless they were keeping watch or something. Great vantage point to observe your home."

"A rug?" Angie studied the log home for perhaps the first time since moving in over two years earlier. A mansion. The two picture windows were enormous, probably eight feet across and nearly twice as high, coming together to form a point directed at their home. She checked her watch, then the sun's position in the sky. "What shape rug?"

"Ma'am?"

"Square, rectangular, oval?"

"They pulled it from the hall—long rectangle, three feet by eight, I'd guess."

"Those picture windows form a prow front like a boat. One faces east, the other southwest. How was the rug oriented?"

The Sergeant looked up at the windows, then down as he considered her question. "One end was pushed up against the eastern window, Ma'am. Does that mean anything?"

Goosebumps swelled on Angie's arms. She looked back at their front door, and then up at the log home.

"Ma'am? Are you okay?"

"Am I okay? A mysterious burglary. Suspicious vehicles, late at night. Refresh my memory, Sergeant. You said you weren't here to alarm me?"

"I'm sorry, Ma'am. But a nice-looking woman like you, living out here. You should know, that's all. If you see anything strange, anything you're not comfortable with, please give us a call."

As the patrol car drove away, Angie slowly backed down their long gravel drive. Leaving her car parked in the circle, she walked along the front of their home, pausing by each window, noting the log home's vantage point. Nearly every window proved naked before that prow front. The only safe room was her study, hidden by the lover's leaves until winter set in.

Angie walked around to the southeast corner of their house and concluded that little of the backyard was visible from the log home. Yet as she peered at the thick dark woods bordering the lawn, she shivered. What had she done to them? This was their home, their sanctuary. Now it was a target. Cyber attacks. Death threats. Spies. Her hands clenched into fists with no one to strike but herself. Damn it. She had to fix this. All of this.

And fixing everything meant telling everything. Boston would be the truth, the whole truth, and nothing but the truth, so help her, God. From Uday's secret drawer in the study, to Gramps's involvement in the judge's proposed deal. All of it. Every last bit.

CHAPTER FORTY-ONE

"Captain Pierce, Mr. Koleshat is already aboard. We'll start loading the general public at…"

Ignoring the remainder of the gate agent's words, Stu hustled down the jetway.

At the cabin door, a flight attendant pointed toward the cockpit. "Getting heated in there."

Stu could hear Carl's raised voice. "With all the due respect…that you deserve…Mr. Koleshat, do I come down to the truckstop at midnight and tell you how to—"

"Carl, I need you to check on the number two main tire." Stu pushed past Koleshat. "Hate to break up this scintillating conversation, gentlemen, but that tire is a safety issue."

"Just a second, Captain, I want to hear what your copilot, Mr. Banks, has to say. It is Carl Banks, isn't it?"

"Yes Sir, That's Carl with a 'C,' and Banks just like the—"

Stu cut him off again. "I'm afraid not, Mr. Koleshat." He turned to his copilot. "Carl, please go check the tire."

Koleshat looked indignant. "Captain, do you realize who I am?"

"Absolutely, Sir, and when it concerns anything but the safe operation of this aircraft, I'll gladly bow to any desire you have concerning our company. But by FAA mandate, you have zero authority in this cockpit. I noticed you arranged to occupy the cockpit jump seat. You won't be doing that either."

"You can't prevent that. I'm—"

"I now consider the relationship between you and my copilot strained, an impediment to the safe conduct of this flight, and I respectfully insist that you make yourself comfortable in first class."

"I can have you replaced, Captain Pierce."

"Yes Sir, but by the time you dig up another captain, you'll be late. Very late. Operations informed me that you went to extensive lengths to arrange for an early departure. Shame to waste all that effort."

"Captain, your copilot ignored my requests for instructions on occupying the jump seat, and he was flipping switches so fast he couldn't have given that task the safe—"

"Do you have a commercial pilot's license? Some other type of professional pilot expertise I should be aware of?"

"No, but I know when something just isn't right."

Stu sat down and started flipping switches. Hands that normally moved methodically, he intentionally darted across the panels at a speed that he hoped made Carl look slow and meticulous.

"At the rate your copilot was.... Well, I feel...."

Stu paused. "You were saying, Mr. Koleshat?"

"Perhaps both you and your copilot need the flight safety department to review—"

The twins came giggling and rambling around the corner, bumping straight into Koleshat. "We came to see the captain."

Cheryl's girls couldn't have arrived at a more opportune moment. They smiled up at Koleshat. "Hi, who are you? We—"

"Mr. Koleshat." Stu cut the twins off before they gave away that he was "Uncle Stu." "Why don't you have a seat in first class, and let me take care of our little passengers."

Looking annoyed, Koleshat squeezed past the twins and headed for a seat.

"Guess who, Captain Stu?"

"No."

"Come on." Twin stamps of feet accompanied their insistence. "Please."

"Absolutely not. You two always cheat. Without your mother here to tell me the truth, I won't do it."

Carl slipped past the two girls. "Well, if it isn't trouble, and worse trouble."

"Hi, Captain Carl."

"I'm not the captain, girls. He always sits on the left side. And captains don't get ordered to inspect perfectly good tires."

"Mom says 'Once a captain, always a captain, the world can't ever take it away.'"

"Always thought your mom was smart. Where's she at?'"

"Way in back. Gave us the last two first class seats."

Stu stared at them cross-eyed. "I can't imagine why."

Daryann stuck out her tongue. Or was it Maryann? "Call Angie. She knows us by voice. Then you have to guess."

Stu pulled out his cell and called. "Carl, pilots' union or not, you finish that sentence about the truckstop and you're fired." He pointed up at the voice recorder. "Koleshat doesn't know much, but he was eyeballing that microphone when he was arguing with me. Choosing his words carefully, too. There are better ways to put the man in his place." Angie's message picked up. "Sorry, girls. Angie's not answering."

"Keep trying. You have to guess," they said in unison.

"Make you a deal. The man that just left before Captain Carl came back." Stu pointed back at seat 2A. "He travels a lot and he gets real bored, kind of like he's stuck in math class all day. So if you promise to keep him company to New York, talk to him about the airline, then I'll try Angie one more time."

"Is he important?"

"Very. He's the airline's vice president of marketing, responsible for deciding how to keep all of our customers happy."

"But we're not customers. We go free."

"That makes you the best type. Since you fly free, you'll only tell him the important stuff. Really, he needs to hear all of your ideas during the flight. Every last one."

"Every one?"

"Yes. It'll be good for him."

The two girls whispered in each other's ears and giggled. "Okay, try Angie again, but if she doesn't answer, you have to guess anyway."

"It's a deal." Stu stuck out his hand. "Shake."

Stu tried three more times. First the home line, then her business line, and finally her cell.

"Come on, Captain Stu. You have to guess. You promised."

Stu looked at them cross-eyed again and pointed. "You on the left, you're Daryann and on the right, you're Maryann."

They burst out laughing and chorused, "Wrong again."

"But my eyes were crossed, so when I said left, it was really on my right, and when I said right, vice versa. So, I was correct."

The laughter stopped. The twins faced each other and conferred. "But we didn't tell you the truth, so you were—"

"Ah-ha...caught you." Stu pointed toward the passenger seats. "Now go sit down—and don't forget your promise." He eyeballed them all the way back to their seats.

"Carl, I'm ready to run the preflight checklist."

"Just a second, Boss. I'm enjoying the show in back."

Stu turned and listened.

"Hi, my name is Daryann, and that's my twin sister Maryann, behind you. Our Mom's back in coach. We just turned nine yesterday, so this is the first time we can sit in first class by ourselves. Isn't our Mom nice? The captain told us you were a vice president. You look rich. Are you rich?"

Koleshat glanced at all the amused passengers around him and forced a polite laugh. Then looked at Stu.

Stu offered him a nod, a flash of lifted eyebrows, and a big smile.

Carl grinned from ear to ear.

"You know what would be cool? If each seat could move around like a wheelchair, then each passenger could take turns..."

Stu tried Angie one last time. Just her message again.

"Engine instruments?" Carl tapped the glass in front of Stu. "You interested in this checklist or not?"

"To tell you the truth. No. I shouldn't even be here. I probably should be home with Angie, but.... I needed something normal, something routine. I just needed to fly."

"Well, if you're going to fly, then let's do it. I wouldn't worry about Angie. I got a feeling she'll be just fine."

"I've called her a half dozen times."

"Trust me. She's fine."

A crackling came from the cockpit speaker. "Captain...Captain." Out on the tarmac, a ground crewman waved up at the cockpit. "How do you read me?"

Stu put on his headset and adjusted the microphone. "Loud and clear. How about me?"

"Loud and clear, Captain. Don't mean to rush you, but with the corporate prince on board, I'd like to get rid of you."

"Can't I leave him here?" Stu chuckled.

"No, Sir. Got no throne," the man laughed. "Please set brakes for chock removal."

Stu set the parking brake and checked the hydraulic pressure reading. "Brakes set. Pressure normal."

The ground crewman took off his headset and ran to remove the wheel chocks.

"Carl?" Stu said.

"Yeah, Ironman." Carl looked at him. "What 'ya need?"

Stu grabbed the yoke with both hands and squeezed. "This...this is real. You always get the truth here. I need this. Make any sense?"

Carl nodded. "The only thing that does, Ironman. Let's fly."

CHAPTER FORTY-TWO

Kashif drove their van slowly through a cluster of half-constructed carnival booths and past a tiny Ferris wheel onto a dirt road. Hosaam was correct. No one gave their vehicle more than a curious glance, just long enough to read the word "Maintenance" that Hosaam had stenciled on the side.

Above the trees ahead, a lone vulture circled. Kashif's thoughts returned to the railway underpass, and his mind was soon a jumble of images—vultures, the dead woman, a robe of many colors, and Tanngela.

"Stop here in the trees, " Hosaam ordered.

Across a small clearing, a man and woman embraced. A long kiss.

"Is this the launch site?" Abbud asked.

Hosaam didn't answer.

The man wore a full beard, the woman a long green dress.

"Are they allies to assist us?" Abbud tried again.

The man spun the woman around. Nudged her toward a giant ball of helium balloons pegged to the ground, then turned away and disappeared into the tree line.

Kashif's eyes remained locked on the woman. With a big smile and a little girl's dashing of feet, she seemed to fly across the road, becoming engulfed in the mass of bubbling balloons. She freed them from their peg, winding the strings about her wrist.

Abbud fired off more questions. "The balloons? Are they a marker? A device to signal others?" He tapped Kashif's shoulder. "Can we launch from somewhere else?"

Kashif ignored Abbud's questions, staring at the woman, his

entire body growing numb, knowing that the only two questions that mattered would never be answered. Why was the woman's hair the precise color and length of Tanngela's? And why was every balloon blue? A low wailing of tongues echoed through his mind.

"Drive, Kashif, before he returns," Hosaam commanded.

Kashif accelerated down the gravel road.

"Good. Now, slow down. Don't startle her." Hosaam reached over Kashif's right arm and gave the horn two quick taps.

The woman turned, her great ball of balloons whirling about her face. Each balloon was decorated with a bright red smiley face on one side and "$2" on the other. She backed away from the oncoming van.

"Stop next to her." Hosaam rolled down his window, smiled, and waved.

Kashif resisted a strange urge to rush out of the van, give the woman fifty dollars, and send her away. A crazy idea. Why would a maintenance worker buy all of her balloons?

Hosaam opened the door and eased out. "Ma'am? A moment, please."

Yes, Kashif thought. This will work. Hosaam will simply claim maintenance work. Fallen tree removal. Loose power lines. Order her to leave the area. But Hosaam wasn't dressed like a maintenance worker.

The woman took a step backward, then another.

"My cousin died fighting in Afghanistan," Hosaam said. "We seek the graveyard."

The woman stopped. "Arlington? That's all the way up on the north side of Reagan National. Get back on the expressway and—"

"Reagan National?" Hosaam's accent grew very thick. "Expressway?" He shrugged his shoulders and walked closer. "I'm a...ghost to your country...a...visitor. And lost." He smiled again, and stepped next to her.

"Oh. I'm sorry." She pointed toward the highway, turning her back to Hosaam.

Kashif's mind flooded with wails.

Hosaam's left hand struck out like a cobra, snatching a wad of black hair. Snapping her head backward, he pressed his knee into her lower back as his knotted cord whistled through the air and coiled around her neck. He grasped the cord with both hands and pulled, spinning and bending at the waist until her back lay flat on top of his, then jerked both fists toward the ground.

Her body lifted into the air, feet dangling, balloons twirling in a mad circle above. The rope dug deep into her throat. After a single violent spasm, the woman's head rolled loose upon her shoulders.

Kashif told himself that everything about this moment was different. His ears weren't ringing from a bomb blast. The air contained not a speck of swirling dust. The woman wore green, not blue. But the balloons were blue, and his body knew no difference. Trapped by hands that wouldn't move to open the door, and legs that wouldn't run, he watched the life leave her as the wails inside him screamed.

Somewhere, a horn blared.

Hosaam dumped the woman to the ground and straightened as he reached underneath his jacket. After a glance over his shoulder to sight the target, he spun and pitched.

The man rounding the front of the van staggered as a knife sunk into his chest.

Above both wailing tongues and blaring horn, Kashif's mind supplied a "thunk."

Toppling, the man rolled once and tried to stand up.

Hosaam delivered a vicious kick to his temple.

The man collapsed.

Bending down, Hosaam knocked the handle to a forty-five degree angle and jammed the heel of his hand hard against the base of the pommel. He twisted the handle left and right before yanking it free. After wiping the blade clean on the man's shirt, he gave Kashif a nod of thanks and slipped it back under his coat. "The horn." Hosaam's hand made a cutting motion under his chin. "Release the horn."

Kashif looked down and saw both his hands pressing the center of the steering wheel. He lifted one hand, and then the other, a little surprised they moved at all. The blaring stopped.

Hosaam appeared at the passenger door. His lips parted and met, forming various shapes. Each time he did so another sound emitted from his mouth.

After several seconds Kashif understood they were words.

"...never anticipated he'd move so fast. Thanks for warning me." Hosaam pointed toward the rear of the van. "Go help Abbud unload the crates."

Kashif's mind reeled, trying to make sense of Hosaam's words. "Crates?" Of what importance were crates? A man lay dead. The woman with Tanngela's hair lay next to him. A moment ago, the man had kissed her. And she ran...a smile lighting her face as she tied the balloons to her wrist. Now, above her lifeless body, the balloons swayed in the breeze.

Hosaam returned to the bodies and crouched low over the woman. He placed a hand on her throat, just below the chin, and rolled her head left and right, studying her face. Across the water, an airliner lifted into the sky and another took the runway. Four more waited in line. Storm clouds were forming to the west, but over the airfield, crystal clear.

Kashif opened the door. He was lined up dead six o'clock behind the departing airliner. Close enough to see the engine's heat plumes roil the cool air. He estimated the distance at 1,500 meters. Well within the SA-14's firing parameters. Hosaam had selected a good launch site. From this range, there was little chance for Kashif to miss. But, there was little chance he would have missed from half a dozen other spots along this shoreline.

He walked around the front of the van to where Hosaam still meddled with the woman's body. "Why?"

Hosaam pointed to Abbud struggling with the crates. "I told you to—"

"I said 'why?'"

"You question me? Is this dutiful? This is the site I selected. While you played at student, I scouted. As you dallied with whores, I planned our—"

"We could have launched from there." Kashif lashed out his arm, pointing at a grove of trees. "Or there." He swung his arm to the right. "Or even back where you commanded me to drive. You never suggested anything like this. I didn't know you planned the murder of innocents."

"Where do you see innocent, Kashif? She walks uncovered. Alone, out here, unescorted. They wear no wedding bands. Whores and sons of whores, all of them. There are no innocents in America. I did not lie to her. My cousins did die fighting in Afghanistan. And so did yours. Do you think she cared?"

"This serves no purpose. Strikes no fear. Will you put signs on their bodies so Americans will know this was done to avenge, to warn, to demand their withdrawal from the lands of Allah? These two need not have died."

"And have you checked the passenger manifest? Do you know that all aboard the airliner are guilty and deserve death?"

"I do what must be done." Kashif pointed at the woman's body. "You studied her face. She's young. Could have found her way to Allah. Bore children and raised them in a house of Islam. But you ended her journey. If I could stop all the killing, I would. Do you feel the same, Hosaam?"

Reaching down behind her neck, Hosaam jerked his knotted cord free and spat on the woman's face. "Go help Abbud. Then load up these Kaffirs. This is your duty. Do it."

Kashif knelt, thumbed the spittle from the woman's face, and freed the balloons from her wrist. They floated toward the treetops.

Hosaam reached for his knife. "Now!"

Abbud dropped a crate to the ground and picked up his sniper rifle.

"Put the rifle down, fry cook." Hosaam brushed past Kashif, shoved aside the van's sliding door, and turned on the aviation radio. "Washington tower, America Airways flight 1285, taxi with bravo. Roger, America Airways 1285, taxi runway one via taxiways kilo and...."

The requests for permission to taxi and the tower's ensuing instructions continued nonstop, reminding Kashif of his mission. He couldn't restore these lives. Their blood was on Hosaam's hands. He had a mission to complete.

Instead of one missile per crate, Kashif found two. "Four missiles? I thought only two per city. Have we such vast resources?"

"Our new mullah has bestowed upon us a great honor. Our target is the priority. Flight 1444. All else relegated to second."

"I thought all teams were to strike as one. Five airports. Targeting a specific flight is not wise. What if it delays or cancels? How will we coordinate?"

"That's our new mullah's concern. We have our orders. Flight 1444. This we listen for. This you will shoot down. That flight is your vengeance, Kashif."

CHAPTER FORTY-THREE

"Hurry." Buzz waved Angie forward. Pointing through the control tower's windows, he directed her eyes to the ramp far below. "Stu's flight has already pushed back from the gate. They should call for taxi instructions soon."

Following Buzz's finger, Angie located Stu's aircraft at the end of the concourse. Of all the things she'd worried about, the weather, getting past security, what length skirt, even the height of her heels, she never dreamt Stu's flight would depart before she arrived. "More than thirty minutes early, aren't they? What about their passengers?"

"These shuttle flights between Washington, New York, and Boston leave every hour. Stu's got a corporate big shot on board. The man had every employee scrambling to get him out ASAP." Buzz pulled out a chair. "Sit right there, Angie. Nice view, huh?"

Nice didn't begin to describe the panorama surrounding her. Through the massive control tower windows, Angie could follow the Potomac southward, clear past the marina and public parks of Daingerfield Island. She could even pick out a cluster of bright blue balloons floating above the autumn leaves. Off to the north, the entire city of Washington, D.C. sparkled in the sun.

Buzz pulled the microphone from the hook in front of her. "Okay, here's how it works. I'm the shift supervisor. I monitor the controllers and intervene when I have to. Everybody in the tower uses a headset. But this old mic works just fine. Hold it to your mouth, squeeze the button on the side, pause for a full second, then talk. Pause again when you're done. Then let go. The pauses are important. Otherwise you'll cut off words at the beginning or end. Go ahead and practice. I've got the system set up so that only I can

317

hear you."

Angie followed Buzz's instructions. "Hey, Ironman, you need…." She choked up and stopped.

Buzz's hand squeezed her shoulder. "It's okay. Stu's told that story more times than I can count. Give it a second, and try again."

She cleared her throat. "Hey, Ironman, you need a hot date tonight?"

"Perfect. You'd sure as hell get a loud 'yes' out of me." Buzz flipped a few switches on the console. "Okay, that mic's live. If you squeeze the button and talk, you're broadcasting to the world. I'll turn up the speaker and give you a nod when it's okay to transmit. It'll be after Stu's headed northwest up the river."

"Buzz? Stu and I…we're having…I'm trying—"

"Angie, I don't need to know. Stu's not been himself for a while now. Just glad you're here."

Angie nodded her thanks. "There's two gift-wrapped packages for you downstairs. Both are the exact shape and size of a case of stout. From me, for today."

"Angie, I can't—"

"You must. Too heavy for me to carry."

"How'd you get them in?"

"Didn't. Just bought, and had them wrapped. Carl got them past security. The man's got skills."

Buzz laughed. "Yes, he does. Most of them no longer appreciated. Whole country's so uptight. Like most of these young controllers. On bad weather days they only talk of crashes, and on sunny days, nothing but the approaching clouds. Almost as if they prefer storms. Sometimes wish I was back in Baghdad. Order them all to shut their traps." He sat down next to her. "But you lucked out. You're working with me. And the conditions are perfect. Clear blue sky over the capital. And Stu's taking off north. Just after he breaks ground, he'll turn left over the Potomac. His wing and tail will frame the National Mall. It'll look like his red, white, and blue jet is flying right over top the Washington Monument. Always gets to me. Make a great photo, Angie. Did you bring a camera?"

Queasiness wrenched Angie's gut. She grabbed her shoulder bag and dug beneath the makeup kit.

She wanted this day to be perfect. Start their lives again. When was the last time she'd photographed Stu flying? Probably not since

9/11. Before those towers fell, a wife could sneak into the cockpit late at night, snap a photo, and steal a kiss. Since then, once the aircraft left the gate, no one got past the cockpit door except flight crew. September eleventh ended her photos.

No. That was just another self-deception. At least she was catching them quicker now. The truth was that the photographs, the special moments she'd normally sought to capture and hold, stopped when she started chasing a rapist and murderer. The photos stopped when Uday started.

Angie pulled out a big, black relic with a fat lens. Her stomach relaxed. "Thanks for reminding me, Buzz. I'm woefully out of practice."

"With a camera? Hell, just point, focus and press."

"No. With truth," Angie muttered.

"Washington tower, America Airways 1444 taxi with information 'Charlie.'"

Kashif hurriedly laid the woman back down on the grass.

Tower answered. "America 1444, taxi runway zero one via…"

"Did our new mullah account for the flight leaving early?" Kashif checked his watch. "We'll be striking a half hour ahead of schedule."

Hosaam beat him to the crates, grabbed a missile, tore off the packing materials and tossed it to the ground.

"Careful! You'll damage them."

Hosaam held the next missile high above his head and glared as if he'd love to crash it down on Kashif's skull. Instead he laid it gently on the grass.

Kashif inspected the first launcher. Hosaam's carelessness had done no apparent harm. From rote, he readied the missile for launch. With each flip of switch the wails in his mind grew louder.

Angie twisted the telephoto lens and focused in on Stu's aircraft as he approached the runway. Hovering in the top right corner of her shot, a bright blue dot clashed with a backdrop of warm autumn tones. Angie slid her chair right and found an angle that eliminated the balloons.

"You won't be able to reach the mic from there."

She slid back to the microphone. "From this angle, there's a big ball of balloons spoiling an otherwise gorgeous photo."

"Forget the photo. Where are the balloons?"

"Of course. I'm sorry, Buzz. Wasn't considering the danger. Look above the trees at the north edge of Daingerfield."

Buzz squinted, then laughed. "If you're talking about the bundle floating over that white van, no worries. Someone flying down there at treetop level already has a much bigger problem than balloons." Buzz shook his head. "Funny, didn't think they allowed vehicles in the park. Probably some sort of maintenance. Looks like standard government issue. Ugly white paint job."

A van? Angie stood up. Beyond the trees, she saw a white vehicle parked in the center of a small clearing. Wasn't that the type of vehicle that her neighbor had reported to the police? Angie increased the camera's magnification to maximum. Located the north shore of the island and panned inland. Booths. Ferris wheel. Trees. Then a blue cluster of balloons. Below them, she found the white van. Looked like two or three people milling about. One with long hair. Maybe a woman. Two more sunning themselves in the grass. Maintenance? More likely, some picnickers.

"America 1444, cleared for takeoff, turn left heading three-two-zero degrees."

After turning onto the runway, Stu pushed the throttles forward and heard a loud warning horn. "Carl, tell tower we'll need a minute."

"Washington tower, America 1444 delaying takeoff for..."

Stu tuned out the remainder of Carl's transmission as he analyzed the problem. Warning horns were just that, a chance to fix something before everything went to hell. Too bad Angie wasn't equipped with one. Stu's eyes flicked over the seven possible causes: Leading edge flaps and slats were extended—confirmed by both the green light in front of him and the overhead position indicator; trailing edge flaps at twenty-five degrees—flap handle matched the indicator; parking brake released—red light was extinguished; stabilizer trim—centered in the green band; speed brake handle—full forward and down. Just in case, he gave the handle an extra nudge. A click preceded the handle's eighth-of-an-inch drop into the proper takeoff position. Problem solved. How many times, over the past decade, had he failed to nudge Angie? Would it have solved anything?

"Roger, America 1444. Takeoff clearance canceled. Do you need assistance?"

"Negative, tower," Carl responded. "The problem's already fixed. America 1444, ready for—"

Stu interrupted Carl's transmission by holding up a finger. He shoved the throttles forward. This time, no warning horn. "Okay, Carl. Go ahead."

Carl picked up where he'd left off. "Washington tower, America 1444, ready for takeoff."

Stu pulled the throttles back to idle and waited for tower to coordinate a new takeoff clearance. Everything here made sense— Carl—the tower—the aircraft. Everything—just as it should be.

Kashif was stunned. Ten seconds ago the missile's growl was loud and fierce, indicating the seeker head clearly saw the engine's heat plume. The strong tone promised a good track to the target. Moments later, the growl softened and went silent. Nothing in his training prepared him for this. He lowered the missile from his shoulder.

"Do you tire so easily, Kashif? Moments from your vengeance."

"I've lost the launch tone."

"Nonsense. Look at the grass springing back up behind the jet. The pilot has pulled his engines back."

"Don't pretend to instruct me. You know nothing of this." Kashif reexamined the launch settings and found a hairline crack in the seeker head. "You broke the glass, you fool. The coolant has leaked out."

Hosaam pointed his AK-47 at Kashif.

"Let him be." Abbud raised his sniper rifle. Clicked the safety off.

Tossing the missile aside, Kashif ran past them both for another missile.

Carl parroted the new takeoff instructions back to the tower.

Stu patted the lucky wings in his pocket, grabbed the flight controls and pushed the throttles forward. Thoughts of Angie slipped away as the jet's speed accelerated. His eyes flitted between the gauges and the runway.

Inside the cockpit, the compressor speeds and exhaust gas temperatures read normal. Outside, he was a little left of the runway's center. A tap of the rudder pedal brought the aircraft's nose back to the painted centerline. Inside, he crosschecked the fuel flows, oil pressures and temperatures. Back outside, four thousand feet remained before the Potomac. As the airspeed gauge increased past eighty knots he shifted his attention mostly outside. Nothing stopped them now except an engine failure, a fire, or windshear. As the airspeed approached one hundred forty knots Stu loosened his grip, readying his hand to leave the throttles. Past that speed, pulling the throttles to idle and aborting the takeoff meant rolling off the end of the runway and plunging into the river.

Rotating the camera's zoom back to normal magnification, Angie followed Buzz's advice. Point and click. A dozen lens shutterings later, she was glad. The first three were action shots as Stu guided the jet onto the runway. The next four showed the long grasses rippling behind the engines. The last five included a passing sailboat, her mainsail running full before the wind, bow cutting the river's water, old world mixing with new. Photos Stu would love. The kind she'd taken when they'd first met...when everything was new.

Angie kept snapping as Stu rolled down the runway. She caught the heat plumes of Stu's jet exhaust disturbing the air, causing a mirage-like optical illusion of a bent and wavy fuselage behind the wings. He'd love that one, too. She felt happy, almost giddy, and young.

Stu released the throttles. All his attention was outside now. If an engine quit, they'd keep going. Cabin caught on fire? Press forward into the air. Goose crashes through the windshield and splatters his skull against the bulkhead? Carl takes the controls and lifts off. With a runway this short, come hell or high water, they were committed to going airborne. He waited for Carl's call.

"Rotate."

Stu eased the yoke back. The end of the runway disappeared. Nothing but water, Washington, and sky.

"Positive rate." Carl's call confirmed they were safely airborne and ready for gear retraction.

"Gear up," Stu commanded.

Carl raised the gear handle.

Comfortably airborne, Stu banked the wings to turn upriver.

A beautiful shot! Stu's jet suspended above the river, landing gear half retracted, National Mall in the background. Angie placed the microphone in her lap and waited for his turning aircraft to frame the Washington Monument. One last photo. Then she would set the camera down and start proving to Stu that he meant everything to her. Show him that nothing in her life much mattered without him. And if that took the rest of her life—so be it.

Angie rotated the camera's focusing ring. Crystal clear. Gorgeous! Her finger got ready to snap. A streak of smoke cut across the view frame and entered the jet's left engine. Stu's wing exploded.

CHAPTER FORTY-FOUR

The aircraft shuddered and rolled left. Reacting not to any conscious command, but rather to decades at the flight controls, Stu's foot pressed the right rudder pedal, starting the wings rolling back toward level.

The amber "master caution" lights illuminated—his jet's way of saying "I need your help. Check my messages." Next to the amber lights, three of the six possible messages were annunciated: ENG, AIR COND, and ANTI-ICE. All reasonably attributed to a simple engine failure, yet the aircraft's initial shudder felt like something worse.

On the instrument panel, most of the left engine's gauges were on the move. RPM, oil pressure and quantity—dropping. Not good. Engine vibration, oil and exhaust gas temperatures—rising. Bad. Fuel flow—steady. Very bad.

The spine-rattling clang of the fire bell filled the cockpit. His jet telling him, "I need your help. Now! Fire!"

Gathering information, Stu's eyes darted across the cockpit. Two more messages were annunciated: HYD and ELEC. Another dozen lights, blue, amber, and flashing red, announced various bits of bad news. And the gauges confirmed his worst fears. Hydraulic quantity—falling. Bad. Fuel flow—increasing. Very bad. Airspeed— slowing toward stall. Disaster.

The flight controls grew sluggish. The aircraft slipped sideways toward the ground.

Stu's mind performed triage on the incoming data, sending the airspeed, altitude, and flight path information directly to his hands and feet while analyzing the lights and messages to formulate a plan.

His foot drove the right rudder pedal to the floor while one hand shoved the good engine's throttle to maximum power and the other pushed the yoke forward. In response to Stu's inputs, the aircraft's nose lowered. The wings leveled. Airspeed and altitude stabilized.

Amidst the cockpit chaos, tower radioed, but the clanging fire bell rendered the words unintelligible. Stu pressed the fire switch, silencing the alarm. A loud pounding at the cockpit door muffled tower's next call.

Responding to the pounding flight attendant, Carl snatched the communication handset from the center console and calmly spoke in flight crew shorthand. "The captain has his hands full. Red emergency. Five minutes. Captain's evacuation command. Copilot's side only."

Short and direct—perfect. The flight attendants now understood the following: The problem was too big to discuss; they had five minutes to prepare the passengers for an emergency evacuation; they were to wait until the aircraft was stopped on the runway and the captain commanded the evacuation; everyone must exit out the right side—away from the fire.

More importantly, Stu now understood that Carl's analysis paralleled his own. Three items stood out. First, this was a modern aircraft with smart engines. Therefore, the instant the fire occurred, the engine control system should have shut off the fuel flow. Second, the leaking hydraulic fluid indicated severed hydraulic lines. Third, an airplane didn't shudder from a simple engine failure. Add them up— something had ripped his left engine apart.

Bird strike? Doubtful. Misplaced wrench? It happens. But those were questions for the investigators. Right now, only the fire mattered.

Expecting the worst, Stu initiated the prescribed emergency procedure by sliding the engine start lever to cutoff. Yep, the fuel kept flowing. He pulled the fire handle, releasing halon into the burning engine. But the exhaust gas temperature remained pegged at the top of the gauge. This fire wasn't going out.

"Carl, tell tower to roll the fire trucks and—"

"America 1444...America 1444...do...you...copy? Missile strike, left wing."

Missile? As if the hand of God pierced his chest, the gap

between Stu's racing heartbeats seemed to lengthen toward forever. The span from first beat to second was more than enough time to analyze the situation. Engine fire—not going out. Hydraulic leak—find it or the flight controls become unmanageable. Missile attack—they never fire just one. Between second beat and third he formulated a plan. "Carl, you're inside, the fire and hydraulic leak are yours. I'm outside, flying and fighting." Stu's racing heart never reached the crescendo of the sixth beat higher, returning to calm and steady as he voiced his plan.

Carl's hands reached overhead toward the hydraulic panel as Buzz's voice came over the radio. "I say again, America 1444. A surface-to-air missile struck your left wing."

"Buzz...I need a clock position."

"Roger, Stu. Launch was from dead six o'clock. Corkscrew smoke trail pattern."

Now Stu's synapses were really firing. Corkscrew smoke trail meant early model Russian. Both good news and bad. Small warhead, but cheap. They could have a dozen down there. He needed speed and altitude to maneuver in the event of further launches. He also needed to turn the jet to shield the good engine. All of that easily accomplished twenty years ago in his tiny F-15, but this behemoth airliner forced him to choose.

He opted for speed and turning—creating larger angles to shield the good engine. But which way should he turn?

What some might call an out-of-body experience was, for Stu, a self-directed mental exercise. From a god's eye point of view, he pictured the aircraft, the airfield, and the surrounding terrain. Where would he position the launch site? This mental snapshot gave him the answer. Turn left, back toward Daingerfield Island.

Stu simultaneously twisted and pushed the control yoke. "Buzz?"

"Roger, Stu. I have you starting a descending left-hand turn. I'm scanning for a second launch."

Stu's eyes split duty between the trees of Daingerfield Island and the proximity of the water below. Deaf to the cockpit alarms, blind to the flashing warning lights, he left behind his pilot body and rode the air as his creator intended. Hands not on a yoke, instead sensing past metal and cable to wings and tail, flexing, shaping, floating through the currents, feeling the molecules bounce from his skin ever faster, the sky whistling past, reminding him, "Quick...be quick."

Stuart Pierce flew hard, bending his aluminum body through the air, nursing out every last bit of flight energy. The river disappeared. Row upon endless row of white tombstones became the focus of his sweep. Beyond the bright grave markers rose the Pentagon and the spot where the 9/11 airliner had crashed, and men had died. Stu didn't hesitate. He toggled the microphone switch. "Buzz, shut them down."

"Roger, Stu, we've stopped all arrivals and departures."

Stu's mind was reeling, his multitasking skills saturated. His hands and feet delicately maneuvered a seventy-five ton jet at the limits of its operating envelope, dancing along a knife's edge of maximum performance where any slight deviation in airspeed, pitch, power, or bank angle would cut the lift and plunge them all to their deaths. And next to him, Carl ran the aircraft's emergency checklist, which required Stu's acknowledgement of the movement of critical switches. And now this too. "Buzz, I mean all of them, Kennedy, O'Hare, Los Angeles, shut the whole country down."

After a brief silence, Buzz replied, "Roger, Stu. Will comply."

Stu's guts wrenched at Buzz's stony response. They both knew what it meant. Within minutes every airplane in the nation would enter a holding pattern until police secured the perimeters of all major airports. Aircraft critical on fuel would divert and land at obscure airfields like White Plains, Madison, and Burbank. Within hours, the skies over America would grow quiet and still. And for only the second time since the Wright brothers, not a plane would fly. September eleventh, all over again.

"Missile launch!" A woman's voice screamed over the radio.

"Allahu Akbar!" Hosaam yelled, and fell to his knees in ecstasy as the second missile screeched up toward the airliner.

Kashif turned his back to the smoke trail and touched a hand to his chest. He rubbed the shirt pocket that held his mother's photo, his mind flashing back over the last minutes, trying to make some sense of what he now felt.

The first missile launch had been easy. Trained for so long to execute the motions, his finger just pulled. But the violent result was something new. The missile rammed home and demolished the airliner's left engine. Pieces rained toward the ground, the larger fragments leaving tiny smoke trails mimicking the dark plume that spewed from the aircraft's wing.

Initially, the jet had rolled left, Hosaam cheering its imminent crash. "You have done it, Kashif! Allah wills their deaths. You are the well-trained instrument of destruction, the righteous hand of Almighty Allah's wrath. Allahu Akbar!"

It had taken all his will power to stop his fist from smashing into Hosaam's gleeful face. Instead, he punched at the airplane in the sky as it righted itself. "They are well trained also, Hosaam. Look, the pilot has regained control." He left the fool staring open-mouthed as he grabbed another missile and sighted on the remaining engine.

Yet, despite the fierce growl voicing the seeker head's promise to track and destroy, the second lauch proved difficult.

"Fire!" Hosaam had commanded.

But as the wails in his mind rose louder than the missile's growl, he hesitated.

"The pilot can't fly without engines!" Hosaam yelled.

He'd gritted his teeth and concentrated on the growl.

"Fire!" Hosaam yelled again.

And so he had. The second missile's trigger was a great weight to pull, but the launch quieted the fool's yelling.

Now silent, Hosaam's arms were raised toward heaven, his face filled with joy as he watched the second missile close in on the airliner.

Sickened by Hosaam's ecstasy, Kashif looked away, his eyes finding Abbud.

The sniper's chin was tucked against his shoulder, eyes squinting up at the sky, face a scrunched-up mask. Of hope or of dread? Kashif couldn't tell. A few seconds more would supply the answer.

"Missile launch, left, eight o'clock," Buzz flatly voiced.

Stu's eyes snatched the latest readings of airspeed and altitude, then snapped left, searching Daingerfield Island. The numbers weren't good. His slight descent had gained him some extra knots, placing him well above stall speed. But he had very little altitude to work with. It would have to do. Jets didn't fly well without engines.

He located the corkscrew smoke trail just above the tree line. Streaking past the northern edge of the island, it turned toward him. Time to surrender the airspeed he'd worked so hard to gain.

Stu lowered the nose toward the white gravestones below, rolled up to sixty degrees of bank and pulled. The aircraft's flight controls bucked and slammed against his palms. But he needed more turn—greater angles to hide the good engine's exhaust. Yet if he pulled much longer, the jet would crash to the ground.

He rough-rode through another twenty degrees of turn, then accepted that this was all she could give him. His jet wasn't lying. She always told the truth. Rolling level, he raised the nose to a shallow climb. The violent bucking reduced to a steady shudder. Soon, she'd flutter to the ground like a falling leaf, the ride down gentle, but death just as sure.

With the warhead upon them, Stu executed the last desperate step of his missile defense. He didn't know if they had altitude enough to recover from this final maneuver, but he was sure that without the good engine they'd all die. Resolute, he raised the aircraft's nose even farther. Rolling up to hide the good engine beneath his wing, Stu chopped the throttle to idle, lowering the exhaust temperature.

The maneuver left his jet in a power idle, nose-high attitude, with dropping airspeed, close to the ground. A place no pilot wanted to be, a situation every pilot was trained to avoid. He was out of airspeed and ideas. Only hope and prayer remained.

For a moment, he thought to pray to God, but God hadn't trained him for this, the U.S. Air Force had. So as the jet pitched toward the ground, he sent a fighter pilot's prayer up to the best of those who'd gone before: Rickenbacker, Bong and Olds. "Screw those lousy, missile-firing pieces of shit," he prayed. Stu could swear he heard chuckling from above.

Four hundred feet from impact, the aircraft's stall warning system activated, a wailing siren interspersed with a dispassionate computerized voice repeating, "Terrain—pull up...terrain—pull up...terrain—pull up."

As the aircraft bucked and slid downward, Stu wished the missile great speed. For once it closed within a few hundred feet, he could add power without influencing the missile's point of impact. Stu's fingers wrapped around the good engine's throttle and squeezed, his knuckles whitening.

The missile flew out of Stu's sight, heading for the fuselage behind him. He slammed the throttle forward as the warhead's detonation shook the entire airframe.

Kashif steeled himself as Abbud cringed. At the sound of the second explosion, the old sniper looked away and stared at the ground, his shoulders slumping.

Turning back, Kashif watched the jet roll, and then drop, disappearing below the autumn leaves.

Hosaam rejoiced and screamed out "Allahu Akbar!"

Moments later, the jet rose back above the tree line, lumbering upward like some great bird, grievously wounded yet refusing to die. Black smoke poured from two gaping wounds on wing and fuselage. Kashif picked up another missile, feeling every bit like a tiny villager hefting one more spear to the kill, but not really sure what he was killing. Not sure that he should.

"Fire!" Hosaam screamed in his ear.

But this time Kashif's finger trembled on the trigger, refusing to pull.

"Fire."

The missile seemed to scream also, an angry tone that begged him to unleash it for the final kill.

"Fire."

As Stu skimmed along above the trees, he caressed the flight controls, demanding from his jet just enough lift to keep them from tangling in the treetops. When he was sure they were well clear, he relaxed the backpressure, letting the nose drop to regain a few more knots. "Carl, where we at?"

"Two fires still burning, Ironman, first class cabin and left engine. All the halon is gone. I've saved enough hydraulic fluid to drop the gear, but that will leave you in manual reversion. She'll be a lot to handle."

"Okay, if the fires won't go out, then they won't. Best thing is land quickly. After we line up with the runway, lower the flaps electrically. One mile out, drop the landing gear and take my throttle. I'll muscle the flight controls. You manage the airspeed. If we get too slow, we'll settle her onto the Potomac."

Stu left unsaid that they still had to cross Daingerfield Island. One more missile launch and there'd be no water landing. No life rafts. Only death. The thought was barely a thought when Buzz radioed, "White van, in the clearing ahead."

Carl pointed out the cockpit window and confirmed that hard trees and not the soft waters of the Potomac would claim them. "Launch tube, twelve o'clock."

Stu spotted the white van. Next to it, three men. One pointed a missile at his jet. As Stu looked straight into the business end of the launch tube he uttered the last word most common to pilots. "Shit."

"Shit," Carl replied.

Although pointless, Stu banked right, and then left, in a vain attempt at something, anything. As he passed overhead the launch tube, he glanced down at those who would kill him and his hopes were renewed by the unthinkable. One man swung his rifle toward another's skull.

Abbud's rifle butt smashed the back of Hosaam's head with a popping crack. Hosaam slumped to the dirt and didn't move. "Fire or not, Kashif. You have a choice."

Kashif targeted the remaining engine, the seeker head roaring its eagerness as the jet traveled the length of the island and flew out over the Potomac. The heat signature dropped off as the pilot banked up to align with the runway, but returned stronger than ever when the aircraft rolled out of the turn and the landing gear came down. Right now...pull the trigger and the airliner would crash. Without engines, and hanging all that drag from the gear, the plane would drop like a stone. Kashif's finger slid back and forth across the trigger, tensing and relaxing. Each time he pulled, Tanngela's smile stopped him. Every time he released, he saw his mother's blue robe dangling from the rubble.

As the aircraft slowed on the runway, smoke poured from the fuselage and engine, collecting behind the jet to mask Kashif's view. The missile's growl silenced. He lowered the launch tube from his shoulder. "Something's wrong."

"Yes, Kashif. Much is wrong."

For the third time, Stu searched the length of the cabin from front to rear, looking for passengers. Flames licked along the ceiling, driving him to his knees as he approached the back rows. Coughing smoke, he sat and dangled his legs out the evacuation door, preparing for his slide to the ground.

"Stu!" a woman's voice screamed.

Thirty yards from the bottom of the slide, two policemen restrained Cheryl. She screamed again, "Stu, Daryann is still in there."

Stu turned, and crawled back under the smoke.

CHAPTER FORTY-FIVE

High heels discarded somewhere on the tower stairs, Angie ran barefoot across the grass toward the burning jet.

Stu emerged from the smoke at the top of the slide. In his arms was a body, small with long hair. No movement—neither his, nor the body he cradled. The firemen screamed at him to jump. But he just stood there—frozen, smoke pouring forth, rolling over his shoulders.

As Angie approached the runway, a police car tried to intercept her, but she cut behind it and slipped in among the evacuated passengers. Sliding left and right, she made her way to the front.

Stu was sitting now. He adjusted the girl's blouse and smoothed her hair. Her head rolled sideways and bobbled free. One of her arms dropped limp below Stu's knee. He nestled her head back into the safety of his bicep and forearm. Tucked her arm along her waist and once more pushed the hair from her face—red hair.

Oh, my God…Cheryl. Angie searched the faces of the passengers.

There she was, struggling with policemen, trying to break free. "That's my baby…my baby." But they held on tight.

Stu slid down and carried Cheryl's child forward.

She looked once at her baby's face and collapsed, searching the ground, looking everywhere, anywhere, but up.

Half a minute passed with Stu standing above her. Waiting, like a figure cast in iron. No matter how much time Cheryl needed, a minute, a day, a year, he'd stand there.

Still looking away, Cheryl reached up toward Stu.

Gently, he lowered her child into her arms.

"My baby…my baby." Cheryl hugged and rocked.

333

Turning away, Stu walked two steps back toward his jet, and watched her burn. Loud explosions filled the air. The fire trucks gave up and retreated.

Stu fell to his knees. Streaks of sunlight knifed through the billowing smoke, highlighting the blood cutting lines down his blackened cheek. His back rounded toward the ground. He lurched forward, the backs of his hands scraping along the tarmac. His duty was done.

"Please officer, that's my husband."

He ignored her.

Carl appeared at Angie's side. "Let her through. She's the captain's wife."

The policeman looked at the broken man on the runway, and nodded.

Angie ran to Stu's side. "Stu, I'm here."

He didn't move.

"Stu?" She rubbed his back. "It's Angie."

His eyes were vacant. Staring.

"Stu," Angie shouted.

"I killed her," Stu seemed to tell his burning jet. "I killed Daryann."

CHAPTER FORTY-SIX

Kashif finished splashing gasoline around the launch site and hopped into the back of the van. He tossed a thermite grenade onto the grass and pulled the door closed. Abbud drove forward. Fifty meters later they stopped.

An explosion preceded a rush of black smoke roiling into the sky. With the launch site sanitized, Kashif yelled, "Go."

Abbud stomped on the gas pedal and sped toward the southern edge of the island.

Kashif checked Hosaam's injuries. Finding blood at the back of his skull, he rotated Hosaam's head about the shoulders, feeling for jerks and pops. The head moved smoothly. Pressing at the side of Hosaam's neck, he counted the heartbeats as his watch's second hand moved from twelve to three. Multiplied the total by four. Eighty-eight. Fast, but well within normal.

He wasn't sure how he felt about that. How would Hosaam react to Abbud's attack?

Hosaam would never confront Abbud directly. Yet how long could Abbud live a life without rest? Constantly checking behind him. Sleeping with one eye open. Everything would be simpler, if Hosaam were dead. Ashamed, Kashif immediately bowed his head to ask Allah's forgiveness, and discovered his shirt pocket torn half away, his mother's photo missing.

With arms stretched wide to steady himself against the bumpy ride, Kashif scanned the van. No photo. Dropping to his knees, he heaved Hosaam on top of the dead man's body and searched the floor. Nothing. Then he rolled the dead man atop Hosaam. Still nothing. He lifted the woman's body and felt underneath. Something.

Tangled in her clothes. Hard edges like photo stock. He pulled and heard a rip, but his hand came away empty.

The van lurched to a stop. The door yanked open behind him. "You will go on from here," Abbud declared.

"I've lost my mother's photo. Help me search." Kashif rolled the woman up on one side. Beneath her, the van floor was vacant.

"This is as far as I go," Abbud said.

Kashif frisked the woman's clothes.

"Do you hear me, Kashif?"

"Tanngela...my friend...my girlfriend saw the photo."

"Hosaam knows this?" Abbud asked.

"Yes," Kashif grimaced. From the woman's torn dress, he pulled a small book, covered in leather, the title worn off. He opened the front. A Qur'an. Wails filled Kashif's mind. "Hosaam murdered a believer."

"Believer...nonbeliever." Abbud shrugged. "Murder is what he does."

"No. Hosaam seeks vengeance, same as I."

"Does he? And what will he say if he learns that you've lost your mother's photo? The photo he knows your girlfriend has seen."

"We're burning the van. The photo will burn with it."

"How do you know it didn't fall out at the launch site? And blow away in the wind. What if the police find it and broadcast your mother's face? Hosaam will say that you must kill your girlfriend to prevent her from leading them to us."

Kashif jumped to the ground. Dense trees surrounded them, the river nowhere in sight. Sirens approached. "Why have you stopped here?"

"I am done. You will go on."

"This is craziness. I won't leave you here."

Abbud pointed at the approaching police cars. "Then stay. And die. If Bin Laden's widow were here, she'd remind you that Americans no longer take terrorists captive."

"But Abbud, we can...."

Abbud braced his rifle against the side of a tree, took careful aim and fired. A hole appeared on the windshield of the first police car, dead center between passenger and driver. The car veered away. Another hole appeared in the same spot on the second car. Four shots later, both cars were stopped well more than one hundred yards off with two flat tires each. The police officers fired wildly at the trees. "Go, Kashif. If I could kill anymore"—he pointed at Hosaam—"I'd kill that animal." Directing his scope at the oncoming helicopter, Abbud pulled the trigger and a spiderweb of cracked glass appeared high above the pilot's head. The helicopter circled away. "Leave, Kashif. The dense canopy will hide the van. And all will converge on my rifle shots."

He squeezed Kashif's shoulder and gently nudged him toward the driver's seat. "My father died before I was born. None of my brothers lived long enough for me to know them. You're the only brother I've ever had. Go now."

Kashif slid behind the wheel.

Abbud slammed the door. "Kashif...say what you have to...to survive. But say the truth about me."

"I'll say you fought bravely."

Abbud shook his head.

"That is the truth."

"Tell the whole truth, Kashif. Anything less is just a lie. And you'll steal from me the only good thing I did with my life. Saving you, without killing a single soul."

Kashif nodded.

"Promise me...say it...the whole truth."

"The whole truth, Abbud...I promise."

Kashif drove toward the southeast end of Daingerfield Island, wiping at his eyes.

At the river's edge, he stopped and listened. In the distance came another rifle shot and answering gunfire. Rousing a groggy Hosaam, Kashif placed scuba gear on his back, fastening the clips at his chest and waist, before shouldering and securing his own tank.

"Abbud?" Hosaam mumbled.

"He fights to cover us. They will kill him."

"Good. Saves me the trouble. Plane?"

"Burning on the runway."

"No crash?" He weakly clutched Kashif's arm.

Kashif easily pushed his hand away. "We must escape." He left Hosaam standing knee-deep in the river and returned to the van. Tore open a box containing several pounds of white phosphorus chips. Spread half along the sidewalls and piled the remainder in the center. Turned the dead bodies until they faced east. Tidied the woman's hair. Entwined their fingers. Asked Almighty Allah to receive these faithful. Two thermite grenades followed.

He rushed to the water and pulled Hosaam beneath waves. After counting to ten, Kashif surfaced to find the van ablaze. The white phosphorus would burn so fiercely that the fire trucks would be unable to extinguish the flames. The van would melt into a pool. No trace of anyone or anything would remain.

Several miles downriver they surfaced beneath a half-dozen circling vultures. Several others tore at the colorful pile on the shore. A loud whistle signaled their train approaching. They hurried beneath the bushes to change into dry clothes.

"I've lost my mother's photo."

"You and your precious photo." Hosaam poked Kashif in the chest. "You know what must be done." Hosaam's eyes questioned his. "If you don't have the stomach...what's your little slut's name?"

"Yes, Hosaam." Slowly, Kashif nodded. "I know what must be done."

"Good." Hosaam turned for his satchel.

For the second time in as many hours, Hosaam received a blow to the back of his head and crumpled unconscious.

Kashif quickly uncovered their satchels, changed clothes, and dumped the contents of Hosaam's backpack. He sifted through the water bottles, energy bars, and clothes, seeking their new identities. Wrapped in Hosaam's shirt, he found a mailer, the seal still intact. Tore it open. Inside were three smaller envelopes. He stuffed the envelope labeled Kashif into his satchel. Money? He'd need funds to survive. Searching every compartment of Hosaam's backpack and turning out each pocket, he found no cash. Opening Hosaam's coin pouch, he shook the contents onto the ground.

A fat roll of green paper bills fell out. He riffled though the wad—mostly hundreds. Had to be thousands of dollars. Kashif stuffed the roll into his pocket. The other items were almost childlike. Locks of hair, red and black and blond, two animal paws, one a dog's, the other burned and shriveled, possibly a cat. And random bits of sheer cloth, black and white—burqa-like material. And the knotted cord. Tangled with it, a piece of shredded fabric—a veil of many colors—the same as the dead woman on the shore.

The wailing tongues raged through Kashif's skull. He staggered backward, cowering low, covering his ears as if the wails rained down from heaven. Abbud spoke truth. Hosaam didn't want vengeance. He wanted to kill. He was an animal. A predator. A psychopath. An abomination in the eyes of Allah.

Hosaam moaned.

Kashif wrenched the knife from Hosaam's sheath and straddled him. Grasping the pommel with both hands, he held it high over his head, wanting to plunge it into Hosaam's heart. But the ululations roared even louder. Was he a psychopath, an animal, like Hosaam?

The train's whistle pierced the air. Kashif felt the rumble, heard the clacking. Soon the train would leave him behind. He slammed the pommel into Hosaam's temple. The moaning stopped.

Kashif snatched the abomination's cell phone from the dirt and dialed 911. At the sound of a voice on the other end, he whispered, "I've spotted the terrorists. Come quick. I can't talk. I'll leave this line open." He hid the phone beneath some leaves and grabbed his satchel.

Bursting from the bushes, Kashif sprinted out from under the vultures, toward the westbound train. He grasped hold of the last ore car's ladder and climbed.

Flopping down on the pile of ore, he lay heaving for air. Above the riverbank, the vultures flushed skyward and scattered. Emergency responders from his 911 call? Seemed impossible. Much too soon. Coast Guard searching the shoreline? This quickly? With dogs, it was possible. Dogs could have followed their scent right into the water. Sent the boats searching along the river. Possible, but not probable. Hosaam? Was he awake and moving along the shore? If the abomination escaped, he'd continue murdering innocents. Kashif pounded his fists into the iron ore, already regretting not killing him, and fearing that he'd learn to regret it even more.

The train curved northwest and climbed a small hill. Above the trees Kashif could see the university's clock tower. Their place.

Before Tanngela, he'd never touched the flesh of a woman who wasn't blood. And to look upon a woman with lust was akin to knifing the Prophet's nephew in the back. But what was lust? Yes, Tanngela stirred him in embarrassing ways. Sometimes sent his body surging out of control. Yet mostly, thoughts of her, the sound of her voice, made him long for talk of family and children, Allah and peace. Through Tanngela's eyes, the whole world became beautiful.

And beneath that clock tower, the bell tolling above them, her lips glistening, he had kissed her. He just had. And she'd kissed back, and held his hand, and they walked and talked for hours, until she invited him to mosque, reminding him who he was. Briefly, he'd forgotten why he'd come to America. Forgotten that his mother was "collateral damage." Harsh was his rejection of her invitation. Harsher still was what he needed to do now.

The clock tower read quarter past five. Tanngela would be in economics class another ten minutes. Kashif removed his shoe and pulled off his sock. Drew the cell phone from his pocket and dialed her number.

After six rings, her message answered. "Allah loves you."

Kashif trembled a small smile and whispered. "No, Tanngela…he loves you."

The beep sounded. "Tanngela, I'm sorry. For everything. I'm leaving for…returning to…I can't see you any…." Kashif coughed, trying to clear the constriction from his throat, but succeeded only in stimulating a coughing fit. He hung up.

As the fit subsided, the phone rang. Tanngela. His thumb hovered above "Answer."

From the west, he heard the whistle of an oncoming train. He spotted it rounding the next bend, perhaps a mile away. More than enough time. He answered.

"Kashif, what's wrong? I'm here."

"Tanngela? I thought…thought you were in class."

"The attacks. Class is canceled. But we're not. We've already organized a rally for tonight. It won't be like 9/11. Not this time. We want you with us. My friends from mosque are coming. We want to show them the beauty of Allah. Even Todd is ready. He's rounding up the men from his fraternity. I need you there, Kashif. Please."

All his resolve wilted beneath the concern in her voice. He wanted to ignore the truth of what he'd done. Wanted to tell Tanngela that he needed her too. She was everything Allah intended.

"Tanngela, listen. You must go…." He'd expected to leave a message—not tell her directly. This was impossible. But if Hosaam had escaped, he'd track down Tanngela and kill her.

"Go? Where?" Tanngela asked.

"The police. Right now. Tell them you need protection. That you knew one of the…."

"Kashif?"

"Tell them…that you knew me. I'm one of them."

"What?"

"The American troops. They called her 'collateral damage.' She wasn't Taliban. She despised the Taliban. Americans killed my mother. I'm sorry. None of that matters. Go to the police. His name is Hosaam. He poses as a cab driver. You saw my mother's photo, Tanngela. He knows. He will kill you."

Silence.

"Tanngela, you must go to the police and tell them everything. If our identities are known, and everything is broadcast on the news, then he has no reason to risk killing you."

The oncoming train's engine rolled past. "Tanngela, I have to go. And you have to go to the police. Right now. Do you hear me?"

The passing train was short, almost gone. A few more seconds and it would be too late. Yet he couldn't let go of her voice.

"But Kashif, I—"

"No. Go to the police."

"Kashif, I love—"

"You mustn't."

"But Kashif, I do. I—"

Kashif dropped the cell phone inside, tied a knot and cast the sock into the air. End over end it tumbled, landing on a load of coal. He watched the train fade into the east.

"Allah loves you, Tanngela," Kashif cried aloud, sinking to his knees. "How could he not?" he whispered. "How could he not?"

CHAPTER FORTY-SEVEN

"Yes, Excellency. I see. Captain Pierce never gives up. But your brother Prince Sadeem demands—"

"No, Taamir, the Ironman...cannot...give up. He does not know how." Uday jammed his thumb down on the remote and leaned back in his hospital bed. The recording reversed, the images spinning backwards. Uday pressed STOP, then PLAY. The jet brushed the top branches of the trees for the tenth time.

"Your Highness, your father has..."

"Strong blood, my father would say of this Ironman. Yet the Ironman's blood is the blood of rape. What would my father say—"

"Excellency!"

Pressing PAUSE, Uday stared up at Taamir.

"Please forgive me, Excellency. I beg you...we must focus on your brother, your father."

"No, Tama. You've done nothing that warrants forgiveness. Always have you served me well. What is it you desire?"

"Your brother, Excellency, demands an accounting of your actions. Your father has removed your diplomatic status as of midnight tonight. Visa revoked. Assets frozen. Roger's office says he is unavailable. We must fly out this evening. This recording must be destroyed. It's been more than two days. The Americans are investigating. You must act."

"Don't fret their investigation, Tama. I'm not some moneychanger's son cowering in a compound. Bin Laden had no oil. I am an Azwad, second in line to The Realm's throne. The Americans will find someone else to blame."

"But your father, he will...will..."

"Annihilate me."

"No, Excellency."

"Yes, Tama. I am unpredictable."

"You are his son. His blood."

"Weak blood."

Taamir frowned. "You mustn't talk—"

"Do not distress yourself, Tama. Yes, I shall return to the sands today. But not like this. If I am to give up my life, then it will be with dignity. Go to my apartments. Bring a robe and turban. I'll smile for the West no more." Uday grabbed Taamir's arm. "And retrieve my signet ring. I left it on the vanity...or perhaps in the safe, but do not return here without it."

"At once, Your Highness." Taamir bowed and hurried through the door.

Uday slid from his bed. Rolling the IV pole behind him, he shuffled to the mirror and tore the bandages from his face. Pressing at the left edge of his lips, he sucked in a quick breath of air at the stab of pain. Eyeing the full bag of morphine hanging from the IV pole, he muttered, "Not yet." To be sure...he'd need every last drop.

Moving his fingers from left to right—just below his nose—the deadness started. Steeling himself against the agony, he tested his practiced smile. Half his face struggled upward, drawing the dead side across, twisting the skin into a lopsided mask, a freak of comic sadness. "So pretty you've made me, Ironman."

Uday left the freak at the mirror and stepped into the outer room. His four bodyguards snapped to attention, eyes staring straight ahead. One by one, Uday stood in front of them, leaning on the IV pole and smiling, then watched their pupils shrink to the size of pinholes, an autonomic reflex of disappointment, disgust, revulsion. A poker tell, the Ironman would call it. "You will allow no one through this door until Taamir returns."

"Yes, Excellency," they answered in unison.

"You failed me before. That failure caused this," Uday pointed at his face. "No one enters this room. Not a doctor. Not a nurse screaming that I'm dying. No one...or you forfeit your lives."

Uday doubted the nurse would make haste. Twice today he'd caused the monitors to call her, then feigned awaking from sleep as she barged in to find everything perfectly in order. The second time he'd cursed her rude intrusion. Yet, threatening his bodyguards' lives provided that final guarantee against interruption.

After shutting the hospital room door, Uday wedged the back of a chair underneath the handle. "You've made me a grotesque beggar, Ironman." Without wealth…without beauty…who would pretend to love him now?

Returning to the bed, he parked the IV pole alongside. "Ironman? A good name for you." Yes, Uday reflected, an iron will upon which he'd broken. "You've taken everything. And yet, you were kind enough to give me the one thing I now most need."

Uday entered the nurses' IV code of one, three, five, seven, and suspended his finger above the up arrow, hesitating as the Qur'an's warning ran through his mind. "…Whoever kills himself with an iron weapon, will be carrying that weapon in his hand and stabbing his abdomen with it in the Hell Fire wherein he will abide eternally forever." Could it be true? Perhaps. And perhaps, it should be. The penalty for weak blood. Uday pressed the up arrow until a steady stream of morphine poured down the tube to his vein. Reaching into the pocket of his robe, he pulled out his signet ring, placed it on his finger and lay down on the bed. One last time he rubbed the star. "Not my star," he whispered, his voice cracking. "Never my star."

Grabbing the remote, he pushed PLAY.

On the television, America Airways 1444 lifted from the runway and turned northwest up the Potomac River. A missile entered the left engine and exploded. The jet recovered, sure and smooth. A minute later, the second missile struck the side of the aircraft, and the Ironman's jet appeared to almost dance, the wings rocking back and forth as it skimmed along the treetops. Uday clapped fitfully as the Ironman cleared the trees again. Vision blurring, Uday's eyelids grew heavy and drooped. Giving up is easy, Ironman…so very easy. Soon, only Uday's hearing remained. He listened for a slide and plunk, but heard only silence.

CHAPTER FORTY-EIGHT

Stu unwound the gauze from his right hand as he looked out the study's bay window. Leaves covered the driveway. Orange. Red. Some brown. The limbs above still held thousands more, all flittering in the sunset. Part of him knew that this was beautiful. His favorite time of year. Always made him feel connected to the cycles of the earth, to something greater than himself. Something lasting. Something that would go on forever. But right now, he didn't care. Couldn't. And that made him angry.

The phone rang. After six rings, Angie's greeting directed the caller to leave a message.

"Hello, this is John Quinn from the *Washington Sentinel Dispatch.* I've left several messages for the hero of Flight 1444. Just wanted—"

Stu grabbed the handset and pounded, scattering pieces of plastic, tiny buttons and lights across desk and floor. As the phone disintegrated in his hand, he felt the sharp edges opening stitches, cutting new paths through his fingers. Stu continued pounding.

"Stu," Angie yelled.

He stopped hammering.

She took what was left of the handset from his bleeding fingers.

"I killed her…and they call me a hero."

"She's not dead, Stu. The doctors say there's hope that she—"

"Bullshit, Angie. I saw her." Stu shut his eyes to stop the staccato blinks. "Just before we pushed back from the gate, I leaned out of my seat to see how much trouble Daryann was giving Koleshat. And she smiled at me—with her 'too big' smile, and her bright eyes. Then the door closed. When I found her, those eyes were blank. No pulse. Nothing." Stuart lifted his hand into the sunlight

345

streaming through the glass panes, and slid his thumb across his bloody fingers, touching each cut. "I couldn't let Cheryl see her that way. Not like that. Plastic shards shooting from her daughter's skull. But some were so deep. Bloody. My fingers kept slipping and slicing. My blood and hers. I kept pulling. I go to sleep pulling. Wake up pulling."

Angie lowered his hand.

"Remove shards?" he rasped. "I know better. You know better. If Daryann ever had a chance, what did that do to her?"

She pushed down on his shoulders, forcing him to sit in the chair. "She's alive."

"Yeah, breathing tubes and needles. She's alive, all right."

Angie bent, pulled his forehead toward hers. Pressed and held, her hands massaging the back of his neck. She released, and kissed his cheek. "Let me get something to clean you up." She left the room.

He leaned his head back and closed his eyes. Sought out the deep powder. Swirling snow over shoulder and neck, extending his legs and lifting, skis rising, floating…weightless, timeless, entering the void, the singularity before the first word, the oneness. Then he opened his eyes and saw the file cabinets filled with tortured faces, his hero shot hanging crooked on the wall, the blood dripping from his fingers onto the diamonds below…. And he knew, he just knew, there wasn't a damn purpose to anything.

Angie returned with a bowl of water and bandages. He passed her as she entered the doorway.

At the great room's wet bar, he snatched the bottle of single malt scotch from the top shelf, poured his tumbler full and guzzled. His thumb picked at the pewter label, covering his name with blood.

"Stu?"

He turned toward the fireplace. "There isn't any damn purpose to this either." He crashed the tumbler into the logs.

Grabbing the bottle, he headed out the back door into the woods. He didn't know where he was going and didn't care. And suddenly, that felt great.

CHAPTER FORTY-NINE

Angie found Stu in the study, his clothes unchanged from last night. Shoes still on his feet. He sat tucked into the corner next to the file cabinets, a wall supporting each shoulder. Staring. Not at her, just staring through the gray morning light at the diamonds in the carpet.

She almost opened the bay window's drapes, then decided he probably wanted them shut. Littering the floor around her desk, she found his hero shot, torn in little pieces. She cleaned up the mess. He took no notice. She didn't expect him to.

After all, what had she ever noticed during the many hours she'd sat numb? Sometimes, it was as though she'd woken from death…found Stu quietly chatting about the deer on the hillside, or the hawk in the sky. Looking down at her body, she'd ponder how she'd ever gotten herself dressed—knowing that she hadn't, and wondered how she'd gotten into the car—knowing exactly how.

She'd never seen Stu like…this. Didn't think he could ever be this. Had no idea how long…this…would last.

Angie brought him warm, buttered toast and hot coffee. Both grew cold, untouched. At noon, she made Stu his favorite sandwich. A thick mound of shaved pastrami on rye, light mustard. By dinnertime, he still hadn't taken a bite. She chastised her foolishness, and brought a piece of cheese, and a glass of water. He ate that. Drank the water.

With the sun dipping low, she left him to prepare for the long night ahead. As she changed into her softest, warmest pajamas, Stu walked past into the bathroom, closing the door. The toilet flushed. Faucet ran. The door opened. He left, never acknowledging her. She wasn't surprised. He probably didn't see her.

347

Angie brought blankets and pillows, laid a set next to him, and curled up next to the grandfather clock. The sun set. Darkness grew. She fell asleep to Granda's voice singing, over and over, "Hush now, don't you cry."

When she awoke in the black of morning, Stu said, "Carpet's cold."

Angie draped his blanket around him, tucking it under his arms.

"Sharp points," he said. "Hard and cold."

"What? Stu, I don't understand."

"Should have swirls, curves, something warm," He shook his head at the carpet, and then up at her. "Why did you tell me about Uday?"

Without hesitation, she answered, "Because you had a right to know…everything you were choosing."

Stu nodded his firm nod, his nod of respect. "I'm sorry about the pedestal, Angie."

"Pedestal?" she questioned.

"You never asked for that," he whispered.

"Stu, you're not making any sense," she said, and immediately regretted saying it. How much sense had she ever made?

Stu returned his eyes to the diamonds.

A lighter dark grew. The sun rose. Angie made coffee. Offered him some. He never answered. As the sun made its way across the sky, she talked to him of the rabbit in the rosebushes, the gusty winds, and the autumn leaves. He didn't respond. He ate more cheese. Drank more water. The sun set. A darker dark grew.

On waking, she brought a basin of water and wiped his grimy face. Kissed his oily hair. Despite "Hush now, don't you cry" running through her mind, she started crying, her tears dropping onto the cuts on his fingers.

He lifted his hand, touched the wetness to his tongue. "Salty," he said, then went back to staring at the carpet. A minute later, he murmured, "Angie," and then went all quiet again.

At lunch, she returned with more cheese and water. Found her desk drawer open, caramel bag empty on the chair, his mouth chewing. Strewn all about him, tiny little wings. "Angie," he said, this time seeming to see her.

"Yes, Stu." She sniffed back a sob. "I'm here."

He just kept chewing, looking at her.

Stu was seeing her now, and talking. She needed to keep him talking…about anything…anything at all. "Maggie called," she told him. "Wants to drop by this weekend. Discuss a job she was offered."

He didn't seem to hear her, yet he remained focused on her face.

"Andrew emailed from Afghanistan," she said cheerfully. "He couldn't say exactly where."

After half a minute, Stu asked, "When did he email?"

"Last night," she answered.

"Then last night," Stu looked down at the diamonds, "Andrew was still alive."

His words hit her like a punch in the gut. For a moment, she didn't care if he talked anymore. Didn't want him to. She wanted to scream at him.

But this wasn't about her. He was the one in need. Instead, she said, "It's dark and gloomy in here."

"Yes," Stu agreed. "Dark."

"I could open the curtains," she suggested.

"Not just yet," he replied.

"I brought cheese. Could make you a sandwich," she offered, but Stu was already gone again, his gaze returning to the carpet. Angie studied him, trying to remember the longest she'd ever stayed with her crows. More than a week, she thought. Maybe two.

"Is that all?" Stu asked, his index finger tapping on the tip of the diamond at his feet. "Gramps and you…behind the mirror? Uday? You've told me everything? Because tomorrow…the next day…I find out something else. Another lie would kill me, Angie. You know that, right?"

Angie knelt in front of him, swallowed, and then swallowed again, fighting against the water filling her eyes. No. Not now. Crying isn't fair.

She removed his hand from the carpet, placing it between her breasts, pressing his index finger against her heart, and then lifted his chin until he looked at her. "You have no reason to believe me, Stu…but no, there's nothing else. That's everything."

His eyes searched hers, darting along the edges, boring into the center, waiting.

She held his gaze. Silent. Unblinking.

He gave her one firm nod, then looked down at his free hand, his thumb rubbing at the dried blood. "Do you suppose Daryann ever thinks of me? Wonders why I didn't keep her safe?"

"Stu...." Angie faltered, not sure what to say.

"She was such a happy little girl." His jaw muscles bulged outward, his eyes blinking rapidly.

Angie remained silent, knowing there was nothing she could say.

"My father was a rapist. A violent man."

"You are not your father."

"But, I am...a violent man."

"No. You protect. You are—"

"Is there a hell, Angie? Does Uday burn there?" Stu looked up at her. No blinking. "Will I...burn there?"

"No, Stu." Angie wrapped her arms around him. "You won't, you won't," she kept repeating, her voice growing harsh, her mind daring God to deny it.

Stu went quiet again.

So did Angie, silently asking God's forgiveness...for everything.

After a time, she got up and opened the curtains. He noticed and didn't complain. She offered him food again.

He shook his head.

"Drink?" she asked.

He responded with another shake. "Whenever my young hurts seemed too much to bear, my mother always told me, 'This too, shall pass.' Does Daryann feel the hurts now? The needles in her veins, the breathing tube down her throat?"

Angie wrapped arms and hugged herself. What possible answer could she give?

"This too, shall pass," Stu repeated several times. "That's a lot of faith, isn't it? She had that, my mother. Does a person like that kill herself? Doesn't seem like she would. But I was flying my F-15 half a world away. Hadn't seen her in a year. Lot can happen in a year. Can't it?"

"Yes," Angie said, her jaw trembling. "Even just five months. An awful lot."

His head fell back against the wall. He closed his eyes.

Pulling Stu's pistol case from behind the Grandfather's bonnet, she hid it behind her back and told him she was going to freshen up. He didn't respond.

Three steps into the bedroom, Angie's knees sank to the floor, the pistol case dropping from her grasp. She folded her arms across her stomach, pressing them against the wrenching and twisting there. It seemed as if Stu was questioning everything he thought he knew. Doubting who he was.

She bowed her head. "Dear God, what have I done?"

Angie didn't mean it as a prayer. Hadn't truly prayed in decades. But suddenly, she felt Granda kneeling alongside her, heard his voice leading her, just as he'd led their nightly prayers countless times when she was a child. "Hail Mary, full of grace. The Lord is with thee. Blessed art thou amongst women, and blessed is the fruit of thy womb, Jesus." Angie straightened her back, pressed palms together, fingers pointing toward heaven, and refrained, "Holy Mary, Mother of God, pray for us sinners, now and at the hour of our death. Amen." Nine more times she repeated the prayer, each repetition further strengthening her resolve.

The index and middle fingers of Angie's right hand slid from forehead to heart, left shoulder and right, forming the Sign of the Cross. "This is about him," she declared aloud. "He has a right to choose...no matter his choice."

She hid the gun in her closet and undressed. In the shower, beneath the steamy water, she broke down as the reality hit her. For the rest of their lives, they'd never be rid of Uday. Photos on the wall—file cabinets at the back of the study—reminders of what she'd done. Even if she took the photos down, and ripped the cabinets out, even if they moved far away, it wouldn't matter. A painting of a mosque, a news story about terrorism, even a veil in a bridal shop's window, every day, another reminder. And herself. Every morning, he'd wake to see her face, the face that betrayed him. How would that ever work?

The strength left Angie's legs. Collapsing to the shower floor, she sobbed until she couldn't sob anymore, then picked herself up and scrubbed until she couldn't scrub anymore. This wasn't about her. This was about him. He had a right to choose.

So many times, he'd taken care of her. Now, she'd take care of him, for days, weeks, months, as long as it took, until he chose. And with that thought, another dose of reality struck her hard. "But why?" she sobbed, thumping her forehead against the glass. "Why would he ever choose me?" The bar of soap fell to the floor. Angie followed, sliding down the glass, curling into a ball.

"You."

Angie's head snapped up.

Stu pressed his fingers against the glass. "I choose you." His voice was clear, tone sure.

The door opened. He stepped inside and knelt beside her.

Angie leaned toward him.

He shook his head. "I'm so filthy," he said, his voice cracking.

Angie picked up the bar of soap and reached toward his chest.

"No. These." He held out his hands, palms up, fingers shaking. "Start here. The blood."

Careful of his cuts, Angie gently washed. "Stu, I'm the one who dragged Uday into our lives. If Daryann dies, I killed her."

Stu's head trembled like it was stuck between nodding yes and shaking no. "Harder," he rasped.

Angie rubbed harder, moving from hands to arms to chest.

"Scrub." He grabbed her hand, digging the soap into his shoulder wound. "Scrub harder than you scrubbed yourself."

Angie scoured until Stu finally nodded, then pulled him beneath the showerhead.

Fully rinsed, she took his face between her hands and looked him in the eyes. "He will always be here, with us."

"Yes," Stu said, his jaw sagging. "Always."

She swallowed several times, fighting the choking in her throat. "And I'll always be here. A reminder."

Stu nodded.

"How can you...." No tears, she told herself again, but they came anyway. "How could anyone endure—"

"I...I can...." Stu looked away, lips parting and clamping without forming words, then finally forcing out, "I will endure."

"Yes...but for how long?" she asked him. How long could any man, she asked herself.

Stu reached up toward her face, his fingers steady. "Until I'm dead, Angie." His thumb smoothed the crease between her brows. "Until I'm dead."

CHAPTER FIFTY

Tanngela was everywhere; laughing from a backyard tire swing, giggling as she chased after the toddlers riding their tricycles, smiling at Kashif from a picnic table, and when the train clacked past the great homes with their high stone walls, she pounded at the gates, demanding their money for the poor and their gardens for the children. Every foolish dream she'd ever spoken of, everything that Tanngela was and could be, shared Kashif's ride west.

In the distance, a billboard came into view—a woman's battered face asking a one-word question—"WHY?" Kashif sank into the darkest corner of the ore car, buried his head in his arms and sought comfort in the Qur'an. Not the harsh verses of mullah and madrasa, but instead the soothing surahs learned at his mother's knee. And with a fervor he'd never known, Kashif begged her beautiful Allah— keep Tanngela safe and reward her with her silly, utopian dreams.

After a time, his mind touched on other prayers—Tanngela's other dreams. But like fingers darting toward fresh-ripped flesh, his mind seized near the fringes of those prayers. Yesterday, she was a part of him. Now, torn away. Forever. She must live out her life without him. But he couldn't yet utter those prayers—the ones he ought to pray.

The rhythmic click-clack of railcar over track quickened to a grinding hum as the train picked up speed. Kashif climbed from the shadows. The patchwork of cropped lawns gave way to what looked like fields of tiny flickering flames, the fading sunlight only powerful enough to fire the golden tassel atop each corn stalk. Kashif grabbed a lock of his hair and held it up to the sun—watched the weakening rays bleed the brown strands red—hair like his father's, and uncles', and cousins'—all of them gone. Every man he'd ever placed his faith in had departed on the dawn trains, the low sun always painting their hair red. Not one of them ever returned. Even those he never trusted, Faiq and the Mullah, they too, were dead. Everyone…taken by jihad.

Kashif scrambled to the top of the ore pile, stood tall, and turned his face to the sun, soaking up the warmth. Straight ahead, due west, all the land glowed orange like some great fire. North and south of him, the cornstalks' tassels briefly blazed in the sunlight, then quickly extinguished as the train left them far behind. This was jihad, Kashif thought, everyone rushing toward the fire of battle, everyone flaring with passion, everyone's life so brief.

Not everyone, he corrected himself. Hosaam might still live. If one could call that life? Anything human in Hosaam had died long ago. For all of Hosaam's talk of godless dogs, Hosaam was the true animal. Kashif felt a pang of guilt, like he'd failed to do what needed to be done. Perhaps the Americans would put Hosaam down.

And what of Abbud? Maybe, after Kashif was well away, Abbud laid down his sniper rifle. Evaded capture. Kashif pressed his fingers into his eyes and wiped away the moisture. No, he was thinking like a child, telling himself comforting lies, the same sort of lies he'd told himself before they'd dug his mother's lifeless body from the rubble. Abbud, his brother in all but blood, had stayed behind so that Kashif might escape…but more so, Abbud stayed behind so that Abbud could escape…forever.

"I am alone," Kashif whispered.

He sat and yanked open his satchel. Pulling out the mailer, he examined the postmark and breathed a sigh of relief. It was dated weeks before the Mullah's camp was destroyed. All knowledge of the information within had likely died with the Mullah and his men.

Tugging off the perforated strip revealed the new identity inside. He shook his head at the irony. It made sense though. His nose was bold, but not big. He had his mother's olive skin and his father's dark brown hair. His instructors had told him that he could easily pass for any ethnicity from Spain to India. And his curls made the Rosenberg on the Social Security card especially easy to pull off.

But Daniel…Daniel Rosenberg? Why not Moshe or Uri? Daniel sounded much too American. A Moshe might make the mistake of saying "in-chez." But a Daniel? Never. Daniel would definitely say "inch-is," just as Tanngela had taught him. Kashif could still see her face, lips gently pursing toward him with each repetition of "inch." When he still got it wrong, she made him close his eyes, took his fingers in hers, and placed them on her lips as she repeated "inches," then placed them on his own lips so that he could feel the word flow. Back and forth their fingers went, lips to lips, over and over again, him pretending he still couldn't say it correctly.

The ore car suddenly jerked and pitched, slowing, as the engine disappeared around the sharp bend ahead, and then reappeared well below, following the tracks switchbacking down the steep hill. Reeds and cattails supplanted the rows of neatly-tilled earth. The engine rolled out onto a long earthen berm, dark waters on either side.

The sun dipped low, entering the swamp. Minutes ago, it was a blazing ring of power dominating the western sky...now just a withering disc, halved and bent, the top half an uncertain shifting of yellow and red, and the bottom half an unsettled churning of ripple and eddy. Both halves, mere mirages, Kashif knew. Fading illusions. The sky half was only a deceptive reflection of a sun already gone, and the water half, just a murky reflection of that false reflection.

Kashif rummaged through his pack, locating scissors and pumice stone. After rubbing the henna stars from his hand, he lifted a handful of hair from his shoulder, set it between the scissor blades...and paused.

Eventually, he could return home. Wait some months, or years, then make his way back to Afghanistan. Yet could he...after Tanngela?

Could he ever really return to that place of veils and burqas and beards? How many of those veils hid smiles, how many burqas covered tears? And all the bearded men, every one of them, pressing his lips together so tightly that his face became a hairy, mouthless mask. And behind that mask, each man keeping secret all those things he could never let his brethren see, the pain and fear and doubt.

Kashif shook his head. No, the truth was that he'd lost his home long ago. His mother was that home. And every haven since had felt like a prison.

The air grew damp as the train accelerated out into the swamp. Fingers of mist floated across the water, reaching toward the berm. Kashif dropped the scissors, rolled up his collar against the sudden chill and watched as the black eddies swallowed the last sliver of false sun. Yes, even his time here in America, this so-called land of the free, had seemed like incarceration.

Until Tanngela. Her smile was never meant for the veil, or her cheeks for the burqa. Cheeks he knew were covered in tears—because of him.

White, wet swirls climbed up the berm and curled round the railcar's iron wheels. Toward the front of the train, the ore cars looked like fuzzy links of chain, wobbling and rattling along behind the engine. At the rear, the last car, marked by its flashing red strobe, whipped around the final switchback curve. Like a link stretched too taut, it straightened, and then seemed to snap, letting go of the broad shore, shooting out onto the narrow berm and into the growing mist.

A shiver ran down Kashif's spine as he accepted that he had no choice, no option, but a new home in America…pretending to be a Jew. Yet the only true comfort he'd felt all these many years was prostrating before Allah. Did Jews ever prostrate before their God? Would Yahweh comfort?

Tanngela could have been…should have been, his new home. Grabbing a tiny lock of his hair, Kashif yanked it out by the roots and rolled it between his thumb and fingertips. Strange. He could feel the skin still attached to the clump of hair, felt the trickle of blood on his forehead, but no pain.

Kashif bowed his head, his chest falling forward against his knees, the clump of hair dropping from his hand. Snatching up the scissors, he snipped and snipped and snipped.

Some time later, he realized that his hands were no longer moving. His fingers lay still, laced through the pile of brown curls at his feet. He studied them, lying there, knew they were his fingers, but he couldn't feel them. Couldn't feel anything. Didn't want to feel anything.

But he saw…saw his shorn hair take on a lighter hue. Then lighter, yet. Silvery. Kashif looked up.

The moon. Bright white, it rose. Full and big, filling the eastern horizon, flooding his body with light. Kashif's lower eyelids welled with moisture just like his mother's used to do.

"Help me, Madar," he cried.

He picked up the pile of curls, and let go. The last strands of his father's hair flew from his fingers out into the swallowing mist.

Kashif hugged his knees to his shoulders and prayed those prayers he ought to have prayed. "Almighty Allah, give Tanngela a good man...and strong sons...and a daughter as fair and righteous as she...."

Ahead, the train's engine vanished into a vast fog.

ABOUT THE AUTHOR

G. Egore Pitir grew up near the shores of Lake Michigan, reading too much, writing too little, and ignoring arithmetic altogether. Naturally, he obtained an engineering degree, flew as a fighter pilot, and then got an airline job. Having successfully faced the math demon in college, he decided to conquer the last item on the list and wrote FACE OF OUR FATHER, a novel exploring how today's clash of cultures permeates every facet of our lives.

While, at first glance, the author might appear to have a lot in common with the main character, Stu, he assures you that they are not one and the same. If he had the energy, the author would rewrite the story and make Stu someone truly noble, like his high school English teacher. Never has a teacher put forth such effort and received so little in return. Stu is taller, stronger, smarter, more compassionate, more honorable, and could last a round or two in a cage fight. The author regularly loses to a seven-year-old girl. In his defense, he argues that she doesn't fight fair. Calls on her brothers and sister for help. Tiny they may be, but fierce.

The author would like the reader to please note his enthusiastic waving of the poetic license white flag. He wholeheartedly concedes to indulging in numerous liberties concerning world politics, religion, military tactics, flight envelopes, FFDO training, and countless other topics. All indulgences are meant to dramatize, to heighten the experience, to fully engage readers in the tale they've written. But not one of those liberties changes the following facts. The world contains over 1.6 billion Muslims and over two billion Christians. These two cultures are clashing. Good people on both sides are dying.

www.gegorepitir.com

FACE OF OUR MOTHER

Chapter Preview

As a young man, Sadeem often prayed for deliverance from lust.
Now, lust was his only prayer.

"**R**oot them out," Sadeem ordered as he rolled his wheelchair to the edge of the palace garden's marble staircase.

"But Excellency, these orchids were cultivated by your great, great grandfather, the irises favored by your grandmother and her grandmother before her. The date palms—"

"Forgive me, Taamir, but times of great crisis require great sacrifice. I will not have our people suffer alone. The Azwads will sacrifice at their side."

"I understand, Your Highness, but surely, the rose bushes—"

"Dear Taamir, your family has served ours for countless generations. Yet if you address me as Prince, or Highness, or Excellency one more time, I will find a whip." Sadeem smiled. "I am simply Mullah Sadeem. I wish no other honorifics."

"Yes, of course, Mullah Sadeem. But the rose bushes, they go back many centuries."

"Very well, Taamir, I am not a brutish man. Consult the gardener and save what you can, but most of these grounds will grow food for our people. I have directed the sprinkler system removed, the piping rerouted. The water will now sprout from palace walls behind me, flow through channels cut in the marble, and tumble down the steps to feed little irrigation streams that wind through the children's playground and out into row after row of bountiful crops. And do not fear. The date palms stay. The local people shall plant and harvest dates, and their children shall float little boats down the streams. Side by side with our people, in mutual sacrifice, we shall see our way through The Realm's crisis."

"Mullah Sadeem, if I may be so bold. All of this uprooting will make little difference."

Sadeem nodded. "I am not a fool. But this little difference is a difference I can make right now. Paying attention to the smallest of details and setting a good example are key to the survival of The Realm. Our people cannot see restructured loans and renegotiated trade agreements, but they will see this garden transformed. Webcams will be installed along the walls to show the workers in the rows and the children at the streams. It is not enough for Azwads to sacrifice. We must be seen sacrificing. Setting a good example is crucial. And, with this uprooting, some few will eat who would have gone hungry—true?"

"Yes, Mullah Sadeem," Taamir replied.

Sadeem patted Taamir on the arm. "You have not commented on my new old wheelchair."

Taamir's eyes slid up and down Sadeem's chair, his look of confusion growing. "Is it antique, Mullah Sadeem?"

Sadeem clapped delightedly. "Good. You see the worn handles, the cracked leather—the details. But no, an antique would have value. I gave mine to an old woman outside the walls and took hers. The news media filmed me as I showed her how to operate the controls. I rolled myself back inside the palace. Examples. Details. Every day you must help me find more. Do you understand, Taamir?"

"I will help you, Mullah Sadeem."

"Good. Thank you, Taamir. Now, as to the beheadings—some details. All executions will be performed on a dais, well elevated, so that everyone in the square can see. I want no bad seats. And all electronic devices must be confiscated. Only official government recordings allowed." Sadeem squeezed Taamir's hand to make sure he had his full attention. "Now this detail is most important. Each city's selectees must be transported to another city, preferably as far from their homes as possible. No one beheaded at home. Too many weepers. A throng of crying women makes for very bad examples. You will ensure this detail."

"Yes, Mullah Sadeem."

"Good. Now what is the status of the Yara Azwad case? She is crucial to setting a good example. The message must be clear. The Royal Azwad family will not spare any of the guilty, even if an Azwad."

"A delay," Taamir frowned. "Yara's mother has obtained Ms. Pierce to represent her. The court has temporarily stayed the decision."

"The case is concluded. The decision, a formality. How can this be?" Sadeem asked.

"Have you read my report on Ms. Pierce? The Angel carries great weight."

"Yes, thanks to my fool brother's mistakes." Sadeem slammed his fist down on the chair arm. "Is there any end to the punishments we must endure from Uday's sins?"

Sadeem rubbed his suddenly weary eyes. "No matter. We will find another suitable Azwad. Root them out, Taamir. There are more. There are always more."

Sadeem spun his wheelchair around and rolled toward the palace doors. "Taamir? The Angel has a celebrated husband, this Ironman. Quite the exemplary pair, these two."

"Yes, Mullah Sadeem? Did you have a question?"

"No. Not now. I must think...think on the details."